SLATS
AND THE
CHANTEUSE

Lee Bornstein

PAGE PUBLISHING, INC.
New York, NY

First originally published by Page Publishing, Inc. 2019

ISBN 978-1-64462-302-2 (Paperback)
ISBN 978-1-64462-303-9 (Digital)

Printed in the United States of America

CHANTEUSE

Ann Sloan stared at the screen. This e-mail would be hers. The wording would be hers. PR honcho Ed Spivey of Spivey & Associates, the magical wordsmith of Hollywood, was going to sit this one out. After all, it was easy. Josh Parker, one of Society's losers, faced the terrible retribution of an unjust system. Convicted of killing a policeman, Josh sat in death row, a victim of the system's need for mindless retribution. And where was the justification for the state to impose death on an individual under any circumstances? But these circumstances were all the more obscene—Josh Parker was innocent.

> Greetings to the Group of Justice
>
> Wonderful news! I want all you activists and other fair-minded persons on this mailing list to know that Dave Shapiro told me that Judge Thompson would shortly announce a new trial for Josh. I want to thank all of you for your tireless efforts in publicizing this injustice. And special thanks to Ed Spezio, whose expertise in DNA and forensics created the doubt that we needed. Of course, the utmost thanks to Dave Shapiro, who capped his

selfless career devoted to justice by his brilliant defense of an innocent man.

Love and justice forever,
Ann

Ann allowed herself a sigh of contentment. How long was it, some twenty years since her last Grammy? Well, it had been her seventh, which, combined with that successful movie career, meant that she and her children and heirs infinitum were set financially. Since she'd become an activist, there were all those White House invitations and sleep-ins (when the Democrats were in power, of course) and causes too numerous to recall. But this was a first, a cause where the Chanteuse didn't just lend her name and reputation to the effort. No, she initially publicized Josh Parker's cause and carried the torch till, lo and behold, the cover of the newsweeklies, the Sunday talk shows, and finally, a new trial.

Ann went to the vanity mirror; she looked as tired as she felt. But it was a good exhaustion, the fatigue of a job well done. She approached the staircase and shouted, "Livonia, please fix my bath, and plenty of bubbles!" Ann strode toward her "gown" closet. She was still bothered by what the mirror had displayed. All those lines, the droopy eyes—fatigue didn't cause it, and sleep wouldn't cure it. More Botox or time for another full pull? Perhaps a few days at the spa at Pebble Beach? Rifling through her choices improved her disposition. Tonight's selection was that velvet and duchess satin gown by Chanel. Add those filigree earrings and only the cattiest bitch would focus on the telltale signs of aging.

The party featured tout le monde, with Harry Connick and Orchestra providing that "easy to listen to, dance to, and continue to chatter to" music so apropos to the mature and well-kept celebrants attending. When Dick LaVerne, that bald-headed pest from *Variety Weekly*, asked, "Where are the Baldwins and Sarandons of this world?" Ann told him that it was precisely his kind of reporting that kept the otherwise sympathetic super celebs away but virtually everyone else in a Hollywood's A-list was there, providing they had the "correct" political outlook. After disposing of LaVerne, Ann concluded the five minutes allocated to the three "pool" reporters, whereupon they were briskly escorted out by several imposing security personnel.

Now Ann could relax and enjoy the festivities. Of course, that crowd of rightwing Fascistic zealots demonstrating 150 yards away could be heard in the swimming pool veranda. Luckily, the party chatter, the martinis, and the moonlit scenery enveloping that green-tinted Olympic-sized pool made the miscreants seem like the faraway pests that they were.

It was nearly ten, and Dave appeared on the bandstand, ready to give the speech outlining the victory so far, as well as his optimism for the new trial. Ann strode toward the head table, where she joined her two sons and her latest flame, Mark Hudson. After bowing to thunderous applause, Ann began sipping that apple martini and turned her attention to the podium as Dave Shapiro was introduced.

The demonstrators were kept behind barricades by an assortment of private security personnel backed up by a detail from the Beverly Hills police, in case things got "out of hand." Prominently in front of the throng were the reps of Hollywood's gossip industry. Reporters from *Entertainment Tonight*, as well as *Access Hollywood* and E! Entertainment Television, were prominent with their klieg lights and microphones as they feverishly hustled for whatever scraps were left out here for those not fortunate enough to be part of the press pool.

With the *LA Times* the only local daily part of the invited pool, Slats Conners, a scribe from a suburban daily, *The Pacific Coast Gazette*, was left to scrounge around the noisy and angry mob demonstrating outside. He buttonholed a graying, beefy gentleman holding a sign under the Retired Policemen's Association banner.

"Hi," he chirped, "I'm Slats Conners with the *PC Gazette*, and you're...?"

"Tim Mulder," the burly man growled, holding his sign even higher.

Slats looked at the sign.

You Want True Justice?
Fry the Bastard

"Can I call you Tim?" Slats attempted his cheeriest smile.

The large man just shrugged while staring at the Bel Air double mansion.

"Tim, how come I don't see anyone here from any of the active police unions?"

"Glad you asked that." Tim Mulder lowered his sign and met Slats's eyes. "Used to be. The unions were as tough on rapists, murderers, and other blackguards as the rank and file. Now... well, it seems all the unions care about is how much money is thrown our way. And since Liberals, Democrats, whatever, fund us best, pay raises, all that, it sort of pays to be, well, what was that phrase from the sixties, soft on crime? But most cops on the beat would still love to see that scum fry, but they have their careers in front of them. Me, I got nothing to lose." He sighed warily. "Of course, they could try and take away my pension..."

"All maybe true," Slats responded, "but *their* point is that he's innocent."

"*Innocent?*" Mulder's cheeks flushed red; his lips trembled. "What have we got? Another OJ? Those OJ guys sure showed the way. Contaminated this, contaminated that. Come on, it's a police station, lab, whatever... What do they expect, Los Alamos, Oak Ridge, Tennessee?"

Slats, furiously taking notes, tried to hide his elation; else this brawny ex-cop might flatten him. *I've already got an angle*, he mused, *and this in just my first interview at the "barricades."* Trying to look stern, Slats offered, "You're saying that the defense team played mumbo jumbo with the evidence?"

Mulder lowered the sign and pulled out a cigarette. "Look, mister, what was that name again?"

"Slats is just fine." Slats flashed his cheeriest grin.

"Okay, Slats, let's forget the tricks they're playing with the evidence. They've got that radical Sloan bitch in every paper and TV show the past year yapping the same thing. Then every like-minded Hollywood star backs her in the media, civil rights organizations join in even though the guy ain't black. They're making it a cause... you know..."

"Cause célèbre?" Slats offered.

"Yeah, that's it, cause célèbre." Mulder finally cracked a smile. "So the media stuff and these high-priced lawyers could convince anyone without a backbone to recommend a new trial."

"You're saying Judge Thompson has no backbone?"

"Worse," Mulder replied, "every political, civil rights, and even environmental group's been picketing his house and office. He just plain cracked. The yella coward."

The "yellow and coward" usage hit Slats like a thunderbolt. This man was probably near sixty, but if the shit hits the fan, 160-pound, lightly built yours truly absorbs the first few punches. His throat suddenly parched, he said, "I can see why..."

"*You can't see shit.* They get high-priced dream team a-holes to mix the facts up, they get every Hollywood and Broadway shithead causing a continuous storm, and then they go to the poetry card, like it makes a difference if I killed a roomful of people just 'cause I write poetry while sitting in death row."

Thankful that Mulder had paused and his jaw was still intact, Slats asked, "You think the poetry's a big factor?"

"Are you kidding?" the big man replied. "They take every people-type weekly and keep yapping about this 'innocent' victim pouring his heart out with poems. All those bonbon-munching matrons and housewives watching *Oprah*, *Rosie*, and the rest of those shitty shows have their hearts broken over this poetry-spouting 'victim' whose only support comes from the Ann Sloans of the world."

Slats thought about all those interviews of Josh on NPR but decided to skip it—but he agreed with Mulders' drift. He was suddenly impressed by the scope of this excop's knowledge. He started to say thank you when Mulder smiled and pulled out a card. "I'm more than an official of a retired police officers' union." He offered the card to Slats:

TIM MULDER
Political Analysis
www.mulderanalysis.com

Both men flashed huge grins. So who snookered whom, Slats pondered as he walked away after thanking Mulder. Slats looked around. A man wearing an Angels windbreaker with a Dodger blue cap had fought his way to the front of the throng. He chuckled at the man's sign:

ANN SLOAN TODAY
= HANOI JANE 1973

Heading toward his car, Slats noticed a smaller but more strident group, most of them college age, affecting that beat-up, long-hair look so prevalent among the rent-a-mob protesters. They were separated from the other demonstrators by additional barricades and police, but Slats was able to make out some of the signs: "Save the Whales," "Jail for Shrub and Dick," "To Hell with Halliburton," "No More Enrons," and of course, "Stop Global Warming."

Approaching the '99 Corvette, Slats decided on that Shell station on Robertson that has the car wash. Don't have to file till Sunday night. Holly's back in town. Why not take her to Huntington Beach tomorrow and watch the Orange County set promenade by one of those chic sidewalk cafes? Holly's probably just as sick as I am of the Malibu–Beverly Hills beautiful people butting into other people's business. As he drove off Sunset toward the Santa Monica, Slats had his mind back on the story. Not much, not much. The Hollywood and intellectual crowd going goo-goo over a poetry-swilling con on death row was getting to be as old as the hills. Where's the hook? Where's the man-bites-dog? Slats sighed. Secondhand sheet assigning a secondhand story to a secondhand scribe? Slats tried not to get depressed. He pictured Holly in a bathing suit.

THE SHVITZ

Ed Spezio looked at his $350,000 Bentley. Hated that metallic gray. But they say, when you get to that level, loud reds and garish greens are out. At any rate, the Honda Civic would be used for tonight's meeting with Glen Tanaka. Got the call from Sloan's personal attorney in Hollywood. Meeting her New York lawyer, Stan Wasserman, tomorrow at noon to arrange fees, expenses, all the rest, over at Wasserman's office on East Sixty-Seventh. *No sweat,* Spezio thought as he told the maid to tell Shirley he'd be home late. Wasserman's been around; he knows the going rate. Ed felt sure Wasserman would agree to the $2,000 a day retainer, with $500 daily for "expenses." They don't like it, let them get another DNA shyster. *But they won't,* he reflected, *they know I'm the best.*

Spezio clicked the garage door open. He parked the Bentley and closed the garage door behind him. He was a little ticked at all the clutter in the three-car garage. Well, next weekend, for sure, cleaning time. He opened the little safe below the toolbox and took out a pair of counterfeit Pennsylvania license plates. He'd affix them over his regular plates at that secluded rest area off the Hutchinson. As he got behind the wheel of the Civic, he thought about his "fleet" of automobiles. Shirley drove the Camry for shopping, the charities, and the rest of those local things. The "cover" for the Civic was that he couldn't use the Bentley or even the Camry because of those shady neighborhoods he had to frequent for evidence and other shit.

But there was a more specific reason. That "shvitz" place. It was at Livonia and Sutter in the 'Ville. No sweat, the car would be guarded. But a Bentley or even a Camry would cause too much attention in such a crummy Brownsville neighborhood. And under no circumstances could he be seen meeting with Tanaka.

Spezio stuck a motivational tape into the player for the well-over-one-hour drive from Scarsdale down to that part of Brooklyn. It was that *Seven Habits* guy; good way to kill time and get the juices flowing for the next trial. It took him a half hour to reach the Bronx–Whitestone Bridge. He'd already shut the tape several times to absorb Covey's "message" and see how he'd incorporate it into the trial strategy. Breezing through the nighttime traffic, he tried WABC. Sterling was hyperventilating over a leadoff triple by Soriano in the home seventh, with the Yankees leading the Rangers, 9–1. *Too boring*, Ed concluded, and he reached to push the *Seven Habits* tape back into the player. Just then, he saw a huge billboard lauding the "Savings" with Sprint. That started the recriminations. He'd only lost half his two hundred grand with Sprint. But his "connections" got him the sweet ride in Enron, Global Crossing, and Tyco. He added to them on the way up, and their eventual total collapse cost him half a million of the original cost basis. Then there were JDS Uniphase, Inktomi, GMCI, Nortel, more 90 percent losses, easily 400 grand. Even Cisco, Microsoft, Dell, Intel got clobbered. Another million. Even the nontechs, GE, and Lucent—*Don't remind me about Lucent*, he remonstrated to himself even as he shouted obscenities at a Mustang that cut him off on the Van Wyck. All together, $3 million down the tubes between 2000 and 2002. He smiled as he recalled badgering Herman Slotnick, his CPA, how long it would take him to write off his losses at the pitiful, allowable $3,000 a year. Easily a thousand years, Slotnick had smirked while reminding him that the stock losses could be offset against gains from other investments. With that good news, they concluded it might take only 750 years.

Anyway, Spezio recalled, he'd been warned about valuations by his guy at Merrill Lynch. But he pigged out at the top of the tech bubble 'cause he had to "make up" for his missing out of the tobacco bonanza. Also, all those CEOs and CFOs of all kinds of companies clearing out with anywhere from half a billion to a billion dollars. Where did that leave ol' Spezio? Desperate to keep up with the fat cats on lousy retainers that, at best, totaled a million a year. Litigation, asbestos, tobacco—damn, that's where the money was/is. So at the tender age of thirty-eight, instead of a possible $500 million or more in liquid assets, down to a lousy twenty.

Ed got off at Atlantic and headed west looking for the Rockaway exit. His mood brightened as he passed New York Avenue. Tenements, ash cans, the city's poor teeming the streets, the stoops begging for a breeze to lighten that dense, sticky August air in the Big Apple. Nobody of any consequence could possibly spot him around here. It got better. As he turned on Sutter toward Livonia, he grinned. It looked like Berlin at the end of the war. Skeletons of once-proud tenements. One so-called yard after another, all littered with the kind of debris and trash one would imagine lie at the seafloor where the *Titanic* went down. He parked on Livonia, one block short of Sutter. Approaching the building, he saw the faded, unlit sign—Gold's Steam and Message. (Everyone welcome.) *Everyone except the cops,* Ed mused.

Gold, the story goes, got his start-up money in the thirties from Murder Inc., and the mob used it as a "shvitz" where they could unwind and talk in the privacy of the steam rooms. As the neighborhood really fell apart, realtors didn't replace the dilapidated buildings, which was great for the mob, 'cause as law enforcement got into the habit of renting a flat and "observing" suspicious locations, there was nothing left close enough for the law to do its thing. The mob's been long gone, but this location still came in handy when Spezio wanted total secrecy. Moe Lipshitz, the son of the founder, Irving, was on duty. Ed always made sure he'd be there when he scheduled a meet. Moe had become a successful CPA and lived in Forest Hills, but he occasionally worked the desk at the "schvitz" for old times' sake. In return, Spezio promised one hundred hours of free legal representation if Moe ever needed counsel. After some small talk with Moe, he was informed Tanaka was already in the steam. While undressing, Spezio was dismayed by the growing paunch in his midsection and the increasingly receding hairline. It all seemed to make his narrow five-foot-ten-frame even shorter.

He greeted Tanaka who promptly announced he had to take a brief shower.

Refreshed, Tanaka strode back in, enveloped in a towel. Spezio couldn't help noticing how small Tanaka looked under that towel.

"Hi, Glen, been here long?"

"Whew, I can see why these places were popular back when. Been here about fifteen minutes, feels like an hour."

Spezio laughed. "That's why they call it a shvitz." He then explained that *shvitz* was Yiddish slang for a "top-flight steam room."

Tanaka mopped his brow. "You're not Jewish, you're Italian, right?"

"Nah, Glen, everyone thinks that. Actually, I'm Portuguese ancestry. Astoria on the island, where Whitey Ford's from."

"Who's Whitey Ford?" Tanaka asked.

Spezio just shrugged. "Where you from again?"

"Sunnyvale, the heart of the Silicon Valley. Though when my granddad worked the land, it was a rural pasture light-years from San Francisco."

Spezio knew Tanaka's family had been rounded up right after Pearl Harbor, but he didn't want to get into that again. "Okay, Glen, all the meetings will be like this one. Moe's always going to be here or the meeting's called off. I don't trust anyone else."

Tanaka indicated he'd had enough, so they both showered and returned to the steam room after telling Moe to shut the steam.

"Look, Glen, everyone knows you're a defense guy since you left the San Jose police force and went out on your own. Still, if the cooperation is too visible, it might cause bad vibes. After all, as a witness, your conclusions are supposedly based on theory, knowledge, experience, and so on." Spezio smirked, "Just 'cause you're going to validate everything I say, we don't want it to appear that you're in my pocket, even if you are."

Tanaka seemed to flinch but continued to stare blankly at Spezio.

Ed looked at his watch. It was a little past eleven. "I've got a six-page printout in my coat pocket for you. I got prosecution experts to tout the prosecution's strategy based on their tactics in the first trial. At the next meet, I'll tell you what Shapiro's planning.

"Meanwhile, the printout counters all their arguments they used in the first trial when we torpedoed all their blood, DNA, and fiber crap. Now, I'm pretty sure we had nullification in that first trial, but you never know about a jury. Of course, that Sloan dame and all the rest of the Hollywood and social glitterati will be out in force again. So even if John Wayne or James Bond somehow made it to the jury, they'd melt by the end of the trial."

"Yes, but…"

"Got you covered, Glen, yeah, even if they're sequestered. Don't forget, Sloan and all the rest will be there every day, smooching with and patting Parker on the fanny every chance they get."

Spezio got up and motioned Tanaka to follow him toward the showers. "Got a good story for your wife, Glen, about why you went out so late?"

Tanaka shrugged, barely smiled. "She's been through this before. She knows cases make for weird hours."

"Good going, Glen." Ed turned off the shower. Tanaka followed him to the locker area.

Ed was dressed and combing his hair when he turned toward Tanaka, grinned bashfully. "Any problems with Parelli tailing you all the way from your house in Little Neck?"

"No problem." Tanaka frowned. "What was it about?"

"No offense, Glen, but Parelli's great at spotting a tail. I couldn't take the chance. Also, I knew he'd remember to attach those phony PA plates while you're parked here. You don't mind, do you?"

"Nah," Tanaka sighed. "You seem to know a lot more about all this cloak-and-dagger stuff. But why PA plates? Why not Jersey?"

"'Cause the cops are always suspicious of Jersey plates at potential crime scenes. Everyone does it. So I figure PA plates take some of the heat off."

Tanaka smiled and shook his head in bemusement. "That's why you're the best."

Spezio's cheeks flushed; he shrugged his shoulders. "Thanks, Glen, I try and earn my pay."

BIG APPLE

Slats peered out the window, mesmerized by the soft waves inevitably dying short of the Malibu coastline. He liked using Steve Castle's office for his brown bag lunch when Steve was kind enough to let him know he'd be out at noon. Slats toyed with a carrot stick while fixated on a seventy footer gently traversing the calm sea.

"Oh, there you are."

It was Flip Fallon, the young copy boy, gofer, whatever, disturbing Slats' Malibu reverie. "Yeah, Flip, what's up?"

"Boss wants to see you, pronto."

"Now?" Slats pleaded, looking at his watch, but Flip was already out the door.

Slats could only mumble to himself, couldn't even get a decent lunch hour at this dump. He took one last bite of that carrot, finished his soda, and headed toward Tom Leary's office.

Slats felt additional pangs of self-pity when he walked into the office and caught Leary leaning back on his chair, nonchalantly peering out the window at that same seventy- footer, sailing so effortlessly along the calm Pacific shore. "Yeah, so you wanted to see me?"

"Slats, how's it hanging?" Leary abruptly lowered his feet from his desk, leaped off his swivel chair, and literally crushed Slats's right hand with that ex-Marine's firm handshake. Slats, still feeling the pain in that hand, marveled over Leary's hard-as-a-rock condition.

Eliminate a few pounds, a few gray hairs, and that granite-jawed face could still win any drill-instructor audition out of central casting.

Slats feigned a worried look. "Is it about the Parker trial?"

"Yeah." Leary grinned. "You've done quite a job considering you're limited to following it on Court TV."

Slats was in the process of gasping a huge sigh of relief when he heard, "How about we send you to New York?"

Slats looked at Leary, who was back on his chair, swiveling back and forth. "When?"

"Now, Slats, now. That means you go see Audrey pronto in Travel and she'll set you up."

Slats watched Leary's countenance turn irritable, but he couldn't help blurting, "But Holly and I got reservations for Caesars at Tahoe next week."

Leary deliberately looked at his watch. "I got a meet with Editorial at one sharp. Audrey'll work out the Tahoe thing. If she can't, someone else will go. My apologies to Holly."

Leary's tone led Slats to conclude that any further protestations were out. "Audrey's got you on a Saturday morning flight to Kennedy. I want you to be settled in by Monday. Your return is open, but you may be there at least a month. She's got you at the Broadway Arms in lower Manhattan, walking distance from the courthouse. Plenty of out-of-town reporters staying there, weekly rate, all that shit, so I want you to do plenty of shmoozing over-the-weekend, maybe pick up some tidbit you missed three thousand miles away."

"What about access and accreditation, Tom?"

"Yeah, Slats." Leary shook his head warily. "They got a lottery system. Depending on your luck of the draw, you should get in once or twice a week. On the days you don't make it, they got closed circuit, better than Court TV, 'cause they'll be showing the jurors. Also, you'll be able to gab with the other reporters in the room."

"Any angles, Tom?"

Leary allowed a tiny smirk. "The News Alliance's been lobbying all over that rags like ours get a chance to compete with the *LA* and *NY Times*, *Wash Post*, and the other big shots. Their point is that with cable, the internet, the US newspaper industry is evolving into local rags like ours, with AP providing the national news, but punks like you dishing the local dirt. Now, here we are in Malibu, only 'cause that heiress willed this space rent-free to Osborne, our founder, 'for the public trust.' So..."

"I'm losing you, Tom." Slats shrugged.

"Getting there, Slats, getting there. First, can ya handle a little stroking?"

For the first time in this visit, Slats sat back in his chair and flashed a grin. "Sure, Tom, I won't stop you."

Tom laughed. "Didn't think you would. Don't let this go to your head, but since you've been filing on Thompson's capitulation on a new trial and since the start of the trial, our circulation's up 40 percent and ad revenue's up almost 30 percent. And... when the circulation increase hits the street, our ad income will soar."

Slats tried putting his hand over his mouth to hide the Chesire grin, but he couldn't help blurting out, "Pay raise, pay raise."

Tom held up his right hand, as if it were a Stop sign. "Hold on, dude, if my aunt Tilly was filing on this, trial circulation would have increased. With that Sloan dame being local and this being the juiciest California case since OJ and those Menendez brothers. The women in our circulation area are going bonkers. They're actually reading the paper every day instead of watching those stupid daytime TV shows."

"Even though the trial's in New York?"

"Right, Slats, but with Sloan and the rest of that Hollywood and TV crowd, the courthouse might just as well be in Santa Monica. That's where you come in. With all that Court TV, the cable shows, there's still nothing like them holding that fish rag in their purty little hands in the beauty parlor. Did you see what Slats Conners says about how Ann Sloan hugged Josh? Did you read what she was wearing? Here, let me read it, a chiffon dress and a blue halter and all the rest of that crap."

Slats shook his head, "Chiffon dress and a blue halter. Tom, you'll never write for the society page."

Tom looked at his watch—five minutes to go before the meeting. "So here's the point, Slats, get as close to Sloan and the rest of the celebs as you can. Even if it's 'no comment' or 'get lost,' our local matrons are gonna eat it up. Did you see what Ann Sloan said to Slats Conners? No, what? Get lost. Really, what was she wearing?"

Slats politely chuckled at Tom's slant. "What about the trial itself, Tom?"

"Getting to that, Slats. You haven't written about the Albert Padilla thing yet. That's a good angle. As we all expected, Spezio's made a mockery out of the fiber-and-blood evidence."

"Mockery? C'mon, Tom."

Tom allowed a harried smile. "Look, Slats, it's not as if we're on the jury. Hells bells, the evidence is airtight. But with that Tanaka testifying about all the historical mess-ups in the Borough of Manhattan, the seeds are planted. That, plus the jury's makeup and the prosecution's in a bind. Add to that the additional nullification because they're starstruck because of Sloan and the rest of the celebs, and well, OJ here we come."

"You're right about that, Tom, five blacks, three Hispanics, and nine women." Tom's face brightened; he giggled and bellowed, "What kind of reporter are you, Slats? That adds up to more than twelve." They both laughed.

Tom picked up the phone. "Yeah, Alice, I'll be about five minutes late. Bring them some Krispy Kremes and coffee and start the meet at one sharp. Lead off with tomorrow's lead. He chuckled. "Right, Alice, I'm a real poet."

Tom allowed himself one brief look out the window. The Blue Pacific seemed as blue and as pacific as always. He wheeled his chair and looked at Slats. "Okay, Slats, Padilla's due back on the witness stand Monday. Shapiro's sure to follow up on that 'submarine watching' incident when he was in high school. Where was that again?"

"Plumb Beach, out on the Belt Parkway," Slats answered eagerly.

Tom got up, adjusted his tie, and put on his jacket. "It's juicy, Slats. Just like they went after that cop in OJ for using the *N*-word, now they're hammering a twice-decorated detective 'cause he kicked this chick out of the car after she wouldn't go 'all the way.' Now, we've all got wives, sisters, daughters, Slats, where we'd be pissed if he did that to them. But damn it, Padillo was in high school, captain of the football team, and used to—"

"That don't make it right," Slats interrupted, grinning.

"Yeah, but got nothing to do with the evidence, which, granted, Spezio and Tanaka did their best to trash. It's obvious Shapiro's gonna make that one incident the biggest story since OJ, Monica, and Saddam combined." Tom was at the door and looked back. "Tell me why, Slats."

Slats smiled the smile of the pupil who can answer the teacher's question. "With the nine women objecting to the rough treatment and the blacks, Hispanics inevitably suspicious of a 'rogue' cop— that, not the evidence, becomes the issue when they deliberate in private."

Tom grinned, opened the door, and looked back at Slats. "Don't let me down in the Big Apple, dude. Earn your pay and expenses. Oh yeah, one last thing. They came up with this broad twelve years after the fact. Don't mess with the Sloan-Shapiro team, they're unbeatable. Feature that."

JOSH PARKER

If people only knew the extent of despair behind these walls
Equal to the torrent of waters unleashed by Niagara Falls
We, the oppressed of society and political prisoners
All await the response of caring Progressives to our call.

Slats's View

Yes, dear *PC Gazette* readers, I already long for our beautiful but brittle coastline, and I miss you all tremendously. As the imposing urban canyons of Manhattan take in the cooler September breeze, the hustle and the bustle of famed avenues such as Madison, Lexington, and Fifth take on a more rapid pace. With the languid torpor of August gone, the "crowd" has returned from the Hamptons, Fire Island, the Cape, and other East Coast escapes. While still too early for chestnuts roasting on an open fire, other signs of a New York autumn are only too apparent. The Yankees are ho-humming their way toward another playoff and the Giants are off to a good start, while the Mets were eliminated weeks ago and the Jets are 0–3.

Yes, dear readers, you no doubt know why I'm waxing lyrical on the Big Apple while you want to read about the trial. Well, as you all know, Judge Shea caught a bug over the weekend and the case will resume Wednesday. The sonnet above my column is but a portion of the latest poem "written" by Josh Parker. The quotation marks hint at the hints I've been hearing that a ghostwriter (either from NPR or hired by Ann Sloan) has been responsible for the prose. But more on that when I come up with something more substantive.

I know, I know, I mentioned her name so you all want to know the latest on Ann Sloan. Well, over the weekend, she dined at La Marquis as a guest of the mayor at the chic eatery's Private Celeb Corner. Before dinner, at dusk, she was spotted in the gardens of the Cooper Hewitt, National Design Museum, where she was seated on sisal benches covered with down pillows at a special showing of the latest Parisienne ensembles from the House of Ralph Lauren. But La Chanteuse was there for all to see showing up bright and early in the courtroom on Monday before we all learned of the judge's relapse on the way in. Flashing a patriotic motif, Ann was resplendent in a red leather Dior suit, a blue hat, and white gloves—no doubt a subtle rejoinder to all those who question her patriotism because of her causes. But it wasn't a wasted trip. She was seen huddling with Josh Parker, Dave Shapiro, and the rest of the defense team. Tomorrow, Shapiro will lead off with his close…

The clamor reached a new level that next day. The usual heavy police and security presence seemed to have doubled. Slats cursed the fates again. There'd be no lottery today. After the automatic admission of the five New York dailies, one paper each from Washington, LA, San Francisco, Chicago, Dallas, and Miami was among the chosen guaranteed access to the proceedings. Today, Slats didn't even rate the closed circuit. He had to settle for the Embassy Hall of the Broadway Arms, with the hotel promising wall-to-wall coverage from Court TV.

The buzz at Embassy Hall turned to dead silence at ten thirty when Dave Shapiro told the judge he was ready for his summation. Slats was impressed by Shapiro's bearing on this big day. Already a Paul Newman (in his fifties) look-alike, Shapiro's stylish gray mane seemed immaculate. His charcoal-blue Italian-cut suit appeared tailor-made, the sum and substance of the successful man on his big day.

After thanking the judge, Shapiro looked at the jury. He seemed to sigh and paused for a moment. "Ladies and gentlemen of the jury, you've been reminded during these legal proceedings, and through countless novels, movies, and TV shows, the awesome duties and responsibility imposed upon you, average citizens trying to administer justice. I won't bore you with the "What is justice?" cliché. But I will remind you of the "reasonable doubt" adage. Since the great Empire State reinstituted the death penalty, society's stake, and the awesome responsibility of jurors like yourselves have taken on awesome dimensions. Whether we agree with the death penalty, and I don't, and whether this was done under the political cover of terrorism, the certainty remains...

Shapiro approached the jury box, hesitated, then took out a handkerchief, and gently applied it to his forehead. "The certainty remains that you, ladies and gentlemen of the jury, have in your power to send a man to his death. Under such awesome circumstances, can any doubt exist? Can a powerful, politically ambitious district attorney eager to embellish his record use any means to erase doubt where it should still exist? Can a police officer eager to erase blots on his record run roughshod over evidentiary matters to assure a conviction?"

Shapiro paused, looked away from the jury, and bolted a glare toward the prosecution's table. He appeared to adjust his tie then turned toward the jury. Slats was impressed by the interlude. He couldn't see the jury on Court TV, but he guessed the jurors were already placing Shapiro at third on his way to a home run.

"Yes, I'm talking about Albert Padillo, the arresting officer. You've already heard the witness from the ACLU testify to the procedural and due process violations of Josh's constitutional rights. You've heard forensics and DNA experts expose countless flaws in Officer Padillo's and the precincts' handling of the evidence. Yes, ladies and gentlemen of the jury, doubt, doubt... doubt that a man of Officer Padillo's character defects wouldn't stoop to just a little body English to assure a conviction? But we aren't talking a pool shot or a pinball machine, we're talking about justice and a man's life.

"Doubt, doubt... if there's any doubt you cannot convict without an eyewitness. Doubt, doubt, if there's any doubt, you cannot send this man to death row. If there's any doubt in your minds… you must send Josh home a free man. Thank you."

"Tom? yeah, it's Slats. Listen, I'm gonna catch the 4:15 flight instead of the noon. I want my story on Greenwald's press conference in the next edition. Yeah, what, I can't hear… Wait, it's the cell… Okay, that's better." Slats moved the chair next to the window. Leary's voice seemed clearer, and he enjoyed watching the legal types scurrying around lower Broadway.

"Yeah, Tom, it was a pisser. He just about admitted he's through with politics and not gonna run for DA again. It's like something the Zucker brothers would do if they made a picture on politics. He blasted everything… all the way back to OJ and Cochran. He blasted La Chanteuse, all of Hollywood, and jury nullification."

Tom said he had a call waiting. Slats leaned back and peered out the hotel window. Not the same as the Pacific view from Malibu, Slats mused, but interesting watching all those ant-like creatures moving about. "Yeah, Tom, you back? Greenwald was really ticked that the entire jury was invited to the reception at the St. Regis after the concert for Josh in Central Park. Right, Tom, they called it the Concert for Josh. What was that? Yeah, Tom, I'll feature Greenwald's legal arguments. He especially blasted the collusion and the tactics of Spezio and Tanaka when the evidence was, in his word, 'airtight.' But, Tom, I know we're limited for space, but I've got to mention Greenwald's defense of Padillo and his heartrending reference to Alice Santana, the dead cop's widow."

Slats jumped up. "What was that? Front page? Tom, you're the best freaking editor that… Okay, no word limit. Yeah, our readers want to know. No, Tom, don't know why it wasn't televised nationally, but I got a transcript. Yeah, Tom, next time we talk, it'll be on Malibu time." Slats pressed the End button on his cell and pushed Start on his laptop.

***

Josh Parker looked at his droopy eyes evincing the past two weeks' hectic pace. *Time to catch up on my sleep*, he reflected, *but when?* It's been parties, interviews, coast-to-coast flights, and more interviews, all carefully monitored by Ed Spivey, that ace PR guy hired by Sloan. Like all forces of nature, Josh figured the hysteria over his acquittal was dissipating, just like the tail end of a hurricane now down to thirty-five-miles-per-hour winds.

Groupies had been hurtling themselves at him at a pace reminiscent of Franky, Elvis, or Mick Jagger, but Spivey said to hold out. "We don't know what Greenwald's up to," Spivey kept repeating. Any of those broads could be a plant, and who knows *what they* might plant. Now that he was off the front pages, life could begin again. *Four fuckin' years...*, he smirked and looked at the mirror again. *Well, four years for killing a cop. Not bad, not bad.* He combed his thinning light-brown hair and took a few moments to clip those visible nose hairs out of his wide, squat nose. Time to get back to Nashville and hang loose. But first, a trip to Vegas. That legal expense fund that Sloan and the rest of those mushy Hollywood types scrounged up added up to about 2 *million.* But Sloan and some other celebs were gonna ante up to more than half of the 4 million or so legal bills. So they promised at least a couple of hundred grand out of the fund, as soon as it could be feasible. Meantime, some kinda legal "slush" fund provided ten grand in "spending money." *I'll give nine grand to Melanie for safekeeping,* he mused. *Meantime, lemme hang loose at the Nugget in downtown. No one who recognizes me there would yap to reporters, not like the Strip.* He called Melanie, but she wasn't home. He left a message telling her what flight he'd be on. He'd spoken to her the day before, so she knew he was coming.

The flight arrived on time at 2:15 PM. By three, Josh, still waiting at the gate, began to wonder. He decided to call her before hopping a cab. He looked up her phone number on his new cell phone and clicked Connect. All he got was her "Sorry I missed your call" message. He grabbed his carry-on bag and started heading toward...

"Josh Parker?" a short, wiry man was in his face. He had the mug and vernacular of an East Coast wise guy, with which he'd become acquainted while at Attica.

"Yeah, who the hell are you?" *First, Melanie's not here. Now this dick's in my face?*

The short man smiled. "I'm Nunzi Calabrese. Melanie was picked up by the Vegas cops for doin' tricks. We're here to drive you to town."

"We? Who the hell is 'we'?" Josh was boiling, but he was confused, scared. *I could pop this dick in the snout, and he's out for a week, but in an airport, after that trial? Was this a setup by Greenwald? A reporter? Vegas cops?* Josh knew he had to restrain himself. Meanwhile, his eyes searched frantically at the few remaining people at the arrival gate. There were two big guys, in particular, who looked like they could be associated with this dirtbag. They were staring at him. The combo of their glares, their plain windbreakers, and the fact that they could be walk-ons as linebackers on any pro football team sent an additional chill through his being. This Nunzi character, at least was a shrimp, and wore a smart herringbone sports jacket over stylish slacks. A *Mutt and Jeffs*, Josh reasoned, or was it the other way around?

Nunzi grinned widely, revealing several gold teeth under an elongated hook nose.

He pointed to the two huge men Josh had spotted. "That's Ralphy over there, with the 'stache. The other guy's called Butch."

Nunzi scratched his eyelid and turned serious. "Ya see that eating area over there? It's virtually empty. Let's walk over and talk."

"Like hell," Josh bellowed, "I'll knock you through that wall first then call the cops. What is this shit, a fuckin' kidnapping? And how the fuck do you know Melanie? I'm going to…"

"You ain't doin' diddly." Nunzi put on his "hit man" glare. He again pointed toward Ralphy and Butch, who, overhearing Josh's outburst, approached them in a slow menacing fashion.

Josh figured they wouldn't do anything at an airport with travelers passing by to and fro. But still, he almost lost control of his bowels. Hadn't been this scared since that first night in Rikers' holding pen.

"The name Turk Worrel ring a bell?" Nunzi's slimy little smirk had a look of triumph.

The down-home name, even with its implications, made Josh feel less anxious. Suddenly, he didn't feel that the next second he'd be shitting in his drawers. Josh slowly followed Nunzi to the edge of the eating area. There were only two couples occupying the widespread tables. The two goons sat between Josh and Nunzi and the other diners.

"You want something?" Nunzi caught Josh's blank stare. "Yeah, why eat a burger at an airport when you're about to hit Vegas? We won't be long."

Nunzi looked foursquare around to make sure no one was within earshot. "Yeah, so you owed the Turk, what was it, $80,000 when they sent ya up for killing the cop?"

"I didn't kill…"

"You're off the fuckin' hook," Nunzi cut in, "save yer fucking arguments for the jury, the reporters, or those Hollywood bitches you hang around. Yeah, we did some business in Memphis and inevitably met the Turk. He said his operation was small-time and he couldn't carry ya all those years you were in the can. Just counting the vig after the first year, Turk figured it had grown to about $700,000. In the three years since then, ya figure about nine million and counting…"

Josh watched Nunzi's sick smile. He watched people ordering food, others walking about the terminal. This wasn't a dream but a fuckin' living nightmare. Nine million? He'd just beaten a rap; now how many people would he have to…

"Well, nine million's a little ridiculous. You were in stir. Not your fuckin' fault. So we agreed to buy out the Turk for half, forty grand. That was two years ago. At normal vig, with *our* juice, we're looking at 10–12 mill." Nunzi pulled his head back, rested the back of his neck against his clenched hands, which provided an ad hoc pillow. He stared at Josh's ashen face, like a teacher only too happy to explain why this "troublemaker" wasn't going to graduate.

Josh began to make a fist under the table. He was about to stand up. Nunzi seemed to catch the drift. "Look, you just got off the plane, so we know you ain't packin'. Don't lose your fuckin' cool. There's no way you can handle me and those two guys."

He pointed toward Ralphy and Butch. "Just relax and lemme explain. The twelve million's ridiculous. You were up the river and couldn't do a thing. We got a rep to maintain. So we charged a normal 10 percent a year for the two years and 2 percent a day since ya got sprung. We rounded it out at $300,000."

"How am I going to—"

"Relax," Nunzi cut him off. He absentmindedly pulled out a Marlboro then realized he was in a no-smoking zone. He fondled the cigarette in his right hand. "We're connected all the way up. I'm not gonna mention any names, but you read the papers. The next time ya read the News or the *Post* and they got headlines "Don this and Don that," *that* could be *the* Don."

Nunzi watched Josh's pallor turn even more pallid. He almost felt sorry for the dude. He softened his tone. "Look, Josh, we're trying to expand out of the usual shit. We've been RICOed and OCIDed to death, a wire under every car hood, every bed, every sofa. It's like when you're shacked up, it ain't just the two of you but some fuckin' Fed or New York investigator in bed with you and the broad."

Josh thought he should have responded to the so-called humor, but his lips couldn't crack a smile. Nunzi looked around again. The nearby tables were still empty. "So we been following your case. We figure if someone's near that Sloan bitch and some of those other weird showbiz types. Well, where there's lotsa loot, there's lotsa loot to be made. If ol' Nunzi Calabrese is seen hangin' 'round Sloan, the Feds get curious. If Josh Parker..." Nunzi grinned.

Josh felt like a load off. They got a plan. I'm gonna live.

Turns out the three goons were catching a six o'clock flight back to Newark. So Josh caught a cab to the Nugget. They had explained that Melanie would be out that night. She was pinched at the gentleman's club where she stripped and did lap dances. The cop was on the take and made penny-ante arrests when it suited someone's interests. In this case, they wanted Mel out of the way so that they have his undivided attention at the airport.

Josh was impressed by this Nunzi and whoever else was behind him. They had a Vegas cop on the payroll. They knew what flight Josh was taking to Vegas. They knew his original name was Jake Pearson and that he had to change it when he killed that shithead head of the gang bullying everyone at the high school. So this Nunzi was definitely big time or at least part of a big-time organization.

What they wanted was for him to supply the white powder, H, and other shit among the Hollywood and showbiz big shots and, once the hooks were in, see what else develops. Nunzi and his boys figured on eliminating the coke dealers those Hollywood types were getting their stuff from now.

Then, in the words of the economists, monopoly. So while in the hole for three hundred large, he now had the backing spadework, everything, for a big-time, big-loot operation.

Josh checked into the Nugget and went right to his room. He called Mel the next morning. She said she was pissed by the arrest but knew Josh had nothing to do with it. Josh smiled and put the phone down. He'd had a lot of tail since getting out, but nothing like Melanie. He couldn't wait for her to show.

A day after the flight back to New York, Josh met Bernie Litke at a noisy restaurant and got his marching orders. He was to meet Jimmy XX, somewhere off FDR Drive, where he'd get his first supply of white powder and H. He was told he'd have two months to start scoring with the celebs. Litke suggested he start with the New York TV and theater types to get his feet wet. Then "We got a suite for you at the Beverly Wilshire starting January." Litke put a one-hundred bill over the check and led them out to the cool Fifth Avenue breeze. "So you got two and a half months to do some good out here. Spring training, so to speak, before you head out to the majors in Beverly Hills. Oh yeah, before I forget, Nunzi wants 10 percent down by next Thursday. That's thirty thousand."

Litke disappeared in the Fifth Avenue hustle in less than a New York minute. Josh was left to contemplate his fate. That damn Turk, I would never have had to pay him. Now, I got all this to deal with. One thing's for sure, Josh vowed, that m——fing Turk's gonna get his. Farming me off to some Sopranos diddleheads with who knows what they got in back of them. Gotti, or some shit like that, only he's dead. Who the hell's paying attention to the new big name. Fuck it, maybe I can get some good out of it. They're calling the shots, doin' the spadework. What the fuck's the good of knowing those dim-witted celebrities if can't get something big out of it? I get in a spot and have to kill a cop, and those imbeciles make me out to be JFK or Mother Teresa. Josh shook his head. *And that stupid poetry, I got a fuckin' D in Slattery's grammar class. How could I write all that shit? Ain't anyone payin' attention out there? Anyhow, next step is for Litke to let me know where I meet this Jimmy XX off FDR.*

Meantime, that groupie, Tanya, who lives in the village, said "Come on over anytime. My roommate's out of town till the New Year."

He hopped into a cab. "Uhh, yeah, Greenwich Village, let's see, 562 East Eighth, please."

Josh shacked up with Tanya for nearly a week. They were stoned throughout.

Booze, coke, speed, and shit Josh hadn't even heard of. The festivities were interrupted just once, when Josh sobered up enough to hail a taxi to his suite at the Lyden Park on East Sixty-Third. He checked his mail and grabbed a grand to finance the rest of the week's spree. When they parted, he told her he wouldn't call for a couple of weeks, "business."

Josh got back on a Monday afternoon and racked out for nearly twenty-four hours. He didn't wake up till noon of the next day. He showered and took a shave. Still "restfully" tired from the long-overdue sleep, he climbed back in bed, grabbed the remote, and clicked the power. That financial network was on, and Josh ignored the numbers and stared at Maria whatever, the Money Honey. Plumb at the peak of the restful repose, the door buzzer sounded. "What the fuck...?" Josh muttered to himself as he slowly ambled toward the door. *Most people call. Who could...* He peeped through the door hole. It looked like a deliveryman holding a bouquet of flowers. An appreciative grin creased his mien as he opened the door. Got to be Tanya, the village beatnik, thanking him for... The deliveryman asked Josh where he could put the flowers. He then took out a receipt form and a pen and handed them to Josh. Josh noticed that the man, wearing a Spatz Florist logo, was a huge dude with ham hocks for fists. Josh began to sign when he thought he recognized... "Say, aren't you..."

The man's huge fist came out of nowhere and caught Josh on the temple near his left eye. The receipt and pen dropped to the floor, followed a millisecond later by Josh. Josh tried to rise, but the room seemed to be spinning. He had to close his eyes and try again. The room still appeared to be convulsing as if at the tail end of a hurricane, but now Josh was able to fathom the situation. The room wasn't in motion. It was the throbbing ache to his head that was causing all this vertigo. After the awful spinning seemed to subside, a new panic ensued. He was seeing double. He tried to get up again, but his body wouldn't allow it. He was helpless. So that's why a guy can't get up by the count of ten. He shook his head, as if he'd just come out of the ocean and had water in his ear. As he regained his senses, he noticed that a smaller man had entered his suite.

It was Nunzi. And the guy who clipped him was one of those bruisers from the airport. "Ralphy," Nunzi said crisply, "get this prick some water." Nunzi helped Josh to his feet and led him to an easy chair. He grabbed the glass of water from Ralphy, handed it to Josh, then pulled up a chair from the dining area. The passage of several minutes and the gulps of water brought Josh back to square one, except for the continued throbbing of the left side of his temple. He suddenly leaped up, put the glass on the table, and headed toward Ralphy.

Nunzi stepped in between. "Ay, dickbrain, sit your ass down. Ralphy'd kill you, and we got all that loot invested."

Josh slowly walked back to the chair. "Know why we're here, ya piece of shit?"

"No." Josh shook his head in a negative manner but also to alleviate the continued aching. "You said three weeks. It's only been two…"

"Who do you work for, ya piece of crap?"

"For you," Josh answered hesitantly.

"Right," Nunzi responded, "and if you worked in a fuckin' office, would you disappear for two weeks and your fucking boss doesn't know *where the hell you are?* Turns out, Jimmy XX has to hightail it to LA and was ready to meet you this week, and you were *nowhere.* Well, we got the cabbie that brought you up here to tell us where he picked you up. Shacked up with that little whore while I'm getting heat from upstairs? We're gonna have to keep you on a tight leash till we at least get our three hundred large back."

By now the room had totally cleared. And the pain had subsided to a dull ache. Josh felt good enough to get his bravado back. "Listen, you fuckin' shrimp, I ain't scared a nothin' and no one. And that fuckin' King Kong over there better kill me, 'cause I keep coming, and there ain't gonna be a sucker punch twice."

Ralphy gladly leaped to the challenge and advanced toward Josh. Nunzi grinned and motioned Ralphy back to the couch. He looked at Josh. "Look, loser, we know ya got balls. You killed a cop, which takes balls, and ya skated, which takes… ahh, luck, lawyers, or getting a bitch like that Chanteuse on your side."

Nunzi pulled up a chair next to Josh. "Yeah, we clocked ya back to your high school when you were forced to change your name. Yeah, you got balls. That's why we're using you. There was this Aryan something…" He looked at Ralphy.

"Aryan Brotherhood," Ralph answered.

"Right, Aryan Brotherhood. But you was on the outs with Whitey something, the leader. So they messed you up real bad. About a month in the hospital. When ya got out, you found a way to get Whitey one-on-one. You got the upper hand and cracked his skull on the pavement. Right so far?" Nunzi grinned.

Josh sat stone-faced while accepting a Marlboro from Nunzi. "So the rest of the Aryans ran for cover, and the school was freaked 'cause it had allowed all them racists to run around like that. So Whitey was buried secretly since he had no family. And the local paper and sheriff cooperated and killed the story. Of course, you had to change your name and transfer to another high school."

Josh let out a smoke ring. "So?"

"So," Nunzi replied mockingly, "we're tellin' you that even though you don't show proper respect, we know we got a ballsy guy on our side. We also know that you're a big hero now, at least to half the country, and therefore, you can go places we can't. But we already told you that. So here's the deal. No organization survives without rules."

Nunzi paused, grinned, and lit another Marlboro. "Certainly no organization in our line of work. So even though you're valuable to us, the rules take over. Otherwise, everything falls apart. Follow?"

Josh, still feeling the ache at his temple, frowned. "No, I don't follow."

Nunzi turned toward Ralphy. "Ralphy, why don't you explain?"

"Sure, boss. To get right to it, what Nunzi's saying is, we don't give diddly how much money you owe us or how much we can make wid ya in the future. Forget about Jimmy XX for now. We see you next Thursday for a down payment. You don't give us thirty large its fuhgetaboudit. Know, what *fuhgetaboudit* means?"

Josh stared blankly ahead.

"I'll explain what it means," Nunzi hissed. "It means we'll either make ya a cripple, or since that bitch Sloan and the papers'll get involved, we'll end it for ya, so that you can't tell the cops 'bout no Nunzi or Ralphy."

Josh tried a defiant grin, but it was no use. The "grin" was weakened by the sledgehammer pounding of his heart, the clammy feeling at the tip of his fingers. He watched Nunzi approach with a piece of paper.

"This here's the phone number of a dummy cell. No one ever answers it. Just leave a message. We'll get back to you. It's paid out of a phony account. So we're untraceable, just in case you're stupid enough to rat. Speaking of rats, one other thing," Nunzi flashed that ugly smile of his, "I feel sorry for anyone nowadays that's got a name like Nunzi Calabrese. That went out with the Mustache Petes. Oh yeah, Butch and Ralphy also made up."

The pair headed toward the door, Nunzi turned back once more, pointed to Ralphy. "We're coming back for the thirty grand, next Thursday, first thing in the morning. What Ralphy done today was tiddlywinks. You don't have the thirty ready for us, you'll end up begging to die."

THE BROTHER

Josh stayed home that night. He ground out the incessant noise of the Second Avenue traffic with one Jack Daniels after another. He didn't care if it didn't help him to figure a way out. He "deserved" to get soused tonight. He pulled out the pack's last Lucky and grabbed a new pack from the carton. He had all his cash spread out as if he was involved in a big-time poker game. A little over $6,000. What happened to the ten grand? A thousand was used up in Vegas before Mel returned the remaining nine. And the two weeks with the hippy must have used up three large. Josh couldn't remember how, but he knew that kind of broad wouldn't have taken him. Must have been all the drugs, boozing; Josh hadn't cared. He was trying to make up for missing four years and to get this new Nunzi problem out of mind. So four grand blown. But even with the full ten, he'd still be twenty thousand short. He thought about hitting on some of the Hollywood types or his attorneys; they'd easily come up with the scratch, but he'd have the bitch of a time explaining why he needed that much cash that fast. But maybe as a last resort… he'd run out of ice and that last shot glass of Jack Daniels put him into dreamland.

He woke up in the pitch-black, and he checked out the luminescent clock. It was just past 4:00 AM. Josh reflectively grabbed the remote and put on the TV. He hadn't had anythin' to eat in quite a while, and now his growling stomach reminded him. He decided to make a grilled cheese and then hit the rack. The old movie on TCM showed Fred Astaire as a sailor. *Sailor, that's it!* In all the parties and happenings since he got out, he'd forgotten that he ran into Andy Anderson, his main man in the Navy.

They'd repaired ships at Mare Island then spent every weekend alley-catting around North Beach, Union Street and other San Francisco hot spots. Apparently, after discharge, Andy moved to New York and had "a few things" on the fire. In a sudden cold sweat, Josh rushed to his wallet—he'd been drunk most of the time. Did he throw out Andy's card? He went through a bunch of old… and then, he found it! Gasping relief, Josh ate the grilled-cheese sandwich and slept till noon.

***

Ramon Cortez was wide-eyed. "No kidding, your name's David Sloan? Right, as all-American as apple pie, but after knowing some-one as Hashtiri, a John Smith–type real name. Well, maybe not outta sight but a little strange."

David smiled. "Why? I don't look Indian, do I?"

Ramon shrugged. "Obviously not, it's just that most of the 'mystics' that I've known usually own up to real names like Horowitz, Goldberg, O'Brien, and so on."

David, sighing, replied, "Good thing you're the only one who knows. Been back in the life for six months, and readjustment's tough enough as it is. Drivers' licenses, rent deposits, living paycheck to paycheck, all those headaches… How do you normal people do it?"

Ramon tapped David on the shoulder. "Listen, amigo, the other fence is green, or whatever that saying is, I've often just wanted to disappear into—what was it again?"

"A retreat." David looked toward the room's closed door, as if ashamed that someone else might hear.

"Yeah." Ramon giggled. "A retreat, but didn't you call it…"

"A Meditation Sanctuary," David cut in, eager to put all this behind him. But Ramon was his one true friend since he rejoined the world, and he had to trust, square up to someone. "Look, Ramon."

David was still smiling, but with an edge. "I'll clue you in some more some other time, but right now…"

"What, did you do something serious?" Ramon's thin dark face tightened, as if there was a secret to be revealed he'd rather not know about.

David caught the tension. "Relax, Ramon, we 'sixteen-hour, $150 a day' PAs got to stick together. It's a bombshell, all right, but nothing like I killed anyone."

"Oh, damn." Ramon shrugged. "And here I am, tired of slaving away as a production assistant and looking for that million-dollar screenplay."

"Well," David tightened his lips, "maybe you can cut me in for some of that million, 'cause I got something better than a murder."

"I'm all ears, want to go out to that Starbucks near here?"

"Can't." David frowned. "Can't let anyone overhear."

"Okay, okay, let's have it." Ramon rolled his eyes.

David took a deep breath. "Ever hear of Ann Sloan?"

Ramon shook his head. "Is this some joke, a quiz show? Who hasn't heard… why when I was *una petito* in San Juan, even my sainted grandma knew only three—Merman, Streisand, and the one and only Chanteuse, Ann Sloan."

"She's my sister."

Ramon flapped his eyelids and shook his head. "*Right*, and the pope, the Holy Father, is my great-uncle." Ramon put his hand on David's shoulder and whispered in a caring tone. "Come on, amigo, what's the *problema*? Tell your Uncle Ramon."

David took a deep breath. "Didn't figure you'd believe me."

Ramon's eyes narrowed; he stared intently. "You're not shitting me?"

"Ramon, I don't have that kind of imagination. Lemme call Reynolds. We've finished the sign-in sheets and the time cards for the extras. What do you think, the first stragglers will be in by three for the night shoot?"

"Ay, David, Reynolds'll have our asses if we pay…"

"I know, I know, Ramon. They were told to be here at four, so we don't pay the early birds. All I'm saying is, we got to be back here by three for the early ones, in case Reynolds hasn't arrived. Meantime, it's one thirty, let's scamper out to that Starbucks down the block."

"What for?" Ramon smiled. "Going to tell me the story of your life?"

"Better," David said haughtily, "going to tell you about me and my sis, Ann Sloan."

David pulled out his wallet, took out a faded photograph, and handed it to Ramon. "She was twenty-five, I was twelve."

"Holy shit!" Ramon was wide-eyed. "She's put on weight, but that's definitely Ann Sloan. And you, you shitbird, you already had that big chin… Umm, yeah, that's you at twelve. Amazing, but why are you slaving…"

David grabbed Ramon's arm. "Let's get a little fresh air. I'll tell you everything, the lattes are on me. Just don't say the name Ann Sloan if anyone's within earshot."

David explained it all—how Ann was bitten by the showbiz bug by the age of six.

By the time she got to high school, she'd outgrown anything Des Moines had to offer. As a sophomore in the High School for Performing Arts in Manhattan, she got her first bit part on Broadway, and as they say, the rest was history. Meanwhile, David explained, even though he thought he'd like show business, the difference in age meant that Ann was already a star while he'd barely entered high school. As he did not have her level of talent, his self-esteem, never that high, plunged further. The parents wanted one "stable professional" in the family, so he aimed to be a CPA. But he never liked it, and by his midtwenties, he took to meditation as a way out. He eventually got so involved he ended up at a *Shasri* in India.

Ann was all gaga since she already had so much loot she'd be able to provide for her ascetic little brother who was eschewing all the trappings of wealth and materialism. She paid for most of his stays, both in India and Vermont, as long as he promised to visit her in Malibu every year or so. Meanwhile, while away, she had to be content with one letter a month and two phone calls a year—further contact would have negated the benefits of the "solitary" and "meditative" existence.

"That's pretty much the gist of it," David concluded, dipping his biscotti into his latte.

"Wow," Ramon gasped. "What a story. But didn't she ever visit you?" David just smiled and shook his head.

Ramon nodded. "But of course, someone like La Chanteuse visiting one of those retreats... too much commotion."

"Anyhow, she still thinks I'm in Ishvash in the Green Mountains of Vermont. She even accepted the thought that I might acquire an orange robe, which would have committed me for life. I've called her a few times since I left, and she's none the wiser. The point is, I don't want her help, for many reasons."

"What about your parents? Why... why won't you let her help you?" Ramon stammered, looking like he had a million more questions.

David took another sip. "Mom and Dad died long ago in a commuter plane... I don't... don't want to talk about it. As for Ann, there's tremendous pressure... I... I just want to make sure I can do it on my own. You know I landed that part in the offBroadway revival of Our Town. If all goes well, if I get reviews, well, I'm on my way. I got a start in showbiz on my own. If the reviews are bad, I'll tell her what's happening, spend a couple of months with her, and go out to Wyoming or something, and study accounting at the ripe old age of twenty-nine."

"What about all that Yogi meditation stuff?"

"It's over with, Ramon, I'm ready to... What do they say on Broadway? Watch out, world. Here I come."

Ramon shook his head and flashed a wide grin. "Million-dollar screenplay, here I come."

David got up and jabbed his finger at Ramon's chest. "Get your own freaking screenplay, leave my life out of it."

As they walked out, Ramon giggled. "Okay, if I say it's a famous brother instead of sister?"

"Why, you...," David mumbled as they hurried back to the set.

***

Josh found a park bench in the northeast corner of Chelsea Park, lit a cigarette, and huddled against the gray cold of a November morning. Within a minute, his cell phone rang, "Yeah, Andy, I'm on a bench facing the swings."

Josh had just lit another Lucky when Andy appeared. They ran toward each other like star-crossed lovers in some soap. "Andy, you a-hole mother, how long's it been?"

"Well, aside for thirty seconds two weeks ago when you were stoned at that party, at least five years, you old has-been—pardon me, famous has-been. Hobnobbing with all those famed Hollywood stars. Lemme look at you. Put on a little weight, heh?"

"What about you?" Josh replied. "A 'stache, cowboy sideburns, and Levi's like you're ranching in Nevada, instead of being a sophisticated New Yorker."

"Easy answer, Josh." Andy led Josh back to the bench. "For some fucking reason, my client base is turned on by the cowboy look. They figure I'm the real McCoy and not some narc."

"What's the client base, and what's the product, you no-good a-hole?"

"As if you didn't know, Josh. The clients are students from NYU and rich broads from some private college out in Riverdale." He held out a bag of white powder. "And," he smirked, "this is the product."

"Just coke?"

"Nah, H too. But you got to be careful with that. Ectasy's really big with those young kids too."

Josh pulled out another Lucky and offered it to Andy, who declined. "So how'd you get started, Andy?"

"Long story. Took some classes at NYU, saw what was happening. Had one scrape with a student competitor, and he disappeared. NYU was all mine. Dealers stood out in a setting like that, inevitably got busted. The village's always crawling with cops. So I moved the operation to this here park, just a cab ride from NYU, and adopted the cowboy look. One NYU dude brought his squeeze from that private school in Riverdale, and she spread the news. So I got kids who pay on the barrel, with no gang bangers, no Mafia or syndicate shit. A clean, safe operation."

Josh tapped Andy on the shoulder. "Sounds like you got it made, you no good fucker."

Andy smiled. "Want in? Oh, I forgot, keeping company with all those movie stars…"

"They got their own political agenda," Josh cut in, "they'll probably drop me like a hot potato and go on to a new cause. Besides, we work good together, and I need some big dough real fast. I'm in."

WRONG PLACE

David watched Reynolds speaking to the director. He glanced at the clock. It was ten thirty. "Damn it," he whispered to Ramon, "we've been here since six this morning. I know this is a wrap, but taking advantage is taking advantage."

Ramon glanced at Reynolds and the director in animated conversation. "Looks like they're excited. Maybe arguing over one more take tonight."

"That's crazy, Ramon. Where the hell is the producer? True, only a third of the extras are left, but they've been on double time for three hours already."

Ramon winced and held his index finger in front of his nose. "Shh, here comes Reynolds."

Reynolds Harding, adjusting his belt to accommodate his ample girth, smiled as he approached the pair. "Thanks for the sixteen hours, guys. Pay the extras till eleven. You guys won't be out till midnight, but that's showbiz."

"Que pasa, Reynolds?"

Reynolds shrugged and adjusted his glasses. "That's a director from hell. Magnus's rep follows him around. He wants a week off to study the dailies with the producer, but he's not happy... I gotta call my wife."

They watched Reynolds heading toward a chair as he dialed his cell phone. "Shit, David, I've never seen Reynolds so beat."

"So what," David smirked. "More money for Metro Casting and a lot more work for us, buddy."

"Yeah, at slave wages."

"Cheer up, Ramon, you survive as a PA on a motion picture with Magnus at his worst, and next, you get to work with Spielberg or Scorsese. Then you get to direct.

You'll be so rich and famous you won't have to write that million-dollar screenplay."

"Right." Ramon sighed. "Meantime, I'm bushed, and we'll be lucky if we're out of here by midnight." He looked around. "Looks like the caterers have flown away the coop. I'm gonna rush down to the diner and get a fresh latte. They'll be filling out their time cards. You can handle till I'm back. Okay?"

"Okay, only it's flown the coop, and get me a decaf double."

"Eeyyy, *caramba*, all those grammar lessons—flown the coop, flown the coop…"

Ramon grinned and hurried out the door.

When he returned, he noticed Reynolds apparently helping David in the midst of a heated discussion over a time card with a scruffy-looking coed type with a long blond ponytail. The line was long, and Ramon felt guilty he'd been away, even for ten minutes. It was now close to eleven thirty, but with three people processing, the sixty-to-seventy time cards would be signed off on in less than fifteen minutes. Ramon couldn't wait. He had a hot one for David.

With the time cards completed, Reynolds went to the costume trailer to help process the stragglers who were still returning the studio's apparel. Ramon watched David stuff the day's paperwork into the respective envelopes, grinning from ear to ear.

David caught Ramon's act. "What the hell you sitting there grinning? C'mon, help me. I'd like to be out of here by midnight."

"I got a biggie for you, David. Ran into Monique at the diner. She had called as to what time was wrap, saying she was there to give someone a lift. She was told not till eleven, so she's been occupying a booth facing our entrance—she can't miss you."

David bit his lips, grimaced. "Did you, did she…"

SLATS AND THE CHANTEUSE

"Relax, amigo, I told her I last saw you assisting on that court-room scene and that you weren't feeling well and probably cut out after the shoot."

David's shoulders sagged; he sighed. "Think she believed you?"

"Nah, I'm a good liar, but not that good. She called you, what, three times on the cell tonight, and you hung up. She can't take a hint, and she's getting hit by a hammer. I guarantee she'll be waiting."

David pursed his lips. "Damn, I hate these scenes. She just won't accept… Well, I told her it wouldn't work…"

Ramon smirked, "What, you giving up, amigo? You said she's a good lay."

"Yeah, compared to what," David blushed, "playing with my wong at the retreat? At any rate, with my big chance in this play coming up, I need solitude or someone I'm more copacetic with. Monique's okay physically, but she's a pain in the butt, and I don't dig her intellectually."

"Okay, amigo, sloppy seconds?"

David shook his head wearily. "Whatever you do's okay by me, pal. I'm just not up to seeing her tonight."

"Say I got an idea, David. There's a dingy staircase out back that's hardly used, except as a fire exit. Go down that way and turn toward Tenth Avenue and there's no way she'd see you, even if she's standing at the front entrance. I've used it sometimes when the elevator's out."

"Ramon, I'll remember you in my will. Show me the way?"

"I will, David, but we'll need a flashlight. That staircase always has rubbish on it, and it's easy to trip. Also, you end up in a dark alleyway, and you got to watch out for the ash cans and shit like that."

"Sounds good, Ramon. Now let's finish before Reynolds gets back."

***

Josh Parker zippered his windbreaker to the top. "Hey, Andy, where you at? Freezing my tail out here."

"Yeah, Josh, I think you're too near something, your cell's cracking. There's the Chelsea Diner, on Twenty-Third, near Tenth. Meet you there in about fifteen. There's an alleyway nearby. I often use it after midnight. There's nothing there but the old maritime building. They built a new one closer to the pier. The old building's used for indoor movie shoots, but they hardly ever go past midnight."

"So what am I supposed to—"

"Just have a cup java, Josh, and some french apple pie. It's the best in the city. I'm meeting some customers in the park—it'll be a quickie. Still, it'll probably be about twenty minutes before I get there. Enjoy the pie."

Josh, muttering, put the cell back in his pocket. Andy's getting to be a pain. Still, he brings me enough stash I can push enough to round up the 30K before I got to see that fucking Nunzio this Thursday.

Josh was on his second cup of coffee and clocking a good-looking redhead shivering in front of that gray, officious-looking maritime building, when he spotted Andy.

"Sorry to hold you up, Josh, but that's my deal, you never know when a customer calls. The young punk said he had a flat. But what the hey, he's a good customer." He led Josh into the alleyway. They stood about fifteen feet from a nearby streetlamp. "Can ya see okay, Josh?"

"Yeah," Josh snapped, "let's get on with it."

"Okay, Josh, I got three packs, a kilo each, of coke, and four eight balls of H."

"What, that's it? That adds up to two fuckin' ounces of H." Josh's breathing was heard over the usual din of nighttime traffic.

"Relax, Josh, you look like you're gonna have a stroke. You got about five ten grand there."

"Didn't I fuckin' tell you I needed thirty grand's worth?"

Andy's heart started pounding. He'd never seen Josh this angry. "C'mon, I thought you were pullin' my dick. You've always been a joker. I didn't think you meant—"

"Of course, I meant it. Don't you fuckin' know me yet?" He moved toward Andy, whose face showed fright as he backed up against a wall. "Well, gimme what you got, on account, then we'll see about—"

"Don't... don't... you know how I operate?" Andy's voice cracked with panic. "My squeeze always shows minutes after a score, and I give her the cash just in case..."

"Well, how much was it?" Josh put his face up against Andy's.

Andy tried shoving him back, prompting Josh to grab him by the shirt collar. "I need thirty grand now."

Andy let go a right cross, knocking Josh back. "I really didn't think you were serious about the thirty. I might be able to round up ten to fifteen—"

"Ten to fifteen? WHERE THE FUCK IS ALL YOUR MONEY?"

"Offshore, we—"

"OFFSHORE? What the fuck does that mean?"

Andy pushed the suddenly befuddled Josh aside. "Don't you know about the narcs, IRS? Where you been? You can't put that kinda loot in the bank." Andy turned and started out of the alley.

"Where the hell you going? Come back here."

Andy turned to face Josh. "Forget it, Josh, You ain't the same. Can't work with you anymore."

"But, Andy," Josh wailed, "I need thirty big by Thursday."

"You in that deep, that scared? Go to that Chanteuse and your rich lawyers for—"

"THERE'S NO TIME NOW!" Josh tried to regain his composure. "I... I... wasted three days counting on you." Andy turned toward the street.

"Come back, ya fuck. You ain't running out on me." Josh caught up to Andy and again shoved him against the wall. "You ain't leaving until..." Josh heard some voices farther down the alley.

"You okay, now, David?"

"Yeah, Ramon, thanks for everything." David, unnerved by the commotion, hurried down the alley toward the street.

Andy, aware that Josh had turned his attention toward the figure heading their way, again broke toward the street. Josh quickly recovered and once more grabbed him by the scruff of the neck and pounded him against the wall. "You ain't leaving till we settle this thing."

Andy kneed him in the groin, but Josh quickly recovered and hit Andy with a roundhouse right—just as David reached them.

"What the hell's going on here?" David, heart racing, realized he shouldn't have said anything. He tried racing past the pair.

Josh grabbed his arm. "See anything?"

"*No*, no… mister, I didn't see…" His heart pounding, his throat parched, David just wanted out. Breathing heavily, he suddenly did a double take. "Say, aren't you…?"

"Who, who am I? You nosy freak. Mind your own…" Josh noticed Andy had slipped away. David tried to reach the street, but Josh caught up to him. He dragged David back into the alley.

"Help! Help!" David screamed at the top of his lungs.

"Shut the fuck up!" Josh slammed David against the wall of the alleyway.

David tried to yell, but Josh put his hand over David's mouth to shut him up. David, unable to breathe, tried moving Josh's hand away. He finally kicked Josh in the shins, giving him a chance to break away. Josh caught up instantly and pounded David's head against the wall. David started moaning, and he collapsed to the ground. Josh, dazed himself, yelled at David to stop groaning. Frustrated by the continued whimpering, Andy's escape, and having to face Nunzio, he began kicking, kicking the body on the ground until it was silent. Realizing what had happened, Josh was about to run out of the alley.

"What's going on? David, I heard screaming. Are you…" Ramon had approached the scene and witnessed the limp body on the ground and a man with a frenzied look head toward him. Ramon froze in terror for a moment, then raced back toward the door, and stumbled up the dark stairs, yelling as loudly as he could. Josh had followed through the door, but the dark staircase and the sound of other voices dissuaded him. Totally unnerved, Josh ran through the alley and out into the night.

JOSH AGAIN

Captain Rick Sullivan looked out his office door. He shouted, "Ay, Stretch, get yer can in here, right away!" Sullivan lit a cigar and calmly watched Johnny "Stretch" Rizzo, all five foot seven of him, enter the office. "Close the fuckin' door, Stretch, and sit yer ass down."

Stretch smiled, closed the door behind him, and picked one of the two chairs facing Sullivan's broad mahogany desk.

Sullivan leaned forward and rested his elbows over his desk. "Whataya got, Stretch?"

Stretch heaved a sigh and opened his palms, as if copping a plea or doing a mea culpa. "Well, no weapon, Sully. No gun, no knife, no blunt instrument of any type."

"Yeah," Mangold confirmed, "all the bruises, contusions, all that shit, from either fists, shoe leather, or the wall or the pavement."

"Wall?"

"Yeah, Sully, it was a narrow alleyway. Mangold's still working on whether the injuries back of the scalp were from the pavement or the wall. Mangold's initial call—a little of both. But he's still working on it. The good news, Mangold's got thirty-seven partial prints and a shot at ridge characteristics."

Sullivan absentmindedly scratched his scalp. "So what do you read, Stretch?"

"Well, it wasn't a planned whatever. When someone uses his fists or stomps a victim to the pavement, it had to be something happening on the spot."

"Like a drug deal gone bad?"

"Probably, Sully. There's the Chelsea Diner, a stone's throw away, where you can wait for someone to show and then walk over to the alley for privacy. Except for the guy that got stomped."

"How's that, Stretch?"

Stretch pulled out a sheet of paper. "The guy's name was Hashtiri. We're still trying…"

"What? What kinda fuckin' name is that? Is he one of them hippies?" Sullivan's jowly cheeks flushed; Stretch rolled his eyes.

"Well, like I said, Sully, we're calling the employer, Entertainment Producers, out in Idaho somewhere."

"Idaho, what kinda shit…"

"Yeah, well, we all can't be in New York or Hollywood, Sully. This Hashtiri—hopefully, they'll get his real name in payroll in Idaho—was a production assistant. Y'know, the guys that shepherd the screen extras around all day and take care of all kinds of crap. Point is, Sully, he was good friends with his coworker. Let's see, ahh, yeah, here it is, Ramon Cortez."

"Well," Sully grimaced, "what does he know?"

"He apparently saw the tail end, and the perp started to chase him up the stairs…"

"I remember that part, Stretch, so when…"

"That's the point, Sully, the guy was taken to Waverly Hospital and put under sedation. When Jillio and Nowitzki went up there the next morning, the guy had already split. And there's no trace of him at his pad in Queens. We interviewed some guy named Reynolds Harding, who works there. His hunch is, this Cortez panicked and went back to PR."

"Shit, Stretch, we had a live witness. Where in PR?"

"Santurce, I think."

"Y'know how many Ramon Cortezes there must be out there? Check with Hernandez, he's got the lingo down pat, maybe he can get the locals."

"On that, Chief. We're also checking Idaho to see if payroll had the next of kin, all that shit."

"Okay, Stretch, you've already wasted an hour of my day. I got other cases." Stretch took the hint and headed out. He was met at the door by an excited Charley Jillio. "Yeah, Jill, what's up?"

"The chief'll wanna hear this, Johnny."

Stretch shrugged his shoulder and led them back into Sully's office. "Yeah, guys, what is it?"

"We got a call," Jillio, grinning, started laughing so hard he bent forward and held his stomach.

Stretch pursed his bottom lip and looked at Sully, who barked, "Who called, and what's so funny?"

"Don't know who called. We traced it to a phone booth in Chelsea. The guy said Josh Parker killed the guy in the alley." Jillio was now composed but smirked as he watched the befuddlement on his bosses' faces. "Look at it this way, we're now in the big time. Oh yeah, the dude said check the forensics, DNA, and so on. That'll prove it's Parker. We got it on tape. Applebaum's checking the tape for voice recognition, all that shit. He's already come up with something."

"What's that?" Stretch sighed. "The dude was scared."

Stretch looked at Sully. Sully got up and kicked at his wastebasket. "Aw shit, Stretch, our precinct. Now, we'll have those Hollywood ghouls and that Sloan bitch down *our* throats. Not that I'm backing down. The fucker skated after killing one of our own. Tell Mangold to skip the universal database on what we picked up at the site. Just check the computer against Parker, and make it priority 1. Have Cassady call the DA to make up the arrest warrant now so we're ready if and when Mangold makes the match. That's all, guys."

Sully picked up the phone. "Joan, get me Adams at precinct 24. If he's not there, get me anyone who worked on the Josh Parker case."

***

Flip Fallon hovered over Slats Conners, who was on the phone. "Just a sec, Holly." Slats put his hand over the phone. "Yeah, Flip,

Leary wants me?" Flip nodded and walked away. "Boss wants me, hon, call you back soon as I can."

Leary, as usual, was leaning back on his chair enjoying the scenic view. "Hi, Tom, I caught the Chanteuse's press release. Can't believe it. How's it go? Déjà vu all over again?"

Leary acquiesced to a slight smirk. "Did you hear she's having a press conference at three this afternoon?"

"Nah, Tom, I hadn't heard. Where?"

"At Spivey's Conference Center in Century City."

"Wow, Century City, I'm really—"

"Keep your eager eyes off those skirts populating Century City, you horndog, or I'll tell Holly on you."

"Aye, aye, skipper." Slats blushed. "Holly's too good for me as it is."

"You got that one right." Leary smiled. "Okay, Slats, first order of business. Heard through the grapevine that Shapiro wants out, going to declare a case overload. He took a lot of heat for letting Parker skate once. My guess is, he doesn't want all that commotion again, no matter what the reward."

"Wow, boss, I'm impressed." Slats grinned. "Picked all that up without hitting the bricks, eh?"

Leary eyed Slats and shrugged. "You don't get to where I am in this business without good, reliable sources. Never burn your bridges, Slats, never burn your bridges." He watched Slats head toward the door. "Be there by two, Slats. Spivey liked your treatment of Sloan in the first trial, so you got a spot reserved. But it's gonna be a madhouse. They might give your space to someone else. Don't blow it. Now git."

Slats grinned. "Going right now. Gonna have a nice lunch in Century City."

"Get outta here."

"I'm gone, boss, I'm gone."

Slats was a half hour early, and he knew he was in the midst of something big.

Cameras from all the nets were there, plus Fox, CNN, and the usual herd of showbizcasters and reporters. Slats was lucky enough to be sitting next to Ann Porter of the *South Coast Daily*, which covered happenings all the way from Manhattan to Laguna beaches. She was busily scribbling down the Chanteuse's "chic" ensemble and gracious enough to share it with Slats. Let's see, from the bottom up, a lizard-embossed leather boot with a one-and-a-half-inch heel, some kind of black slacks with "stitch detailing," and a black leather frog-closure jacket with a faux Persian lamb collar and cuffs. Ann told Slats what *faux* meant, adding, "Not to worry, your female readership will know."

With everyone seated, the noise abated, and the cameras set, Ann Sloan strode to the podium. She got right to it. "With the Ashcroftization of our justice system, the wholesale attack on the environment, women's rights and the poor, capricious foreign adventures, and tax cuts for the rich, our nation has reached a new low in civility. Synthesizing the despotic turn in the affairs of our nation is the calumny of the power structure's war on the innocent. Josh Parker may be one man, but he symbolizes what can be achieved when the forces of justice unite to fight the oppression of the system."

The Chanteuse paused for a sip of water. Slats noticed how rapt the audience of the third estate was. Was it the impressive celeb at the rostrum, or did this crowd buy the idiotic pablum being dished out? He figured it's the former. This gathering can't be that stupid.

Duly refreshed, Ann Sloan continued, "I won't attempt to enter the legal domain today, but all of you here are certainly aware of Josh's recent travails. He served four years for killing a policeman, a total frame-up. After so many caring persons entered the fight to end an innocent man's ordeal, justice was served, and he was freed after a new trial. Now, repressive forces in our society, still smarting from their defeat in their first frame-up, are attempting it again. Rest assured, Josh, all the Progressive forces in America and, for that matter, throughout the world will take up your cause."

Cal Brenner, the nationally syndicated talk-show host, known as the new Rush, asked the first question, "Yes, Ms. Sloan, a two-part question. First, why frame Josh, in particular, to begin with, let alone again? And second, if no matter what prints, DNA, fibers, and so on are found, if the defense claims they were planted or some such, how can the prosecution ever prove its case to someone like yourself, let alone a jury?"

"I'm glad you asked that, Mr. Brenner." A slight smile creased her lips. "After taking so much criticism for so long for countless wrongful incarcerations of African Americans and other people of color, the oppressive forces no doubt decided on an end run by like-wise framing a WASP. As for the second part, Mr. Brenner, I have full faith in the everyday citizens that serve on juries to reach a just conclusion based on the evidence or… falsity thereof."

Brenner tried some follow-ups after Sloan hissed a thank-you for all the attention he brought her on his show. Spivey, however, interceded and kept things moving. The questioning lasted well over a half hour, and toward the end, Slats noted, Spivey no longer answered just the "tough" ones. He'd moved Ann over and answered them all, crisply and curtly. Their problem, Slats guessed, was the absence of Shapiro, lending credence to the rumors that he'd had it. The more the questioning centered on Shapiro and his role in a new defense of Josh Parker, the more terse Spivey was, as he seemingly couldn't wait to call on a new questioner, "Next."

As he wandered out of Century City, Slats no longer focused on the well-turned ankles scurrying to and fro. He was trying to remember the name of that legal reporter for the *Chron* up in Frisco. He was a graduate of Hastings Law and was sure to have a good guess on who'd replace Shapiro. Slats wanted something before facing Leary tomorrow. *Call the Chronicle and look like an idiot asking the name of their legal beagle or go to Lexis Nexis?*

That night, near midnight, a shades-drawn black limo approached the guard gate at the Chanteuse's Bel Air estate. The limo was parked near the gate, and an automobile from the mansion picked up the occupant, Dave Shapiro, and his chauffeur.

The chauffeur was deposited in one of the libraries and given his choice of drink and movie fare. Shapiro was led into the study, where he was greeted by Ann and Jeff Hudson.

Ann rushed toward Dave and bussed him on the cheek. "Dave, so wonderful to have you here. Mind if Jeff sits in?"

Dave looked at Jeff, who was decked out in a black waffle-textured robe over silky white pajamas. "Legally, you're not married, he can testify…"

"Oh, Dave," the Chanteuse did her best Bette Davis, waving her arms back and forth, "how you do carry on."

"Hi, Dave." Jeff shook his hand. "Anything on ice in here, or should I call Harold? He can fix—"

"It's okay, Jeff." Shapiro chose a plush leather recliner. "Scotch on the rocks is just fine."

"Coming right up. Dave." He looked at Ann. "Can I freshen your drink, hon?"

"I'm fine, baby, just fine. Just take care of Dave."

The chimes in that Old English clock announced 1:00 AM, and Dave was on his second drink. "Sorry, Ann, I could smother you with details of all the cases I got on my plate. Sure, I can farm them out to associates, but when they pay those big bucks, they naturally want the big man for their money." Dave caught Ann and Jeff rolling their eyes as they looked at each other. "Okay," he snapped, "if you think there's more to it, you're right."

He looked at his suddenly focused listeners and calmly sipped some more of that J&B. "I got contacts at the precinct handling Josh. Turns out they got a lot more than the first time. Spezio and Tanaka, if you use them again, got their work cut out." He watched the expressions of shock on Ann's and Jeff's faces. He got up and helped himself to some more ice cubes. "And that's the least of it. Apparently, someone called the precinct sounding scared to death and said that Josh killed that kid. Of course, Ann, I'll be glad to share what I have with whoever you hire to see if the prosecution provides all this in discovery."

Ann was starting one last "Can't you think it over?" when Harold appeared and announced that the chauffeur had just concluded viewing Shane. "That's it." Dave shrugged. "Felix gets real cranky when he's bored, and it's too late to start another movie."

Jeff hugged Ann after Shapiro left. "I'm so furious. What an attitude, after that fortune in fees we sent him." She wiped off some tears and rested her head on Jeff's chest. She slowly led Jeff back to the couch. "I made him the most famous attorney in the world, and this is how he repays me?"

"Well, is Johnny Cochran available?" Jeff tried a little humor.

"We'll get someone, Jeff, and someone good. If there's one thing I've learned in life, you can buy a lot with a lot of money. Now let's retire, Jeff dear, I need love right now real bad."

They walked toward the bedroom arm in arm. "Jeff, darling, aren't we due to hear from David at that retreat pretty soon? He always calls in July and before New Year's."

"Right, hon, and New Year's Eve is in two weeks. Why mention it?"

"Well, because that young man that was killed had one of those Vedic mystic-type names. You know, just like David uses."

"Well, hon, they don't read the papers in that place in Vermont, so David and the rest of them won't be getting any bad vibes."

NNM

Ann Sloan managed to get Dave Shapiro to meet her one more time. They lunched at Dejeuner, one of those Tony French bistros that continually seem to surface along Beverly Hills' restaurant row on Sunset. It was small talk over old times and cases until the delectable desert tray showed up. Ann bit into her napoleon and went to message. "The jury was only out two days in the past trial, Dave. We won it going away. They've got it in for Josh. It's now a symbol. They *have* to get him. I'm sure that's why they planted—"

"Ann, please." Shapiro held his right hand up. "First of all, my practice is here in California. Sure, I'm licensed in New York, but there was too much bicoastal hassle last time. Barbara was a dream, putting up with it, but with the kids in college… Ann, it was a one-shot favor. Look, Spezio lives in New York, give him the top chair. Glen Tanaka's ready to move up, he's got a law degree and—"

"Dave, I'm counting on *you*. I deserve the best, Josh deserves the best."

Shapiro leaned back and took another sip of coffee. "Ann, let me explain something about defense attorneys. We get a bad rap, and I guess we always will. It's the nature of what we do. But no matter what the public thinks about so-and-so getting away with it, beating the system, skating, if you will, believe me, most of us won't take a case to free a defendant if we know he's guilty. If he's going to plea, of course, it's our duty. But that's different, he's still going to serve time.

But if we know, but for sure if I know, that the client is guilty of a capital crime, I will not be a party to setting him free."

"But, Dave…"

"Please, Ann, let me finish. What's wonderful in jurisprudence is that most of the time, if the client maintains he's innocent, most lawyers won't know for sure whether the client's guilty or innocent until well into the trial. Of course, under such circumstances, we'll push the envelope for our clients. But there's a difference, some of us won't take a case if we know…"

"Dave," Ann gasped. "What are you saying?"

"Josh was guilty the first time, Ann. Yes, I directed Spezio and Tanaka, and they did a great job. And we threw all kinds of extraneous stuff at that jury, including you, Ann. Midway through, when I had already realized I was defending a guilty man, I did that hatchet job on that police officer. I… I… still can't sleep…"

Shapiro stopped because he saw Ann hyperventilating. Her heavy breathing, accompanied by a staccato of mini shrieks, had already grabbed the attention of nearby diners. As Shapiro got up to help her, he noticed the waiter and the maître d' rushing toward Ann. Shapiro tried to pat her back, but she brushed him aside, yelling, "I'm all right, I'm all right!"

She eyed the maître d'. "Andre, please call me a cab."

Andre looked at Shapiro, whose flushed cheeks betrayed his embarrassment. "Yes, Ms. Sloan, right away."

Ann picked up her purse, shot a daggerlike glare at Shapiro, and followed Andre toward the front. Dave Shapiro tried to ignore the stares and whispers surrounding him as he stared blankly at the check and finished his coffee.

***

Ed Spivey had a lot on his plate. Ann, his principal client, was under sedation and in seclusion. Her condition wasn't helped by the fact that her LA attorney, Stephen Fine, was vacationing with his family on a yacht off some Greek Isle and would only respond to "emergencies." So Spivey had to combine e-mails with picture phones in long-distance confabs with her New York attorney, Stan Wasserman. Stan was confident that Spezio could handle top chair but promised he'd check with some top criminal attorneys to see if they'd be "available." Spivey sighed; he knew Wasserman was putting him off. No topflight criminal lawyer was going to go through the pain in the ass of getting a guilty man off twice. Opprobrium from the law and order half of the nation if you win and a blow to your reputation if you lose. Spezio, on the other hand, despite his age and track record, was still hungry. That would overcome his inexperience as top dog in a major criminal trial. He decided to wait two more days for Wasserman to call back. If Wasserman doesn't call, Spivey decided, he'll recommend Spezio to Ann.

Hopefully, Ann would be lucid by then. Meantime, there was that firebrand, Tom Crosby, who's latched on to the Chanteuse's skirt and planned a bicoastal demonstration against the establishment using Josh Parker controversy as a linchpin. He wanted Ann to lead the Hollywood contingent at the Bowl while he resurrected the demographics of the Vietnam era for a huge simultaneous rally at the Ellipse in Washington. In studying the activists of the Vietnam era, Crosby apparently had been most impressed by the New Mobe that took place in 1969, nearly bringing the capital to its knees, hence the New New Mobilization, or NNM. *Very cute*, Spivey concluded. If that young agitator decides to grow up and join the wicked system, his way with a phrase would fit right in at Spivey & Associates.

His stomach growling, Spivey looked at his watch. *Nearly two, time flies when…* He heard a knock.

"Yes, come on in." It was Rhea Simpson, one of the firm's bright young associates. "Yes, Rhea. You look like you got something important. I was just about to go to lunch, but I can order a sandwich if—"

"I think you better order a sandwich, Mr. Spivey." She smiled and grabbed one the soft foam chairs facing Spivey's ornate desk. She crossed her legs, exhibiting a delicious set of gams. Spivey tried not to look as he picked up the phone. All this harassment shit… "Yes, this is Spivey. A Western on sourdough toast, mayo on the side, and a Diet Coke."

He leaned back on his chair. "Yes, Rhea, what have you got that's so important?"

She tossed her head back, allowing her close-cropped reddish hair to flutter as if caught in a soft breeze. She rearranged her notes while absentmindedly scratching that pert little nose of hers.

"Yes, Rhea?" Spivey tried to focus as he forced a smile.

"Mr. Spivey, I've been working with Jim Donaldson on the Ann Sloan account, and we're picking up some strange tidbits that go well beyond the usual loonies attracted by a big media circus."

"Such as?" Spivey was back to business.

"Well, you know Slats Conners, the reporter that—"

"Yes, Rhea, that hack that works for that fish wrap up the coast. I liked what he did on the trial. What about him?"

"Well, he was checking Hastings Law School in the Bay Area to get a clue on who might take Shapiro's place if the rumors were true, and he spoke to a reporter for the *Chronicle.*"

Spivey's antenna was activated. He leaned forward.

"The reporter said word is, some of the New York tabloids are checking around about the victim in the latest Parker flap. Seems his employer knew him as Hashtiri, a Hare Krishna–type refugee from one of those meditative retreats, we think, in Vermont. So…"

"Well, fine, Rhea, that's a good human interest for someone like Conners, but how does that—"

"Mr. Spivey, the buzz is the guy's real name was David Sloan. Isn't that Ann's brother's name?"

"Well, sure, Rhea, but you know how many David Sloans there must be?" Spivey's heart started to thump. He was hoping that was all, but he dreaded that someone of Rhea's caliber would have more.

"Well, the *Chronicle* reporter got a call from a reporter for a paper in Santurce, Puerto Rico. Seems they knew each other back when. Turns out there was some panicky guy in Santurce who told the reporter that this Hashtiri, a.k.a. David Sloan, is Ann's brother."

"Yes, Rhea, a lot of freaks are always attracted to these kind of things." Throat parched, Spivey tied a swig of water. He looked at Rhea, dreading.

"His name is Ramon. He worked with the victim. He barely escaped and is scared to death."

"Is that the guy that called the precinct?"

"No, Mr. Spivey, the man who called the precinct had Anglo diction. This Ramon is reputed to have a thick Latino inflection."

Sheryl knocked and came in. She deposited the Western and the soda on the side of Spivey's desk. "Thanks, Sheryl." He handed her a ten-spot. "Tell him to keep the change." Spivey eagerly bit into the Western, as if the eggs and veggies would spare him from any more thunderbolts from Rhea. She politely waited for him to digest the first mouthful. "Go ahead, Rhea."

"Well, Mr. Spivey, the Santurce reporter got this character Ramon a lawyer. The reporter knows there's no way to speak directly to Ms. Sloan and that they have to get through a gaggle of screeners just to speak to you." She paused and tried to look calm. Maybe she was succeeding, but Spivey knew something awful...

"Jim and I have concluded that all this is not a crank, and we better let that lawyer get through to you."

Spivey, breathing hard, shoved his half-eaten sandwich to the side.

"I'm sorry, Mr. Spivey." Those delicious little lips just oozed compassion. "I can imagine what this'll mean to her... if it's true."

Spivey told Rhea to arrange the phone call. As she closed the door behind her, Spivey was already thinking ahead. Call Hudson on his cell and arrange to meet. Spivey figured Hudson would have to be there and already braced when he tells Ann the awful truth. Hearing someone that close's been killed by someone you set free would be enough to derange most people. But emotional divas, chanteuses, whatever, you'd probably need a twenty-four-hour suicide watch.

***

Tom Crosby had found a quiet spot at the French Hotel on Shattuck. He eschewed one of those lattes that made the place so popular. Black coffee for a while, he decided. While he didn't give a damn over such "bourgeoise" concepts as personal appearance, his increasing midriff on a narrow five foot eight frame might make his appearance the issue instead of the issues. He looked at his watch and frowned. He was about to grab a *New York Times* when Phil Upshaw finally showed. "You took your sweet time," Crosby sneered, ignoring Upshaw's outstretched hand and frozen smile.

"C'mon, Tom, you said around ten, it's only ten fifteen. I met Dinella about the posters and shit, and well, it's complicated."

"What's complicated?" Crosby was still in the glaring mode.

"Ow, shit, Tom." Now Upshaw joined in the glaring contest. "You're figuring half a million? I know most of us make up our own signs, but you can't count on the message. You said yourself you want something new, catchy, to dazzle the TV people. What if they still show up with the 'no war for oil' b.s.? You think Dan Rather features *that* at six that night?"

Crosby succumbed to a slight smirk. "You got a point."

"And not only that, Tom, we can't make the signs up out here. No matter how many buses we charter, they'll take up too much room."

"So work it out with Silvera. He works on the Hill for that independent that represents the Eugene area, right?"

"Right. But he's got a full-time job."

"Don't hand me that, Phil, and don't let him hand you that. Tell Silvera I expect him and any other Progressive staffers to help out. Besides, the way things are looking, we'll be delayed till spring, 'cause of that Chanteuse idiot. So we'll schedule it when Congress breaks. That way, we might get half the Hill to help out."

Crosby got up, refreshed his lukewarm coffee, and opened a pack of sugar. "So what have you heard about Sloan, Phil?"

Phil scratched his forehead and sighed. "Looks like we'll have to go to the Nancy Light card. She's not a heavyweight like the Chanteuse, but she used to be married to Larry Pearson, and she picked up some of his radical rap."

"Yeah," Crosby smirked. "Pearson, the Cable Comic, played Berkeley a few times. What ever happened to him?"

Phil rolled his eyes. "Married Light. Now he's got the big dough and doesn't have to work cable or comedy dives."

"He gets the dough." Crosby giggled. "She gets lessons in radicalism. Why do all those showbiz types crave the world of politics?"

"Well, I don't know about the men, Tom, but with the women, it's easy. It's like when you score with a babe and fill her up with 'Oh, baby, you're beautiful,' all that crap. What's the inevitable reply?"

"I got it," Tom smirked. "Why don't you love me for my mind?"

"Right, Tom, and when they become the one in a thousand that make it big, they must have some degree of guilt and need to prove intellect so they have to attach to causes like peace, the environment, and—"

"And Josh Parker?"

They both giggled out loud.

Phil quickly resumed a sober pose. "Just a couple of complications, Tom. We still can't get Sheen, Sarandon, Baldwin, and other old-timers to take a more conspicuous role."

"That' s okay, Phil, we already got Light for Sloan. Who cares if Sheen sits at home every night watching reruns of *West Wing*? There'll always be new stars trying to prove their gravitas. We won't be short on the Hollywood end."

"I agree. Looks like the Chanteuse is going to be a problem, though."

"How's that?" Crosby frowned.

"Well, Tom, word is, at first, she couldn't believe it was her brother. She spent nearly two months in New York. She dismissed that Puerto Rican guy as a 'government' agent. Apparently, they came close to having to unearth the body before she caved in to all the DNA, fiber stuff. Evidently, it matched some old clothes her brother had left at Sloan's mansion. The easiest part for the DA, I heard, was convincing her of the computer matches they had on Parker before and what they picked up at the scene."

Tom bit his bottom lip. "Can't Spezio and Tanaka use the one out of 10 million stratagem?"

"Sure, Tom. It worked with OJ and was part of the Parker jury's justification for letting him walk. But would that kind of argument sway you or me or someone directly involved like Sloan? You read about that emotional funeral at St. Patrick's? Well, word is, she vowed to nail Parker if it's the last thing and all that malarkey."

"Tsk, tsk." Crosby glared straight ahead. "Not only do we lose our star ally, but we're new confronted with a star enemy. What's she up to now?"

"Phil shrugged. "Last I heard, she's still in one of those plush Betty Ford–type spas recovering."

"Well, Phil, maybe it'll help our cause. Did you know she was a racist, a homophobe, and an anti-Semite?"

"Is that all?" Phil grinned.

"All for now, Phil. Unless we eventually need more. Get Fiore, the Lexis Nexis guy, to get started on it. We'll throw so much shit at her from so many directions some of it's got to stick. Before we're through, she'll join Bush, Ashcroft, and Limbaugh in the Progressives' Hall of Shame."

He noticed Phil's dubious expression. "What is it, Phil?"

"I know we can hatchet and get the usual suspects to join the feeding frenzy, but…"

"But what?"

"C'mon, Tom. That's like trying to pin that shit on Ted Kennedy, Ralph Nader, or Hillary. She's spotless, showbiz and all that."

"Funny you mention Nader. Didn't Gore call Nader a racist in the 2000 campaign?"

"WHAT!"

Crosby giggled, adjusted his horn-rimmed spectacles. "Easy, Phil, don't blow a gasket. No, he didn't call Nader a racist. He called Nader's health plan racist." He watched Phil's startled expression. "If you can do that to Saint Ralph and get away with it, where's the Chanteuse in comparison?"

"Well, she's been at every benefit, AIDS, the homeless. She slept over when Clinton was in the White—"

"Please, Phil," Crosby shook his head, "you still have a lot to learn. You don't think the Chanteuse ever employed a chauffeur, a sleep-in maid, a gardener?"

"So?" Phil looked puzzled.

"So you remember those two women that sank as AGs before Reno got the job? What was their undoing?"

"Yeah." Phil smiled. "They didn't pay social security or something for the maids, and..."

"You don't think—"

"But the Chanteuse's handlers wouldn't be that dumb after they saw what happened."

"Right, Phil, but even if we can't nail her on social security. How much did she pay them? Ten dollars an hour for a maid, twice the minimum wage. WHAT! Who can get by on 20K a year when you're trying to raise a family in the LA area? Oh, Ms. Sloan, did you pay them ten an hour because they're black, Hispanic, Asian? And what about the gardener? Was he Hispanic? How much was *he* paid? And was he legal? We'll get something, guaranteed."

"But, Tom, we don't have the funds or person power to..."

"No sweat. Ever hear of Bill Mellon?"

"The asbestos *and* tobacco guy?"

"The very same." Tom grinned. "He's in with us, on the q.t. Yeah, Mellon, Caldwell, & Cunningham, the biggest tort firm in the world. And you know Frommer & Sons..."

"Those reprehensible private eyes?"

"One and the same. They'll do anything Mellon wants. He pays, they always get results. Even if they have to..."

"But why is Mellon in with us?"

"It's those right-wing Fascists who, while railroading innocent citizens like Parker, try and legislate against trial lawyers who are only trying to compensate victims of corporate greed and negligence." Crosby watched Phil roll his eyes. "Maybe, Phil, maybe. But people'll buy it as long as they can identify with the lottery winners. Just take those jurors in Mississippi. They'll vote liability no matter what. With Ol Miss in the bag, only forty-nine states to follow."

They watched rain-soaked Berkeley types surround the counter for the warmth of hot java. "Brrr, looks like one of those bitter February storms. Y'know, Tom, before I hooked up with you, I used to eat my heart out bombing out with every babe in sight. Was a time I'd kill just to be *near* someone like Elly for five minutes. Now that she's in my hip pocket, I got ten to twenty stunners literally all over me every time I'm organizing a new protest. What is it about this shit that turns them on?"

"Don't know, man. I think the Beatles once sang about that. All I know, I was twenty-seven and still hanging around Sproul Plaza till I found this demonstration shit. So I went from a drifter, loser, who flunked out of Cal, to top dog in the New Mobe. I even heard *Time's* going to feature me in a cover story the week of the New Mobe."

"Wow."

"Yeah, not bad for a guy in predental who failed both qual and quan."

9

TECHNICALITY

Tom Crosby bit into that juicy eight-ounce hamburger amid the hub-bub at Clyde's. *Say one thing for the venerable Georgetown hangout*, he mused, *you can't beat the atmosphere and that basic All-American chow.* He reflected on how tired he was of all the tofu, yogurt, sprouts, and the rest of that idiotic cuisine meant to convey a "message," let alone a healthier lifestyle. "Mmmmm," Tom sighed as he bit into that succulent, medium-rare beef deliciously smothered with sautéed unions and mushrooms. Another swig of the Sierra Nevada combined with the exhilarating view of the buzz and the flow at this Washington landmark and Tom spaced out. He felt so light-headed as that potent brew worked its magic. He thought about the trip, with all the noise and activity as a mellow backdrop.

The Mobe was a blast, the coverage was great, and we were about 20Gs in the black. Tomorrow's the big farewell dinner at the Specialty Sprouts, before we all head our respective ways. Meanwhile, for the sake of sanity and the real world, I got a night off by telling them I'm meeting with a potential contributor at his Georgetown home.

Sure beats going to the movie up Wisconsin Avenue to see *Che Died for Us All.* Meanwhile, speaking of meeting someone, is that lanky blonde at the bar with that creep, or is he just hitting on her?

Two days later, Tom was at the Starbucks at United Dulles terminal, with a dozen or so other Mobe participants from the Bay

Area. They were catching the 11:15 to SFO. Tom still had to return to DC in several weeks to follow up on the legal tangles. He figured it was time to catch up on the West Coast happenings. "Hey, Sandra, watch my carry-on, will you? I gotta make a call." He grabbed his coffee and moved to a quiet area of the lounge.

"Yeah, Phil, Tom here. How'd it go at the Frisco end? The papers hardly covered—"

"Tom, is that you? You okay? Yeah, Tom, absolutely too good to be true. We used some of the same shit we utilized when Bush invaded Iraq. We also got the National Lawyers Guild to coordinate the attorneys doing our paperwork again. It's a breeze. Just like then, we got Harrigan up the wall. None of us are paying the one-hundred-dollar fine, and they can't take us to court 'cause the court system would be so clogged Roto-Rooter couldn't help. Even better, we got a lapdog SF Court Commissioner to threaten to dismiss charges against all 1,700 protesters due to a technicality."

"Technicality? No kidding, Phil, what was it, and can we use it out here in DC?"

"Don't think so, Tom. DC doesn't have a DA like Harrigan, doesn't have the *Chron*, the *Guardian*, and a board of supes that'll—"

"Check, Phil, guess I'm currently on the wrong opposite end of the Left Coast. So what's the technicality?"

"Well, in the first fifty cases similar to the 1,700 arrested, the prosecutors violated due process by crossing off misdemeanor charges on the citations and writing in lesser charges, such as jaywalking, instead of filing new cases… Hey, Tom, you drunk out there? It's not *that* funny."

"Check, Phil, it's just that I know where you're heading. Harrigan's not going to pursue the cases 'cause of the cost. Probably one of the reasons he reduced the misdemeanors to infractions to begin with."

"Yeah, Tom, that and the fact that no one in Frisco wants to see any of them punished either by fine or doing time."

"That's where you got me, Phil. DC isn't as scared shitless of arresting anyone, even with the clout of the local Progressives and the large number of African Americans. Plus, they got DeLay and

Ashcroft and the rest of the congressional Neanderthals watching everything they do. So I'm going to contact Mellon's outfit. They got a big office here in DC in the K Street corridor. The best litigants in the world should be able to handle this little fuss. If not up their alley, they can easily refer us to other shysters. Either way, won't cost us a cent. Part of their pro bono crap. Ain't that a scream?"

"Sure is, Tom, can't you hear me giggling three thousand miles away?"

"Yeah, well, the giggling's got to end soon. We raised Cain over Josh Parker and naturally had to throw in Iraq, the Palestinians, a woman's right to choose, prescription drugs, you know, the whole spectrum, just like you guys did out there."

"So what's your point, Tom?"

"The point, dear Phil, is that I'm going to have a depressing flight back. The heart of everything we've been doing lately revolves around that Parker guy. Now that the noise is over, there's no more demonstrations, protests, all that shit. We got to get to the nitty-gritty of proving Parker was framed."

"You worried?"

"Listen, Phil, from what we all heard, the cops got a lot. At least enough to convince the Chanteuse. Now we got to bring her down without losing the rest of Hollywood. Plus, we got to prove it was a frame."

"Prove it was a frame? We got cause to worry, I guess."

"Stop that groaning, Phil, we got the lawyers, we got the noise, and in a pinch, we always got NPR. I'll use the flight to do some deep thinking. The SEIU got me one of their first-class tickets and—"

"Why, you lousy, spoiled bast—"

"Relax, Phil, I'll save some caviar for you."

***

Ann Sloan was delighted to be leaving the spa. She dialed her cellphone. "Jeff? It's Ann. Where are you?"

"Ann, I thought you'd be at the Knowles Spa till next week. You know I was planning to pick you up."

"I know, Jeff, but Carter Reynolds, who lives so close, was visiting his sister and offered me a ride." She looked at Carter. "Jeff says hello."

Carter, his eyes still focused on the road, replied with a smile, "And a big hello back."

"Did you hear that, Jeff? Good. Well, you see, since I've got the medical okay to leave, I couldn't help but accept. Suddenly, three more days of that regimen seemed superfluous, and when you told me that the servants are back at full strength, 'home sweet home' never seemed sweeter. I'm dying to get back into the swing. And hopefully, I'd surprise you. You know I love surprises. Unfortunately, you're not home. I was hoping to catch you in bed with a beautiful blonde. Then I'd have an excuse for the press and the nosy public in case I had a relapse."

"I know that's why you wanted to surprise me, darling, but one beauty at a time in my life is about all I can ever handle. I'm on my way right now. I'll have the cell on speaker so we can 'parlais' as I drive home."

"By the by, where are you?"

"At the club, darling. I'm on my way."

Jeff put the cell back in his pocket. He looked at the tall, raw-boned redhead stretched out on the bed. "Thanks for keeping quiet, Laura. I'll definitely speak to Millstein about that part in the new HBO movie."

Laura slowly crept to the edge of the bed and absentmindedly fondled her slippers. "What if I'd let out a giggle?"

"Well, I would have said it was one of the young waitresses. She must have heard a joke or something."

"Waitresses at a men's club?"

Jeff walked toward Laura and kissed her on the forehead. "Affirmative action, sweetness, affirmative action, it knows no bounds. Nothing's sacred anymore."

***

Tom Crosby took the BART out to the Walnut Creek station. He caught one of the taxis parked adjacent to the station. "McCovey's, please," Tom mumbled. The cabbie nodded and dropped him off in front of the bustling restaurant named after the Giants' great. Tom gazed at the brown-orange facade meant to replicate PacBell's exterior.

Within a minute, a short, wiry man wearing a blue blazer approached him. "Crosby? I'm Stu Frommer, one of the sons in Frommer & Sons." His smirk seemed to indicate that Stu thought this frivolous intro was a good icebreaker. He put out his hand. "Thought I recognized you from the photos."

Tom, while shaking Stu's hand, cast a wary eye toward Stu's companion, a hulking young man whose two-day fuzz added to the menace in his mien.

Stu put his hand on the man's shoulder. "Tom, meet Dave Worziek. As you can see from looking at him, a man like me needs a guy like Dave around in plain sight. Might hopefully discourage some 'get even' a-hole, well, from acting like an a-hole."

They drifted past the hostess to a quiet corner facing one of those ubiquitous TV screens.

"Try the baby back ribs, Tom, they're great. It's on me."

"Great." Tom grinned. "Then I'll have the full slab."

The fresh-faced waitress appeared in no time with three Anchor Steams and took the order.

Stu poured some more of the brew into his glass. He glanced toward Dave. "Look, Tom, Dave's going to be paying with his cell phone while we're here. He might make a quiet call or two. The rest of the time, he'll be playing blackjack or football on that silly phone. Plus, even if he were paying attention, I trust him with my life. Clear?"

"Clear," Tom replied. "But first, Stu, when you called me, you said you'd explain why we're meeting out here in White Bread country."

"Sure did." Stu's lean face allowed a slight grin. "Look, Tom, every reporter in the city knows me. They see me talking to the New Mobe guy, and it takes the lead in the C section of the *Chron*. People in my business don't need that. I know what you're thinking. Why not in my office, a suite in a hotel, or some nondescript Chinese chophouse on Clement?"

"Makes sense." Tom shrugged. "But why the Creek?"

"Should we tell him, Dave?"

"Huh, not following, Stu. I got a 14, and the dealer's showing an 8. Do I hit or stay?"

Stu grinned. "Asking the wrong guy, Dave. Bet I've easily left 100 large at the wrong end of those Vegas blackjack tables."

"Okay, Tom, nothing hush-hush or sinister. I got a suite about five minutes away at the Renaissance Hotel. There's a lights-out yoga teacher at the health club there. And she's got all this shit going on this side of the tunnel. What can I say except 'Bye-bye, Frisco. Hello, East Bay.' Besides, there's advantages. These hicks at the *CC Times* haven't caught my act yet. *So…* even though I'm keeping my condo near PacBell, a lot of my business is done out here. And speaking of business, we got a plant shacking up with that Ann Sloan sycophant, Jeff Hudson."

Tom's face lit up; he was about to answer when the waitress, sporting that 44 on the back of her outfit, showed up with three platters of succulent-looking ribs. They quietly watched her efficiently deposit the huge platters in front of the three diners. Tom noticed that though the server looked as delicious as the ribs, Stu was barely checking her out. That yoga teacher must be something, he figured. "Before I commend you on the Hudson exploit, one question, Stu."

Stu wiped his face after discarding an empty rib. "What's that?"

"Why are they all wearing 44 on their back?"

"You got to be kidding me, Crosby. Didn't you know that was McCovey's uniform number? Didn't you grow up out here?"

"Nah." Tom shrugged. "Grew up in Great Neck, New York. Never followed any of that, the Mets, Yankees… My parents had me studying Marxian theory in my spare time. They intimated that baseball was just another opiate of the masses."

Stu seemed to grimace and roll his eyes.

"Yeah, Savage was right on that one. I'm one of those Red Diaper Doper babies. It's pretty stifling to have Commies for parents. That's why I jumped at the chance to go to Berkeley. And all that Commie lingo has come in handy with all this demonstration shit."

"Great Neck? Isn't that a wealthy suburb? And your parents were Commies?"

"Check." Tom grinned. "Not much different than Marin County today."

"You got a point there, Tom. All that wealth, all those hot tubs, and Chairman Mao would win in a landslide in Mill Valley." Stu glanced at Dave. "Dave, just about finished? Why don't you take fifteen for a smoke? There's a McDonald's real close, you can grab some coffee."

"Sure, Stu," Dave shoved his plate aside and took one last swig of the Anchor Steam.

They watched him head out.

"Okay, Tom. We got fifteen minutes to get to heavy-duty. I trust Dave with my life, obviously. But up to a point."

Tom tried to nonchalant Stu's pitiable metaphor. He stared at Stu as if he had his rapt attention.

Stu handed Tom a creased piece of paper. He watched Tom stare at it. "The dude's name is Felix Urbina. Lives in Adams Morgan."

"Adams Morgan?"

"Don't sweat it. The first time he'll meet you will be at the Key Bridge Marriott."

"Why not Dupont or Thomas Circles?"

Stu frowned. "Got to be kidding me, Tom. Too much's going down in those places, ranging from undercover cops to Feds, narcs."

"Yeah, but I fit. I still look like a college swell."

"Maybe," Stu sighed. "But Felix'd make our pal Dave look like a faggoty poetry professor."

"That big?"

"Not the size, the face. Central casting looking to cast a mean Columbian drug dealer, he gets the part in a walk."

Tom's hand trembled as he held the beer mug. "Is he a dealer?"

"Used to be. Crossed someone down there. Or vice versa. He lost the power struggle. Had to hightail it up here. We found him. He's good. Does what we want. We pay enough so that he doesn't need sidelines. At any rate, he'd stand out at Dupont Circle." Stu took out nine-hundred-dollar bills. "Here, I want you to rent a car so you can drive to Key Bridge. Also, buy yourself a suit and wear a tie when you meet Urbina. You'll both look like businessmen closing a deal or something."

"What are we…?"

"Bring a cell phone. Better yet, buy a new one when you get to DC. You'll talk every day. Whatever legal problems you can't clear up, just tell Urbina. He knows enough people out there to grease things. If he can't, he'll still take care of…"

"What do you mean?" Tom gasped.

"Don't worry about it." Stu grimaced. "It invariably doesn't come to that. We got enough money and enough connections. One cop was seriously maimed by a rock at one of those demonstrations. Another was killed, but it's not clear if it was a heart attack or what. So far, the *Post* has buried this shit on page A17, and no one reads the *Wash Times*. What we don't want is for this to get to trial, where publicity is going to hurt our PR. Don't forget, we're the good guys. It's the damn Bushies et al. who are trying to distract attention from the Progressive forces' attempts to expose Bush for Halliburton and other sins too numerous to enumerate now."

"Wow," Tom gasped. "You sure got the jargon down pat."

Stu smirked, appreciative of Tom's compliment. "Urbina's our liaison with some jury consultants, judges, and other 'fixers' in the DC judiciary system. Don't contact me till you get back. I'll be talking to Urbina every day. So you focus on speeches, TV appearances, and all that crap. Urbina'll fix you up with a new PR guy to get you the TV and radio spots now that we can't count on Spivey anymore. After the legal shit's cleared up, I'll start working on the Chanteuse. We got to bring her down. We all set?"

"Sure," Tom replied. He placed his trembling hand under the table.

Stu grinned and reached for his cell. "Dave? Yeah, we're finished. Stay by the Golden Arches. I'll pick you up, and we'll drop Tom off at the BART station." He put four of those new crisp twenty-dollar bills over the check, and they left.

10

THE TAPES

Stu dropped Sharon off at her yoga class. She bussed him on the cheek. "Stu, hon, when am I going to get you in here?"

"One of these days, baby, one of these days. I think I've got to unwind a little before I get twisted into a pretzel."

"Coward," she teased with that dynamite smile, "you know that in my classes, everyone can go at their own pace. How many times have I told you that you'll gain time in the long run since reduced stress levels lead to increased productivity?"

"Got it, got it," Stu replied. "Meantime, let me use the next ninety productive minute to catch up on my phone calls and other business. I know you don't eat after the class. But if I get hungry nursing my CC and soda, do I order my burger with or without onions?"

Sharon blushed. "Without onions, you rascal. I think I'll be in the mood to—oh, hi, Eric." She watched the wiry blond six-footer enter the workout room after he acknowledged her with a wink.

"Who the hell was that?"

"Oh, come on, hunk." She ran her fingers up and down his cheeks. "You know I don't like them that young and immature. One thing, though," she grinned, "he sure can tie himself up in a pretzel."

Stu simulated an angry scowl.

"Down, boy." She grinned. "Make that last drink soda without the CC. I want a sober lover when we meet again."

He watched her move that derriere as she sashayed past that large glass door into the workout room. Besides that damn Eric and a few other stray males, lots of goodlooking, leotard-clothed pussy in that room, but no one in Sharon's class. He looked at his watch and drew a deep breath. "It's 7:30. Won't see her till 9:15 at best." He sensed some movement in his groin area. "Down, boy," he repeated her admonition. "Save it for later when it counts."

Stu reviewed some work on his PDA and was on his second drink when he checked his cell's voice mail. He called Laura first. "Yeah, it's me. Can you talk?"

"It's cool, Stu. I'm home alone."

"Okay, what have you got?"

"He told me they're going to that annual Actors' Fund Ball a week from next Thursday in Newport Beach. So for sure, they'll be taking Wyton Drive to Beverly Glen, then to Sunset and the Freeway."

"But are you certain?"

"Positive, Stu. He had me over just once when Sloan was recuperating. The maids, butlers, whatever, were either off duty or sleeping in separate quarters. We got there 2 AM. Left before 7, in advance of any of the help reporting for duty. He had to take the San Diego to take me back to Manhattan Beach. And that was the route he selected."

"Thanks, Laura. Try and see him sometime next week to make sure. Meanwhile, I'll start working on it."

Stu asked the bartender for some ice. He checked Crosby's voice mail: "Back in Frisco. Thanks for all your legal help in DC. Everything was greased. No one's doing time, and there's still $17,000 left over after we paid the fines. Call me whenever."

Stu smiled and decided business was over for the time being. *Let's see. About forty-five minutes before she's finished.* He put away his cell and PDA and waved at the bartender. "Ay, Lee, let me have the patty melt with a Diet Coke."

"Patty melt comes with onions, Stu. Aren't you waiting for Sharon?"

Stu grinned. "Remember you in my will, Lee. Tell the chef to make it mushrooms instead of onions."

Sharon had an 8:00 AM class at Diablo Valley College, and she was gone by the time Stu woke up. She left a note thanking him for a "great time" and added she'd be calling him before noon. Stu sighed and wondered how much longer he could swing with this gorgeous babe. He'd been around, had the sophistication, the money... Still, how long before some younger Eric or equivalent sweeps her off her feet?

He dialed room service for some OJ and a bagel, and he pressed Pedro's name on his cell.

"Padgett Motors, can I help you?"

"Service, please. Pedro Ramirez."

"That's extension 44. I'll connect you."

"Yeah, service."

"Hi, Pedro available?"

"I think he's working on a transmission. Who's this?"

"Patrick. Could you tell him to call me?"

"Sure, Patrick, what's the number?"

"He's got it. Thanks a lot."

Stu was perusing the *Chron* in the hotel lobby when his cell rang. "Hi, Patrick, Stu around?"

"Quit the clowning, Pedro. You know it's always Patrick whenever anyone else is involved."

"Okay, Stu, is it the deal you were talking about?"

"Yeah. You sure we're set?"

"No sweat, Stu. I've done it in the past. I already got recorders attached beneath the dash and, if they're outside, under the front grill and under the plate in the back. So we'll record it whether they're inside or outside in the front or back."

"It's been recording all along?"

"No trouble at all. We just wind back from the end. Don't forget they'll have the car towed to the garage. I'll grab the tapes then."

"But are you sure the car will stall?"

"Ay, it's no problem. It's worked before. I'll be parked half a block away. When they leave, I'll follow and, at the proper time, activate the magnet we attached next to the distributor. The car's got to conk out, max ninety seconds."

Stu looked around the lobby and patted his forehead. "Isn't there a chance they'll recognize you when you tail them?"

"Nah, it'll only be a block or two, and I'll be dressed like one of those illegal gardeners, fake 'stache and all."

"All right, Pedro, I'm going to hop a plane down to LA. No, no, don't pick me up at the airport. I'll meet you at that diner in Manhattan Beach. Get the LA Western area map. According to my info, they'll be taking Wyton toward Beverly Glen."

"Yeah, Stu, I know Wyton. Good, dark, quiet spot."

"Well, they're heading to some awards show, televised nationwide. So it won't be dark."

"Right, but it's quiet. That's more important. I'll do a couple of drive-bys, to make sure there's no surprises."

"Good. Save one of those trips for me. I'd like to see the setup."

"Okay, bro, call me when you know your flight."

"I will. Are the dudes you got reliable?"

"Ten big ones apiece, for one night's work, they'll be reliable. With what you're paying me and those ghetto blasters, you must have a lot of the old mahas behind you."

"You got it, Pedro, money's not the issue. We got deep pockets." Stu skipped the fact that by "deep," he meant the overflowing pockets of the Mellon lawyers. No need to get into all that with Pedro. "By the way, you think you'll be okay if they figure it's you who caused the whole fuss?"

"Nah, it's cool, Stu. When the car won't start, they'll call AAA. The driver might try the battery, and when that doesn't work, he'll simply tow it. We do all the work in his Bent, so I know they'll ask to have it towed to our shop. I'll be in first thing in the morning and remove the tapes and the magnet before anyone else looks at it."

"Sounds good, Pedro. Looks like we're going to have one hell of a bonfire event."

"Bonfire? What do you mean?"

"Never read Wolfe's *Bonfire of the Vanities*?"

"Nah, Stu, what's your point?"

"Tell you about it when I get to LA."

RADIO SPOT

"Yessiree, Stan Morgan, your answer to Rush, Shawn, and Savage is back on the air. Hope you all had a wonderful weekend. As you devoted Morganheads know, I usually eschew guests, but today is an exception. For the second time, we have the one and only America's number one diva, the Chanteuse, Ann Sloan. I'm hopeful there'll be time for Bushwhacking or Cheney-mongering, but I'm sure Ann wants to start with topics closer to home. Welcome to the show, Ann. You certainly look good today."

"Thanks, Stan, you're so kind. And how have you been?"

"Hotter than a firecracker, Ann, or about at that level of intensity that, that would be President Howard Dean was after Iowa. Oh, pardon me, just a little housekeeping, Ann. All you folks out there can reach me at 1-800-M-O-R-G-A-N, and the e-mail's on my website. But please, folks, hold the calls till the second hour. The first hour is reserved for the one and only Chanteuse."

"Wow," Ann tittered. "A whole hour with Stan Morgan. I hope I don't let you down."

"You won't, Ann, you won't. Something tells me this is going to be quite an hour."

"Now, to start with, Ann, I'd like... Wait, there's a call for me? We got the best screener in the business, Bruce Applestein—Brucy, Brucy, live up to your rep. I thought I said no calls... What? The Reverend Spotsworth Abernathy of the Abbysinian Baptist Church?

I apologize, Bruce, the Reverend is always welcome, no matter what the circumstances. Put him through."

"Hi, Stan, am I on the air?"

"Hello, Reverend, always a pleasure. How are things in Compton?"

"Fine, Stan, just fine, although something *is* on my mind."

"Great, Reverend, love to hear it, but we have a little difficulty. Could you turn your radio down?"

"Oh, sure, Stan, I always forget that."

"Think nothing of it. We do have Ann Sloan here today, and I promised her the first hour and—"

"That's why I'm calling, Stan, there are some rumors hitting the community that are very disturbing."

"About Ann?"

"Precisely."

"Hello, Reverend, ahh, so pleased to talk to you again." Ann was wary, and her voice displayed her unease.

Stan interjected, "Well, now that all the hellos have been dispensed with, can we get to something of interest to our audience?"

"Glad to, Stan. To my utter astonishment, I have heard reports that Ann Sloan, who, until recently, had been one of the shining lights against the extremism of the Fascistic corporate establishment, has been guilty of uttering shocking racial slurs."

"WHAT?"

"Easy, Ann. Let the Reverend finish. Go on, Reverend."

"Well, Stan, I don't have all the details, but the occurrence is beyond dispute."

"What, what is this about, Reverend? I've never ever in my whole life uttered—"

Morgan interrupted, "Uh, perhaps I can be of help, Ann. Sorry to cut you off. It seems that a tape has been sent in to me, anonymously, of course, and from what I've heard, Reverend Abernathy has due cause to be offended."

Ann, sitting several feet away from Stan, moved her chair back. "I can't believe I'm hearing this. What tape?"

"Okay, Ann, and I'm as shocked as you are, Reverend Abernathy. Roll it, guys." Stan Morgan smiled as the tape went out over the airwaves.

"*What's the matter, Jeff?*"

"*Don't know, hon, the car was serviced last week. It just petered out. Hard to believe. I filled the tank yesterday. Tell you what, Ann, call information on your cell and get AAA. Meanwhile, I'll check out the front and the tires. Might be something obvious.*"

"STOP THIS, RIGHT NOW!" Ann shrieked.

Stan Morgan, a smirk lingering on his face, motioned to the control room. The tape stopped playing. "Get hold of yourself, Ann, the public is entitled to and shall know the truth."

"I know what you're referring to, and it's outrageous that we were recorded."

"Maybe, Ann, maybe, I believe in civil liberties as much as the next person, probably more so, but the public has a right to know."

"But—"

"Look, Ann, I sure didn't record this. But since it was sent to me, do you really believe I'm going to cover it up?"

"I want my lawyer," she wailed, literally.

"Okay, folks, we're going to pause for several messages. Right now's a good time. Looks like the Chanteuse is under the weather."

After several spots, Stan Morgan improvised with several PSAs before announcing, "We'll be back with a lengthy segment after these words." Stan was in a bind, but he reasoned that the audience, instead of being ticked by all the commercials, would grow in both interest and size as the buzz grew over the Chanteuse's plight, if and when she returned to the air.

Stan continued to converse with Reverend Abernathy while the commercials aired. When the broadcast resumed, Stan told the Reverend, "Well, we're back on the air, Reverend, and I'm not going to deprive you or the audience of Ann Sloan's comments."

"I'm all ears, brother, I'm all ears. Certainly as aghast as I've been by the rumor, the actual words will pierce like a stiletto, but I'm up to it, Stan, I'm up to it."

Stan pointed to the control room. "Okay, Cliff, pick up with the last sentence aired."

"Might be something obvious."

Stan made the "cut" sign to Cliff. "Okay, folks, that's when Jeff Hudson, who was driving the car, was getting out to see why the car had stopped while Ann was calling AAA."

"Wait, Jeff, come back in the car."

"Why, I just want to check—"

"Jeff, don't you see those two young black men? They're wearing gang jackets. And what are they doing around here?"

"Hon, they probably saw us stop, and they want to see—"

"Jeff, get in here! I'm terrified!"

"They're probably coming over to help us."

"Jeff, is the car locked? Good. I'll call information for—"

"No need, Ann, I just remembered. It's 1-800-AAA-HELP."

"What street are we on? They're sure to ask. Oh, *why* is no one outside?"

"It's embarrassing. I take this street all the time for the freeway, but I don't know the name... Maybe if I walk to the—"

"What, are you crazy? You're not leaving this car. Oh my, they're coming over."

"Ann, calm down. Why are you giving me the phone?"

"*Call the police.* I'm terrified. Call 911, or something like that."

"Okay, I'll—"

"Jeff, they're banging on the window. Don't roll it down. What are they saying?"

"I think, 'Dude, can you help us? Our car's stuck. We wanna borrow a cell phone.' I... I couldn't make out the rest."

"It's a trick. Oh, Jeff, don't open up. Dial 911 already! Eek! The one with the red bandanna is coming over to my side. He's banging on the window!"

"You didn't help us, you racist honky!"

"Jeff, they're... they're walking away."

"Yeah, hon, but not before the red bandanna guy gave us the finger. Okay, I'm dialing 911."

Stan motioned to the control room. "All right, folks, I think we've heard enough. Reverend, are you still there?"

"Yes, Stan, and can you imagine my chagrin? Here are two, I assume, young African Americans. And because they're dressed in ghetto attire, they are made to walk away into the night with no one in a rich white neighborhood to help them. All they asked for was a cell phone to call a relative or AAA, and these people wouldn't even roll down the window. Outrageous!"

"But, Reverend, fair's fair, now that we've heard the tape, there's no evidence of Ann using racial slurs."

"Stan, racial slurs are piercing, but no worse than the evidence that members of the African American community are treated with suspicion and contempt."

"Stop this! I can't believe that in all my years of fighting for justice… Where did you get the tape?"

"Like I said, Ann, it was anonymous. I'll get the postal people and the FBI—"

"Stan, how could you have surprised me like this?"

"Sorry to have waylaid you like this, Ann, but you know the nature of this show. That's why the ratings—"

"Ratings? Oh, Stan, how could you?" Ann got up and motioned to the control room. Someone opened the door to let Ann out.

Stan, smiling from ear to ear, leaned back on his leather chair. "Reverend, you still there?"

"Yes, I am, Stan, and obviously shocked by these events."

"Well, Reverend, show some of that compassion you're famous for. All transgressors need forgiveness."

"Amen to that, brother, amen to that. But I'm not sure the public will be as forgiving."

"With those wise words from the Reverend, we'll pause for some messages before we open up the phone lines."

CHANTEUSE'S RUINATION

"Holly, that you? Sorry, I thought I was calling Slats on his cell."

"No problem, Tom, Slats's out fishing by the brook. Didn't want his bucolic contemplation intruded upon by any ringing."

"Guilty as charged, Holly. Where do I serve my sentence?"

"Tom, don't be silly. We've actually been up here six days, and this is the first time you've called."

"Holly, Holly, what am I gonna do with you? You got my number and then some. But give me credit for the six days."

Holly grinned, and the smile was reflected by the lilt in her voice. "We're way ahead of you, Tom. We're all Tahoed out anyway. The next lodgers are checking into the cabin by noon tomorrow. We'll be talking about the Chanteuse the minute we hit Interstate 5."

"Aha, so you're way ahead of me. Been reading the papers, catching Fox, CNN?"

"Well, of course, Tom, when you're living with a reporter, there are no vacations from the news. And don't feel guilty, Tom, Slats loves the glitz and prestige of covering the Sloan happening. He was hoping you'd call."

"You're not just saying that? Jenkins had the initial call, but I'd prefer Slats. Just double-checking you all haven't gone NoCal on us."

"Not a chance, Tom, we miss the smog, the crowded freeways, and all the rest SoCal has to offer. What would we do without it?"

"Holly, you're a pearl, and way too good for that good-for-nothing."

"Exactly what I remind him of all the time. Want Slats to call?"

"Nah, it's cool, Holly, only if he doesn't expect to be in bright and early on Monday."

"Take care, Tom." Holly closed the cover on the cell phone. She lowered the chaise to a virtual prone position. Holly smiled as she applied a new layer of suntan lotion. Slats never did like the startling white areas around the upstairs and downstairs private parts of her body. *What a break*, she mused, latching on to this one-family-at-a-time cottage with a secluded backyard, perfect for sunbathing in the nude. The fading four o'clock mountain sun began to chill Holly's naked body. She put on a robe and dozed off.

"Here I am, boss man, 8 AM and tanned, relaxed, and ready to go."

Tom Leary took one last look at the coastal fog and the fierce morning waves pounding the Malibu shoreline. "Looks like you did get a nice tan. Did you get to play much?"

"Nah, Tom, the good gambling's in the South Shore. When you commit yourself to the North Shore, it's forget the slots, blackjack, all that. Holly sunbathes most of the time, and I fish. Real relaxing. We find a nice restaurant every night and—"

"Okay, enough, Slats. What is this, the travel section of the *Sunday Times*? Do any thinking on the road?"

"Yeah, Tom. The *San Francisco Chronicle* covered it pretty good. The whole thing's too goofy. She was obviously set up in a ham-handed way. So the people that did it didn't give a damn how awkward it looked long as the Chanteuse is down for the count."

"So earn your pay, Slats. Who was it?"

"Well, everything was copacetic with regard to the Chanteuse till it all went haywire when her brother was killed by, pardon the expression, her hero."

"Which means? Let's get to it, Slats." Tom's tone evinced annoyance. "Well, the way I see it, Tom, there were all kinds of stories coming out against her since she, for lack of a better word, flipped. Not only was the 'movement' bruising her, but Nancy Light, admittedly not the icon Sloan is, has replaced her as their leading spokesperson in the press, protests, meetings, etc."

"Now we got it. The only question is whom you mean by 'their.'"

"Well, much as they're trying to hide it, the Frommer bunch got their dirty little fingers in the equation."

"Right, Slats." Tom leaped up from his chair, walked up to Slats, and jammed his index finger in Slats's chest. "It's their slimy MO from here to Thursday. The only question who they report to."

"Christ, Tom, I'm a reporter, not a detective."

Tom smiled and walked back to his swivel chair. "Look it up in the dictionary, dude. They're synonyms." He wheeled and turned toward the window displaying a brightening sky. "A good reporter's a good detective. A reporter doesn't get his copy from a wire service. We got a shot here, Slats. A Pulitzer's in view."

"Come on, Tom, how do we compete against—"

"Slats, I earned this office by what I know. The *Times*, the *Chron*—they go on to new things: the economy, Martha Stewart, the latest war, elections, all that hard-news shit. We, on the other hand, focus, like that proverbial laser beam, on the one and only Chanteuse. And it's just not that glitzy, gossipy crap. Something big is going on here, way beyond the Chanteuse, showbiz, and those stupid protesters. Now go get us that Pulitzer, dude."

"Whew, anything else, Captain Queeg?"

Leary ignored the sarcasm and returned to his chair. He leaned back and replied, "Yeah, have something on my desk by COB Friday."

Slats headed toward his desk. He turned on his desktop. The time appeared. It wasn't even nine yet. He decided to skip his stock portfolio and went right to Google. He looked up Frommer—lots of listings. *But which is* my *Frommer? Wonder if Google has a subheading for Slime Pits?*

Slats eventually found Frommer & Sons. Between Google, LexisNexis, and some legal websites, he retrieved more than enough references. Most were familiar. Everyone knew they did the dirty work for many of the offbeat, big-time, big-money legal disputes. They even were involved as gumshoes for one side or another in divorce and other sex escapades. Although that outfit in Frisco that "reportedly" handled the dirty work for Clinton's bimbo eruptions got the bulk of those cases. Still, Frommer's name had popped up more than once with reference to all those protests the Chanteuse was directly or indirectly involved in. *So Frommer's as good a place to start as any. The key, though, dirtbags like Frommer never do anything on their own. There's usually a loaded client pulling the strings. Trouble is,* Slats sighed, *the big law firms that employ these shitheads keep the relationship confidential for all those obvious reasons.*

After lunch, Slats tried the five largest law firms he could think of. He started with Mellon, Caldwell, & Cunningham. It took two hours, but as expected, he wasn't able to find a connection between Frommer and Mellon. He similarly had no luck with Farrel, Levine, & Schwartz. *Pointless,* Slats concluded, *only the IRS would be privy to any payments between the likes of Mellon and Frommer. And there's no way they're going to divulge anything of that confidential nature to the likes of me.* Of course, the Frommers were all over the tobacco and asbestos lawsuits, and that connected them to Mellon, plus another half-dozen legal jackals that latched on to those gold mines. The question remained, when it came to the Chanteuse, who was funding the Frommer's pernicious behavior?

Slats went to the paper morgue next floor and asked Pam for every local paper for a full week after the Chanteuse's fiasco. An hour of leafing through the papers didn't lead to anything he didn't know already, but there was a mention of an interview with a Phil Hedges, the service manager at Padgett Motors on Sunset. *As good a place as any to start,* Slats concluded. He thanked Pam and went down to get his jacket.

He pulled into Padgett Motors at a quarter to four. Slats was happy to see the service area was open till midnight. Compared to that, four was early, and like any good bloodhound, Slats wanted his meat right now.

What a fancy place, Slats thought. The lounge featured three types of coffee, real cream, Krispy Kremes, a plasma TV, and comfortable seating all around. *So this is what it's like when you're rich. Even the gal that came out with the inevitable "Mr. Hedges will be right with you" had the look of a still-undiscovered Hollywood starlet.* Several minutes after the last "Be right with you," Hedges appeared and led Slats to his office.

"You're a reporter, did you say?"

"Yes, and it's about that Ann Sloan deal, and I'm—"

"Don't mean to be short with you, Slats, but we've already talked to the *LA Times* and other papers, and the cops were here several times." Hedges stole a glance at his watch for emphasis.

"I understand that, Mr. Hedges, but—"

"Phil is just fine." The all-American grin on his young face seemed to make amends for his abruptness.

"Well, Phil, sometimes time and distance from an event can lead to—"

"I read you, Slats. Naturally, our service department is always busy as hell, specially before five, but what can I do?"

"For starters, who worked on Sloan's car? Anyone in particular?"

"As a matter of fact," Phil's cheeks displayed a blush, "there was one technician who always worked on Ms. Sloan's automobile, Pedro Ramirez. Unfortunately, he left about a month after all that hullaba-loo. I guess all the fuss got to be too much."

Slats's heart started pounding. *This might mean something.*

"'Left,' you mean another dealership?"

"No, went back to South America, somewhere."

"Mexico?"

"No, not Mexico."

"How do you know that, Phil, if you don't know where he was from?"

Phil smiled. "'Cause he once got into a lunchroom fight with someone of Mexican ancestry after Pedro was sprouting off about all the Mexican wetbacks living off the fat of the land."

Just fine, Slats concluded, *it would have been tough enough to trace him in Mexico. Now it could be anywhere in South or Central America.* Slats sighed, "Bet you're going to tell me he gave no reason for leaving."

"Well, except for the Sloan hassle, it doesn't figure."

"Doesn't figure? How's that?"

"He left entitled to three weeks' vacation and a bonus near 10 percent of his annual earnings. Would have been about 6K in his case."

"Well, isn't he entitled to—"

"Know where you're going, Slats, but our industry has so much turnover that there is no vacation, vacation pay, or bonuses unless they're still on the payroll."

Slats grimaced and nervously rubbed his hands together.

Phil grinned. "I'm at the same conclusion a hotshot reporter like you arrived at."

"How's that?" Slats gasped.

"Money was no problem."

Slats leaped to his feet. He grabbed Phil's right hand. "Thanks, you've been a big help." Slats headed toward the door then turned. "Doesn't the employment app ask for birthplace?"

Phil shrugged. "C'mon Slats, in this PC climate, we're lucky we can still ask their names."

"Social security number?"

"Slats, you're a reporter. We can't give that out. You've got to know better."

"Yeah." Slats shrugged. "And his previous address?"

"Not without his permission." Phil strode past Slats and opened the door to his office. "Can you find your car okay, Slats? Or can one of our sales reps interest you in a Bentley, Porsche, or a Jag?"

Slats grinned and put out his hand. "You've been a big help. When I get my bonus, I'll check out one of your Jags. Even with a bonus, a Bentley's out of reach."

Slats, pulling out of the dealership, suddenly felt inadequate tooling around in an aged Corvette. *Better not tell Holly about the Padgett Motors visit, or she'd start asking about getting a new Porsche or Jag. Right, as if our bank account could stand* that *shock.* Entering the Slauson cutoff, Slats focused on what he got out of Hedges. The key was, this Pedro suddenly departed, leaving all that potential loot on the table. Ergo, two potential conclusions: one, maybe Pedro did do something to the car to make it conk out exactly where the "setup" took place; two, if Pedro did indeed tamper with the vehicle, whoever put him up to it gave him so much money that he could chuck his job, bonus, and the good old USA. Who's got that kind of loot to throw around? Right, the Frommer Slime Pits and whoever's funding them.

When Slats got back to the office, he called Spivey & Associates to get Jeff Hudson's phone number. He was referred to a Rhea Simpson, who told him their clients' phone numbers were confidential. "Anything I can help you with?"

"I doubt it," Slats replied. "Thanks for your help."

Slats put the phone down and looked around. Leary looked like he was staring out the window at the magnificent coastline. *Does that guy ever work?* Slats figured no point in discussing anything with Leary at this point. He looked at his watch. It was 5:15 SPM. *Hmm, so they don't have bankers' hours at Spivey.* Still, he decided it was too late to call. But Slats was determined to call Spivey first thing tomorrow and see what he could get out of the chief honcho himself.

CENTURY CITY

Six phone calls, all screened by one of his flunkies, and Spivey's ignored them. all. And it's been three days since the first call. "He'll get back to you real soon, he'll get back to you real soon. What was that number again?"

Yeah, right, real soon, like when hell freezes over or Berkeley votes Republican. After a gloomy dinner punctuated by Holly's "are you a man or a mouse?" taunts, Slats, appetite gone, left a third of her eggplant casserole on his plate. "Why don't you put it in the fridge, Hol? There's too much left to throw out."

"Like hell," she growled as she emptied Slats's plate into the garbage bag. "The fridge is too packed as it is."

"Jeez, Holly, all you did was defrost and microwave the egg-plant. Why the heat?"

Holly, rinsing the dishes, sighed. "You know, Slats, some-times… you won't get off the dime on our relationship, and that's fine. I like the lack of commitment myself. But you know, after four years, maybe my ego wouldn't mind if you at least popped the ques-tion once."

"Is that what this is about?"

Holly wiped her hands, turned toward Slats, and shook her head. "Slats, what have we been talking about tonight?"

"You mean earlier? That I'm in deep shit. Can't get to see Spivey, and to report to Leary tomorrow, and all I got is some missing mechanic. Is that it?"

"Oh, that's it, all right. Slats, you're in your thirties. When are you going to show some, get up, and go? Oh, Slats, part of your charm is, you're so easygoing. You never turned me off like all those pushy yuppies trying to impress me with their so-called credentials—their incomes, their portfolios, their Maseratis. *But there's a limit!* Slats, just when are you going to stop coasting?"

"Holly, baby." He moved toward her and hugged her. "I never looked at it like I'm coasting. I got a good job—till they outsource it to India."

Holly pulled way, grimacing.

Slats, like all those comedians whose jokes fall flat, mumbled, "Nothing."

Holly toyed with her apron before putting it back in the kitchen. She came back to the living room and stared at Slats sitting on the sofa. "Like you say, Slats, and I agree, Tom's a topflight editor and a great guy. But he's got a boss too. How long do you think he's going to stick with you when you report to him tomorrow with nothing except an AWOL mechanic?"

Slats sighed. "C'mon, hon, at least I came up with that."

"That's not enough," she almost screamed. "I'm not an editor, and it's obvious to me. And you say Leary's been around like forever."

"Well, he's not quite fifty," Slats replied softly, "but it seems like he starred in the original *Front Page*."

"*Front Page*. That's it! Jack Lemmon, Walter Mathau—nothing stopped them."

"That was the second one, Holly. All I remember from the first one is Rosalind Russell." He grinned. "First thing tomorrow, Holly, I swear, I'll front-page everyone at Spivey and get to see the big man himself."

"He probably won't give you much, but at least you can tell Tom you didn't take no for an answer."

"Holly, you're the greatest."

Holly smiled and shook her head. "Right, Ralph Kramden, go back to driving that bus." She puckered her lips. "I'm sorry I went postal, sweetie."

Holly, her lissome long legs visible through her housecoat, approached Slats and stuck one of her thighs between his legs, rubbing up against his groin. She kissed him hard, wet. Even without her heels, she was slightly taller than Slats, prompting him to stretch mightily to meet her lips. They stumbled to the couch and embraced another minute until Holly gently pushed him away. "Not so soon after dinner, lover boy. Bad for the digestion."

Slats watched her head back to the kitchen. "Well, it won't be tonight, angel. I need all my beauty sleep. Like I said, first thing tomorrow, Spivey's office. I'll show you who's coasting."

Holly smiled that sensual smile of hers. Her long blond hair seemed to obscure her eyes as she walked toward him. He got up, and they embraced. "I'm sorry, Slats, sometimes things get to be too much."

They kissed again. Slats never tired of putting his arms around her slim waist. "Holly, you're an angel, even if you weren't putting up with a jerk like me. You don't ever have to apologize, you've given me so much. Tonight got anything to do with your job?"

She gave him a quizzical look. "Everything's fine with me, Slats. At least we got one paycheck that seems safe. Tonight the subject was you. So what's on TV?"

Slats was able to find a sixteen-dollar early-bird special at a lot about a ten-minute walk from Century City. He winced when he accepted the four singles in change, hoping Leary would okay the expense. Plus, you go to one of those Century City coffee shops, and it's a ten-spot for just an English muffin and some coffee. But it wasn't even seven thirty. He figured on a nearly two-hour stay sipping coffee and perusing the *Times*. They probably don't open till nine, and half past nine's the earliest he thought he could attempt to barge past the receptionist.

Then it hit him. He'd probably have to sign in, show he had an appointment. All this terrorism shit. Well, he reasoned, a big mouth and a press badge can usually overcome man-made obstacles. It seemed to take forever, but it was finally nine. The place had half-emptied at eight, then some more at eight thirty, and now there were virtually no customers left. Slats glanced at the check. The coffee and English came out to $8.37, including tax. With all the refills, he figured give her twelve bucks and keep the change. *Egad, twenty-eight bucks, and I haven't even reached Spivey's office yet—from which I'll probably be thrown out on my butt anyway.*

As Slats entered the Century City complex, his anxiety diminished as he scanned all the talent scurrying about. *Damn, what hotties populate this part of town. Plus, as opposed to the freeways, you can see what they got.* He was back to business, and his heart started pumping as he saw the guards and the sign-in sheets. He clipped his press badge to the lapel of his sports jacket.

"Yes, can I help you?"

She was a tiny and middle-aged Filipino, probably, with a good-natured smile. But that beefy guy with the gun in the visible holster didn't appear as friendly. Slats grabbed his badge and held it close to the lady's face. "I'm Slats Connors with the *Pacific Coast Gazette*. Here to see Spivey & Associates."

"Do you have an appointment?"

It came out "appoytmente," but Slats decided this wasn't the time for lessons in diction.

"No, miss… ahh…," Slats leaned over to glance at her badge, "Ms. Isabel Ramos."

She smiled and blushed while the guard began to scowl.

"I'm sorry, but you need…"

Slats looked right at the guard "Look, you can search me or call my office. Here's the cell phone. I'm a reporter on an important story. I got to get up there."

The guard cracked a slight smile. "I sympathize with that. Sign in right here." He pointed to the airport-type metal detectors. "Okay, now deposit your keys, belt, change, anything with metal. I'll wait for you."

"Ah, let's see. Thanks, Bruce." Slats turned back toward Isabel and waved as she grinned in return. He went through the detector, picked up his belongings, and was dutifully "frisked" by Bruce.

"You're okay." He smiled. "Good luck with your story."

Slats headed toward the twenty-fifth- to seventieth-floor bank of elevators with a spring to his step. Damn, those two were nice. If Spivey's pissed and tracked it back to them, they could be canned. Nah, a PR guy would never do that. Bad PR.

Slats pushed 45 on the elevator. There was one pudgy, bald-headed accountant type riding with him, along with three gorgeous dames. The small blonde with the short skirt had pushed 36. The elevator whooshed up there so fast he couldn't even appreciate… Well, maybe, hopefully, the elevator would stall? He was next, and 45 lit up in a few seconds. The other two luscious ones were in back of him—he daren't sneak another look. Glancing at the gaudy Spivey & Associates office entrance, Slats admonished himself. *You hopeless bastard, the biggest moment of your career's coming up, and all you can think about is pussy. Gonna mention the elevator trauma to Holly when she asks about your day? I thought not.*

Slats took a deep breath and opened the glass door. The receptionist looked up and flashed a cutesy smile. "Yes, can I help you?"

"Yes, I'm Slats Conners with the *Pacific Coast Gazette*, and I'd like to see Mr. Spivey."

The receptionist appeared to scan her computer screen. "Do you have an appointment? I don't see—"

"Well, actually, I don't, but this is important, and I did call, and no one—"

"What is this about, Mr. Conners?" The cutesy smile was definitely gone.

"It's about Ann Sloan. I got some news Mr. Spivey can use, and maybe he's got something I can use."

The receptionist's expression turned businesslike. She picked up the phone and pushed an extension. "Rhea, there's a reporter out here." Slats could hear a voice at the other end but couldn't make out what, but he did hear the receptionist say, "Ann Sloan." She put the phone down. The smile, while no longer cutesy, was back. "Please have a seat, Mr. Conners. Ms. Rhea Simpson will be right out to see you."

Slats sat down at one of those plush, foamy reception area chairs. He picked up *Fortune* magazine and tried to hide his elation. *Well, Holly, talk about a man or a mouse. This mouse is starting to smell the cheese.*

It took less than a minute. This enchanting little thing approached him. "Hi, I'm Rhea Simpson. I hear you're a reporter." She smiled and held out her right hand.

Slats, obviously losing his cool, jumped up from the chair, tossed the magazine haphazardly on the end table, and shook her hand. Blaming himself for leaping from the chair, tossing the mag., and perhaps holding on to that soft little hand a little too long, Slats felt weak in the knees. The best he could come up with was, "Pleased to meet you." He thought she noticed how uncomfortable he was, because she hit him with a forgiving, dazzling smile.

"Well, Mr. Conners, would you like to follow me to my office?"

He was tempted to answer, "Is the pope Catholic?" In this case, he had two reasons to feel giddy about following her to her office. He was in and without an appointment. And who wouldn't want to be in an office with this little thing who, remembering the old Dangerfield line, you look up *cute* in the dictionary, and there's her picture. There were a few turns, a lot of busy-looking young professional types, blondwood paneling, lots of plants and flowers, and finally, a door marked "Rhea Simpson, Senior Account Executive."

She held it open. "Won't you please come in?"

By now, Slats was over the comfort of getting past the reception area and, as in the elevator episode, admonishing himself for his lustful thoughts. This seemed to be too easy.

She faced him behind a relatively small desk that seemed pretty uncluttered for a senior account exec. The desktop computer was over by the left side of the desk.

"Mr. Conners," she began, "may I call you Slats?"

Is the pope Catholic? Slats mumbled to himself again. He replied weakly, "Well, sure."

"Good." She grinned. "Please call me Rhea."

"Okay, Rhea, I was wondering if…"

"First of all, I want to apologize on behalf of Mr. Spivey and the firm for not getting back to you sooner. Our appointment manager took sick, and it was several days before we could track her down to get her password. As soon as we realized you wanted to visit us, we called back, ah, about 8:30 this morning. Someone called Holly answered with a recorded message. You'll see our message when you get home. We didn't have—"

"Bad timing." Slats shrugged. "Both our cell phones were out, and we've been too busy to go to Sprint until I got a new battery late yesterday... Well, I'm sorry for any inconvenience."

"Oh, it's cool, Slats. All's well that ends well. Now, Ann Sloan is one of our most valued clients, and if there's anything—"

"Well, yes, Rhea, to begin with, I called your office, and a staffer told me Jeff Hudson's phone number wasn't available."

"That was me." She blushed. "We, of course, would never give out Ann Sloan's number or e-mail, so with Jeff's relationship with her, we maintain that proprietary confidentiality as far as he's concerned also." She paused and scratched her nose. "Err, that didn't come out quite right. What I meant is that when Ann and Jeff are represented by our firm, we handle everything. Someone wants to reach them, they come through us."

"I understand that, but I'm sure we've both got the same goal."

"And what would that be?"

"Finding out who set the Chanteuse up and why they did it."

That pretty little face took on a more serious expression. She reached for her phone and pushed one of the extensions. "Mr. Spivey? Yes, he's in my office. I think now would be a good time." Rhea put the phone down. "Mr. Spivey will join us in a moment, Slats. Can I get you some coffee?"

"No, no thanks." Slats smiled.

The door opened almost immediately. Ed Spivey grinned and approached Slats, who rose to shake Spivey's outstretched hand. "Hi, I'm Ed Spivey. Followed your stuff on Ann and the trial. I'm very impressed."

Slats appreciated Spivey's attire. He wore what looked like one of those sage-colored short-sleeved chambray shirts with khaki slacks.

Pretty cool, Slats reflected. *Well, maybe it's dress-down Friday.* "Thanks, Mr. Spivey." They both sat down facing Rhea.

"Can you put me up to speed, Rhea?"

"Yes, Mr. Spivey, Mr. Conners would like to get Jeff Hudson's phone number. That's about all we covered, ah, except for the fact that Mr. Conners says he has some information for us."

Spivey looked at Slats. "Did Rhea explain that we can't give out that kind of information?"

"Yes, she did," Slats grinned, "dutifully."

"Well, Mr. Conners, may I ask why you want to contact Jeff and, of course, what pearls you have for us?"

"Slats is just fine, Mr. Spivey. Rhea and I are on a first-name basis."

"Okay, Slats, what do you have?"

"I had a hunch that took me to Padgett Motors. Found out there was one mechanic who religiously worked on Hudson's Bentley, someone named Pedro Ramirez. The service manager told me he hightailed it out of the country right after the Sloan-Hudson debacle." Slats noticed Spivey and Rhea glance at each other.

"The reason I wanted to reach Hudson was to see if he had any idea where he ran off to. The Padgett guy told me somewhere in South America, but not Mexico. I mean, the car conking out so close to where they live, everything recorded. A lot looks fishy."

"And you think—"

"Well, Mr. Spivey, the tapes had to be in the car. Who else but—" Slats didn't finish the sentence. He just eyed Rhea and Spivey with a satisfied smirk.

Rhea responded, "Very perceptive, Slats. That's what we suggested to Jeff. He just couldn't believe it at first." She looked at Spivey, who seemed to nod. "I guess you'd like to reach Ramirez to find out who backed him on this. So do we." Rhea paused and glanced at Spivey.

"Thanks, Rhea. So, Slats, we're about as deep in this as you are. One thing, though, Ramirez is from Spain, Basque Country, not South America. His English is virtually perfect, came here at the age of six. Apparently, his father was a Basque Nationalist, and he emigrated to New York to escape Franco's police."

"Impressive," Slats cut in, "but how do you know all this? And why the South America fake-out?"

Spivey looked at Rhea, as if to get approval from his associate. He clasped his hands together and smiled. "We never found out for certain, but we assume he returned to Spain and left again due to a criminal matter and the so-called South American fake-out can only help him keep his prior life a secret. We check out anyone that comes in daily, weekly, or monthly contact with Ann. Of course, then, that includes Jeff Hudson. You understand, Slats, that someone as famous as the so-called Chanteuse can attract many malefactors with who knows what on their minds."

"I didn't realize your services were that comprehensive."

Spivey's eyes narrowed. "Of course, we stick to public relations, our specialty. But in looking out for the best interests of our clients, we do, when required, obtain the services of, how do I put it, specialists."

Slats displayed a nervous grin. "Like the Frommers?"

Spivey looked at Rhea. "Go ahead, Rhea, I've been monopolizing the conversation, and after all, it is your office and your account."

"Thanks, Mr. Spivey." She scratched that pert, upturned little nose of hers again. "The Frommers are the largest and probably the best. But they have so many, shall we say, interests, that we never know when the so-called worm will turn. We prefer smaller outfits who will always value our business."

"Well, if I may ask, Rhea, are you hinting at what I'm trying to find out?"

"How's that?" she blurted out.

"I've been trying to figure out who backed Ramirez in that automobile taping fiasco. My conclusion, the Frommers." He caught them making eye contact again. *I must be on to something*, Slats thought. "I figure the Frommers are big enough and ornery enough to pull off this escapade, but the big challenge is who, in turn, is pulling the strings on the Frommers."

"Go ahead," Spivey cut in, "you're on a roll."

"I figure those kings of lawsuits, the Mellons."

"Anything more than a hunch?"

"Well, no offense to your Chanteuse, Mr. Spivey, but this whole Josh Parker stunt always struck me as a crock. Sloan was involved, but why would so many so-called Liberal activists stick their necks out for a thug like Parker? And where did this 'movement' get its muscle, organization? This isn't prescription drugs, abortion, racism, war, where the base is readily activated. Something big had to get these 'activists' out there."

"Besides their being richer than Warren Buffett or Donald Trump, which means financing this is chump change, what makes you think Mellon, Cunningham, and Caldwell have an incentive to be involved in this?"

Slats hesitated. He drew a deep breath. "We all know about the litigation crisis. Apparently, the party of Roosevelt, Truman, and Kennedy has now become a front for unlimited lawsuits. To keep the momentum going, the Mellons have to continually invent crisis, causes, whatever, to activate civil Libertarians, women's groups, minorities, anything to keep the pot boiling, so to speak."

"I'm not clear," Spivey interrupted. "What's all this got to do with the Democrats and Harry Truman?"

"Well, Mr. Spivey, the way I see it, the Dems are caught in a bind. No one with half a brain or love of the USA can be in favor of all this legal frivolity, but the party is in hock to the trial lawyers. They can only think of the next election. Meanwhile, the Mellons get the right venues, the right juries, judges—the sky's the limit."

Spivey frowned. "Mellon has all the money he'll ever need or dream he'd ever need."

"Right, Mr. Spivey, but sometimes the cause, the legacy, the life's calling obviates financial considerations."

Spivey looked at Rhea. "Pretty impressive discourse, don't you think, Rhea?" She grinned and nodded.

"No offense, Slats," Spivey continued, "but you sound more like you're leading a seminar for grad students at Georgetown or Stanford than being a reporter for a suburban daily."

Slats smirked. "Well, Mr. Spivey, when I'm not working, watching football, or forced to watch chick flicks with my girl, Holly, I read the *WSJ* daily, *Newsweek* weekly, and *Fortune* monthly. I also haunt a ton of strange and political websites. And oh yeah, when I'm in the car, I tune in Rush."

"Nuff said. We don't want to give this young man a swelled head, Rhea. So, Slats, where do we go from here?"

Slats shrugged. "Looks like we got the same goals. Well, I mean, you want to protect your client, and I want to find out what happened to her and who's behind it."

"Good, Slats. You and Rhea will contact each other whenever info pops up that's of mutual benefit. Of course, anything that's been said up to now, or you hear from us in the future, stays between your ears. Clear?"

Slats didn't like the sound of the clear, where Spivey went from sounding like an urbane PR exec to a Mafia-type gunsel. Still, he couldn't disagree. "Clear, Mr. Spivey, nothing that comes from you or Rhea will end up in the *Gazette*."

TRAINEES

There was a buzz among the staff and students on that gray, chilly January morning. The rumor mill had it that Mr. Mellon himself would visit the premises and observe the trainees. The classroom was located on the fifth floor of one of those typical, brick-layered, nineteenth-century office buildings prevalent on Maiden Lane, near the canyons of Wall Street. The law firm of Mellon, Cunningham, and Caldwell purchased the 175 Maiden Lane location in 2001, bought out the remaining tenants, and used it strictly as a "training" facility.

The facilitator, George Fields, was directing an attractive tall blonde and short, pudgy young man with glasses who were engaged in role-playing. "Okay, Cindy. You're at the copy machine. Lenny, you're dropping off some mail. Go."

"Hi, Cindy. You sure look good. Haven't seen you all day."

"Hello, Lenny, nice seeing you. Thanks for the compliment." Another blonde in the class raised her hand.

"Yes, Julie?"

"Well, Mr. Fields, if Cindy's at a copy machine, someone else is either hanging around within earshot, or someone who wasn't noticed could have passed by."

"Meaning, Julie?" Fields blinked as he noticed William Mellon himself at the door quietly taking a seat in the back of the room.

"Meaning that Cindy is supposed to lead Lenny on when there's no one around. When a potential witness is nearby, Cindy should act curt and look annoyed."

"Good, Julie." Fields beamed. "Can you elaborate?"

"Yes, Mr. Fields. The object is to lead this loser on when they're alone and look like you're being annoyed or, to put it legally, harassed when there are witnesses."

"Thanks, Julie. You see, class, the object is simply to collect on a sexual harassment suit. In order to do that, we simply need one set of witnesses and one set of nonwitnesses. Those who have seen Cindy being bothered, annoyed, harassed, whatever, by character like Lenny *and* those who have *not* seen Cindy leading him on."

Mellon rose; Fields nervously pointed to Mellon's presence in the rear of the room. "Class, this is William Mellon. Anything in particular, Mr. Mellon?"

Mellon slowly walked to the front of the room. He was nearly six feet tall but seemed shorter due to his enormous waist. He'd apparently left his suit jacket in his office. He sported one of those light-blue Armani shirts with huge white cuffs and a solid white collar. A bright-red tie with soft blue dots and golden cuff links and several huge finger rings added to his image as a wealthy executive. "Didn't mean to interrupt, George. From what I can see, you're doing the usual topflight job, and it certainly looks like you've got a bright, attentive class." He walked to the front of the class and looked at the young ladies who were seated. "Would you all mind coming up here?"

Without hesitation, they all marched to the front of the room. The well-coifed, well-groomed young women looked like the typical receptionists at glitzy-offices setting back in the sixties when attractive women filled their decorative roles in American commerce prior to marriage. Fields, though, knew Mellon could give a rat's ass about their decorative capacities. They'd been carefully selected, prepped, and advanced to this stage of the Mellon plan. *Which ones,* Fields wondered, *if any, would be disposed of today, Trump style?*

"Well, four blondes and two brunettes," Mellon observed as the Stepford-type gals grinned self-consciously. "Starting from the left, could you all count off, beginning with one, please."

Mellon watched carefully as they counted off. "Number 4, could you remain standing? The rest of you can sit down."

Mellon looked at Number 4, who, while smiling nervously, couldn't hide her anxiety. Mellon waited until her audible breathing had subsided. "What's your name, please?"

"Sheryl Waters," she answered.

Fields thought Sheryl seemed hesitant, as if looking for a lectern or something to lean on. But there she was, all alone, with no support, physically or morally, while facing the top litigator in America today, who, incidentally, was also her ultimate employer and held the key to her future. Still, Fields was proud; she passed the first test. She gave not her real name but her Mellon-provided name.

"Ms. Waters, why do you want to work for San Francisco Water and Power?"

"I feel that energy and a scarcity of natural resources will shape the agenda for the United States and the world in the foreseeable future."

"I see. Well, we all like to feel that we're doing something important. I notice that you're from the New York area. Why move to San Francisco?"

"I've had family move out to the Seattle area—it's a close aunt— and the Bay Area has the advantage of being in the same time zone but sufficiently far away so I can do my own thing when we're not visiting. Besides, who wouldn't want to live in the San Francisco area, cost of living aside?"

A slight smirk creased Mellon's lips. He looked at Fields. "All right, Number 4, you may sit down."

Fields suppressed a grin. One of his pupils had passed the Mellon hurdle. "Why don't you sit down, George? I'll take over from here. Number 4 came through okay, and that can only reflect positively on your training methods."

Fields sat down, meeting the appreciative stares of his pupils.

Mellon's expression turned dour. "You did a good job of thinking on your feet, Number 4. George, even though you just sat down, could you please stand and explain what was illogical about what just went on?"

"Sure, Mr. Mellon." Fields beamed. "First of all, if a topflight litigator wanted to relocate from, say, Colorado to New York and join the Mellon law firm, it might be expected that the 'why do you want to relocate?' question might be asked. However, it would never be asked of a civil servant applying for a tedious data entry position for a dull agency like DWP. All you do is pass the civil service test, then demonstrate your data entry capacity, and you get selected."

Several hands went up. Fields pointed to Number 4. "Yes, Sheryl?"

"Why San Francisco? What if there are no openings, and what if I don't do well enough in the test?"

Fields looked at Mellon. "As they say on those quiz shows, I'll save the first for last and let Mr. Mellon answer. There *will* be openings, Sheryl, several weeks after you've moved out there. And with your intelligence and capacities, you're already more qualified than most when it comes to data entry. In other words, you're a shoo-in to qualify for a job that pays about 1 percent of what your earnings capacity will be once you've pulled off the con and can go back to your former identity and use your legal background."

There were appreciative titters of laughter.

"So you're letting me answer the San Francisco part, George? Well, thanks for your confidence. No, you won't be asked questions that can trip you up at an interview for that kind of job. It's when you're out with the girls, TGIF, as doughty as you will attempt to appear, the other gals are sure to wonder and ask, what's a stylish young lady with your class doing in a place like this with a job like that? That's what we don't want. We can't take a chance on a witness called for the defense finding a hole in your past. You've got to sell who you are to sell the sting." Mellon looked at George. "George, have you mentioned the Great Escape yet?"

George grinned. "It was on the agenda for this week, Mr. Mellon. But since you're here today, I have a feeling you're going to tell us about it."

"Right you are, George. You anticipate me well. I enjoy telling the Great Escape tale because the lesson is the key to what could trip any of you up in your upcoming assignments. The Great Escape came out in the early sixties. It was a film about downed Allied airmen in World War II and their continuous attempts to escape German prison camps."

Mellon paused, poured himself some water, and continued. "Most of the prisoners were British, and the ad hoc leader, a wonderful actor named Richard Attenborough, was the mastermind of the attempt as a massive breakout, hence Great Escape. No matter the training, Attenborough kept emphasizing that if your false papers were those of a Frenchman, *always* think in terms of French so that you'll never slip back to your native English."

Mellon went back to the little table that held the pitcher of water. He refilled his plastic cup, slowly ingested the refreshing water, and deliberately walked back to the center of the classroom. Fields successfully hid a smirk as he observed the trainees in awe of the master. Was he really that thirsty, or was this just another lawyer's trick to enthrall a jury?

Mellon smiled. "I'm sure by now you all know how this ends. Attenborough and a companion, posing as French businessmen after the escape, endure several close calls on trains, and now they're about to board a bus to take them beyond the massive dragnet looking for the escapees. A gestapo-type inspects their papers and, in French, tells them they can board. As they reach the entrance to the bus, the suspicious Gestapo official suddenly shouts out 'GOOD LUCK!' in English. Attenborough, of all people, responds *in English*, 'Thanks.'"

There were some appreciative murmurs in the classroom. Mellon, now looking grim, continued. "Do not giggle at what I'm about to say. We've invested too much. Attenborough's faux-pas would be the equivalent of Bill Mellon or your instructor, George Fields, making a similar mistake." Still looking grave, he looked at Fields. "Sum up today's lesson, George."

"Surely, Mr. Mellon. Any CIA operative or law enforcement official working undercover knows that one slipup means his or her life. Our stakes are not *that* high, but the success of your careers and, ultimately, the survival of this firm depend on your remembering this lesson."

"Mr. Mellon."

"Thanks, George. I really enjoyed this visit. Anything else before I go?"

Number 2 raised her hand.

"Yes, you have a question?"

"Yes, Mr. Mellon, I was wondering, why San Francisco?"

"In what regard?"

"Well, just that it's so easy. Where's the challenge?"

"Good question. Yes, it's easy, especially with regard to the harassment issue. When it comes to police or fire departments, all it takes is one blink from us and they offer 20 mill. But we've played out the protective services. That's why for the Bay Area, we're focusing on the Department of Water and Power. One wouldn't expect a burly policeman or fireman to inadvertently be 'insensitive' to a female at DWP." Mellon paused for the appreciative giggles. "Of course, if we can't find a panting young man to lose his marbles around a beautiful blonde or redhead. We can always," he smirked for effect, "hire one. But first, we try it legit.

"The other challenge in an otherwise-accommodating environ-ment is the fact that the City of San Francisco is about 300 million in the red. To get them to cough up 20 mill without a fight under those circumstances is where the challenge lies. Don't forget, future associates, one-third contingency of another 20 million here and there means about as much to this firm as a dollar tip to a server at Starbucks. But we have to keep growing as a firm. I worry about all our futures—the current partners, future partners like perhaps some of you, and the well-being of our families. There are only so many billions left in asbestos, tobacco, and the drug companies. Growth, class, growth. We never stop."

Another hand was raised. Mellon pointed at her. "Question, Number 5?"

"Yes, sir." She rose and inadvertently touched her long-tressed auburn-tinted hair. "If San Francisco is some 300 mill in the red, how do we collect even as we win the judgment?"

"Good question, Number 5. I conclude that you've taken some eco classes prior to law school. But in this case, it's poli sci. that matters. You see, class, back in '75, before all of you were born, the City of New York was teetering on bankruptcy. President Gerald Ford, even though he felt New York got what it deserved because of its profligate ways, was forced to cave to the pressure, and the Feds eventually bailed out the city.

"Similarly, several years later, Chrysler and Lockheed were bailed out because their demise would cause too many job losses. So cities like San Francisco, who love to help out women who've been harassed, they'll find the money—from the state, the Feds or by raising taxes. But we, class, we *will* be served, no matter the economic or political conditions. And one final note: California law has zero tolerance. Any harassment will be treated as the employer's fault, even if the employer had no knowledge.

"The rest of you ladies will be assigned to cities as varied as Detroit, Baltimore, San Diego, where we'll get you into one of the protective services. Those cities may not be as accommodating as San Francisco, but any suit emanating from fire or police can't help but be successful. Thank you for your time."

He turned toward Fields. "Thanks, George. You've got a promising bunch of associates here." With that, Mellon was out the door.

NOB HILL

Scott Slotzky was drained. Coming off that sixty-hour week at that Microbiology Conference in Tucson and not getting home till Sunday afternoon was bad enough. But on top of that, this Monday's been the mother of all blue Mondays. In at seven, home past eight, with virtually no break for lunch. Unless those half-dozen aspirins for that hell of a daylong headache count as nourishment. So what's that, thirteen hours? *Be* thankful it's just a ten-minute walk to work, or we're looking at a fifteen-hour day.

He sat on the couch with his dress shirt and tie still on. Scott lazily fondled the remote and checked out ESPN. Julie's got a class Monday nights, and it's too late and too Monday to get together with someone else for a bite. He headed toward the fridge. *Let's see, which Healthy Choice is the winner tonight? Herb Baked Fish? Nah, tired of seafood.* He reached for a Weight Watchers' pizza. *Hmm, chicken on top, looks like the winner.* He heard the phone ring.

"Stuey, hon, it's Mom. I've haven't heard from you in—"

"Ma, gimme space, all kinds a things going on up here. I swear I was going to call as soon as—"

"Scotty, baby, that's not what I'm calling about."

"Oh, oh, Ma, sounds serious when there's something on the agenda bigger than my not calling enough. Is it all that political hassle? I thought your stay at the spa—"

"You got me, son. I'm fine emotionally, but Spivey and others thought that now's a good time to sort of stay out of the limelight but still be an hour's away from the record companies, agents, all that. They suggested Scottsdale or La Jolla, but I figured if I'm going to leave Beverly Hills, why not hang with my eldest in a nice cosmopolitan city like San Francisco?"

"That's great, Ma. Need a place till you get set up? I got room."

"Don't be silly, Scotty. Jeff found me a furnished flat in a high-rise on Jones Street."

"Jones Street, where's that?"

"Nob Hill. Isn't that the place to be?"

"Well, you could say that, but for me, SOMA's where the action is."

"SOMA? I've never heard of it. Is that the Italian section in town?"

Scott almost said, "SOMA's for people in my age bracket." But he wasn't that pooped. "Oh, it's a redeveloped area in the heart of the city, south of Market. Market's San Fran's Broadway. Hence SOMA."

"Oh, that sounds delightful, Scott, so in addition to your pad, I'll be seeing an exciting neighborhood."

"Looking forward, Ma, looking forward. Jeff coming with you?"

"Too many irons in the fire, Scotty. But he'll be up every weekend or else—that is, after the first weekend, when I want to have you all to myself. How's Allen? Have you heard from him recently? I haven't received an e-mail in nearly a week."

"Well, he did call a couple of days ago. He's been real busy. He knows we talk five minutes, most. He said he'd call you when he's got an hour to spare. It's not easy, with the two-year-old, the time difference."

"So he picks his brother over his mom. What is this world—"

"C'mon, Ma, don't start."

"I bet it's that wife of his, Susan. She always sounds so distant."

"Ma, be fair. It's been hell with their both working and Connie still not ready for preschool."

"Ohhh, I'm going to lose it, Scotty. Why won't you or Allen accept any help from me? I swear, you both take after your father,

Irving, with that Slotsky streak of being obstinate and independent. That's why he left William Morris and started his own agency."

"Ma, you and I have been through this before. And their need isn't money. Was the time, the sitter, the sleepless nights, the commute from Falls Church into DC. That's the hassle, not money."

"That's another thing, Scott. I still haven't had an explanation about where's he's living."

"Where he's living? What does that mean?"

"Well, I don't know much about that area, but I thought all the proper people live in Georgetown or Montgomery County."

Scott tried not to breathe hard. "Ma, I swear, sometime—haven't you heard of McClean?"

"Of course, I have, Scotty, but I don't want my granddaughter growing up among military types or right wingers."

"Ma, unbelievable. Where do you get your ideas? It's got to be more than Hollywood. Okay, one last time. Georgetown's no place for children, and Montgomery County's too far north. Allen works near Capitol Hill. Suburban Virginia's the best commute."

"Okay, son, no more arguments. Pick out a nice restaurant and get a corner table. No publicity. Just want to treat my boy to a top-flight meal. Also, I need to be with family, after losing David."

"I got just the place, Ma. It's Postrio, that Spago guy's San Fran outpost. The class is there, but there's no paparazzi hanging on the outside, like at Spago's."

"You're *so* grown-up. Can't wait, son. And come with an appetite. Last time, you didn't order an appetizer. If the bill's under one hundred dollars, I'll be disappointed."

While getting the details on his mom's flight, Scott frantically wondered whether he could get the maid over before she sees the digs. He checked his notes—"4:15 arrival Friday." Plenty of time to get the maid in here in time. Meantime, what's the deal with that Jeff Hudson only coming on weekends? Scott was almost concerned, but he concluded if that tidbit had meant anything, he would have caught it in his mom's tone of voice. But she seemed comparatively relaxed.

While adding a call to the maid to tomorrow's AM schedule, Scott wondered if he should bring Julie along to Postrio. Nah, certainly not right away. She still doesn't know ol' Scott Slotzky is the Chanteuse's youngest son. Was going to find the right time to break the news. Now, after seeing Julie for four months, Armageddon's at hand—or certainly flying up from LA. Scott looked at the freezer again. It was nearly ten—too late for any pizza. It might affect his sleep. Instead, he fixed himself some humus with avocados, opened a bag of soy crackers, and opened a can of Coors. The beer relaxed him immensely. He absentmindedly began dipping the soy crackers in the humus container. He contemplated what he'd say to Julie about the plans for the weekend. He figured the second time he takes Mom out to dinner, Julie comes along, or she'll suspect that "mom" is just another babe.

He checked his watch. It was ten fifteen. Julie's got to be out of class and driving home. He pushed her number on his cell. While he heard the ringing, he thought about when he'd tell Julie that his mom was Ann Sloan, the famous Chanteuse.

***

This was going to be something special. Leary wanted a meet over lunch. He said he had "business" in the Beverly Hills area, so "I'll meet you at Juniors around one." *The good part*, Slats figured, *I get a lunch on the paper, maybe see a movie star, and don't have to trek into the office till the end of the week. The bad part? Well, if I were to show up with flowers, wouldn't Holly suspect that I'm feeling guilty about something? Or to recall that old maxim, there's no such thing as a free lunch.*

Prepped for some new chore or assignment, Slats was resigned to his fate when he got to Juniors at five to one. For some reason, it wasn't that crowded, and Tom was already at a table when he waved. Slats walked right over and noticed Tom had nearly polished off a Coors. Slats looked at the virtually empty bottle. "Been here a while?"

"Nah, Slats, just five minutes. I drink fast, though."

Slats started to say something when Leary cut in. "Man enough to finish a hot pastrami?"

"In this place, I don't know, Tom, but if I only finish half, I'm sure Holly would enjoy the other half." Slats felt a knot in his stomach. Leary usually gets right to the point—not like him to make all this small talk. Slats was already picturing a meet with Hanson, the union steward, to fight tooth and nail for his job. *Cut the panic*, Slats berated himself, *there's no indication anything's wrong.*

The bored-looking waiter had appeared. All of ten seconds had lapsed, and the waiter's eyes were already rolling to beat the band. You could almost hear the sigh of ennui. *Well*, Slats thought, looking in the direction of the waiter, *hope you have a better day at a casting call tomorrow.*

"Bowl of matzo ball soup and the gefilte fish appetizer," Leary chirped.

Leary and the waiter both stared at Slats. "Hot pastrami on rye, no mayo, mustard on the side, with a side of slaw." Slats was proud of the way he had barked out the order like a drill sergeant on the first day of basic. But the waiter still seemed jaded.

"To drink, Slats, what to drink?" Tom grinned.

"Oh yeah, cream soda, and make that pastrami lean, please."

The waiter shrugged and took off.

"Wow, Slats, cream soda and lean pastrami. You're a real maven."

Slats blushed. "Grew up in Fairfax. Dated a lot of Jewish chicks. Plus, there was that deli there."

A waitress appeared with Leary's second bottle of Coors. They both watched her pour the contents into a glass.

"Something going on, Tom?"

Leary grinned. "What makes you say that?"

"It's not just the lunch. It's the way you haven't said anything of substance yet."

"Can't put anything over on you, eh, Slats? Well, you read me good, Slats. I'm feeling guilty because I don't want to be the cause of any friction between you and Holly."

Slats watched Leary drink his beer. "Another trip?"

Leary's cheeks flushed red. "Well, not too far, Slats, but maybe for a while."

The waiter appeared with Tom's soup and Slats's soda. "Then it's not New York again?"

Leary frowned. "What's the latest you've heard on our ongoing Chanteuse soap opera?"

Slats paused while the waiter dropped off Tom's appetizer and his humongous pastrami sandwich. "Well, I heard that she wanted to lie low for a while, but not go the spa-rehab route again. Sort of a compromise, La Jolla or Scottsdale, leave the heat of la-la land, but be close enough for business, so on, let alone that Hudson guy."

Tom smiled. "You're good, Slats, you're good. The paper isn't wasting its money when it treats you to a lunch at Juniors. Thing is, it's San Francisco, and she's already moved up there."

"What? When, and how did you…?"

Leary bit his bottom lip, Clinton style. "I got a confession, dude. Spivey and I go back a long way. Remember when I mentioned sources?"

"Yeah?" Slats dropped his sandwich and stared directly at Tom. "You scooped your own reporter?"

"Take it easy, Slats, take it easy. Don't say or do anything you'll be sorry for."

"I expected something to come out of this lunch. Frisco's a great town, after I square it with Holly. But you knew Spivey? After I wet my pants trying to get to see him?"

"Relax, Slats. First of all, don't ever say 'Frisco' when you're up there. The locals don't like it. Second, Spivey and I go back a long way. The brotherhood of Gyrenes lasts a lifetime. Been seeing him at special dinners, occasions, the Marines Memorial Officers Club. Even went to his eldest daughter's wedding."

"Still, Tom, you could have—"

"Slats, that week that you got into Spivey's digs, I had no idea your trail was heading in that direction. 'Sides, you don't want anything handed to you on a platter. And as far as Spivey's concerned, I don't call in markers until I'm up against the wall. We hadn't reached that point yet, not by a long shot. Look at the good side, Slats, you impressed a big shot like Spivey, made me and the *Gazette* look good in the process, and apparently accomplished something else."

Slats relaxed when he caught Tom's impish smirk. "Accomplished? Like what do you mean?"

"Spivey apparently has a real cutie working on the Sloan account. He said he thought he caught some sparks between the two of you."

Slats tried not to look defensive, but he knew he was showing vibes of a cornered bear defending her cubs. He forced a weak smile. "Yeah, Rhea Simpson, the gal working the Sloan account is sort of cute." He caught Leary trying to restrain a giggle. "What's your point, Tom?"

"Well, Slats, Spivey told me she's going to be in the Bay Area as long as the Chanteuse is. And as I heard when you were in Spivey's digs, you agreed to share and coordinate information helpful to both our causes."

"Right, but I'm a pro, Tom. You think I'm gonna fuck with a Pulitzer, fuck with you, or fuck with Holly 'cause I'm a hopelessly horny bastard who's got only one thing on his mind?" Slats watched Leary cut off a large chunk of the gefilte fish, busy digesting the mouthful as if determined not to answer."

"Listen up, Spivey and Leary, those two DOMs don't have to worry. I'll be focusing on my job like a laser beam." Slats tried to sound convincing, but losing one's temper didn't help. Besides, his groin area was already active picturing dinner in some romantic hideaway in the Marina with that little cutie-pie.

"Would next Monday be an inconvenience?"

"Well, the faster I face Holly, the better." Slats shrugged.

"Attaboy, Slats, we'll be setting you up in Haddon Hall, one of those weekly residential hotels just like we had for you in New York. It's on Sutter, near Union Square, breakfast and dinner included, and *no* visitors of the opposite sex."

"Well, this being San Francisco, how about the same sex?"

Tom shrugged off Slats's lame response. "I think what they mean is no hankypanky, period. They got someone at reception twenty-four hours." Leary watched Slats, who seemed at a loss for words. "On the other hand, that Simpson lady's staying at the W near the Moscone Convention Center."

"The W?" Slats almost screamed.

"Yeah, Slats, well, that's the difference between a second-rate paper barely in the black and a first-line PR outfit representing the likes of the Chanteuse." Leary waved for the check, looked at Slats, and grinned. "Well, when it gets down to 'your place or my place,' in this case, it's going to be her place."

Slats rose from his chair and made a fist. "What's the legal ramifications of cracking your boss in the snout?"

Leary reached for his credit card. "C'mon, Slats, who's gonna be the best man at the Slats-Holly wedding? Love ya both. Wouldn't tease you like I do if that weren't the case."

Slats was barely paying attention to the heavy three o'clock traffic on the Santa Monica. *Stop off and get something for Holly? Right, like this is a movie and you're Cary Grant. Forget it, this is one time that stupid cliché applies—just be yourself.*

Slats was watching one of O'Reilly's rants on the *Factor*, which put him in the right mood in case breaking the news to Holly resulted in verbal fisticuffs. On the other hand, she didn't seem to mind his trip to New York—but that was high-profile, lasted just several weeks, and there was no guilt. In other words, no Rhea Simpson on that one.

Slats's heart was pounding. Would his guilty conscience give him away?

The phone rang. Traffic was a bitch. She was still twenty minutes away. Holly said she wouldn't be cooking dinner tonight. She asked if he wanted to pick up some Chinese. When he answered yes, she told him to get the Warm Duck Salad for her.

Slats leaped at the opportunity. "Sorry for the traffic, hon, but we got something to celebrate. Going up to Frisco to follow the Chanteuse. And you can come up some weekends and—"

"That's a celebration? You know the way things are going, I can barely get away and—"

"I'm on my way, hon." Slats clicked the phone shut and went into the kitchen to look for the "Shanghai delight" menu. Well, that didn't go so well, but at least the subject was broached over the phone. Slats heaved a sigh of relief. If he had introduced the subject of the trip in her presence, she might have caught something in his manner, disposition. Now, if an argument ensues, any stress he displayed would look like it resulted from the brouhaha.

Sure enough, no sooner was Holly in the door than she blurted out that the traffic was the least of her troubles this fine Tuesday. Henrietta Wilson's mom was in an accident and hospitalized. Henrietta was rushing out to Tucson for who knows how long to be at her side. And Ruth Aurelia's been out with the flu for nearly two weeks. "Now, I've got to still do all the billing and collections, but also help out with the sign-ins and appointments. Harry Feldman, DDS, is going to be a zoo the next few weeks."

All this meant that Holly would have to come in weekends to catch up. That meant no chance she'd be going up to Frisco and problematic for Slats to come down on weekends until some of the MIAs return. Slats kept interrupting, mumbling platitudes like "Things will work out, we'll at least talk on the phone," "Thanks, Henrietta and Ruth, whoever you are. Your timely misfortune got me out of a potential hole tonight," and "A virtual green light in Ms. Rhea's direction."

UNION SQUARE

Slats observed the performers and mimes do their thing as he crossed Powell, heading up Geary. *Man, the Bay Area sure is costly compared to SoCal,* he reflected. *First, they have all those tolls on the bridges. Now, you can't even traverse Union Square without getting hit by panhandlers who want your money, or so-called entertainers who want the same thing.*

He passed the Curran Theater and the attendant excitement in San Francisco's mini version of the Great White Way. He knew he was close. The hotel clerk had said the Clift was one block past the Curran. He told Slats the Clift had a classy bar where "you won't feel out of place."

"There's good talent unless you're inclined the other way, in which case, there's the Castro where you can always—"

"I'm just out to get a drink," Slats had cut in. "It's my first night in town. Just out to get some vibes. I live with a gal, and—"

"Sure, sure," the hotel clerk had smirked. "Have a good time."

Slats thought he'd been a little too defensive, but who knows if and when Holly might run into this hotel dude, and… *Enough,* Slats chided himself as he noticed how parched his throat had suddenly gotten. *You're that paranoid, and so far, Holly has nothing tangible to get pissed about. Right, so far, so far…*

Slats entered the Clift Hotel and was impressed by the laid-back elegance of the lobby. Nothing garish here, unless you include that huge Cinderella Chair, but you knew you were in a class establishment. He passed the receptionist and walked up to the bar. Slats spotted a hip-looking restaurant beyond the bar area's lounge that seemed to possess the kind of electric buzz found in trendy eating places. The bar and surroundings had all the accoutrements of a first-class joint, with mirrors, murals, and decorative seating arrangements throughout the lounge area. Slats noticed a couple of balding expense-account types grab their drinks at the bar and head toward the lounge. He quickly sat down on a barstool visibly vacant after the departure of the businessmen.

This place looked too stylish to order a beer, so Slats called for a Stoli and tonic. When just two dollars were returned from his ten-spot, Slats knew he was in the land of expense account and expensive living. He deliberately took the twist out of his drink with the stirrer and put it on a napkin. He took a sip and turned around to catch the flow. About 60 percent men this Tuesday evening, and it looked like about half the women in the place were hooked up. Still, after downing some more of the drink, the few comely strays scurrying to and fro put Slats in a mellow and hopeful mood.

"How's the scenery look to you?"

Slats turned to the dude to his left. "Hey, I'm no interior decorator, but I'd say a lot of dough went into this establishment."

There was a pause. They both laughed. "But I bet you weren't referring to the built-in scenery. My name's Slats." Slats held out his hand.

"I'm Stu. Nice meeting you. You from these parts?"

"California, but la-la land. Malibu."

"Wow, Malibu."

"Nah, I'm not rich." Slats blushed. "Just taking advantage of some of that rent control that headed northwest from Santa Monica to parts of Malibu. How about you?"

"Been living out here a few years," Stu answered. "Got a condo near PacBell."

"Talk about wow." Slats grinned. "Don't know much about these parts, but I do know SOMA's big now, and you're near PacBell to boot. But don't they call it something else?"

"SBC Park." Stu shrugged. "But most of us haven't given up on calling it PacBell. You on the loose?"

"Just a couple of weeks or so. My squeeze stayed in Malibu."

A tall, well-built brunette wedged in between Slats and Stu. "Excuse me, guys, hard to get his attention?"

Stu looked her over. "Oh, it's Brian. He's pretty good. He'll get you in no time. What would you like, if I get his attention first?"

"Lavender martini." She saw Stu grab a twenty lying among the loose bills spread out in front of him. She put her hand on his right shoulder. "Oh, that's all right, ahh…"

"Stu." He grinned.

"Right, Stu." She blushed. "Nice of you to offer, but I pay my own way."

"Well, can I offer you a seat?"

"Thanks anyway, Stu, again, but I was late, and I'm with some friends from the office." She pointed to two gals sitting at the far end of the lounge.

Brian was quick and fixed the martini promptly while Stu caught Slats winking appreciatively at him.

"Enjoy the evening, guys." She turned after a few sips of the martini and started heading back toward…

Stu grabbed her left arm. "You can't walk away until I accomplish one thing."

Her ever-present smile turned to a frown in an instant. "Now, Stu, don't spoil things. You've been a real sweetheart until—"

"No, you don't understand. All I want is to know your name before you go back to your friends is all."

"Oh, no problem, Stu." She grinned. "Traci, Traci Eyre."

Stu let out a sigh. "Thanks, Traci. Now I know who I'll be dreaming about the rest of my life."

Traci emitted a slight yelp. She put her martini back on the bar counter. "My gosh, that's… that's… Why, that's the best line I've ever heard." She reached into her purse. "Here's my card. Doesn't matter whether you or I have significant others. What just transpired definitely calls for us to do lunch, a least once." She rushed off toward her party, delicately balancing the martini. When she got there, she kept pointing toward Stu, no doubt rehashing the best line she ever heard.

Stu had a slight smirk on his face as he glanced at Slats while putting her card in his shirt pocket.

"That was brilliant, Stu, brilliant. Where are you from, the East Coast or something? That was so smooth."

"I'm from all over, Slats. Been back East a lot, though."

"Well, it sounded to this bashful California beach dude like something like Scorsese or one of his *Goodfellas* would say."

"Well, Slats, I got a hottie I'm shacking up with in the East Bay, but this gal's got a bod that looks like it won't die. I'm sure I'll find an opportunity to do lunch."

"By the way, Stu. What's the card say? What does she do?"

"Media consultant, whatever that means. Never heard of the company."

Stu stared at Slats. "What about you, Slats? What brings you up here? You in sales? A convention?"

Slats shrugged. "Speaking of media, I'm a reporter."

"Reporter? For the *LA Times*?"

"'Fraid not, Stu. A regional fish wrap called the *Pacific Coast Gazette*."

Stu's eyes narrowed. "The sheet that's been covering the Chanteuse?"

Slats swallowed hard. He tried to maintain his composure. He put his drink down lest he display his anxiety with a shaky hand. He replied softly, "You, ah, get down to LA much?"

Stu looked like he'd just announced "four ladies" while taking a pot away from someone who had declared a full house. "It's my business to follow anything written about the Chanteuse."

"Yeah, how's that? You also a reporter, a writer or something?" Slats inadvertently came close to making a fist.

"Small world." Stu grinned. He held out his hand again. "Stu Frommer, of Frommer & Sons."

Slats's being seemed to drift into space. The vodka no doubt had some effect. But what's happening here? Is this an out-of-body experience? An incredibly realistic dream? How can you so nonchalantly meet someone you so completely hate by reputation, especially the first day you're in town, covering the Chanteuse, the very person this Frommer is dedicated to bringing down? Slats reluctantly shook Frommer's outstretched hand. "I've heard of you, obviously."

Frommer left a five-dollar bill and some loose change for the bartender. He collected the rest of his money and got up. His manner turned brusque; his grin was replaced by a frown. "You seem like a nice guy, and I know you didn't follow me here 'cause it was spur of the moment after an appointment didn't show at the St. Francis. If we meet over business in the future and if, well, things don't go smoothly, I assure you it won't be personal."

Slats tried to be assertive, but his voice cracked. "Is this, ah, some kind of white-collar-type threat?"

"Don't be silly, Slats. Our business is sort of amorphous. We google and dot.com any big name in the news. Whether it be Dick Morris, Bill and Hillary, Michael Jackson, Kobe, anyone rich and/or famous where our services might, err, be required.

"Naturally, that includes the Chanteuse. Interesting what's been going on with her lately, especially her moving up here for a while. Of course, our only interest is from a professional standpoint. When it comes to Ann Sloan, we have no fish to fry."

"But you could in the future, couldn't you?"

"Well, of course, Slats, why else would we invest time and effort in the research if we can't be ready to jump in if and when our services our required?"

"And what do your services consist of?"

Stu shook his head and smirked. "Reporter to the end, eh? Bet your editor'll be proud of you. I told you, Slats, our services are nebulous, and since we're private, we don't have to disclose anything more. But if your *Gazette* can ever afford our services, we'll tell them if we can perform whatever they request. Bye, Slats, enjoy your time in the Bay Area."

Stu started to head out but abruptly turned back to Slats. "Slats, why the long face? We got a camaraderie going here."

"Camaraderie?"

"Sure, Slats, one that's lasted thousands, if not millions, of years. Two humped-up males with only one thing on their minds. I ended up getting the shot at Traci, but we were both out for the same thing. We shared what guys have been fantasizing and wanting from the Stone Age, to the Roman gladiators, to any locker room today."

Slats sighed and showed a slight grin. "And that is…?"

"Tail, Slats, luscious tail."

"Something told me that'd be your answer."

Slats breathed heavily as he watched Frommer walk out. He quickly downed the remainder of his drink and waved to Brian; he wanted another. As he toyed with the ice in the empty glass, he could hear the thump, thump, thumping of his heart. Talk about the *Goodfellas*, that *was* a threat, wasn't it? And what is this about our services are required? Isn't it similar to the Sopranos saying they're going to do some work on someone or for someone?

Slats eagerly attacked his second vodka and tonic. His fear reminded him of how he felt the first time he experienced a horror movie as an eight-year-old. *How can this happen? What are the odds? Of course, as Frommer mentioned, I wasn't followed*—because I didn't follow him. *So that leaves the possibility he followed me.*

But my picture doesn't appear in my column, so how would he know what I look like? Plus, I walked over here right after the hotel guy told me about it. It took less than ten minutes. Even if he was in the lobby and asked the hotel guy where is he going, Frommer wouldn't have had the time to race past me and be that far advanced with Brian drinks-wise. No, it was some fucking coincidence, like out of Hitchcock. Now, what the hell do I say to Tom, to Spivey, to Rhea, to Holly? Who's going to believe… I got to tell Holly. We share everything—bingo. For the first time since Frommer left, Slats felt a sense of relief. *If I tell Holly this convoluted, unbelievable story, it will be proof that I was out on the town*—on my own.

He quickly downed the remainder of his drink and headed out. The invigorating San Francisco wind chilled his body but also helped end his gloomy mood. He almost caught himself whistling as he buttoned his jacket to fight the cold in the air. *Think I'll have one of those pizza slices in that place on Powell. Then I'll call Holly and tell her what happened.* Describing a "stag" night in Baghdad by the Bay couldn't help but put Holly at ease and make it all that much easier to make that play for Rhea. His body warmed as he pictured Rhea doing whatever in that room at the W. *Yeah, right, since the Stone Age, all we can think about is tail, luscious tail. You got that one right, Frommer, you bloodsucking a-hole.*

By the time Slats had downed the pizza slice and Diet Coke, it was near eleven, and he decided it was too late to call Holly. He'd already called her after checking into his dump, so he figured he'd call her at work in the morning after he'd broken the news to Tom about running into Frommer. He also considered calling Rhea but concluded the late hour also made that a no-no.

The next morning, Slats made a beeline for the nearest of the myriad Starbucks in the Union Square area and was halfway through a bear claw when he figured it was a good time to call Leary. It was nearly eight thirty, so he reached for his cell. Turned out Leary was hardly phased.

"Like most cities, Slats, San Francisco has certain sections that cater to particular demographics. For young, straight horny a-holes like you and Frommer, there's only so many sections. There's Cow Hollow, the Marina, SOMA, and of course, Union Square. Starting the weekend, a young stud will be checking out the other three areas known for upper-scale singles. During the week, like on a Tuesday night, prowlers like you and Frommer might retire to one of the Union Square hotels for a drink after a tough day's work. So forget Hitchcock. With Frommer in town, the odds of you being in the same place aren't that much of a long shot. Although the fact that he was seated right next to you, well, what can I say? Maybe there's a little bit of Stephen King creeping through that Dashiell Hammett SF fog."

"Wow," Slats had replied, "not only my boss, but my mentor. Is there no end to your talent?"

"Lemme clue you on a little secret, Slats. Back in the seventies, when I was young and carefree, me and the guys would fly up to Frisco on a Saturday night, the PSA fare was only nineteen dollars. We went through everything and everybody, trying to hook up with some of those chic sophisticates that populate that kind of area. We were up all night and grabbed the first PSA morning flight back to LA."

"Wow, again, Tom, am I supposed to report all this in *People* magazine?"

"Shut your hole, wise guy. That's when I met Lenore. She was up from Palo Alto, and she was doing the town, in the center of it all, Perrys."

"No shit, Tom, you met Lenore at the one and only Perrys?"

"Yeah, dude, met the mother of my three kids at the original singles bar. Lenore still has loads of friends in the Bay Area. When we're up there, we do the town. That's how I know what's happening now."

"Wow, Tom, can I say wow for the third time?"

"No, you can't, wiseass. This is California, and three strikes and you're out. I got some people waiting, Slats, back to business. How you going to follow up on this Frommer dude?"

"Haven't figured it out yet, Tom."

"Well, since you're in liaison with that Spivey babe, you better let her know right away so she can inform Spivey."

"Gee, boss, do I have to talk to her?"

"Get outta here, horndog, and don't forget what we're paying you for while you're up there, and don't forget Holly pining for her lover back home."

Slats heard the click. He clicked End on his cell and pushed Okay for Phone Book.

Right, he figured, *call Holly. But first, let's see. Rhea's cell. Got to call right off.*

Assuming she's out of her hotel room by now and certainly past her morning OJ. After all, the nemesis of her client's sniffing around, coincidence or not.

She told him she was in the W lobby having some coffee and a muffin. When he broke the news, she didn't seem that concerned. She said she'd inform Spivey. "But we know he's from the Bay Area, so it's not that unusual that you ran into him. I'll be sure to tell Mr.

Spivey about his 'threatening' behavior, but if anything, it looks like he rattles easily, which should only make our job that much easier."

Slats loved that. Did that mean, by implication, that Slats, this maiden's Sir Galahad, slew the bad guy? His reverie was shattered when she told him she'd be taking the Chanteuse to Calistoga for some tasting in the wine country and a full day's spa activities in that geographic area's soothing and healing waters.

As he got ready to dial Holly, Slats figured, *Not bad, not bad.* Rhea gets paid big bucks, and part of her job is to spend a full day in the wine country getting spa treatments with a celeb.

Slats went back to his room to get his laptop and repaired to another Starbucks to google around the Chanteuse, the Bay Area, and any interconnection between the two by any media types in either LA or SF. He figured he might not hit pay dirt till the Sunday paper when the Pink Section was sure to have a full-page spread and interview with the Chanteuse, as customary with any visiting celebs. On the other hand, even though she'd appeared in the Pink Section on past visits, she might refuse this time around, since this trip wasn't to promote anything but to get away. Well, whatever the Chanteuse's decision this time around, it was sure to be heavily influenced by her walking chaperone, Rhea Simpson. Slats couldn't help but smirk. What an assignment!

He spent nearly two hours googling and then checked out the refurbished lobby of the famed St. Francis Hotel before returning to his dump of a hotel. After dropping off his laptop, he figured on lunching at the venerable Lefty O'Douls, a San Fran institution without any of the panache of the kind of eatery that, that evil Frommer dude and that sexy wench would be doing lunch in.

He was there in five minutes and spent a few moments looking at all the old-time baseball photographs, especially Joe D. and Marilyn, who had a DOD ID listing her as Norma Jean DiMaggio, obviously while she was on tour in Korea. *Too precious, too precious,* Slats mused. *Wonder what that Norma Jean photo's worth, comparable to the Mantle rookie card...*

Just then, the local news channel droning in the background actually sounded that pathetic "This just in" message that comedians inevitably love to mock. The announcer continued: "A massive demonstration on Route 29 in the heart of St. Helena tied up traffic on 29 all the way back to Rutherford in the south and Calistoga in the north.

"Apparently, the demonstrators were protesting the appearance of Ann Sloan, also known as the Chanteuse. We now have Shirley Babitt, our reporter at the scene."

Slats sighed. He didn't know whether to be happy that he's up here for a juicy story or sorry for that sweet little Rhea who's in the middle of all this.

"Yes, this is Shirley Babitt standing in the center of St. Helena, the heart of California's bucolic Wine Country. A detachment of officers from the California Highway Patrol have finally brought order to the area. Some sixty protesters have been issued citations, and I think about twelve have been arrested. Some five minutes ago, I recorded an interview with Tom Crosby, noted Bay Area activist who led the protest.

"Tom, can you tell us what this is about?"

"With pleasure, Shirley. At one time, Ann Sloan was considered one of the many in the entertainment industry striving with fellow Progressives to shift the nation from the dark abyss of the Bush/Cheney/Ashcroft repressive era to the light of what America and any Progressive society should be."

"Well, Tom, with the Chanteuse's background, what could have changed that—"

"Didn't mean to interrupt, Shirley."

"Oh, that's all right, Tom. I thinking that our viewers are wondering how a Liberal icon like the Chanteuse could suddenly be in such disrepute among activists like yourself."

"That's a good question, Shirley, and I'm eager to answer. Starting with her coldblooded betrayal of Josh Parker to her appearance on the Stan Morgan show, where she revealed a shocking degree of pure, unadulterated racism. We cannot allow her visit to Northern California to stand without a response from caring Progressives eager to—"

"Well, Tom, we really don't have that much time in this report."

"There's also racist policies with domestics in her employ. Please reach our website at www.crosbyprogressives.org."

"There you have, it, Mark. Back to you."

"Thanks, Shirley. This is Mark Castilla returning you to your regularly scheduled programming."

Slats was going to order one of those filling meat sandwiches. Now, downing the first few sips of an Anchor Steam, he decided he was hungry enough for an entire meat plate. *Potential writer's block, go away and come back another day. I got enough ammo to at least get started on a column or two. That'll keep Leary at bay while I figure out how to move on that sweet little thing. She'll sure need some cheering up after this Calistoga disaster. That quiet little eye-talian place on Chestnut? Best calamari ever. Hopefully, they're still in business.*

DINNER WITH RHEA

Slats figured the commotion had died down sufficiently by noon of the next day. He decided to call. "How's she doing, Rhea?"

"Oh, fine, Slats. Though that scene in the wine country was frenetic. She was hyperventilating so badly we called an ambulance. They concluded she didn't require hospitalization, and they gave her some antihyper whatevers. They then drove us to the nearest pharmacy, where the druggist filled out some prescriptions."

"Really? The ambulance people write out prescriptions?"

"Who knows, Slats, someone on board must have had the necessary degree, but she got all her medicine, and her physical recovery was so fast that she insisted we have lunch in St. Helena. Of course, after all that, the Calistoga spas would have to wait for another day, if ever."

"That's a shame. Rhea, you could have had an idyllic day of sun and mud baths, and—"

"Well, all's well that ends well. She felt good enough to stay with her son last night. Tonight she's going back to her place on Nob Hill."

"So she's over the hump?"

"Well, she's no longer breathing hard, her blood pressure is back to her normal high level, but emotionally, it hit her hard."

"You mean the demonstration?"

"Well, she was already reeling from the death of her brother at the hands of you-know-who. Then there was the Stan Morgan radio disaster, and now this Crosby guy whom she'd never heard of. Add to that the ice she's been receiving from the Hollywood and media elites, and you've got one miserable woman. Slats, you, you're not going to write any of this, are you?"

"Come on, Rhea, cut me some slack. Like that ambulance story, I could have gotten that myself if I did the legwork. All the rest of it is common knowledge. But if you want, you can stop filling me in on Chanteuse trivia. What I find myself, I won't have to worry about implicating you as a source."

"Now, Slats, no need for this. Please cool your jets. I'm... I'm trying to be helpful."

"I realize you have a job, but my job is to protect her. Don't forget, the reason we've come this far is that we're both on her side. I'm assuming that's still the case with you. Besides, everything I've told you in this call has been as a friend, not as a career woman. You asked me how she was, so—"

"You're right, Rhea. That was the first thing I asked when I called. But that wasn't what I was calling about. It was more personal than business."

"Oh?"

"Well, Rhea, it's been nearly a week since I'm up here, and we still haven't gotten together. How about dinner tonight? I know this great Italian place on Chestnut, and—"

"Chestnut, where's that?"

Slats's heart soared like that proverbial eagle. She didn't say no. "Well, if that expression's still in use, it's a yuppie section of the city called the Marina."

"Oh, the Marina, I've heard of it. That sounds like fun."

"Great, what time would be good for you?"

"Oh, about 7, but I do have to keep the cell on. She feels free to call me anytime before 11."

"So meet you at the W? We can take a cab and—"

"No, Slats, I'll drive. The company's paying for a car. Might as well use it and learn the city. I'll swing by your place and call you when I'm there."

Slats was ashamed of the place he was staying at, but there was no sense arguing. It was a fifteen-minute walk to the W, and besides, if this is the first of many, she'd eventually see the dump anyhow. "Okay, casual, right?"

"Oh, by all means, I get tired of heels."

Slats tried some humor. "Say, I resemble, I mean, I resent that statement."

"What statement?"

"That you're tired of heels."

"Aha, I've got a comedian on my hands."

"Once in a while, Rhea, once in a while, I hit pay dirt."

"Well, speaking of pay dirt, don't be getting mushy on me, Slats. Let's keep it on a professional basis."

Slats, whose heart no longer soared like an eagle, was glad they were on the phone, so she couldn't hear his sigh or see the deflated look on his face. "Oh, sure, Rhea, professional all the way."

She was right on time, and in less than ten minutes, she made a left on Chestnut off Van Ness.

"Looks like the parking won't be easy tonight. Chestnut looks tight as a drum."

"Oh, I've got it covered, Slats. Have we reached Pierce yet?"

"Coming up next block. Why Pierce?"

She grinned. "The concierge said there's a four-story indoor metered city lot, in case we had trouble... there's Pierce. What do you think, a left?"

She turned left, and there was the parking structure.

"Hats off to the concierge. I've got plenty of quarters." Slats saw Rhea pull into one of the empty spaces on the second level. He hoped enough BS would make her forget to ask, "You've been to this great restaurant and don't know about this big parking garage on Pierce and Chestnut?" Bad enough she was probably thinking it. Well, he'd taken a cab that other time... Good excuse, but not good enough. What guy wants to feel a loss of control early on a first date?

Slats liked beer with Italian food, but when the waiter asked "House wine?" he looked at her and nodded yes. Everyone knows gals love wine with a meal. Slats feigned like he was turned off by the wine after the waiter offered a taste, which got a giggle out of Rhea before he looked at the waiter and said, "Just kidding, it's fine."

The waiter didn't seem impressed by this byplay, but that didn't matter; her reaction did matter. They touched glasses and talked about how that gesture was reminiscent of those old Hollywood movies where the man (i.e., Paul Henreid) lights and puffs on two cigarettes at a time before offering one to the woman (i.e., Bette Davis).

Too bad smoking's no longer chic, they concluded. That led the conversation to the tobacco suits, which led to Mellon, the king of asbestos and tobacco, and inevitably to the man of the hour, Frommer.

He grabbed her hand and smiled. "Can we forget about business at least until coffee?"

"I'm for that," she grinned as she looked at her hand, "but you did promise you wouldn't get mushy on me."

He slowly removed his hand from hers. "God golly, Ms. Molly, I wasn't getting mushy. Just had an urge to touch, that's all."

She smiled a smile that seemed to make him float. Or was it the wine? Probably both. "I… I guess I can't hide the fact that you wiped me out the second I saw you."

Rhea reflectively scratched her nose and sipped some wine. "That's lovely to hear, Slats, and I do think highly of you. Really, I do. But I'm up here with our firm's most important client when she's at her most vulnerable. I can't get into an affair right now."

The "right now" gave him an opening. "And when we get back?"

A flush overtook her countenance. "We'll see, we'll see. Gee, where is that food?" She chewed on a slice of bread after peppering it with olive oil. She pointed toward the kitchen. "Which one was our waiter again?"

Slats nodded and smiled slightly. "I get it. Trying to change the subject. Well, I don't blame you. I really never planned to put you on edge. This was, err, is supposed to be a fun evening. Perfect timing, here he comes now."

The waiter deposited the two calamari specials on the table and asked, "Is there anything else?"

"We're fine, thanks." Slats evened out the marinara sauce over the pasta and juggled some calamari and pasta around his fork. "Hope this is as good as it was last time."

Rhea took a bite of the calamari. "Uhhm, it is good. Now, Slats, can you tell me about your relationship with Holly?"

All he got was a limp kiss on the cheek as she dropped him off at Haddon Hall.

Parking was a bitch, and even that pause for a moment of tenderness caused all kinds of honking from the oncoming traffic. "Thanks a bunch, Slats. It was fun. Talk to you soon."

Thanks a bunch? Didn't that go out with Gidget? He pictured those silly SoCal beach movies, and then he realized he never even asked where she was from originally.

Pathetic, Slats, pathetic. Well, if and when it does come up, he could always state that expression like "Thanks a bunch," and her lack of an accent made him assume she grew up in Southern California. Still, pathetic. Spend three hours in a romantic hideaway, finish off a bottle of house wine, and never even ask where she's from. Five minutes of reminiscing about what they spoke about for three hours, and all that wine caught up to him. He fell asleep with the lights on. He woke up around 4:00 AM, no doubt due to the lights, and had trouble falling back asleep. *How could I have not asked her where she grew up?*

Finally, it was seven, and that perky Courie was grinning on the tube, and Slats was still moody over last night, so after the weather, he switched to Fox. Lathering himself with Foamy, he did a quick self-analysis. All this second-guessing over last night was BS.

You're fucking steamed because instead of an orgy on her bed at the W, all you got was a limp kiss on the cheek like this was a first date in high school. Naturally, he nicked himself. *Cut the crap, Slats, all this moaning like a lovesick teenager comes at the wrong time. You got a shot here at something big. Holly was right. Stop coasting.* Make something of yourself.

Holly, Holly. Rhea had blushed after uttering that dagger, no doubt seeing Slats's discomfort. He tried a flippant "Holly, who's Holly?" But neither side was fooled. Rhea obviously didn't want to cause any more embarrassment, and Slats, caught off guard, decided to drop the subject till another time. Studying his razor cut, he absent-mindedly put some aftershave over it while he decided on when next to call Holly and when to "explain" Holly to Rhea. No doubt she got it from Spivey, who, in turn, got it from Tom. *Thanks a bunch, Tom. Wow, who ever said life was easy?*

By the time he got his slacks on and was buttoning his shirt, he remembered—he'd mentioned Holly at that initial encounter with Rhea and Spivey. Well, that gets Tom off the hook, maybe. Nah, not maybe, guys might forget a tidbit about relationships at a serious business meeting, but not gals. To them, being aware of and following relationships is as important as following Bonds' home run chase is to guys.

He decided this was a good day to partake in Haddon's Continental Breakfast. Plain food and aimless conversation with other lodgers couldn't help but take his mind off a sudden ton load of dilemmas. No angle yet for this week's dispatch down to Tom and, naturally, of greater importance, a good chance of losing Holly while hearing that dreaded "We're just good friends" from Rhea. *A bird in hand, Slats, a bird in hand. What the hell are you doing, Slats? You'll end up with nothing.*

Right, bon appétit, fella.

SFDWP

Slats couldn't wait to break the news. He dialed Tom's cell.

"Yeah, Slats, what's so important to disturb my reverie on the Santa Monica? What? What the hell's DWP?"

"Why, Department of Water and Power, what else?"

"Oh, that sounds cosmic. So what the hell have you got, Slats?"

"Sounds like something out of a Russ Meyer x-rated flick. You got two beauties at SFDWP in a helluva hair-pulling catfight."

"Sounds great, Slats, but since we're not in the movie business… oh, you want to turn our proud little *Gazette* into a Left Coast version of Murdoch's *New York Post*? C'mon, Slats, what have you got?"

"Well, boss, some bloggers up here are coming up with some interesting conclusions."

"Bloggers? What about the papers?"

"Well, I don't think the Lefty papers up here want to touch this, but eventually, they'll have to. Just like the *Times* and the *Post* after trying to ignore the Swift Boat Vets."

"Why the hell don't they want to touch it? Got something to do with Kerry, Hillary, or the mayor?"

"Worse, boss, it's lawyers."

"'Cause two babes had a spat? I don't get it."

"I don't have all the details. Those bloggers love to write thousands of words, but apparently, Drysdale's leading the way."

"Drysdale, yeah, I've downloaded his stuff. The guy's to the right of Savage, Limbaugh, all the rest. Is he off on some tangent?"

"Maybe, boss, his theory is that they're both undercover lawyers out to make a harassment score."

"What? How'd he come up with that?"

"Well, it seems that before and after the hair pulling, they were throwing all sorts of legal terminology at each other. Not the kind of vocabulary usually associated with data-entry operators."

"That was their job?"

"Yeah, Tom, and Drysdale's come up with a hell of a conclusion." Slats could hear Tom's sigh.

"I'm listening, Slats, I'm listening."

"Well, Tom, it seems they were both hitting on this creepy mail boy, and—"

"Two sexpots hitting on a creepy mail boy?"

"The theory, Tom, is that he'd start flirting back, and then, bingo, sexual harassment suit."

"Slats, I think all that fog and whatever you're up to with Rhea had muddied that old bean of yours. Why the hell was it a tandem?"

"No, Tom, that's the point. They both were up to the same thing, but definitely not working in tandem."

"We're not touching this, Slats."

"Agreed, not with a ten-foot pole," Slats replied. "We'll let Drysdale become the next famous Drudge. He's a wonder."

"Must be, how'd he come up with his conclusions?"

"It seems both photos were sent out over the blogger's website. One thing led to another, and someone who went to law school recognized one of them. It wasn't hard to put two and two together after that."

"What's our interest, besides prurience?"

"Well, Tom, the one that was ID'd apparently works for Middleton and Burnitz."

"Those shysters out of Palo Alto?"

"The very same."

"Well, that's still of no use to us."

"Except for one thing—Drysdale and the other bloggers are feverishly working on a theory."

"What's that?"

"That the other legal babe works for Mellon."

"How'd they come up with that?"

"Well, the photo of the other sweetie was cyberspaced and came up empty. Some lawyers and law professors were consulted, and the only firm that successfully hides the identity of their nontrial lawyers is the one and only Mellon."

"Okay, so you came up with something. But don't forget, Slats, we're financing your San Fran jaunt to finish up the tale of the Chanteuse, not to get involved in some glamorous clash, ahh, no matter how much it aids our circulation."

"What was that, Tom?" Slats sensed Tom could pick up his grin despite being four hundred miles down the coast.

"You win, joker, see what you can dig up. I can just see the grin on your face. But I'll wipe it off, Mr. Conners. You're just going to have that much less time with that Simpson cutie-pie, 'cause I expect you to spend full time on the Chanteuse. Anything extra on those legal gals comes out of your free time. Are we clear?"

"Clear, boss man." Slats was sure his sigh could be heard all the way down to Malibu.

"Well, we'll see just how clear it is," Tom sounded triumphant, "when I see just what you send me every Friday. Bye, Slats."

"Wait," Slats cut in, "don't go yet."

"What is it, Slats? Traffic's getting heavy."

"Well, Tom, getting back to Russ Meyer, can't wait to see what those babes look like. So far, the *Chron* and the other papers have ignored the whole deal, so obviously, no pictures, and Drysdale isn't volunteering the one photo he's come up, which he's probably looking to sell it to *People* or some similar magazine. On the·other hand, they didn't commit a crime, so ordinarily, they probably both would have skipped town already."

"You think so?"

"Nah, Tom, probably not. As badly as the politically sympathetic local DA wouldn't want to mess with the likes of Mellon, region 9 of the Bush Justice Department would do anything to nail the administration's public legal enemy number 1. They'll probably come up with some Federal statute to hold them. Meanwhile, bet those cool dudes at the *Chronicle*, Mattier & Ross will come up with something in tomorrow's paper. They must be arguing with the Marxian editor right now. Mattier & Ross will win the argument. Even Commie rags know they need circulation to stay in business."

"Hey, Slats, don't be so hard on that comsymp rag. They got a good sports section. Even stole Scott Ostler from our area. Plus, they got both a good TV and movie guy… Whoops, traffic's picking up, I better hang up. Keep in touch, Slats."

***

Derek Burnitz's chauffer picked up William Mellon at SFO and headed south on 101 toward the executive airport facilities near Half Moon Bay. Mellon always liked a trip to the coast, especially Northern California. It invariably seemed that the climate was an improvement over the East Coast, no matter what time of the year. However, this trip was shaping up to be a ball-breaker. Burnitz knew George was aware of the DWP ploy. Hell, he trained the skank, but Burnitz wanted it mano a mano—no one else involved.

"Don't worry, Bill, you won't lack for company if I start to bore you." Burnitz had cackled. "Middleton and Burnitz, while still not at the level of your firm, can come up with many 'companions,' whether directly under our employ or, more probably, from an 'escort agency' in hock to us for keeping them on the right side of the law."

"Ah, we'll surely dine once, Derek," Mellon had replied, "but any other free time, I'll be looking up old contacts in the Bay Area." *Right, as if I'd be careless enough to spend time with a bimbo supplied by Burnitz. Good try, Derek, good try.*

Mellon was driven all the way to the hangar, where Burnitz, grinning from ear to ear, waved a hello. Mellon didn't appreciate the grin for this serious meet, let alone that stupid white suit and cowboy hat, where this idiot was trying to emulate either JR from Dallas or Tom Wolfe.

Burnitz, all six foot four of him, rushed to shake Mellon's hand in a hardy Texas style. "Hi, Derek, thinking of pulling up stakes and moving to Texas? That Bush blankety-blank really ruined it for us there."

Burnitz looked puzzled. "Moving to Texas?" Mellon looked him over up and down.

"Oh, the outfit," he bellowed as he pointed toward the plane, "you can't get on and off a beauty like this and wear a pedestrian suit." Burnitz reached up and touched the right wing. "It's a beaut, isn't it, Bill? A Gulfstream El500, the latest 'personal aviation for an exec on the go' right here." He jabbed at the wing for emphasis. "I memorized their brochure." He grinned. "All aboard."

Mellon noticed a grounds-crew type had just attached a portable staircase and dutifully stood by to grab Mellon's arm as he started to climb on board. Mellon quickly settled into one of the plush tan leather seats in the spacious plane. He watched Burnitz talk to the pilot. *Bad enough I've got to go through a session with this jerk settling the DWP fiasco. Now, in addition, I've got to put up with the old high school taunt: my dick, ah, my Gulfstream is bigger, newer, and better than your Learjet?*

The taking a ride on this impressive plane for "privacy" was a crock. Two billionaires would never have a problem finding privacy. Mellon figured it's Burnitz's way of reminding number 1 that he was close behind. A good way to prove that would be not minding the cost of all those gallons of aviation fuel on a pointless flight.

Mellon heard the hum of the engine and watched Burnitz approach.

"Martini? No butler, chef, or cabin attendant on this flight, but the martinis were premixed, and we've got some delightful cold sushi from the best caterer on the peninsula." He pointed to the martini vessel on the spacious bar, next to a large serving tray containing the sushi. "And there's the utensils, serving spoon, and as you can see, plenty of napkins and ice."

Mellon responded with a blank expression.

"Oh, have no fear, Bill, you'll be hungry once you start on a martini. Here, let me bring you the first one."

Mellon took a sip and decided to approach the sushi bar. He wasn't that hungry, but he already had visions of the ebullient Burnitz stuffing the sushi down his esophagus like a mom stuffing castor oil down the throat of a wary child.

Burnitz pointed to one of the windows on the right side of the plane. "Isn't that precious, Bill? Just look at that coastline. I think we just passed Pebble Beach, and isn't that Monterey Peninsula a beaut? Observe how that jutting coastline meets that calm Pacific. Except for maybe the Rockies, best damn view in the Continental US."

Mellon nodded politely as he munched on a California roll. Was that Rockies comment a chance to bring up that time-share in Telluride so he could drop every name in the Hollywood book from starlets to famous producers? To head off the possibility of a repeat of that tiresome event, Mellon decided that the prelims were over. He selected several edamames and a salmon roll and selected one of the eight seats. After a perfunctory peek out the window, he looked at Burnitz, who seemed to be feeling no pain as he jiggered his glass, mesmerized by what little martini remained. "All right, Derek, are you pleading no contest so we can wrap this up before we land?"

Burnitz greeted Mellon's smile with a huge roar of a laugh. "Can I, in my cowboy outfit, head you off at the pass? Can ah, can ah?" he said, doing a dead-on imitation of Carvey's "Can I finish, Larry?" rendition of Ross Perot.

"Go ahead." Mellon shrugged. "You got a lot of explaining to do."

"Oh, so I'm the defendant. Is that the way this is going to play out?" A hint of a scowl showed in Burnitz's visage, rapidly erasing image of the jocular cowboy in the white outfit. "First of all, what's the three most important words in real estate?"

"Come on, Derek, quit the clowning and get to the point. This isn't *Boston Legal.*"

"Location, location, loc—"

"All right, get to the damn point, will you?"

"Don't interrupt, Bill. I was about to make a valid point. We're out of Palo Alto, for Christ's sake. This is our territory. Haven't they heard of harassment in New York or Jersey?"

"Derek, you know damn well that *we* have no geographical limits. We are number one. We get fat, everyone else gets well, including Middleton & Burnitz. My god, Derek, you've gotten so healthy following our tobacco and asbestos trail that those three additional zeros went on to your net worth before the IRS could separate you from the masses. And what about all those mass drug actions? We've both gotten so fat that we don't even bother with that Vioxx bonanza."

Burnitz smiled sheepishly. "You sure about that?"

Mellon scowled. "You agreed we'd stay out and let the new mean and lean outfits get their own score."

"Easy, Bill, our firm's not involved directly, but if some of the secondary firms want to thank us by paying a percentage of the settlement, hey, one-hand washes, and all that malarkey."

"What you're suggesting smells to high heaven, Derek," Mellon hissed. "Remember one thing. Doesn't matter how much Limbaugh, Bush, and all those yahoos come after us. No matter how ridiculous those asbestos, tobacco, drug settlements appear, the public knows that *they* benefit. If not this time, maybe next time.

"Meanwhile, enjoy the good luck of all those who've won the lottery. Maybe next time, it'll be me or some member of my family. But what you're doing, that doesn't help the public, and that Limbaugh can—"

"Enough about Limbaugh, and don't you lecture me, Bill." By now, Burnitz's affable front had dissipated, and that mean-spirited, hard-core courtroom demeanor was front and center.

"We've already finished our second pass back over Half Moon, Mr. Burnitz. Want me to descend or another pass down the Coast?"

Burnitz picked up the intercom. "One more pass, Alex, I think another half hour's about right."

Burnitz put the intercom back in place and poured himself another martini. He sat back down without having offered to replenish Mellon's glass.

The gloves are definitely off, Mellon smirked to himself. This next half hour should really be something.

"Where was I? Oh yes, we had $700 mill in billings last fiscal year, give or take. We're near three bill in total worth. Just 'cause you're number one, or were number one, you're not dealing with schoolboys, Bill." Burnitz finished with the kind of glare you'd never see in a courtroom, too likely to turn off a jury.

Mellon caught and brushed off the "we're number one" jibe. *You are and will always be second rate, Burnitz. All those fancy millions and billions you just boasted about consisted of your jackal firm splitting the kill after we blazed the way.* "Have it your way, Derek. Hard enough to control an obstinate teen, let alone a—what was it—3-billion-dollar law firm?"

Burnitz offered a weak smile. "You saying I'm obstinate?"

"Enough, Derek," Mellon replied. "We've got less than a half hour. Let's clear up this harassment mess."

"Right, and like I made clear, the Bay Area's *our territory.*"

"Please, Derek, where'd you come up with this territory crap? Legal representation doesn't have boundaries. What is this, the American League?"

"You're the one that's twisting things around, Bill. We're not talking about representing a client. We're talking about where we implement a scam. When it comes to that, San Fran's ours, Manhattan's yours."

Mellon roared a deep laugh. "You've got a point, Derek. Sort of Capone's got the South Side and Moran the North Side, is that it?"

"Yeah, right." Burnitz's wide grin had returned.

"In the future, let's get some paralegals to keep in touch in a general way about another move like this DWP thing. Make sure this hassle isn't repeated."

"Right, sort of like a Kennedy/Kruschev hotline. Meanwhile, how do we extricate ourselves from this mess?"

"Not easy, Derek. The Feds apparently want a pound of flesh. They've got a trumped-up charge holding our gals within fifty miles of DWP till they figure how to make life miserable for us."

"The Feds can't be gotten to."

"Right, Derek, speaking of Capone, damn Justice Department, just like the Untouchables. But ahh, we've got enough friends in Congress. We'll get them to apply heat, especially the House. How many did we elect with trial lawyers' muscle and funding? Meanwhile, they can only harass us. They've got nothing."

"Unless one of our gals pleads or goes to the tabloids."

"Well then, Derek, it's our job, isn't it, to remind those ladies the legal frat sticks together and has a long memory. We both picked the best of the best for this little scam, right? They'll both know which side their bread is buttered on."

"Perfect timing, Bill. Alex is starting to descend. Look out the left side. There's Half Moon Bay, and if you look to the right, you can see the San Mateo Bridge connecting to the East Bay. Beautiful, isn't it? Next time, bring your camera."

"It is beautiful, Derek, but I'm hoping there won't be a next time, if you catch my drift."

"Loud and clear, Captain."

They heard Alex on the intercom. "Mr. Burnitz and guest, please make sure your seat belts are fastened. We land in three minutes."

THE OB-GYN

Scott Spillman entered the well-appointed lobby of the Mellon Building and approached the Guard Station. He passed those either signing in or being checked out through the detection devices. He flashed his special ID badge at Dale Ogden, who smiled. "Have a nice weekend, Mr. Spillman?"

"Yup, how about you, Dale?"

"Couldn't be better, Mr. Spillman. Have a nice day."

Spillman headed toward the last bank of elevators. It was the Express to the eightieth-floor complexes. He pressed 82 for executive suites. He was patted down as soon as he exited the elevator. Another guard told him to hold his arms up as he was frisked by another uniformed guard at the entrance to Mellon's individual suite. *Things must be getting real hairy*, Spillman thought. He couldn't remember the last time he'd been up here, but the precautions sure have escalated.

Mona Kline smiled as he entered. "How are you, Mr. Spillman?"

'Fine, Ms. Kline, I was—"

"Mr. Mellon was expecting you at nine." She looked at her watch and blushed. "Obviously, he's running late. He's still in the conference room on the eighty-first floor. Have you had breakfast? I'm sure the chef and staff at the exec dining room on the eightieth floor is still—"

"I'm fine, Ms. Kline." Spillman gently patted his stomach. "Couldn't eat another thing."

Spillman picked out one of those ostentatious lounges in the anteroom and was perusing an article in *Forbes* when he noticed it was twenty past nine. He turned toward the door and saw Mellon, looking distracted, open the glass door holding a pile of papers. Mellon noticed him and headed toward him. "Scott, how are you? Sorry to keep you waiting. It's been a bitch of a Monday."

Spillman tried to answer and rise simultaneously, but the chaise was so plush and soft…

Mellon held out his hand. "We try and impress visitors with the plushest this and that, but talk about utilitarian, will you—$6, 000 for a lounge chair and you sink so deep you can't even get up without assistance." He opened the door to his office. "C'mon in, Scott."

Scott selected another comfortable leather chair facing Mellon's desk. But thankfully, this one had a harder bottom, so Spillman was confident he wouldn't need help from the Old Man when it was time to rise again. He watched Mellon absentmindedly shuffle the papers he'd brought up from the meeting.

"Anything special at the meeting, Mr. Mellon?"

"Now, Scott, you know better than to…" He caught Spillman grinning.

Mellon laughed. "It'd really be something if one of my main gumshoes is naive enough to think that I'd reveal anything that—"

"Just trying to make small talk, Mr. Mellon. Still, I concede when things are getting portentous. Idle chatter sometimes doesn't fit."

Mellon looked at Spillman, sighed, and pushed a key on the intercom. "Mona, short of an emergency, hold everything for the next half hour." He leaned back on his high-topped chair, folded his arms, and smirked. "Okay, Scott, what have you got?"

Spillman spent close to ten minutes outlining all the recent problems with regard to malpractice and the ob-gyns. The main focus seemed to be Pennsylvania.

"All right, Scott, so how big is the organization?"

"It covers four counties in the middle of the state, Mr. Mellon."

"Including Pittsburgh and Philadelphia?"

"No, sir, that seems to be the point. Historically, they didn't trust that the city slickers would take into account any disparate views of the country bumpkins."

"Well, can't they be had?"

"Doesn't look like it. Dr. Craig Beltran insists there'll be no compromise. Any ob-gyn who doesn't follow the exodus out of the state would be considered an outcast, a traitor."

"I think I'm getting a little confused here. I thought Beltran had committed suicide."

"No, sir, it was physicians Gordon and Foulke who committed suicide. In Beltran's case, it was his wife who took her own life."

William Mellon gasped. "That's why he's so militant?"

"When you've lost everything and are some $40 million in debt... Well, obviously, he's lost his house, so he sent the youngsters back to Arizona and he's staying with a colleague in Scranton."

"So we can't get to him?"

"Not to be flippant, sir, but we'd have to come up with 40 mill plus, and even then, we'd never overcome his hatred. Plus—"

"There's a plus? *Pardonnez mois*, but hasn't this person suffered enough?"

"Well, Mr. Mellon, I realize that you've got national and inter-national concerns that occupy your time, but if you recall, we have the *Rolling Thunder* litigation under which anyone who has felt the 'heartbreak' of knowing someone whose childbirth has had 'com-plications' has the right and obligation to file additional suits. As a result, Beltran is about $360 million in hock, and there's a potential for a billion—"

"Well, he can't flee the State's jurisdiction, can he?"

"Oh, I don't think he intends to flee. He's vowed to stay and appeal to the 'last breath' or whatever dramatic phraseology he used."

"Well, he can't possibly succeed, can he? Not only is the law on our side, but don't we have practically every appellate judge in Pennsylvania in the bag?" Mellon noticed Spillman wince. "Well, lighten up, Scott, when I say 'in the bag,' I don't just mean pay-off-wise, I mean politically in the bag."

Scott blushed and displayed a wan smile. "Well, naturally, most of the judiciary in Pennsylvania and nationwide sees things our way. Still, not every judge in the State will concur with our outlook. Plus, I hear rumblings he's considering an eventual appeal to the Supreme Court."

"What? Outrageous! We can't fix *them*. Plus, they're tipping in the wrong direction even as we speak. Oh, why, why did we ever allow that damn Bush to get in?" He watched Spillman shrug. "Well, thanks for your input, Scott. I'll take it from here."

Mellon watched Scott leave the room. He appeared beat, not from fatigue or anything related, but he appeared down psychologically. Spillman was a top lawyer and the firm's top "unorthodox" operative. *Time to replace a top operative who's showing a conscience— or is it fatigue or nerves? Nah, he's still a good lawyer, and all that info on the Beltran threat's invaluable. He'll stay for now. Still, I'm not sure I want to continue this with Spillman. He's good at inquiry and analysis, but how good is he at solving problems? Maybe Frommer and all the lowlifes he employs? It's reached the point where certain steps have to be taken, and obviously, when it comes to violence, it's to be confined to a need-to-know basis. The real blast in all this, how did I let it get this far?*

We own quite a few counties, several states, and of course, the media is sympathetic, except for that damn Wall Street Journal and that reprehensible Fox News channel. I was focused on stopping doctors from leaving litigious jurisdictions. Now, it looks like Beltran is going to have to be stopped, period.

Mellon rang for his chauffeur. He felt the beating of his heart. *Maybe we're going too fast, juggling too many areas? Maybe consolidate all the tobacco and asbestos windfall? Maybe relax, buy a ball team like Angelos, the other asbestos guy? No, got to keep going. I'm sixty-six. Who knows how much time is left? Still, anxiety's only natural.*

When it comes to killing someone, there's always the possibility… something goes wrong. That damn Beltran.

Arthur was there in no time, almost too quickly. "Where to, Mr. Mellon?"

"The club, Arthur, but drive slowly, I've got thinking…"

Arthur reached the first Stop sign and turned on the sound system. "Say when, Mr. Mellon."

"Go back to that classical station, Arthur, I think it was two back. I need some classical music. Helps me solve things."

"I got it, Mr. Mellon. That's 103.7 on the FM, good choice."

It sounded like Debussy or Saint-Saëns. Mellon leaned back on the on the soft, plush brown leather seatback of the Lincoln. He closed his eyes and took in the music. One of the keys, of course, was keeping the ob-gyns in line by keeping their insurance carriers solvent. Naturally, this meant "convincing" the state regulators to allow premium increases to cover the actuarially predicted payouts while at the same time allowing the supportive political hacks to yell murder over the greedy, gouging insurance carriers. As for the doctors, they naturally raise their fees to be able to cover the resultant "obscene" malpractice premiums, and the only ones hurt are wealthy expectant mothers. The minorities' costs are probably covered by third parties, and at any rate, who's going to sue their doctors? Unfortunately, that Timlin SOB went overboard in going after Beltran. Now this thing is becoming too impolitic. Even friendly politicians have to take notice when ob-gyns start leaving the State en masse.

An additional goal, probably through a referendum, California style, was to have a reinsurance-type fund sitting in Harrisburg because no malpractice coverage can cover the jury's beneficent awards. This way, he reasoned, medical types don't have as much worry that we'll go beyond their insurance and eat into their savings and homes. Mellon recalled that Davidoff had recommended something along those lines several months ago, but he was focused on that sexual harassment scam. *Maybe*, Mellon figured, *if we were faster, we could have headed off this Beltran deal... well, if we can get it passed in time for this November.* It'll take about 40 mill for the ads and another 10 to keep the legislature from making too much noise.

As for that damn Beltran, I highly respect Scott, but I still think we ought to work on Beltran before finishing him off. For that, I'll use the "services" of Frommer, if that avenue doesn't work and we have to terminate... Well, Nunzi, that Mafia reject who handled Josh Parker, will have to do the job.

ALL THOSE THREATS

William Mellon walked Nancy Chavez to the limo. He was preoccupied and barely paying attention to Nancy's excited babbling. She was flying first-class to Paris at the request of Justine Mellon, who just couldn't abide by those "lazy" French maids.

Justine, a socialite from Day One, ran through maids faster than, well, J-Lo through fiancés. For some reason, Nancy, who'd been with the Mellons for nearly a decade, was able to withstand Justine's demanding style with her ever-present smile. When they reached the limo, Mellon handed her 5,000 Francs in case Justine forgot to have a chauffeur waiting for her at Orly.

She excitedly shook his hand as she entered the limo. "Zanks you so very much, Meester Mellon, for evereething."

He blushed. "You've got your passport, English-French dictionary?"

"Made up a leest and checked it many times, Meester Mellon. If I wasn't eeficient, Mrs. Mellon would have gotten reed of me just like…" She put her palm over her mouth and giggled.

Mellon nodded and cracked a slight smile. "Right, there's a reason why you've lasted. Give my love to Justine and have a great time." He watched the limo merge with the East Fifty-Third Street traffic as it quickly reached the red light on Madison. He turned toward the town house steps. Nancy must have really appreciated the "give my love" statement. It was no secret there'd been no close contact between him and Justine for easily a decade. Some thirty years earlier, the prim Justine Abernathy, then twenty-five, had jumped at the chance to latch on to the already-wealthy and highly esteemed trial lawyer so she could continue at the spending lifestyle to which she was accustomed, especially after her father, Duke Abernathy III, had blown most of what was left of the family shipping fortune in a series of unsuccessful bond and business deals.

Mellon, while not too turned on by the gaunt, somewhat attractive, always dieting doyenne, similarly felt that marrying into the Abernathy clan could only help in his unceasing quest for financial and social advancement. It couldn't have turned out better. After three years, what little sex had existed virtually ceased, as Justine "discovered" Europe and saw how popular she became as the cultured but money-lacking Europeans discovered the "culture" of her Yankee gelt. In no time, she became the patron saint of many "struggling" artists in Paris's Left Bank while hosting a slew of parties on the Right Bank out of her fashionable manse in the Ninth Arrondissement. She returned every September for the start of New York's social scene and inevitably was back in Paris after the New Year. All this meant that for nine months every year, Mellon didn't have to be all that secretive as he pursued all the pleasure that his wealth and position could obtain.

Not that Nancy wasn't discreet, but the only other "sleepover" help was Harold, the butler/chauffeur. And he was like a brother. He might turn on his boss under CIA questioning, but otherwise, he was as loyal and tight-lipped as any employer could hope for. So whatever excesses his sixty-six-year-old body could bear, his Fifth Avenue mansion would accommodate him in the coming weeks. Mellon walked into his study and reviewed his messages. E-mails and phone calls, mostly from Frommer, but also from Frontiere and some of the cyberspace sleuths, all focusing on one topic: *threats.*

Hate mail, threats, whatever, had always been the bane of litigants. But someone like Mellon, who'd had so much success in class action suits, created too many enemies to keep track. Still, the past month or so had seemed special, or so it appeared to Frommer, Frontiere, and the others who were the first to read these invectives.

Mellon kept one e-mail account the old-fashioned way. It was the office account, and one of Mellon's young aides sent a CC of every threatening message to Frommer and Frontiere. He had two other accounts, strictly for personal messages, but they were routinely compromised and had to be changed more than Mellon liked. Although he had secretaries at the office "screen" his calls, the situation at home was more than a pain. All calls were picked up by a monitoring service before coming through, and all this was too much for Justine, who finally acceded to using a cell for most of her incoming and outgoing. Such was the baggage associated with the daily life of a billionaire, several times over. Even Justine came to realize that much.

But she was living the gaudy life in Paris and couldn't care less what billionaire/husband/litigants had to go through to maintain her lifestyle. Mellon stopped thinking about Justine. He checked his mail. The forwarded message from Frommer seemed especially alarming. He looked at his watch. Nearly ten—that meant it wasn't quite 7:00 AM in the Bay Area. He knew Frommer was in the midst of a hot and heavy playboy existence. But for what he was being paid, he couldn't complain about being awakened while shacking up. It took only two rings, and Frommer was on.

"Hope I didn't wake you, but your message seemed especially frenetic."

"No problem, Mr. Mellon, I was up at six and just about ready to call you."

"Okay, what's going on that's so special?"

"Well, we're pretty sure there's been one source, although Frontiere says the cyberspace sleuths have detected decoys probably to throw us off. You know, just like misleading flares in a wartime battlefield."

"And?" Mellon's tone elicited some irritation.

"And they're way too specific for our taste. Twelve e-mails and seven phone calls referred to next week's visit to Coit State where you're to receive that honorary degree."

"Coit State? But that hasn't been in the papers yet, how could they—"

"That's the point, Mr. Mellon, they want to show their reach. Whoever they got to at Coit is beside the point. They're just playing mind games. They want you to suffer—mentally, not physically."

"So the threats weren't physical after all?"

"Brace yourself, Mr. Mellon, it's like one of those sickos that would make Hannibal the Cannibal seem normal. Oh, the physical threats are all over the place all right. But for now, I think they just want mental harassment. Otherwise, why warn you or us? You'd have been a sitting duck at Coit without our being alerted."

"So you think I should beg off the Coit event?"

"Well, pardon my French, Mr. Mellon, it's not my ass directly on the line, but I say show up. You don't want them to think they've got you on the run. Word could spread to like-minded yahoos. No, keep the date. Frontiere'll send four of his best operatives. They'll be visible, and they look mean. Plus, we'll have the Cassady Agency checking every arrival within fifty miles."

"That sounds very efficient, but will the hotels, car rentals, airlines cooperate?"

Mellon heard Frommer chuckle. "Maybe not, Mr. Mellon, but what we have to fill in, well, we have ways. Don't forget, your slush fund for this type of work still has $67 million, we'll do what we have to."

"Sounds good. So what's next?"

"We're all in this 150 percent, Mr. Mellon. We got the numbers, and we got the talent. By the way, you know the Frommers have an office on Madison and Fifty-Seventh. I share everything with my brother Phil. If you need anyone in the same time zone, he'll be there for you, within five minutes. And if the Coit thing or anything else heats up, I'll be out there in no time. You can count on that, Mr. Mellon."

"I have counted on it, all these years. And so far, Frommer & Sons has never disappointed me. How's it going out there with the Chanteuse?"

"We're setting up the next phase, slow but sure. Want us to speed things up?"

SLATS AND THE CHANTEUSE

"No need, Frommer, no need. The political people aren't even sure whether we can get any more mileage out of mangling her."

"I read you, Mr. Mellon. An hour a day from here on in with Frontiere, the cyberspacers, and Brother Phil, until this threat thing subsides."

Mellon chuckled. "Doesn't leave much time for your other clients, let alone all those California 10s."

"They don't all look like Bo Derek, Mr. Mellon, although sometimes—"

"Easy, Frommer, easy, you'll have me on the next flight out there. Keep in touch."

He clicked the cell phone shut as he heard Frommer utter goodbye with a laugh. Mellon walked the phone to the battery stand when he heard a thud. His heart pulsated so severely he had to sit down. Then he realized the noise came from the servant's entrance as Harold was showing the new cook the kitchen. It wasn't right for the top barrister in the land to be so jumpy. What would a juror or, worse, a reporter think? The so-called threats had taken their toll. Well, there was the normal security and, of course, Frontiere's operatives. But this called for a sleep-in of another kind. He punched P on his cell and reached Palmeiro Protective Services. Someone answered on the first ring.

"Palmeiro Protective Services, may I help you?"

"Yes, I'd like to talk to Carlos Palmeiro."

"I'm sorry, but he's not available. Can someone else help you?"

Mellon was irritated by her perfunctory tone. "This is Mr. Mellon," he barked. "Page him."

"Yes, Mr. Mellon." Her voice now reflected Mellon's authority. "Do you want to hold on or—"

"I'm not holding on. Just tell him I'll be waiting for his call."

His phone rang in less than two minutes. It was Palmeiro. "Mr. Mellon, what can I do for you? It's been a while since—"

"I need someone over 24-7 for the immediate future. I want your best, most experienced operative."

"I'm sorry, Mr. Mellon. My two best are in Capri and won't be back for about a month."

"Capri? What the hell are they doing there?"

"A long and, as you understand, confidential story, Mr. Mellon. But if you want the best Palmeiro has to offer, you're looking at, I mean, talking to him."

"Meaning?"

"Meaning, I just don't run Palmeiro, I'm still out there when required, especially for special clients."

"Fine, Carlos." Mellon's tone lost its edge. "How much time do you need before—"

"I can be there in two hours."

"And be ready for an indefinite 24-7?"

"That's why you're paying for the best, Mr. Mellon, it's all part of the package. Our lives are completely subservient to our client's wishes and needs. As you know from the past, Mr. Mellon, there'll be two of us, plus two others to spell us when the 24-7 gets too confining. But you'll get to meet us all at the outset. We wouldn't ever want you to be uncomfortable by seeing a strange face."

"Fine, usual fee?" Mellon heard Palmeiro agree.

"Okay, when you get here, I'll fill you in. By the way, I'm having dinner guests tonight. They should be gone by 11. So be here by 11:30, but call first, I don't want you to show while they're still here and have to explain who you are."

"I understand, Mr. Mellon. ETA 11:30 and I'll call first."

Mellon put the phone down. He could hear his heart thumping amid the hum of the Fifth Avenue and crosstown traffic. It was a strange and uncomfortable feeling. It had never been like this. There'd always been threats, finger-pointing, but as long as it wasn't organized crime, what was there to worry? They were all rich tobacco, asbestos, drug company execs—they're going to risk it all by hiring a hit man? Not likely. Plus, Mellon was always the young one—one conquest after another as his fame and fortune grew. The ride up was exhilarating; any danger was part of the thrill, the excitement.

Now, being on top, for a while, and in his sixties, Mellon could visualize the end, but even that wasn't as bad as that clammy feeling of fear that enveloped him. He tried to fight it, but his heart pounded even more. He decided to look in the mirror. Good show, it doesn't show. Well, that's half the battle. He rang for Harold, who was there in just about a minute. "How's the new cook?"

Harold shrugged. "She's eager, good references, but it'll be some time before we know. Anything else, Mr. Mellon?"

"Yes, Harold, a toasted almond, double on the J&B."

Harold's eyes widened. "Before dinner?"

Mellon looked at Harold as if he was about to begin a cross on a key witness. He didn't want to let on that he needed the jolt of the Drambuie and scotch. He held out his hands. "Yeah, Harold, getting tired of martinis."

Mellon sat in the study watching *Elmer Gantry* on the big plasma TV on the wall.

He toyed with the ice as he felt the warmth of the scotch filter through his body. In just a few minutes, he felt drowsy. He put the movie on mute to catch a little shut-eye. He fell asleep.

"Hey, wake up. What you doing here, boy? Can I help you?"

"What, what do you mean?"

"I mean, boy, you're in the lobby of the South Coast Country Club. For members only. This ain't Rockaway Beach. Now let's see your membership card, or you got five minutes to—"

"Hey, I belong here, I—"

"You didn't show me your card. Now you got two minutes to amscray, or you'll go out feet first and on your ass."

"I work here."

The man grinned at the youngster. "Really? Doing what?"

"I'm a parking jockey, on lunch, decided to check out the lobby, and I guess I fell asleep."

The man reached inside the side pocket of his green blazer and pulled out a pager. "Richardson? Yeah, it's Bellknap. Got a kid here, says he parks cars for us. He was asleep in the lobby when I found him. Huh, no, I'll check. What's your name, kid?"

"Billy O'Shea."

Bellknap shouted "Billy O'Shea" at the pager.

"What? You hired him? Get over here, Richardson, pronto."

Bellknap shut the pager, looked at Billy O'Shea, who rose from his seat and started to walk out.

"Where the hell you going, kid?"

"Back to work, I—"

"No, you don't, you just wait here." He looked at O'Shea, who appeared uncomfortable just standing there. Bellknap grinned as he saw Richardson rushing toward them.

"Yes, Mr. Bellknap?"

"It's this kid, here, Richardson. He's through. You pay him off and take care of the paperwork, all that shit."

Richardson, a chubby man in his forties, tugged at his jowly cheeks. "Why, Mr. Bellknap, what's he done?"

Bellknap glared. "Are you questioning me? Some more lip and you'll join him."

Richardson, now trembling, blurted, "I… I didn't mean anything, Mr. Bellknap. It's just that I hired him and he seems—"

"He seems what? I'll tell you what he seems. He's got the wrong body language, the wrong spoken language, and the wrong name. He's like an Irish thug, straight out of *Hell's Kitchen*. Not what our clientele is paying $50 a month and an initiation of $750 to rub shoulders with. He was on the center lounge, for Christ's sake. What if Mrs. Horton or some other socialite sat next to this? Is this what 1950s Long Island's newest and most exciting country club has come to?"

O'Shea, whose face looked like it would explode, started toward Bellknap. "Hey, who the fuck you think you're talking to? I got rights."

Bellknap grinned and met O'Shea halfway. "Listen, you low-life hoodlum, every twenty seconds, you reinforce my original estimation of you. Touch me once, Paddy, touch me once, and I'll kick your ass in self-defense and then make sure you spend the next twenty years in the hoosegow."

O'Shea backed off a mite and looked at Richardson.

Richardson shrugged slightly. He put his arm around O'Shea's shoulder. "Come on, Billy, let's go to my office before things get out of hand."

Bellknap watched them walk off. "Give him one week's pay. I don't want no labor lawyer hassling us about—"

"Speaking of lawyers…" O'Shea, suddenly grinning, had turned to face Bellknap. "I'm prelaw at Hofstra. My adviser had just convinced me, last week, that it was impractical, with my background, having to work, and all."

"Beat it kid, I'm losing my patience."

"Yeah." O'Shea's grin had widened. "But count on this, Bellknap, you'll see me again—five years, eight years, how long it takes. You'll be my first case when I hang up my shingle."

"Get the fuck out before I really lose my temper." Bellknap watched O'Shea turn around again and walk out with Richardson.

O'Shea sat in the small and cluttered office and watched Richardson pour through some forms. "I… I'm sorry, Mr. Richardson. I hope I didn't get you in trouble with that Bellknap SOB."

Richardson smiled warily. "Earning a living's never easy, Billy. Well, I don't spend fifty hours a week down in some coal mine, on the waterfront, or loading crates off trucks. I work in a beautiful country club, no heavy lifting, so to speak. So if a Bellknap comes with the package, I think of my family, the mortgage, and I don't hate myself for taking the kind of shit no human being should ever have to take."

"Gee, Mr. Richardson—"

"Better late than never, please call me Jerry."

"Oh, right, Jerry. It looks like I've got a lot to learn. Worst part, that mother's got me covered, as we say in Elmhurst. I got to learn to get rid of the rough edges, forget about kicking his ass, look at the total picture."

"You're learning fast, Billy. And the best part, don't forget your ambition. Go to law school, no matter what. As for me, when the war ended, I figured I had to make up for the three years in the Navy. So I married my high school sweetie, went right to work to support our first kid, and… well, you can figure the rest." He handed Billy a check.

"Wow, Mr. Rich… I mean, Jerry, this is the same as my two weeks' pay."

"Well, Billy, bad enough he fires you with no notice. One week's pay is BS. He'll never know the difference."

O'Shea folded the check and put it in shirt pocket. He rose and held out his hand. "Thanks, thanks a lot, Jerry."

"Sit down, Billy." Richardson smiled. "I still got five minutes to give you. Now when the next Bellknap gets in your face, you can't change your name, but you can use another version of your name."

"Huh?"

"Look, Billy, when you check out your birth certificate, you'll see you're registered as William O'Shea. No doubt you haven't introduced yourself as William to anyone you've met since your mommy insisted you be called William O'Shea at your confirmation." Richardson grinned. "Am I right so far, or at least in the ballpark?"

"You're right on, Jerry. If I'd ever introduced myself as William, from PS 76 in Red Hook right on through Elmhurst High, they woulda thought I was some faggot and have loads of donnybrooks on my hand. How do you know so much, Jerry?"

"Well, I grew up in Brooklyn, Bay Ridge, it's all the same. No one wants to be introduced as Rodney Farnsworth II."

Billy laughed and shook his head. "You got that one right, Jerry."

Richardson turned serious. "But now you got to think like a grown-up, Billy. Bellknap would have probably treated you bad under the circumstances. But what if you had said your name was William O'Shea? Different ring, right?"

"Yeah, Jerry, that does sound more grown-up."

"Now let's get to the tough part, Billy, I mean, William. I don't want you to be ashamed of your Irish heritage. But in this day and age, except for Boston, and with deference to Mayor O'Dwyer, most Irish are still on the outside, looking in."

"Yeah, but—"

"Please, Billy, let me finish. When my granddad got off the boat from County Cork, he found guys named Flaherty were greeted by signs saying 'Dogs and Irish Need Not Apply.' He was proud, but he had seven kids that had to be fed. Flaherty became Richardson."

"Wow, Jerry, I can see how you understand—"

"What I'm leading up to, Billy, when you get out of law school, and the law firm's filtering through hundreds of apps, how fast do you think William O'Shea's going into the circular file?"

Billy frowned. "You're saying…?"

Richardson nibbled some peanuts and raisins. "I'm saying things are a lot better than when my granddad, rest in peace, had to change his name to get any kind of job. You won't be facing that, thank the Lord. But think ahead, you've graduated law school or tried to be an intern, how do you think a top law firm would react to an app from a William O'Shea?"

Billy winced, "I think you got a point, Jerry."

Richardson grabbed another bunch of the raisins and peanuts, started chuck-a-lugging, paused for the soda on his desk. "Oh, I'm sorry, Billy, want some? My wife thinks I eat too much junk when she's not around."

"Gee, thanks, Jerry, but I think I'll wait till I get home."

"Can't say I blame you. Yesterday she packed some fresh fruit, cantaloupe, melon… Hey, I got it. Mellon, William Mellon, how would that look on an app?"

"Huh?"

"But I mean 'Mellon' with two Ls. There's this insufferable a-hole at the bank the country club deals with. Rodney Mellon, a textbook-stuffed shirt, but wouldn't that name fit in anywhere? How does William Mellon sound? Richardson grinned. "Mellon, Mellon, William Mellon, Mellon. How's it sound? William Mellon, Mr. Mellon, Mr. Mellon."

"Mr. Mellon, Mr. Mellon, please wake up, your dinner guests called to say they're on their way."

Mellon bolted up and rubbed his eyes. "Wow, Harold, have I been out all this time?"

Harold grinned. "No one can say I don't make a potent toasted almond, Mr. Mellon."

21

ASSAULT ON K STREET

Phil Frommer picked up the phone. It was Rincon, an operative at Frontiere, who told him to tune CNN right away and catch the feed from a local station in DC. Frommer clicked the remote.

The young newscaster was excited. "This is Stan Halloway of WTOP, Washington, reporting. Our cameras are focusing on the crime scene. Err, Mr. Oswalt, do you have a comment... ahh, no comment? Well, that was Huston Oswalt, who seems to be in charge of... Ah, yes, Cindy, back to our anchor, Doris Maddux, in our studio."

"Thanks, Stan. This is Doris Maddux in our studio on K Street. To summarize to those just tuning in, it has been reported, but not confirmed, that Matt Thompson, who heads the DC offices of the nation's largest law firm—Mellon, Caldwell, & Cunningham—has been shot and severely wounded. To repeat, the latest we have is that he has critical wounds, but no confirmation that—"

Phil clicked the TV shut and reached for his cell. It was already ringing. "Yeah, Stu, someone at Frontiere called me. I was just tuning CNN. How bad is it?"

"They went into a shell, Phil, said to wait for a statement. Guess they don't trust us since we're not part of the firm. The key is that the lead detective, someone named Oswalt —"

"Oswald?"

"No, Phil, don't get into your Grassy Knoll hysteria. It's Oswalt, with a *T*. Anyway, Oswalt earned himself 100K, easy, by letting me know before anyone outside the Metro Police Force that the perp left a note to the effect 'No more lawsuits for the Mellon parasites, Thompson's just the first…'"

"Was that it word for word?"

"Nah, Phil, it rambles on just like any psycho sicko with a lifetime of grievances. Oswalt said he was afraid to e-mail me the full contents until it's officially released to the press. I'm already on the way to SFO. In the meantime, I want you to get over to Mellon and put plan C into effect. What? Yeah, I know Palmeiro's over there. When the Frontiere contingent gets to Mellon's place, they'll explain plan C to Palmeiro. If the Palmeiro crew wants to be part of it, okay. Otherwise, they can scram. Even better, let them scram. They don't have to know shit about plan C. Clear, Phil?"

"Crystal, bro. I'm heading right over. What about the press?"

"That was covered once before, Phil. Mellon's got an in with the local precinct. The whole block's going to be cordoned off. Besides, that'll make those ritzy Fifth Avenue neighbors happy, since they just love their privacy."

"Okay, Stu, I'll call the limo service right now. Have a good flight." Phil looked at his phone and took a deep breath. He felt his lips tremble. Thompson shot? Who the hell expected it would come to this? His finger shook as he pressed East Side Limo.

Phil was frisked by a Palmeiro employee even though Mellon had okayed him. "We'd frisk your mother under these circumstances, Mr. Mellon."

Mellon nodded. "Safety first, I guess." He looked at Phil Frommer. "Met you once, with your brother, Stu. How long ago was that?"

"About two years ago, Mr. Mellon, at some dinner."

"Right, I remember now. You guys sure look alike, although he was a little shorter than you. So what's plan C?"

Frommer tentatively looked around the room.

"It's okay, Phil. I trust Palmeiro with my life, obviously."

"Right, Mr. Mellon, but just like Palmeiro couldn't be careful enough about frisking me, I'm not sure we want Palmeiro's outfit to know the details of plan C. On the other hand, it's your fees that keep both the Frommers and the Palmeiros in business, so it's your call, Mr. Mellon."

Mellon shrugged and looked at Palmeiro. "I guess he has a point, Palmeiro. Hang around till I depart in the limo. You'll be paid till Sunday—the full compliment of four. Just stay close to your cell phone. I may need you at any instant."

"Thanks, Mr. Mellon. We all appreciate your generosity, and we're always at the ready."

"Not at all, Carlos. The Mellon firm appreciates the fine efforts of you and your associates." He looked at Palmeiro as if to say, "You're now out of the loop. Why are you still here?"

Palmeiro caught on. "Thanks, Mr. Mellon." He motioned to two of his associates. "Let's go, we're out of here."

Phil Frommer and Mellon watched the Palmeiro group leave. "Okay, Phil, clue me in on plan C."

"We got three limos from East Side Limousines, Mr. Mellon. Three of Frontiere's best went to East Seventy-Seventh Street to pick up the limos. As soon as it's dark and the police have sealed off the block, the limos will pull up. There'll be two men with your height and build who'll enter your house. You'll all be given ski masks and then enter separate limos."

"Why the ski masks?"

"They might have your home under satellite, Google, or direct observation. If they're not sure that's three limos, they have to worry about tailing. The limos will head to three different locations in Manhattan. About a quarter mile from the destinations, a Frommer associate will take over and make the final delivery."

"Very James Bond–ish, but why the switch in drivers?"

"Because one of the drivers could flip."

"No offense, but why wouldn't a Frommer operative flip?"

Frommer blushed. "'Cause they'll all be Frommer first cousins. No amount of money can overcome that."

Mellon grinned appreciatively. "Good thinking. Can you clue me as to where I'll be holed up?" Mellon watched Frommer's blank, worried expression. "Come on, Phil, there's no one here but me and you."

"Mr. Mellon, no matter how many times this place has been swept, a tiny listening device could have been put in anytime and anyplace in your home."

Frommer smiled. "When the time is right, you'll know, if you don't actually get there first."

Mellon sighed. "If I'm out of sight, what's the press—"

"You're in seclusion—that word covers a multitude of sins, and with the Thompson incident, fully understandable."

"By the way, how is Thompson?'

"A lot of medical mumbo jumbo, but the gist is, the bullet entered near the heart, and the last word was 'critical but stable.'"

"Well, that's good. Let me know if there's anything—"

"I read you, Mr. Mellon, he's at Georgetown Medical Center. Last I heard, Dr. Matt Skowron, cardiac surgeon, is attending."

"Is he good?"

"I checked it out, Mr. Mellon. He's neck and neck with the top guy at Walter Reed who's on call if a similar thing happened to the president."

"Good. But what about Thompson's family?"

"The DC Metro Police will be guarding Thompson indefinitely as long as he's hospitalized. As for his family, there's a Bethesda-uniformed officer that'll be stationed in front of the house for several weeks while several Frontiere people will be on guard thereafter."

"How long?"

"How long? Hard to say, Mr. Mellon. What with Thompson and his family being African American, if, well, if anything should happen, there'd be a hell of an outcry: 'Billionaire white lawyer scrimps on protection for black man and his family, while the white man is securely holed up at some undisclosed Manhattan location or, more succinctly, Katrina II.'"

Mellon shook his head and sighed. "It's that out-of-control media. What is this world coming to?"

"I get your point, Mr. Mellon. Yes, the mainstream media is securely on our side. But immediate ratings and circulation always, well, not always, but they invariably trump editorial opinion and the natural bias of reporters and newscasters."

"Meaning?"

"Meaning I'm sure you've heard the refrain 'If it bleeds, it leads.' Well, so far, the local politicians and civil rights leaders haven't found a racial angle, but you know someone would only be too happy to stir the pot, if an excuse could be found."

"As it is, Phil, there's elements out there accusing us of giving Thompson the DC slot for 'show' purposes. Well, it was a natural fit, you know, the symbiotic relationship between the Democratic Party and African Americans. And by giving Thompson the legislative liaison position, we were just sealing the deal, so to speak."

"Right to all that, Mr. Mellon. The upshot, there'll be a slew of releases by Frommer people as to what a valuable asset to the firm Thompson was/is, how much he's missed, and how we'll not rest till the perpetrators are brought to… yada, yada, yada."

"Will that be you or Stu?"

"Oh, you mean the releases, Mr. Mellon? Nah, we have a bevy of wordsmiths led by Sally Dellasandro, and we expect—"

Phil's cell phone rang. "Yes?"

"They're here, Mr. Frommer."

"Good, let them in."

Phil closed the phone and looked at Mellon. "They're at the door, Mr. Mellon. Plan C, here we come."

Stu Frommer arrived at JFK three hours after Mellon was dropped off at the secret location. A Frommer cousin was at the airport and whisked Stu to a new condo on First Avenue, near 51st, not far from the United Nations. Phil Frommer met him in the lobby while the cousin drove home. The brothers hugged.

"How are things on the Right Coast, Brother Phil? Looks like we're under the gun and about to really earn our pay."

Phil pointed toward some lounge chairs near the entrance and away from the reception area. They sat down. "Lotta details, bro, lotta details. His wife's not important. She's in Paris and oblivious to all. His butler and cook are staying at his Fifth Avenue mansion and will contact our Manhattan office if she should call, but she probably won't. Sometimes they don't communicate for a whole month. Mellon's already called his son and daughter on their cells to clue them as to what's happening. He gave them my cell number if they feel they have to call him. We can't trust their talking directly while plan C's in effect."

"Good thinking, Phil, whoever it is or they are, they seem sharp. It's still not sure, Phil, but we got someone leading the pack."

Phil's eyes lit up. "No shit, this fast?"

"I don't consider it fast, Phil. It's been a while since the threats escalated, and a ton of man-hours, but we think it's Beltran."

"Beltran, that shithead from Pennsylvania? But how sure are we?"

"Well, Phil, that sort of thing can never be as certain as a math equation, but you know Pascerelli was chief code breaker at Fort Meade, he made the call."

"Based on what?"

"Aside from the fact that Beltran was the odds-on favorite since he followed asbestos, tobacco, and pharmaceuticals in Mellon's crosshairs and was the only one to publicly threaten the Mellon firm before he disappeared?"

"Right, Stu, so you don't have to be Sherlock Holmes or Dick Tracy to figure out the culprit. Why are we spending millions on Pascerelli and the handwriting experts and all the rest?"

"First of all, dear brother, the fees are bumped up to Mellon. What's a million here or there to Mellon? The only ones who pay attention are his accountants or auditors."

"A million?"

"Well, I haven't kept close tabs, but Silvestri says about half a mill has gone to Pascerelli so far, the bills are still coming in, and that doesn't count the others."

"So what do you figure for Operation Sleuth, about two million?"

Stu sighed and leaned back on the comfy chair. "If we're lucky and Beltran's the guy."

Phil looked at his watch. "Well, Mellon must have radar know-ing you've arrived. Guess it's time to go up there. You're going to break the news on Beltran?"

"With the proviso that there's still one in ten that we're wrong."

"He's going to ask what we plan to do about it."

"You mean if we find him? Well, prior to all this, we were try-ing to find him to shut him up or buy him off. But since he fled Scranton, the elusive MF is turning into another Osama. Of course, before we only had two of Frontiere's people searching. Now, we're going to increase the Frontiere contingent and maybe," Stu paused for effect, "use the mob."

"The mob, Stu, do we have to?"

Stu grinned. "Don't look so bent, Phil, you know we can keep our shirts clean."

"Still, why do we have to...?"

"Look, Phil, didn't mean to cut you off. The bottom line is this: Frontiere's people can play rough but won't kill on a whim, like a mobster. This is one time the corporate mentality doesn't work to our advantage. We have to find him and fast. Mellon's our meal ticket. And guaranteed, if a friend of a friend has to talk, a mobster can be a lot more persuasive than a private dick."

"Huh?"

"Simple, bro, who are you more likely to open up to faster: Sam Spade or Al Capone?"

"Okay, you win, Stu, but like you said, keep our skirts clean."

"Is it skirts or shirts?" They giggled.

"Hey, Phil, one more thing. The DC police are going to be on the lookout, as well as the Bethesda law enforcement. Then, I'm sure someone'll find a reason to make it interstate so the FBI can join in, plus all those looking for a reward."

"A reward? How much?"

"Dunno, Phil, but it'll be plenty."

"So where am I staying, bro?"

"Got your usual suite at the Carlyle, but Alice says you're wel-come to stay over and—"

Stu grinned. "I like the scenery in and around the Carlyle."

Phil shook his head. "Same old Stu, when are you gonna settle down? It's not fair you get to buy toys for nephews and nieces and I don't."

Stu's cheeks flushed red. "One of these years, Phil, one of these years. Meanwhile, too much fun."

Phil looked at his watch. "It's past eight. He must be finished with dinner by now. Let's get up there."

Phil approached the receptionist. "We're here to see Paul Snider."

"Is he expecting you?"

They nodded.

"Who shall I say is calling?"

"Stu and Phil."

"Stu and Phil what?"

"WHAT!"

Phil, wary that Stu was about to jump over the counter and grab the geeky, bespectacled clerk by the throat, answered, "Jones."

The receptionist, sensing the mood, picked up the phone. "Yes, Mr. Snider, this is Michael at the desk. There's a Stu and Phil, err, Jones to see you."

Michael heard a roar of laughter from Snider. "You may go right up, gentlemen. It's unit 1620, the first bank of—"

"Yeah, I've been here before. Thanks, Michael."

They got to the elevators and watched the lights flickering the message of when each would reach the lobby.

"Why were you so nice to that faggoty creep, Phil? I was ready to deck him."

The spacious elevator door opened. They watched themselves in the mirror as the elevator whooshed up to 16. "C'mon, Stu, he doesn't know who the good guys are. We want a guy like that to be careful."

"You're right." Stu sighed. "It's been a long flight and a tough couple of days. Believe it or not, bro, after a drink at the Carlyle, I'm heading right to the rack."

"Is this the terror of both coasts losing his touch?"

"Not by a long shot, Brother Phil. But I'm tired, and we easily got two hours covering the bases with Mellon. Hey, who thought up Snider?"

Phil blushed. "Kravitz, our CFO. I asked him if he were writing fiction, what would the last name of his main character be?"

"And he said 'Snider'?"

"Yeah, his dad was a rabid Dodger fan, and Duke Snider was his favorite." Stu smirked. "And so it goes, some Beltran shithead's out here looking for William Mellon, and the only way he'll hit pay dirt is if he finds the Duke of Flatbush."

"Well, we do the best we can, Stu." He pointed to the left. "C'mon, Stu, 1620's that way."

THIS WEEK

It was Sunday night, and Tom Leary was listening to the basketball game while driving home. He switched radio stations during a Laker time-out. Listening to KFI, he heard Drudge report that William Mellon, of the "controversial" law firm of Mellon, Caldwell, & Cunningham, was to appear on the next cover of *This Week*. Drudge assumed that Thompson's shooting underscored the past decade's hullabaloo over tort reform and the "excesses" of trial lawyers. He suggested that Thompson was an easy first victim but that Mellon, who was in seclusion, was the ultimate target. Drudge said that after the "following" messages, he'd return with an analysis of Hillary's chances in '08.

Leary shut the radio and called Slats. "Hi, Holly, is L'Enfant Terrible there?"

"Hi, Tom. Sunday night, close to nine, he'd better be. Hold on, Tom, I'll get him."

She looked at Slats and held out the phone, grinning. "Can you imagine, Slats, it's Simon Legree, not Tom Leary, bothering the one and only curled up on his couch on a Sunday evening."

Slats groaned and got up. "Very funny, Ms. Holly. I just hope I'm still laughing after talking to Mr. Legree."

Slats grabbed the phone and sat on the chair next to the end table. "What's this? You're calling me on a Sunday night? A severe

LEE BORNSTEIN

enough wage/hour violation without the additional factor of my missing any part of *Desperate Housewives*."

"Relax, Slats, I was in the car saving Lenore a trip to Trader Joe's and just heard on Drudge that Mellon made the cover of *This Week*. So no home telecommuting tomorrow, dude. I want you in first thing. This has got to affect where we go from here."

"Will 6 AM suffice, boss?"

"Quit the quips, Mr. Conners. Around eight will do, and no surfing at your desk. I mean in my office by eight. Bye."

Slats returned to the couch. The TV was still on mute while Holly dangled the remote. "Mellon made the cover of *This Week*. So I got to be in the office first thing tomorrow to see where we go from here."

"Hmm," Holly scoffed. "So that means less time on the Chanteuse watch with Spivey and all those Spivey employees?"

Slats grimaced. "Are you on that again, Holly? I told you there's nothing between me and Rhea Simpson."

Holly got up. "Put *Desperate* on the VCR. I'm taking a shower."

"C'mon, Holly, don't get started—"

"Slats," she hissed his name like she was aiming a dagger, "I can understand a young stud, and I'm being magnanimous here. I can understand a young man in heat letting the moment overcome him. Water under the bridge. Who knows how I'd react if I was on the road and had a similar opportunity. I'm sure that—"

"Holly," Slats wailed, "how many times have I told you that there's nothing—"

"SLATS! Just don't insult my intelligence. These things happen. You're here now, tonight, Sunday night, like any faithful husband or lover. That's enough for me. Just don't think I don't know something's been going on. Now don't forget to tape *Desperate*."

Slats watched her enter the bathroom. He was glad she'd run off to take a shower.

And the taping command meant that she's going right to bed. *Okay for you, Slats.* The equivalent of sending naughty Tommy to his room without supper. So Slats has had his supper, but she was sure to be asleep or feigning it by the time he turned in. The result was the same. Naughty Tommy went to bed on an empty stomach, and Slats went to bed empty, well, in another way.

Blast, Desperate's started already. Slats pressed the Record button. He watched that little strumpet, Eva Longeria, up to her latest she-nanigans, but he couldn't concentrate. Holly's suspected or known all along? Well, she'd hinted before. But that was like any soap opera, de rigueur. Well, there's nothing to know or suspect. Nothing's hap-pened, yet. Still, he was glad she'd run off to the shower. He wouldn't have known how to lie after being surprised like that. Damn, how'd she find out, or is she still guessing? The plumber was hitting on Terri Hatcher, again. Or was it the other way around? He toyed with the ice in his crème de menthe and grinned at the absurdity of the unfolding developments on the screen. He'd relaxed enough to start thinking about what to suggest to Leary in the morning. Focus back to the Frommer's as opposed to the Chanteuse? That would mean less time around… He felt a pang; damn, he had it bad for Rhea.

With the 'eight o'clock sharp" admonition, Slats didn't want to be late. For a change, Leary wasn't observing the Malibu waves. As Slats approached, he saw Leary wave him in through the glass par-tition. After brief hellos, Slats picked his favorite chair. It was ten to eight.

"Nice weekend?"

"It was, till about 8:45 last night."

Leary shot him a serious look. Then he grinned. "File a fucking complaint to the NLRB."

"I'll keep it in mind."

"Well, while you're keeping that in mind, what's your mind say about this?" Leary picked up the latest edition of *This Week*, and there was William Mellon, America's biggest and richest lawyer, right there on the cover.

Slats got up and took the magazine out of Leary's outstretched hand. Beneath the huge sketch of Mellon was the caption "MELLON ASSOCIATE SHOT! WHAT'S BEHIND THE SHOOTING? WHO'S NEXT?"

Above Mellon's likeness was the heading "Sen. Joe Biden and Iraq, Ticket to '08?"

Slats grinned and tossed the newsweekly back on Leary's desk. "Looks to me like the *Pacific Coast Gazette* may have some new priorities."

Now, Leary assumed his usual stance of leaning back on his high-back swivel chair and clocking the endless Pacific Ocean surf attack the Malibu sands. "Oh really, like what might those new priorities be?"

"Well, Tom, through no fault of my own, I'll bet that our circulation fallen in the past month."

Leary leaned forward on his chair and looked at directly at Slats. "Well, that's a good guess, or do you have an in at circulation?"

"Common sense, boss. People are getting tired of the Chanteuse. Nothing big's happened since Hollywood and the Libs turned on her. The women are no doubt back to concentrating on what's up with J-Lo, Jen, and Britney."

"Even with our age demographic?"

"Well, it's just not teenagers who give a shit about who's going with who, who's divorcing who, and so on."

"Great analysis, Slats, if we ever run a strictly gossip column, you're in line." Slats winced. "Thanks, but no thanks, boss. I'd quit first."

Leary leaned back again and stared out the window. "So you've had twelve hours, well, minus any time with Holly. What'd you come up with?"

"Wow, boss man, you give me too much credit."

Leary grimaced. "C'mon, Slats, let's hear it."

"Well, on my way in this morning, I called a friend at Hastings. He's an early riser and, coincidentally, was already starting off the week checking the bloggers."

Leary looked at Slats. "And anything?"

"Well, Tom, it's what the legal beagles have been opining virtually since the shooting, that Thompson was a good first target, 'cause he's, in effect, a PR guy, never worked cases, so he doesn't have any personal enemies. Ergo, there was hardly any protection."

"Ergo, where'd you come up with that one?"

Slats grinned and pointed to his noggin. "Hey, don't sell me short, Mr. Leary. There's a lot up here."

"Okay, Einstein, so?"

"So the conclusion is that the dude on the cover *is* the ultimate target but that, as long as he's alive, the issue remains alive."

Leary smiled wanly. "And the issue being all those ridiculous lawsuits?"

"Well, not just the suits, Tom, but the payouts. How many industries have to go under? How many employees have to lose their jobs?"

"Easy there, Slats, you sound more like an advocate than a disinterested observer."

"Well, you know me, boss man, I do have views. But they stop at the water's edge. They would never affect my reporting, you know, just like Dan Rather and Katie Couric."

Tom grimaced and held up his right arm. "Enough already. It's too early on a Monday morning for this old bean to absorb your so-called witty asides."

Leary glanced at his watch. "So what do we do?"

"Well, I have heard that Frommer flew Back East, where he and his brother provided the 'seclusion' for Mellon, except, of course, in this case, seclusion doesn't mean a Garbo I don't want to talk to the press, but rather I don't want to talk, plus no one knows where I am."

"So he's hiding for his life?"

"Just about. As to how long, probably not much longer."

"Why's that, Slats, if, as you and the bloggers say, he's scared shitless?"

Slats shrugged. "I think the consensus is that the longer he's out of sight, the longer the lawsuit guys are in the spotlight, and nobody would want that—no matter the industry or the issues involved."

"Unless, of course, it's someone like the Chanteuse, where publicity's the foundation of a successful career."

"Right, but just like the Chanteuse doesn't welcome pub about her personal life, the lawyers don't relish stories of their being threatened as opposed to stories about their successful cases."

"Good point, Slats, so where do we go from here?"

"Dunno, boss man, maybe another trip to New York?"

Leary winced. "I look forward to meeting with Mr. Big on the ninth floor to approve your travel expenses like going for root canal."

Slats grinned. "And a root canal's a lot less expensive."

"Well," Leary sighed, "the Big Man's looking to be bought out by the McClatchy chain."

"Meaning?"

"Meaning, while he watches every little penny to make the balance sheet look better, he knows the more gloss we bring, the more chance of being bought out."

"So?"

"So make a fuss, Slats, make a fuss. You scoop a story that's picked up by the nets, the cable news, the *Times*, the *Journal*, and you get the Pulitzer, the fame, and yes, the broads, while I land on my feet in case we are bought out."

"So?"

"Gee, some reporter I got here. His vocab is limited to one two-letter word. So as you so eloquently put it, get rolling."

Slats took a deep breath and turned toward the door.

"One more thing, Slats, don't forget to get your hands dirty."

"What?"

"Dirty, you know. Be part of it. If they're gunning for Mellon, let them gun for you too. Y' know, Slats, don't just report it, live it." Leary grinned. "Don't look so pale. If it comes to that, I promise I'll be at your funeral. And I bet you'll have a Ms. Holly and a Ms. Rhea attending and mourning. What more can a guy look forward to?"

"Gee, thanks, boss, I never realized I had that much to look forward to." With that, Slats was out the door.

DR. CRAIG BELTRAN

Slats worked through lunch reviewing his database on bloggers. He googled some of the promising ones under "political/politics." That comprehensive list was whittled down through a batch of key words: *legal, lawsuits, Beltran, Frommer, Mellon, Crosby, Chanteuse.* He settled on three bloggers and hustled over to the research section where Vic Lopat seemed to be toying with a Frappucino. "Hi, Vic, liquid lunch?"

"Oh, hello, Slats. Yeah, I guess more thirsty than hungry this noon."

Slats looked at the disheveled Lopat. His shirttail was out, hair uncombed, and he probably hadn't shaved in three days. Well, Slats concluded, research might be boring and a dead end, but no one's gonna get on your case because of your appearance. He put a printout on Vic's desk. "I got three bloggers here, Vic, along with their backgrounds and their areas of interest. I typed out a little summary of what we're after right now. It's gone beyond the Chanteuse and all those trials. Now we're after anything at all on this Beltran character and that Mellon law firm."

"Nothing on Frommer?"

Slats smiled. "You got a good memory, Vic. Yeah, throw the Frommers in. You'll probably come across them no matter what. But in this project, the key is Beltran and Mellon."

Lopat looked up at Slats as if he was going to…

"Don't even ask." Slats grinned. "Unless there's something big on your plate from upstairs, the answer is 'as soon as possible.'"

Lopat shrugged. "My plate is clean. Coming right up."

"Which means?"

"I don't know, Slats, a couple of days?"

"Thanks, Vic, I'd appreciate anything you can do." Slats headed toward the elevator and took one more peek at Lopat, who seemed to be dreamily lost in that Frappucino.

Slats was ticked. He'd seen Lopat at lunch on Tuesday, and it was past ten, Friday morning. Any second now, Leary, the venerable Marine DI, would be on the phone barking, "What the hell you got for me, Slats?" Slats toyed with his blueberry muffin, wearily sipped some lukewarm coffee, and tried Yahoo. Just as Yahoo News flashed on his screen, the phone rang. Slats's heart began pounding. He turned and saw Leary wasn't in his office. The pounding stopped. Maybe it's Holly.

"Hi, Slats, it's Vic."

Just the dude I needed and wanted, Slats mused. He leaned back on his chair. "Whats'ya got, Vic?"

"I'll send you a Word appendage, Slats, but I can summarize it if you want to meet."

Slats sighed the sigh of contentment. "Free for lunch today? It's on me."

"Well, gee, Slats, an offer I can't refuse. The diner?"

"Nah, Vic, it's always too crowded and noisy. We don't want to be shouting 'Beltran,' 'Frommer,' or 'Mellon' above the din, do we? What about the Mexican place? It's spacious, and they got a garden, and it's not that windy today."

"Wow, Slats, splurging for the Cantina Manana?"

"Yeah, Vic, the waitresses are worth the price of admission, and I can sense you got something good for me."

"Well, I won't be coming empty-handed, Slats."

"That sounds promising," Slats crowed. "Noon sound good?"

"Noon it is, Slats. Be at your desk then."

Lopat got zonked with at least three margaritas, but who was counting? Slats felt that his two margaritas no doubt affected his ability to keep score. At a quarter to three, Slats was sufficiently aware to call Leary and left a message that they were at the cantina, that Lopat had done his usual thorough job, and that all the info would be shared with Leary first thing Monday morning. With that, bring on the burritos, the black beans, and the tacos, all the way till TGIF time when the youngsters come in to let off steam after the end of another week.

Maybe it was the margaritas, but Lopat displayed a surprising sense of humor. Their table didn't draw one of those Latina hotties with those red roses attached to the ruffled, low-cut white blouses, but Latrice, the black knockout who waited on them, had a personality to match her looks. When Lopat asked her what part of Mexico she was from, she answered, "The southern part, the *deep* southern part."

Slats knew it was too late on Friday for Lopat, especially in his condition, to head back to the office. He told Lopat he was in no shape to drive, so he gave him twenty dollars to cab back to the office. Slats said he was going to walk to that Starbucks a block away, clear his head with one of those Grande things, take notes, and make Lopat promise him that he wouldn't leave the office until he was good and sober. "And oh yeah, lemme have that Word appendage before noon on Monday."

Slats was in by eight Monday morning. He checked his mail, and sure enough, there was a message from Lopat with an attachment entitled "Here It Is. Good Luck, Slats." Slats beamed. "I'm gonna put in a good word for Ol' Lopat. Maybe Leary will be touched and offer Lopat bonus." *More likely*, Slats concluded, *Leary'll say, "His pay is his bonus."*

Slats rushed to the print room and gulped when he saw nothing had been freshly printed. Donahue of Accounting was waiting and offered, "Relax, Slats, there's a little backup. I think that's mine coming out now." He walked to the second bin, pulled out six or seven pages, and said, "Sounds like yours is coming out of the first bin right now."

Slats watched Donahue walk out; he went to the bin and grabbed the bottom page.

It was entitled "Summary of Research regarding the Mellon, Beltran, Frommer Case." Slats smiled as he stapled the remaining five pages to the title page. *Now the question is whether I can digest this shit before Leary gets here.* He figured he had a little less than an hour.

Slats was rehearsing his monologue when he heard, "It's a five-day week, Slats, last I checked. So all day Friday in some cantina isn't part of the deal."

Slats turned and watched Leary slowly turn and head toward his office. "Gimme five to check my e-mail, then come on in, Slats, and… oh, yeah, better have something worthwhile for me."

Slats smiled smugly as he watched Leary sit down and stare at his computer screen. Let's see, give a topflight report and get every Friday off? The only question, start off with Beltran or Mellon? *Easy,* Slats concluded, *Beltran, the new name's going to be headline news.*

Slats opened the door to Leary's office tentatively. "Ready for me, boss?"

Leary waved his left hand impatiently. "C'mon in, Slats." He briefly turned back to the window to catch some of the languid waves approaching the shore. He looked at Slats. "Okay, what did Lopat and you come up with?"

Slats shrugged and held out Lopat's report. "Want a verbal summary, or do you want to peruse Lopat's findings?"

Leary winced. "Peruse? Another five-dollar word? Gimme, gimme, I'll peruse later. You're the Sherlock, or Shylock, on this story. I want your report."

Slats rose and handed the pages to Leary, who glanced at the title then looked at Slats.

Slats cleared his throat, eliciting a grin from Leary. "Gee, Slats, don't get nervous. It's only Speech 101."

In response, Slats had to get his own dig in. He held out his hands. "Look, Ma, no notes." *Well, that fell flat,* Slats concluded. So he jumped right in. "With a guy like Mellon, you can easily whittle down the usual suspects to about a thousand. But the timing and some other hints that Lopat and I are not sure of, we're both convinced that Mellon, Frommer, et al. think that some guy named Beltran, a gyno from Pennsylvania's the guy."

"Never heard of him." Leary sighed. "How'd he beat out the other 999 suspects?"

"Good question, Tom. It is on the record that before he disappeared off the face of the earth, Beltran, more than once, threatened Mellon and others like him."

"Oh yeah, Slats, I think I remember, wasn't he head of some professional medical group in PA who got wiped out due to some dubious malpractice? And wasn't there something else?"

"Right," Slats sighed. "His wife then committed suicide."

Leary frowned and leaned back on his chair. "That's more than enough motive."

"Good point, Tom, unless some other enemy of Mellon figures the same thing and concludes he's got a green light as long as Beltran's threats are on record and he's disappeared."

Slats spoke for ten minutes straight, highlighting what he felt was important in Lopat's report. He knew it was the right time to conclude when he noticed a hint of boredom in Leary's demeanor. *There won't be any more hassle over a whole Friday afternoon at the cantina*, he concluded. Plus, a victory on the report. Slats's mood had already turned from trepidation to ennui. He started daydreaming about.

"So who did you say was in the hunt besides Mellon's honchos?"

"Well, the FBI, the PBI…"

"Huh?"

Slats grinned. "That's the Pennsylvania Bureau of Investigation."

Leary shrugged. "What will those bureaucrats think of next? Continue."

"Well, about six or seven agencies in the tristate New York area, Lopat wasn't sure." Slats noticed Leary's puzzled look. "Well, Tom, you know there's all these interagency bureaucracies… well, like the New York, New Jersey, Connecticut, Interagency Task Force, and—"

"Whoa, Slats, did you say 'inter-' or 'intra-agency'?" He caught Slats grinning. "Wipe that grin, wipe that grin, or—"

"The answer, my friend, is written on the wind—the answer is both."

Leary's stern demeanor was falling apart; a slight smirk crossed his visage. "Lord, have mercy. Is or are there no end to all this bureaucracy bullshit?"

"Not if they can help it, boss man, not if they can help it. I think it was summarized by Lopat on page 7. There's about fifteen state and local—"

"What about the Feds?"

"Well, Tom, the FBI doesn't want to talk about its caseload, according to Lopat. My view, for what's it worth, is that Mellon et al. got enough juice to even get an unfriendly administration to allocate resources to help a sworn enemy like Mellon. My guess, for what it's worth, is that the FBI has got to do a perfunctory hunt for this Beltran character. But you can bet it's not getting the attention or follow-through as the hunt for Osama and his Al-Qaeda crew."

Leary leaned back on his swivel chair, put his feet on the desk, and stole a look at the Malibu shoreline. "Slats, Slats, what am I gonna do with you? Every fucking time I come at you loaded for bear, you always manage to disarm me." He leaned forward and waved his index finger at Slats. "One of these days, Slats, one of these days, I'll get you yet."

"So what do I do next, boss?"

"Well, Slats, we can't compete with *ThisWeek, Time, Newsweek,* and even busybodies like the *New Yorker*, let alone the *New York Times'* interest in publicizing and finding an enemy of their sue forever legal hero."

"Which means?"

"Which means, see what you can do about getting the Chanteuse in this, and—"

"C'mon, Tom, that's a stretch, and she's played out." He caught Leary looking at his watch. *Whoops, this session's coming to an end,* Slats concluded.

Leary rose from his chair. "I'm going to write an e-mail to Lopat congratulating him on his fine effort as soon as I digest this report. As for you, Slats, think of something. And like I said before, if you have to, become part of the story. Later."

BELTRAN IN BERKELEY

Beltran decided it was finally time to check out the infrastructure of the famed crazy pen aptly called Berserkeley. It had been three months since he'd decided that the best place to hide, hang, and plan was the Capital of the Loony Left. (Somewhat like Osama hiding out in the endless labyrinthine spaces of the Pentagon?) It was a Tuesday afternoon, and everyone was out of town or out doing something. He looked at his watch. It was a quarter to two. He squeezed into the tiny bathroom and glanced in the mirror. There was a time when the two-day fuzz on his cheeks was unconscionable, let alone his disheveled hair.

Instinct made him pick up the brush and comb. He smirked and chucked the idea. *Better to fit in, my dear. Maybe I'll do better than Little Miss Riding Hood.*

He drifted down to Shattuck and passed the French Hotel, where he'd already had a coffee with Alma. Well, she looked the Berkeley hangout type without trying. But the place was too small. It was hard to inadvertently discuss any "business" without the risk of being overheard. Beltran crossed the street, passed the bookstore, and entered the Jewish-style deli. *Mmm.* He smelled the pastrami and those knishes. Bad timing, he'd already had lunch. *Some other time,* he figured. He turned the corner and saw this other place. It looked like the perfect venue to hang and catch the indigenous vibes. He walked up to the Starbucks-like counter. He saw all those

Frappuccino-type drinks on the board. He felt like something frosty, but he figured, despite his shaggy appearance, it would make him appear too yuppified. So he ordered a plain latte, no whipped cream. He blanched when he was informed of the price. Wow, these people rebel against the system but are willing to hand over three dollars for a cup of coffee in a dump like this?

He found a table and looked at some notes. They were all on index cards with a simple code—N stood for Mellon, G for Frommer. Not too hard for Ultra or the CIA to crack, but hopefully, these Berkeley types and the bozos chasing him weren't in that league.

He'd been there about ten minutes when he saw her. She was smiling at him. If this were twenty-five years ago, he thought, before Marie, before the children, before all this. *Nahh*, he concluded, *too scruffy, too political, and I'm past fifty*. Still, if she cleaned herself up, it's been a while. Shacking up would help in the deception but increase the chances of a mistake tenfold. *No*, Beltran concluded, *it's been a while, and it'll be a lot longer*. But what was number one on a young man's agenda twenty-five to thirty years earlier had to take back seat now.

She approached him. "Like this place? It's more active than the French Hotel. More buzz, more activists." She held out her hand. "I'm Daveda. This isn't a pickup, it's just that I've never seen you here before, and," she held out some flyers, "there's a rally this Sunday in SF at the Civic Center sponsored by the San Francisco Area Gay, Lesbian, and TransGender Coalition."

Beltran tried to suppress a smile. He looked at the flyer. It was headed SFAGLTGC. Wow, how silly can you get? He virtually bit his lip to keep a stern appearance. "I'm Manny Rivera." He looked as if he were studying the flyer. "Hmm, this Sunday, may not be able to make it, but—"

"How about next Saturday?" she asked breathlessly. "It's for Hezbollah." She handed him another flyer.

He barely glanced at the new flyer before folding it and placing it in his shirt pocket.

He figured that if he read how they're selling Hezbollah, he might really crack up laughing or, worse, show anger at the absurdity of it all. "Yes, next Saturday might be easier for me." He reached into his shirt pocket as if he was about to pull out the flyer. "Is it also in the Civic Center. On a weekend, it's pretty easy to—"

"Well, actually, no, Manny, it's in People's Park here in Berkeley!" She seemed to wait for some feedback and caught his blank expression. "You see, as Progressive as San Francisco is, the powers that be don't feel that SF is ready for Hezbollah."

Well, bully for San Fran, Beltran thought, *maybe there's some hope for the politics of that stylish, scenic, politically weird city yet.* "Yes, well, no matter how Progressive an area appears, there apparently are reactionary elements everywhere."

That seemed to establish his bonafides. She really seemed impressed. She held out her hand, "Oh, I forgot to formally introduce myself. My name's Daveda, Daveda Lefkowitz."

Beltran hesitated but decided to plow ahead. "Lefkowitz, isn't that a Jewish name?"

"Yes," she said proudly.

"Well, pardon my probing," he stumbled, "but don't you feel squeamish about backing Hezbollah. I… I mean being Jewish and all…"

"Oh, not at all," she responded. After all, peace trumps any ethnicity." Beltran tried to look like he was on board, but his expression betrayed him.

"But, Manny," she exclaimed, "it's not a question of religion or anything like that. It's just that Halliburton and reactionary political forces are creating false enmity among peace-loving peoples throughout the world."

"Well, I'm Catholic, so I never kept up with all this Jewish-Israeli/PalestinianMuslim stuff. But doesn't it go back over fifty years, I mean before Bush, Halliburton, and all that? I mean, not that I'm defending Bush or Halliburton, but I think Roosevelt or Truman was president when all that Mideast stuff hit the fan." He felt he'd gone too far. She looked puzzled. He thought he caught a frown on her face.

He did like how he was able to pull off repeating "I mean" figuring that was Berkeley Speak, despite his middle-aged appearance.

"Ehh, Truman?" she mumbled. "I think I've heard the name. Was he a secretary of state or an activist?"

He decided to get serious before he lost his "bona fides."

"Well, the main point, Daveda, as you no doubt know, is that it doesn't matter who's president, whether it's Halliburton or some other oil company, the US has been in the pocket of the oil interests, it seems forever, and it *must stop now!*"

Daveda's face lit up as if she'd just been singled out for a commendation in kindergarten. "Oh, Manny, you're so smart. I... I mean naturally... I mean, you're new at this, and yet look at all you know."

Beltran was tiring of this charade. If this little knowledge impresses her, heaven help us and heaven help these pathetic "activists." He looked for a way to conclude. "Ahh, pardon me, Daveda, but how did you know I'm new at all this?"

"Well, Manny, it doesn't take long to recognize the activists at all our protests and rallies... On the other hand, sometimes there are thousands, just an educated guess."

"Well, Daveda, you guessed right. As you can tell from my age, I've dropped out, hating every moment I've been part of the military industrial complex."

Daveda's face seemed to glow with compassion. "Oh, Manny, not to worry. We've all grown up in this imperfect society. It's up to us when we see the light to fight to make this a better society, a better world."

He wanted to respond, but he was fascinated by the way her head shook as she gave her plaintive lesson in worldly civics. As if she was six years old and admonishing her favorite doll, who hadn't seen the light according to the doll's six-year-old mommy's worldly wisdom. This simpleton was getting to him. He felt some movement in his groin area. Without a doubt, it was time to go. He took one more sip of his half-finished latte, got up, and held out is hand. "Well, Daveda, thanks for all the valuable insights. I hope to see you soon, either here or at some demonstration."

"Oh yes," she gasped, reluctant to let go of his hand. "I'm sure we'll see you somewhere."

As he walked out, Beltran glanced at the disheveled types, with their beards, 'staches, or goatees, wasting a weekday afternoon, apparently jobless in the most dynamic economy in the world. Most looked too old to be students. Besides, he'd already checked out the fact that most students hung out at places closer to the Cal Berkeley campus. *What a waste*, he mused, thinking back some thirty years when he'd put in one-hundred-hour weeks as an intern. That was a waste also, but at least he was engaged in the start of something big—a career in medicine.

He walked back to the place, checked the mail, and bounded up the creaky staircase. Everyone seemed to be back: Alma, Broderick, Dennis. "Hi, gang, where's Willy?"

Alma answered, "Based on your note, he went to the French Hotel. He wanted to cover something with you."

"Yeah, well, mistake there." Beltran shrugged. "I discovered a new place right near there and… Say, why didn't he call?"

"You know Willy." Broderick grinned. "Afraid someone's going to listen in, and apparently, it was big—"

"WHAT?" Beltran fumed. "Doesn't he know all our cell lines are secure?"

"Right." Broderick shrugged. "I've explained it more than once, but you know how he worries."

Beltran frowned. "We can't handle worriers in what we're up to. I know we're all lawyers here, except for me. What kind of law was Willy in?"

"Ahh, I think he was a staff lawyer for the Bergen County Child Protective Services." Alma hesitated and added, "Err, maybe it was Hudson County. All those Jersey suburbs ring a similar bell."

Broderick grinned. "I'm from Falls Church, Virginia, a suburb of DC. I wouldn't know a Bergen from a Hudson from a Smith or Jones. You from near there?"

"Bethpage, on the island. Sort of far." She laughed. "But over the years, there's always one or the other reason to head out to Joisey."

They all laughed at her affectation. Dennis chimed in, "If what's bothering you is that Willy has no big-time trial experience, you've got a point, Mr. Beltran."

"Well," Beltran shrugged, "trial experience or not, going after a delinquent mother's a lot different than taking on the likes of Mellon or Frommer." He watched them nod nervously. "Don't get me wrong," he added, "I appreciate everything you've all given up to help my cause. So I'm eternally grateful to Willy and," he felt a lump in his throat, "to all of you."

They looked at each other. Alma seemed to be voted the designated responder. "We appreciate your kind words, but let's not forget, we're more in this to save our noble legal profession than to help you."

That seemed to lift the tension. They all grinned.

Beltran frowned. "Your... your giving up... giving up so much more than could be asked of anyone. Even though all of you won't be involved in the violence part of this gig and, of course, never meet anyone who will, you're still all liable to the ultimate legal penalties if, as expected, things don't go perfect."

"We're all in your boat," Alma responded. "We've all given you that confidential written summary of where we were in our lives when we decided to chuck it all and go with you." She looked around the room and showed a weak smile. "Of course, I know what my circumstances were. I assume we're all in about the same boat."

"Yeah." Dennis grinned. "And let's hope that boat ain't developing a leak." More nervous laughter.

Alma looked directly at Beltran. "So, Manny, we're all getting a little tired of hiding behind computers. What's next?"

Beltran smiled. "Catch that, folks? She called me Manny. No one, leastways at the moment, is looking for any of you. But everyone's out looking for Dr. Craig Beltran. The less anyone ever mentions my first or last name, the less chance it'll happen in public when who knows who might put two and two together and run to the nearest tip line." He watched all of them nod defiantly, as if I'd be stupid enough to inadvertently give you away. Alma appeared anxious to get an answer. "Sorry, Alma, but for now, you're all going to continue to be tech jockeys. Captain Tumult's the head of Operation Lethal. Until we get an update, everything's on hold."

"Well," Alma looked at Beltran, "I think I can be sure of one thing."

"What's that, Alma?"

"I never knew what you looked like, except for some black-and-white photos in the papers. Of course, your hair wasn't blond, you didn't have the beard, and my guess is, you're wearing contacts to change the color of your eyes."

Beltran shrugged and held out his arms in a "you got me" gesture. "No offense, Alma, but if you figured out Espionage 101, it'd be a cinch for a rookie from the bureau. The key is luck and that the average Joe or Jane Blow isn't thinking about me or my situation and, if aware when the news broke, forgot about it by now."

"And the luck?" Alma smiled.

"Well, the luck is that as big as bureaucracies are, the chances of randomly running into an FBI agent are, well, infinitesimal."

"Unless they get a tip," Dennis broke in, "and are zeroing in on you."

"Exactly, Dennis, and that's where all you computer wizards with your phony trails, and living here in the heart of the enemy—"

"Sleeping with the enemy?" Alma grinned.

"Well, Alma, let's just say 'sleeping within the enemy.'"

There was a knock on the door, and Willy walked in. "Hi, guys, and gal." He laughed. "You can stop talking about me."

Beltan watched Willy take a seat. "We were, Willy, we were. But not for long. Next time you're looking for me, skip the French Hotel. I found a new place nearby. Didn't even catch the name. I'll take you there real soon."

Willy looked puzzled. "Anything special?"

"No, just that you all should be aware of SFAGLTGC rally."

"The *what?*" Alma was the loudest, but they all expressed their bewilderment.

Beltran smiled and sighed as if he was teaching a class of 'slow' students. He walked toward Alma and handed her the flyer. He walked back to his chair, suppressing a grin.

"Well, of course," Alma boomed, "the San Francisco Area Gay Lesbian and TransGender Coalition. It's been a long day, folks. I knew that one all along."

Beltran held up his hand, interrupting the catcalls from the others. "Maybe we ought to attend? When in Rome…"

"Aha," the still-flustered Alma responded, "and when the cops break up a melee and blow our cover?'

"Like I said," Beltran grinned, "maybe we ought *not* attend."

Beltran met them all Sunday night at this busy Mexican dive off Ashby. The place had many advantages. It was brassy and loud, and half the customers spoke Spanish. It was also good for those on budgets because the beers were cheap and the wait staff was prompt with the chips and salsa, giving a fifteen-minute head start before one had to order, on a half-full stomach.

Everyone was sufficiently trained to wait for the pitcher of beer to appear before engaging in serious conversation. While gulping water to wash down the salsa and chips, they talked aimlessly about who'd seen the most of the Academy Award nominees so far. Alma won hands down, it figured, a girl. It took about twenty minutes on that busy night for the waitress to show up with two pitchers and record the orders. Beltran watched her walk away while checking out the nearby tables. Everything looked kosher.

"I'm meeting Captain Tumult for lunch tomorrow in SF. Are any of you perchance going to be in the city tomorrow?"

They all shrugged or looked blank. Willy cupped his ear, as if he'd had trouble hearing. "Did you say tomorrow?"

"Yes, tomorrow," Beltran answered.

"No, sir, no SF for me tomorrow."

Beltran allowed a slight smirk. "Good, then there's no chance of anything unforeseen like one of you inadvertently walking into the same restaurant, a hint of recognition, Tumult, like any shady operator, gets antsy, wonders what's up, and who knows what happens next."

"Been watching too many CIA spy flicks?" Alma giggled.

"Maybe, maybe not." Beltran shrugged. "The main worry is how many of those flicks were based on someone like Tumult."

"Especially if he's the dastardly villain?"

"Right, Dennis, right now he's our hero, but in his line of work, the distinction between *dastardly* and *heroic* is fluid."

"What restaurant, Farallon?"

"Don't know, Alma. I'll call him when I get off BART." The next morning, Beltran caught a 10:30 AM train. He arrived at the Embarcadero Station at eleven fifteen, and after taking the escalator to the street level, he walked over to the entrance of the Hyatt and called Captain Tumult.

"Hi, I'm in front of the Boulevard, you know where…"

"Yeah, I know, I'm at the Hyatt. See you in about five."

They'd already met twice in the past three months, so there was no difficulty recognizing each other. They were ostensibly on the same side, but they greeted each other warily as if it was the first meeting of a CIA operative with an alleged KGB turncoat.

"Hi, Captain. You selected quite a trendy place."

"Hadn't thought of it that way, Beltran. Just figured it's on the corner and I'd be easy to spot." Tumult allowed a wan smile. "Checked out the area. There's a nice sushi place right around the corner."

Beltran looked dubious.

"It's also a full service Pan-Asian restaurant."

"Sold America." Beltran grinned.

They were both toying with their sakes when the waiter took their order.

Captain Tumult watched him walk away and looked around, seemingly appreciating the din of the noontime crowd. He leaned forward. "We're not getting close to Mellon. They're doing a great job of leaking false leads. My guys are running around like Keystone Cops. There are at least four condos, just in Manhattan's Upper East Side, where he owns a minimum of three floors. All the high-rises have basement garages where at least a quarter of the residents have those black tinted limos. He could be shopping daily at the local Grinaldi's, and we'd never know the difference."

"Well, do you need—"

"This isn't a plea for more money or men," Captain Tumult cut him off. "Just trying to explain the lack of progress."

Beltran frowned. "What about the Frommers?"

Tumult allowed a hint of a smile. "The Frommer dick who lives in the city enters all four of those buildings at least once a week. Of course, with the doormen, front desks, shit like that, we can't follow him right in. He knows it, we know it. He's toying with us, and it's getting tiring. Our guys make out like they're plumbers, cable guys, but they're ready for anything. A couple of our guys have been detained by the cops as potential burglars. You don't think the cops are in with the Mellon/Frommer gang?"

"The richest lawyer in the US, let alone New York—yeah, I'd think he'd have one or two cops in his hip pocket."

Tumult grinned. "Don't look so worried, I've handled tougher than this. We'll break through."

Beltran swigged his sake glass and took another sip of the virtually empty glass. "Speaking of 'tougher than this,' when you do catch up to him, no qualms about finishing him off? I mean, I've got every reason, but for you it's a profession, a business."

Tumult shrugged. "The cause is just. It's not like I'm targeting Mother Theresa, and the pay's great. What more can a workingman hope for?"

They both grinned as the waiter showed up with their courses.

They enjoyed about ten minutes of silence as they chowed down. Beltran used the silence to study the "ferocious" captain. He seemed "perfect" for his profession: about five foot ten, average weight, receding hairline, never considered for the cast of Sopranos. *Who would expect...?* he wondered what Tumult's frontline hit men looked like.

Tumult smiled and lit a cigar. "This bother you?"

"No, Captain, go right ahead."

Tumult leaned back. Watched the smoke head toward the ceiling.

A maître d' type approached. "Excuse me, sir, but under California ordinance, there's no smoking allowed inside the establishment."

Tumult grinned. "Sorry, sir, I should have thought of it. It's just that I do a lot of traveling and—"

"I understand, sir, we get a lot of out-of-staters, and so this happens often." He took an ashtray out of his pocket and put it on the table. Everyone laughed.

Tumult put out his cigar on the ashtray. "I never even noticed there wasn't an ashtray. You know the old adage, 'A fine meal is followed by a fine cigar.'"

It seemed to be the line the restaurant employee was waiting for. "We appreciate that, and for any inconvenience, can I order some after-dinner drinks on the house or an order of complimentary egg rolls?"

Beltran and Tumult looked at each other. "How about two Napoleon brandies?"

Tumult looked at Beltran, who shrugged. "Two brandies sound just fine."

"Coming right up. Sorry for the inconvenience."

They watched him walk off. "Whew, talk about customer relations. I bet you'll be back here often."

"Nah, Captain, the maître d', or whoever he was, is bound to remember me. Can't chance it."

The brandies arrived in a flash. They both took a sip. "Everything okay in Switzerland?"

Tumult looked around and assured no one was within earshot. "Looks good so far, Beltran. Withdrew 50K just for the exercise, went smooth. Looks like there's 3.4 mill in the account. Square with your figures?"

Beltran swigged some ice. "Sounds about right."

"Well, my expenses are hitting the fan. Got a dude setting himself up in Bern. He'll start making major withdrawals next week."

"That's what it's there for," Beltran replied.

Beltran perused the just-arrived check. "They didn't charge for the brandies." Beltran deposited four twenties over the bill and waved for the waiter. They both looked in the direction of the missing waiter. "Mind if I ask you something before we go?"

"Shoot."

Beltran smiled. "Your response is appropriate. How'd you get into all this Godfather/Sopranos/CIA-type BS?"

The waiter showed and scooped up the twenties. Beltran waved his hand. "Keep it."

"Thank you, sir. Hope you gentlemen visit us again."

They watched him walk away. "You in a rush? I got about ten minutes of nursing my brandy left."

Beltran eyed his watch. "A little past two. Just as long as I'm on the BART before rush hour."

"There's an outdoor eating area about a block away." He grinned. "It's not connected to any restaurant, so I can finish my cigar in peace."

As they exited the restaurant, a stone's throw from the Bay, they both seemed refreshed by the cool, crisp air. "Nice to get out, eh, Beltran? No matter how nice the dining experience."

They found an empty bench, and Tumult pulled out a fresh cigar. They watched the passing parade for a minute. "If you don't mind, Captain, it's obvious you don't have the look of someone in your profession. How did it start?"

Tumult smiled, leaned back on the bench, and watched some cigar smoke disappear into the atmosphere. "Well, I grew up in Brooklyn, Bensonhurst, not that far from where Mellon grew up, in Red Hook."

"Really?"

"Yeah, small world, ain't it? Can you believe that Mellon, raised in a hellhole like Red Hook, and then Elmhurst, and look at him now. America, you're beautiful." Tumult noticed the quizzical look on Beltran's face. "Oh right, you wanted to know about me. Well, I was an average middle-class kid looking forward to an accounting degree from Brooklyn College and, of course, having all the fun in the world that was possible for someone like me to have."

Beltran appeared to wince at the way that last sentence came out.

Tumult took another puff, seemingly mesmerized by the passing scenery. "So I meet this unbelievable babe at the on-campus snack shop, and I won't let go until I get her phone number. So she finally relents, and I'm, like, floating in heaven. She goes through the nice meeting you b.s. and waves goodbye. I'm in my reverie about thirty seconds when one of those know-it-all, obnoxious dicks comes over and says 'Ay, dude, you don't wanna go down that alley. She's connected.'"

"Connected?"

"Yeah, Beltran, connected. You know, like in the movies, the Mafia, organized crime. All that shit. So I go into the mind-your-own-fuckin' business, you dick, or I'll kick your can out to Canarsie."

"Canarsie?" Beltran suppressed a smile.

Tumult shrugged. "It's a part of Brooklyn, people used to talk that way. So he beats it, but I start wondering. She did have an Italian name. I call her that night, and we set something for Saturday night. Meanwhile, there she is again the next day lunchtime at the same snack shop." Tumult played with his cigar and took another puff. A frown creased his brow. He looked at Beltran. "You're my employer, paying me bigger bucks than I ever thought I'd see. So I owe you an explanation. But as we get into… into, ahh, nefarious events, I may have to pull my punches. After all, there are—"

"Don't sweat it, Captain," Beltran cut in. "It's all those contributors who are your boss. Not me. Some financiers arranged the Swiss crap, and all sorts of millionaires—maybe some with a B—just sent those big payments in there, and here we are."

"I appreciate the distinction, Beltran, so I got a lot of bosses. But you're the cause, and I'll bet there's hardly any altruism involved."

"You mean the donors?" He watched Tumult shake his head. "Well, most of them *are* selfish. They have a lot to lose. You produce, acquire wealth, here come those legal pirates ready to take it away."

"Through the courts?"

"Right, through the courts. Although quite a few contribute out of patriotic reasons. They don't want to see this country go down this path. Most of my volunteers fall into that category—virtually all lawyers, not happy with what's happening to their noble profession."

Beltran looked at his watch. "Well, past three. These old legs could use a seat."

Tumult grinned. "Got you covered. Rush hour's on its way. I'll let you know what's happening." He caught Beltran's frown. "Not to worry, it'll be unintelligible to an ordinary person. Plus, I'll supplement the e-mails with calls. We'll be moving in about a week."

"New York?"

"Nah, it's a dead end right now. We'll go for the soft underbelly. Maybe the Bay Area, y'know like Churchill attacking the Germans through the Balkans and then Italy." Tumult grinned. "Two wars, and both didn't make a difference. But a great concept."

Beltran rose and held out his hand. "Well, Winston, nice seeing you again."

Tumult watched Beltran head toward BART. "Hey, Beltran, I still owe you a finish to your question. Y'know, how non–Central Casting became a Soprano."

"Right, Captain, you didn't get far."

"Tell ya what." Tumult grinned as he lit a new cigar. "I'll e-mail you. It's easier that way. There's no way you'd turn on me. You're the hunted one, so you need me more than I need your paycheck. Still, there's things that maybe… Well, if I'm writing, I can see if there's anything I don't want out."

"Understandable," Beltran replied.

"Good, it'll be good to reminisce. Make me feel like a kid again. I'll be using one of my Asian accounts. Why don't you send me your best e-mail address to my moniker that begins CTUM@—"

"Yes, Captain, I have that information."

"Good, all I ask is that you don't share it with anyone and erase it as soon as you've read it. You look worried, Beltran, nothing to it. It's just that in this business, you can't be too careful. You'll love reading it as much as I'll love writing it."

"Book of the month?" Beltran grinned.

"Yeah, sort of a combo of *The Godfather* and *Casino Royale*."

"Can't wait. Any exotic Bond girls?"

"Oh, sure, but you'll have to wait for the movie." He waved to Beltran. "Hope you get a seat. We'll have another meet when I can report something tangible."

Beltran got a seat on the BART heading toward Richmond. He wondered what would be in the e-mail he'd receive from Tumult and the joking over the topic as they parted. Tears welled in his eyes— these volunteer kids, Tumult, any rapport, any connection to the human condition, any humor, any smiles, anything to keep him sane enough to gain retribution. He shut his eyes and wondered where his children were hiding. He received recorded e-mails periodically to assure him they were all right. For their safety, Beltran had agreed it best he didn't know where they were. There was always the danger of his capture and some "truth" serum or whatever. But they were okay; the last message had been received several weeks ago. And the senders were doing a good job of camouflaging the origins. He felt better and wiped the teardrops from his cheeks. He then thought of his dear departed Marie, silently wept, and once again swore revenge.

Several days later, Beltran received the e-mail.

> Hi, I'll make it short and sweet. You remember I told you about that "connected" babe. Well, I saw her four or five times over two weeks, meeting her near the college each time. I knew this was "movie" material when she wouldn't let me pick her up or drive her home.
>
> She kept putting me off about meeting her parents. A girl that age wouldn't be that afraid of her parents. No way. It had to be something else. Turned out it was the eldest of her three brothers. Must have been a question of keeping her in the "family," if you get my drift.
>
> Probably some big shot in the organization had his eye on her and the bro figured he'd move up if he kept her available, or something like that.
>
> The bro met me coming out of my house one day, went into his song and dance, and when he saw I wouldn't budge, he started making a fist while mouthing the penultimate "This is your last chance, BS." I, pardon the expression, beat

him to the punch and, as we said in Brooklyn, "kicked his ass." I went back upstairs and told my parents I had to "skip town," sort of told them what happened, and warned them to be careful, but not to worry. If the mob killed "innocent" parents, it would bring unwarranted "heat" and be bad for business.

I called the sweet babe and told her I was leaving for "everyone's" sake. She seemed to understand and told me to be careful. I drove down to Miami, got involved with some Cuban émigrés, and eventually did some "jobs" for them v. some Castro types, and when that was finished, they said I had a "flair" for this type of work. They connected me with a firm in South America protecting millionaires from all those kidnappings. After a few years, I became a honcho in one of those Blackwater-type companies. And like all Horatio Alger stories, I eventually founded my own company.

Talk to you soon,
The Captain

Beltran was fascinated by the e-mail. But any way someone becomes a Captain Tumult, there'd have to be a similar explanation. He wondered whatever happened to the babe and Tumult's parents—he also couldn't place the name Blackwater. Then it hit him: it was that special-ops company that made all those headlines in Iraq.

Captain Tumult

Tumult was enjoying the view of the Oakland Hills from his suite on the twenty-seventh floor of the Hyatt Embarcadero. He closed the curtain, sat down, and was reaching for the TV remote when the phone rang. "Yes, I'm expecting him. Let him on up." In what seemed like hardly two minutes later, Chase Wright was at the door. Tumult greeted him enthusiastically. "Enjoying the Bay Area?"

Chase smiled. "Oh, it's been a couple of weeks. I'm finding my bearings."

Tumult led him toward the window and drew the curtain. "Like the view?"

"Majestic." Chase grinned.

Tumult eyed Chase. Tall, blond, muscular, and in his late twenties, Chase appeared suitable for a lead in a surfer movie rather than employed as one of his operatives. Might not blend in with the scruffy protest types, but complications are part of the drill. "Okay, Chase, all set for your Berkeley debut?"

Chase shrugged. "I've boned up on my politico speak, so to speak, like cramming for a final. Ready to go, Captain."

"Good, Chase. Can I peek at your cheat sheet?"

"Sure, Captain." Chase handed Tumult a printed 8"×11" white sheet.

Tumult looked at the sheet for a moment. "Okay, Chase, you know Crosby's the main dude and that his crew hangs outside that Peet's on Vine near Shattuck."

Chase partially raised his hands as if to effect a Stop sign. "It's not my first operation, Captain, and Feliz has reviewed all the particulars with me twice."

Tumult's face showed some blush. "Yeah, well, you know Chase, unlike so many other walks of life, ours requires the ultimate in prep time."

Chase's eyes narrowed. "Piece of cake, Captain. Of course, when there's no set script..."

"I read you, Chase, all my operatives are chosen on cojones and ability. You're not lacking in both." Tumult admonished himself for being a pain in the butt to a valuable asset. *You turning into a Nervous Nellie in your middle age?*

Tumult called room service for a late breakfast, and they spent the next hour reviewing "parameters" of the game plan. "You're not at the Claremont?"

"Nah, Captain, fancy digs make me nervous. I'm in some dump off Shattuck. Here's the card if you can't, or don't want to, reach me on my cell."

Tumult walked Chase to the door. "Good luck. You know how and when to keep in touch?" He caught Chase's nod. "Good, I'll be down in about five minutes. A little stroll down to the Ferry Building. But we don't want to chance being seen together in the lobby. All those cameras. You never know."

Chase shrugged. "I understand, Captain. Talk to you soon."

Chase spent the weekend checking out the assigned area. He gazed appreciatively when passing the unpretentious Chez Panisse, the famed Alice Waters dining spot. He drove back to the motel, showered, and went to the nearest Berkeley BART Station, where he promised himself dinner at Tadich's seafood joint, followed by a night of hitting the spots in SOMA. On Monday in the AM, work begins.

Chase arrived at the corner of Peet's around half past ten Monday morning. It looked like the usual suspects were hanging around. The weather was frosty with that summery Bay Area chill Chase had gotten used to. Still, most of the dudes wore sandals without socks. Besides the lack of shoes, beat-up jeans, loose-fitting shirts, and beards pretty much summed up the look outside the coffee shop. As for the gals, Chase didn't pay attention to the clothing. They looked okay, but nothing he'd lose sleep over. He had two names: Phil Upshaw and Tom Crosby. Chase had seen their grainy photos in newspapers covering large demonstrations. He wasn't worried about recognizing them. The latest intel was that they'd forsaken the French Hotel and this was their new spot.

Once he was "in," they'd surface, unless they were out of town.

He walked in and took several minutes to lounge around the area featuring samples of the day's coffee. He poured some coffee into one of those tiny sample cups. "Is this good stuff?" he offered to a tall blonde standing next to him.

"You mean the Columbian?" She smiled.

"No, I mean Peet's. Never heard of it."

"You must be a stranger. Everyone in the Bay Area knows Peet's."

She was still smiling. Should he start something? Nah, it's important to start talking, to get in. But aside from her height and bare midriff, she seemed shabby and plain, nothing like what he'd seen in SOMA and North Beach. "Well, you're right, I am from out of town." He held out his hand. "Name's Carlton, Carlton Munson."

"I'm Rachel." She grinned. "Rachel Longley." She seemed reluctant to let go of his hand.

"I don't see the cream."

"Oh, it's over there." She pointed toward the window.

He held the tiny cup in his right hand. "Thanks, Rachel. See you around."

He watched her join a mixed bag of Berkeley types at a corner table. He quickly looked the other way before she peeked in his direction. A meeting of the eyes leading to a Jen Aniston sitcom scenario wasn't what he wanted right now. Meeting her was sufficient. He had to get "in" with this crowd, and fast. He scoured those inside Peet's and those pontificating outside, coffee cup in hand. No sign of Upshaw or Crosby. He joined a couple of dudes who, amazingly, were talking about the A's. He nonchalanted a few opinions and withdrew after emphasizing that he was from the East Coast and, therefore, wasn't aware enough to know when and if Eric Chavez would live up to his potential. Chase tried to turn the topic to oil company "greed," but the cats seemed obsessed with the state of the A's infield. "Nice chatting with you guys. Name's Munson, Carlton Munson." Well, he now had a couple of centers of influence. All the better when Crosby and Upshaw were present.

He spent Tuesday at a Starbucks with his laptop engrossed in MoveOn.Org and Daily Kos websites, absorbing all he could. On Wednesday, he arrived at Peet's slightly after ten and was delighted to see Upshaw and Crosby in conversation outside the store.

Good fucking luck, at least those SOBs weren't out of town or, worse, found a new playground. He was fourth in line at the counter, and the two or three minutes seemed like an eternity. When he was next up, he stole a peek at what the two were drinking. Looked like ordinary to-go cups of coffee. Yeah, revolutionaries wouldn't be caught dead with a Frappuccino. He ordered a "small" coffee in one of those Styrofoam cups and quickly added some half and half so his tongue wouldn't burn and "casually" strolled outside. He carefully took a sip through the small hole in the coffee lid and longingly looked for those dudes more obsessed with the A's infield than making revolution or undoing global warming.

Chase edged to within earshot of the Crosby-Upshaw conversation. The topic was illegal immigration or, as the pair described it, the nativistic oppression of "undocumented workers." *Thank you, MoveOn*, Chase mused. *That was conveniently topic A yesterday.* Chase approached them. "Hi, guys. Couldn't help overhearing your discussion."

They looked at him warily. Crosby added a hint of annoyance.

No sweat, Chase concluded. If this were the Bada Bing part of Joisey or any ghetto across the land, a hint of annoyance would be the least to expect when barging into a conversation. But this was Berkeley, where, theoretically, violence wouldn't even be a last resort. "I've been looking into this so-called illegal immigration issue, and

I think many Progressives, including the *Chron*, the *NY Times*, and *MoveOn*, have omitted a central point."

Upshaw appeared puzzled, but Crosby had one of these "Who is this blond surfer telling activists like us what's important in any issue, let alone the immigration issue?"

Chase held out his hand. "Oh, pardon the interruption, guys. Name's Carlton, Carlton Munson."

They both shook his hand but didn't offer their names. Their glares implied, "We're listening. Get on with it."

"Yes, well, here's the thing. First, let's get to the obvious. Everyone—well, at least 99 percent of Mexicans are Latinos, Hispanics, however you want to describe them."

"Which means?" Crosby retorted, as if he should be impressed by a "Who is buried in Grant's Tomb analogy."

"Which means," Chase smiled, "that you don't have any Texans, WASPs, Republicans, whatever, oppressing the people as we are so unfortunately aware in this potentially wonderful land of ours." Now he had them. Upshaw seemed enthused, and Crosby appeared to have lost his hostility.

"So here's the deal, guys. You've got a beautiful, scenic land full of natural resources, industrious people, more tourists and more petroleum per capita than even the USA. So why would so many millions be driven to the hardships of desert crossings and living in the shadows under corrupt and greedy employers?"

"Opportunity?" Upshaw asked.

"But that's the point. You know that there's massive unemployment in the USA because of the greedy Anglo-Saxon employers. So why would there still be so many more jobs here than in a Progressive society like Mexico?"

"You got me," Crosby sneered, returning to his earlier hostility.

"Halliburton," Chase boomed triumphantly. "You think Cheney and Halliburton are confining their activities to Iraq and the Middle East? No, sir, they're sucking the blood out of Pemex and the Mexican people."

"Pemex?"

Chase looked at Upshaw. "The nationalized Mexican oil company."

Upshaw winced. "But if it's nationalized?"

Chase sighed and looked at Crosby for support. Bingo, he got it.

"I think what he's trying to say, Phil, is that Pemex is nationalized in name only and that Halliburton is calling the shots and—"

"And the profits," Chase interrupted.

"Right." Crosby grinned. He offered his hand. "Name's Crosby, Tom Crosby."

Upshaw smiled. "I'm Phil, Phil Upshaw."

While shaking Upshaw's hand, Chase tried to minimize his slight smirk. He felt like grinning from ear to ear, but they might catch something, like he's putting them on. *You won, Chase, you're in. The simpletons fell for it.* "Hey, nice talking to you guys. Didn't mean to interrupt. I'm new in the area. Hope we can 'parlais' some more in the future." With that, Chase drifted back into Peet's.

Crosby watched Chase disappear. "What do you think, Phil?"

Phil sighed. "Dunno, Tom. The dude was way over the top. I mean, we all know about Cheney and Halliburton but that they control the Mexican oil and all that."

"Question is, does he think that because, as activists, we have talking points, we believe everything we say?"

Upshaw shrugged. "Maybe he figures we're the Progressives and he's trying to get in good, make friends and all that. He said he was new."

"Make friends? Phil, are you kidding? Did you see that guy? He walks down the street, and he's got ten foxy ladies climbing all over him."

"Yeah, Tom, perhaps. But maybe he's gay."

"What, that's like saying Britney Spears or Paris Hilton are into gals instead of guys."

"What do you mean, Tom?"

"I mean, this guy gets pussy too easily to—"

"Jesus, Tom, what about Rock Hudson and—"

"Phil, you're getting on my nerves, I can tell."

"So now you can tell by looking at someone. I'm sure our gay comrades would love hearing that one."

Crosby hurried to a receptacle and threw out his coffee cup. "Don't start, Phil, don't start. The dude's not gay. I don't know what his game is, but I got a feeling he'll be around again. Could turn out good. Fresh face, new ideas. He *is* over the top, but he knows how to, ahh, 'parlais.' Let's see what he's got on his plate."

They moved to the outside receptacle and discarded their cups. "See you later, Phil. Got a full plate this afternoon."

Phil waved. "Okay, Tom, see ya. Say, you think we should check this guy out, err, with Frommer?"

"If we get involved, Phil. No sign of that as of now. Later."

Chase showed every other day for the next two weeks. He invited Phil and Tom to lunch at that kosher-style deli nearby, explaining he was "stuck" in Berkeley on a consulting gig and had plenty of expense accounts and that it was on him. He also said his client had given him three A's tickets for a Tuesday against the Tigers and ask if they would they like to come? The pair didn't seem that enthused about baseball, but the "free" tickets carried the day. The A's were winning a laugher, and Chase did his best to maintain their interest by continuing the Berkeley speak of the day to these Berkeley activists.

A week later, he arranged cocktails at the Claremont with three stylish young ladies who were "leaving early next morning" to get back to their hometowns now that their consulting stints had ended. The ones that Phil and Tom were paired with had "boyfriends" back East but were so happy for the "pleasant" company on their last night in town. Chase was satisfied. He had whetted their appetite. He was now ready for his move.

When he got back to his rented car, he called Tumult. "Hi, Captain. Free to talk? Yeah, well, it went great, great. Those three babes came through with flying colors, if that phrase still applies. What? Yeah, the dudes were properly disappointed but bought the story that they had significant others back East. Yeah, give Feliz my cell number. No, no, Captain, I've met him several times. He's already e-mailed me her picture. What? Well, hard to tell how old the photo is. But even if it's been a while, she's one of those cute little senoritas that will always look young, well, until she starts looking old."

Chase heard Tumult's cackle. "No, Captain, I'm no Robin Williams, but what came out a joke is true. A lot of those cute little Asians and Hispanics continue to look young until... All right, Captain, I'll keep you up-to-date."

Chase e-mailed Feliz and arranged a meeting at Chase's motel room—not risking the outside chance that they'd be seen in a local restaurant by Crosby or any of his cohorts. They showed around noon on the following Tuesday. Chase was impressed by the babe. She had that sexy, sensuous smile and all the physical attributes that a ninety-pound package like that could bring to the table, or rather to the nearest available bed.

Conchita Rivera was her name, which, Chase figured, was probably the female Hispanic equivalent of John Smith or Tom Jones. Chase enjoyed the irony fixated on her "stage" name while he's using the Carlton Munson moniker.

They spent a good part of the hour-long meeting assuring Conchita that the plan was foolproof. Feliz would show before she had to "do it." Chase and Feliz ended the meeting discussing Conchita's English, or lack thereof. It was decided she knew enough, especially the key sexual and financial words. Chase and Feliz agreed that Feliz would prep her until she knew the plan inside out. Nothing complicated, but she had to be assured help would come in the nick of time.

Chase had exchanged cell phone numbers with both Tom and Phil, and he waited till nine that night to call Tom.

"Hi, Tom, busy day? Yeah, well, something just came up I'd like to tell you about over dinner tomorrow night. What? Good question, Tom. Not an ounce of business, strictly pleasure. The deli? Good. See ya around 7. Oh yeah, just one thing, Tom, don't mention this to Phil. It's for one guy, and I selected you. Nah, nah, Phil's a cool dude, but I can tell who's the honcho at that Peet's and the rest of Berkeley. Don't let it go to your head, Tom. See ya tomorrow."

Feliz had provided a sexy photo of Conchita, legs spread out over the side of a huge bed, making her look like a comely, if very young, pro. The picture was signed "Love, Estella."

Holy shit, mused Chase, *doesn't anyone use their real names now-adays?* Now there was another potential hitch to the plan. Chase quickly concluded that if he should slip up and call her Conchita, he'd say that was her nickname.

Chase waited until the waitress had taken their orders and brought the beers to pull out the photo of Conchita, a.k.a. Estella. "What do you think, Tom?"

Tom blushed, not sure how to answer. "She's nice, awful nice. Your girlfriend?"

"Well, let's just say I knew her in a biblical sense, once or twice. Believe it or not, now she's play for pay. It's a long story, and I sorta helped her out of some legal scrapes, and now we're kinda good friends. Ordinarily, she charges $1,000–$1,500 per session and—"

"For… for how long?" Crosby gasped.

"Oh, obviously, that's good for all night, if the John prefers it that way."

Crosby didn't seem to know what to say next.

"The point, Tom, is, I met her back East, but most of her family's in California, and she always said if I'm ever out here to look her up."

"Which means?"

"Which means, Tom, that although we're just friends now, she's always said she'd charge a lot less for any friends of mine, to repay me because I refused any payments for my time helping her with her legal problems."

Crosby unsuccessfully tried to hide a wide grin. "How much less?"

"About a hundred bucks, give or take. Of course, there'd have to be a tip for that kind of rate."

"Oh, oh, sure," Crosby croaked.

Chase took a sip of his beer. "So, Tom, are you on?"

"On?"

"Yeah, you want to spend a night with her? At one hundred dollars, I mean."

"Well, gee, Chase, I appreciate the offer and…"

"Look, Tom, being away from everything, I mean, I've met some bimbos and some real nice babes in Frisco, but it's all transient. You and Phil have filled a big void. I wanna pay you back. I'll find a way to thank Phil later."

Tom paused while the waitress deposited the overstuffed sandwiches. They nodded affirmatively when she asked, "Is everything all right?" Tom watched her walk away. His cheeks reflected a sudden blush. "Assuming you're not an undercover for the vice squad?"

Chase was surprised but recovered quickly. "Right." he grinned. "We're gonna spend a month going after someone with no indication of vice, and then when we get him, he's got the best case for entrapment in history."

Crosby stammered, "Err, I mean, what I meant was, I'm sort of a public figure, and you never know if—"

"Holy shit," Chase exploded, "you try and do a favor, and this is what—"

"No sweat, Carlton, I appreciate the offer. Count me in."

Chase noticed Crosby's anxiety. He decided to remain on offense. "Hey, Tom, what is Carlton shit? I thought I told you my friends call me Carly."

"Sure, Carly, and don't think I'm not appreciative."

"Don't sweat it, Tom. I'll call you in a few days." He pulled out his wallet and made sure he pulled out the visa card that said "Carlton Munson." He waved to the waitress for the check.

Chase called Crosby two days later. "You free Thursday night?"

"For the gal?"

"What else, Tom, what have we been discussing?"

"Like I said, Carly, I'm down. Where?"

"Probably the Claremont. I'll see if I can get a good corporate rate."

"She… she doesn't have her own place?"

"Well, in the peninsula, Tom. She's coming out here as a favor to me. So keep Thursday night open. I'll call to confirm."

They met in the hotel lobby at nine fifteen. It was scheduled for nine, but Tom had problems figuring out the parking. They shook hands, and Crosby apologized for being late. "No sweat," Chase responded. "Relax and have a great time. She's in room 415."

Crosby's face flushed. He pulled out some Trojans. "Err, not as good this way, but what with AIDS and who knows what else—"

"You didn't have to," Chase cut in. "She's got all that shit. She'll go anyway you want to." He patted Crosby on the shoulder. "There's the bank of elevators you want. Have a blast. Call me when you get a chance." Chase watched Crosby push the elevator button. He turned and walked out.

Crosby pushed 4, and the elevator door whooshed open in no time. He gulped and looked at the hallway directories. He found the corridor for 415. His heart started pounding. Why was he doing this? He had a steady and continual choice of new talent from the groupies. He got to 415. *Why, you MF? Because she's a babe, she's a pro, and I'm getting a bargain.* He rang the buzzer.

"Yes, who izz eet?"

The voice had a Hispanic inflection. He pictured her photo. A flush of desire overwhelmed him. "Err, Tom, friend of Carlton, ahh, Carly."

"Just a meenute."

She opened the door and looked great. Better than that damned photo. His dick exploded. He was afraid he'd shoot his wad before taking care of business. How embarrassing would that be?

"Hello, I'm Estella, and you're Tom?"

He nodded.

"Would you like a dreenk?" She smiled, pointing to the table near the curtains loaded with a large room-service type bucket of ice and what looked like a fifth of scotch, vodka, and tall bottles of tonic and club soda.

"Sure, Estella, why not?"

"Wheech one?" she almost screamed while giggling.

"Ahh, gin and tonic." He quickly realized there was only vodka and scotch on the table. He grinned sheepishly. "Err, I guess vodka and tonic." He wasn't sure about the drink. What the hell are they going to do? Talk? He wanted to get it over with. His dick had deflated, and for a panicky moment, he thought maybe he'd come and didn't realize it while listening to all her heavily accented yapping. He saw her tentatively preparing his drink and was about to assert his manhood and volunteer to pour the drinks himself but instead pointed to a closed door. "Is that the bathroom?" She nodded yes.

The second he got in, he lowered his trousers and felt all around. It was dry. He hoped she didn't hear his loud "Whew." He didn't have to go, so he spent a few minutes combing his hair and washing up. When he came out, she handed him the drink and said, "Now I'm goiiing een so I can get ready in preevate?"

She seemed to be asking for assistance, so he said "pryyyvate."

"Zanks." She giggled. "Pryyyvate, I'll be right back."

He sat on the side of the bed and started to undress. By the time he was down to his shorts, he noticed his pole was as erect as a pole. Now he couldn't wait. Just picturing her coming out of the bathroom… his heart was pounding. She came out, waved to him, and grabbed the drink she had prepared for herself. "Help mee relax." She giggled. "When we finish the dreenks, then…" She sat on the side of the bed near the phone. She took a sip and exclaimed, "Oh, I have messaaage? Do you care if…"

"Go right ahead," he whispered.

"Yes, 415, zank you very much." She looked at Tom and pointed to the big armchair. "You seeet? Finish dreeenk, then we begin. All right?" She asked him where he was from, what he did. He mumbled some innocuous replies and was getting antsy.

It'd been years since he paid, and as he recalled, they couldn't wait to get it over with. But maybe at this level…

The doorbell rang. She ran to the door. "Who eees eet?"

"Security," a voice boomed.

A look a panic enveloped her pretty features. "Oh, poleeece?"

Incredibly, instead of the usual "just a minute," she opened the door just wearing the flimsy top and bottoms of a typical Frederick's of Hollywood special-occasion undies. Crosby was flabbergasted, but it quickly got worse. A stocky, swarthy Hispanic-looking man in his midthirties entered and shouted "Estella!" and then what sounded like Spanish curse words of which he thought he made out the word "diablo."

Crosby was additionally amazed when the man addressed her in more than passable English. "Get out and wait for me in the lobby, whore from hell."

"But, Feleeez," she wailed, pointing to the closet.

Feliz looked at Crosby, who had just finished putting on his slacks. "You stay where you are," he hissed. While observing Crosby, Feliz dashed to the closet, picked out a blouse and skirt, threw the items into the bathroom while grabbing her by the arm and pushing her in. "I give you two minutes, you shame to the family. Wait for me downstairs."

Feliz walked between Crosby and the door that Crosby was too petrified to approach while Feliz looked in his direction. In no time, Estella had dressed, and while clutching her high-heeled shoes, she streaked past Feliz to the door. "VANAMOOSE!" he roared as her tiny frame rushed by him into the corridor. He closed the door and approached Crosby. "You know how old she is?"

"Say, look, ahh, what's your name?"

"Fuck you, fairy, that's my name. I said, you know how old she ees?"

"Look, mister, an acquaintance, Carly, err, Carlton, he arranged—"

"She's seventeen, man, seventeen. I don't know if to call the police or keeyl you myself."

Crosby could no longer stand. He was afraid to make it to the armchair, so he sat on the edge of the king-size bed. He wanted to confront Feliz. Feliz—that was the name he had heard, but his heart was pounding, his lips dry, and terror gripped him. He looked long-ingly at the phone that was on the other side of the bed. He tenta-tively pulled out his cell phone.

Feliz rushed toward him while Crosby rose from the bed. "Let me have that," Feliz sneered. Crosby instinctively pulled it back, like a child eager to hold on to a toy. They were both in the five foot eight height range, but there was no question. Feliz was burly and played the part of tough guy well. Crosby had managed to avert fights since junior high, and he was scared even then, even in the affluent envi-rons of Great Neck. Now, he'd settle for any charge, any judge's sentence—please, let a pig show up. Anything but being at the mercy of this Feliz. Alone in a hotel room.

"I said, let me have that phone."

"But why my phone?" Crosby wailed.

"Leesten, you cojoneless fuck. I'm not asking for your wallet, your money. Just give me that phone. I'll count to three."

Before Feliz could start counting with one, Crosby shoved the phone into Feliz's hand. "Can... can I go now?"

Feliz allowed a disdainful smirk. "After you give me your name and address."

"Why... why do you—"

"Because you have dishonored my family. I should keeyl you, but maybe we'll find a better, ah, arrangement. I ask for cell phone, so if you give bad informacion, we, err, I can track you down." He smirked. "Also, would anyone in your phone book want to hear the story of your violating a young senorita?"

Crosby, who had been ready to leave after giving up the phone, plopped down on the side of the bed again. His shaky legs no longer supported him. Now, he was on the wrong side of everything—shakedowns, blackmail, who knows what else, the Chanteuse, and so many others. Now he was in their shoes. His reverie broke when he saw Feliz approach the lamp table, where he grabbed a pen and hotel notepad.

He handed the paper and pen to Crosby. "You write," he barked. Feliz reacted to Crosby's blank stare. "Your name, address, and phone, *stupido*." He watched Crosby's shaky hand start to write. "Both phones, *stupido*, this phone and any plugged in home."

Crosby handed him the paper.

"All correct, senor? Don't forget I have this." Feliz waved the cell phone directly at Crosby's face. His smile gave way to a sneer. "And now, you can go."

CHASING FROMMER

Crosby stopped at the convenience shop of the hotel and grabbed a cold bottle of Coke. He looked longingly at the glass double doors leading to the outside while waiting to pay. His panic overtook him. He leaped to the front of the line, threw two dollar bills on the counter, and rushed out. As he bounded through the doors leading out, he worried that he'd hear, "Mister, two dollars isn't enough for the Coke." He hadn't wanted to stop for the Coke, but his throat was so parched that for the moment, hysteria over Feliz had to take second place to bodily needs. He got to his car in no time and quickly started the engine while keeping the Coke bottle between his knees. He didn't take the first gulp until he stopped behind the two cars ahead of him waiting to pay the attendant in the booth. The joy of that cold cola cascading down his windpipe was mitigated by the fear of Feliz appearing at his window. He looked warily around, and it took a horn blast from an impatient driver behind him to remind Crosby to move up to the pay booth.

When Crosby reached home, he instinctively checked to see if there were any phone messages. Gasping for air, he didn't recall whether his cell had his home number, but he was listed. You just had to call information. But did his cell have his name? Who pays attention to such things? Did that bitch—he'd already forgotten her name—remember his name? He put what remained of the Coke in the fridge and pulled out a can of Coors. He devoured it as if it was a shady oasis at the end of a dry, sandfilled desert. His heart pounding less, he pulled out another can and sat on the armchair.

He looked over the mess that was his living room. He shut his eyes. *Relax, dingbat, let's analyze this.* The first thing is to call Carly and get an explanation, but it was too late tonight. Fuck it again, Carly's number was on his cell. There's no written record. He didn't remember what motel Carly was at. The only thing, get a good night's sleep and show at Peet's in the AM. If this wasn't one of Carly's heavy consulting days, hopefully, he'd be there.

Crosby arrived at Peet's earlier than usual, hoping to be involved in conversation if and when Upshaw showed. He also didn't remember if he told Phil about the assignation, but in either event, he wasn't in the mood for Phil's usual BS. He considered it slumming, but he had no choice but to crowd into the group discussing the A's. *Discussion* wasn't appropriate terminology; it was more a screamfest between one dude and the rest as he shouted, "Can't you guys spell? I was talking about Haren, not Harden!" Crosby tried the look of pain evident on the faces of the targets of the vocal blast. But he had an additional reason to look perplexed and/or pained: he had no idea who the hell Haren and Harden were. Another two minutes, and he moved on. Facing Upshaw this AM was no worse than another moment not knowing what mental midgets were talking about.

He wandered back into Peet's and absentmindedly added chocolate powder to his lukewarm coffee. Half the tables were occupied by singles, and no one looked familiar.

He grabbed an A section of the *New York Times* and sat down. While perusing the editorial page, he heard, "Tom, glad you're here." It was Carly.

Tom blushed and fidgeted, like it was the first day of kindergarten. Suddenly, he rose. "Did you hear?"

Carly stopped him with a shush sign. "Let's get the hell out of here."

Crosby couldn't have agreed more. He reached the door with a bounce to his step way ahead of Carly. He couldn't wait to tell Carly about the weird happenings, about this Feliz character, about the cell phone. Apparently, Carly was aware of something. He handed

Crosby two fifty-dollar bills. "I'm really sorry, Tom, I'm at a loss to figure—"

"Who the hell is this Feliz?" Crosby cut in.

Carly looked around as if to say, "Do we want this crowd outside of Peet's and the rest of Berkeley to hear every detail?"

Crosby caught the drift. He clammed up.

"C'mon, Tom, let's walk over to my car. Let's talk about this. I'm so sorry."

Crosby followed Carly to the car so dutifully it reminded him of the first time he followed his mommy through the zoo. Like his mommy, Carly would solve this riddle, this dilemma, this Feliz thing.

They arrived at the rented silver-toned Lexus, and Carly held the passenger-side door open as if Crosby was a broad and his date. "Why don't I drive you to your pad so that we can have a drink or something and discuss this in privacy?"

"Sounds good, Carly, I'd be especially embarrassed if anyone I know overheard any of this shit. But gee, Carly, I'm walking distance, we don't have to—"

"You want me to walk back here? I still got work today. It's just that I heard what happened, and I figured I owed you."

Crosby nodded, got in, and directed Carly onto Shattuck. They drove two blocks when Crosby directed, "Hook a left at the light and start looking for parking." It apparently was the right time on a weekday, and spots were plentiful. They walked up one flight of the two-family house and entered Crosby's large two-bedroom pad.

"Pretty nice." Carly grinned. "Berkeley rents?"

"Rent controlled, the only way to live." Crosby headed toward the cluttered kitchen. He peeked into the fridge and looked at his watch. "Nearly eleven. Too early for a beer?"

"No way, Tom, it's never too early for a cold one."

"Coming right up. Want it in a glass?"

"C'mon, Tom," Carly answered, "just hand me the can. What am I, some broad at a bar?"

"Sorry for the slight, Carly." Crosby grinned as he plopped down on the sofa opposite Carly. They opened their beer cans virtually simultaneously, and Crosby chugalugged his beer like, well, like someone who had just escaped a hotel room with a dude named Feliz menacing him. "So what's it all about, Carly? I thought you knew that gal from way back."

Carly took a sip of beer and put the can on the lamp table next to his chair. His demeanor turned serious. Crosby caught Carly's frown. He didn't like it. It quickly got worse. Carly squeezed the can, looked at the label, and glared at Tom. "Coors Light? What the hell is this? I thought we all were Progressives around these parts."

Crosby, heart pounding, had been expecting some version of Feliz II based on Carly's scowl. *Now the joke—it was a joke, wasn't it?* Everything would be all right. That broke the ice. Now, with the tension lifted, Carly would set things straight, for sure. "Okay, Carly, you got me on that one." He grinned. "Just don't report me to the *Berkeley Gazette.*"

"Glad you enjoyed that, Tom." Carly looked impassive and toyed with the beer can.

Crosby started to fidget again. He'd been waiting for Carly to set things straight. *Nothing* was happening. Tom sensed something was wrong, but he went ahead. "So what gives with this Feliz, Carly, and the whole setup?"

Carly took another sip and squeezed the can some more. He seemed to look past Crosby as if he were daydreaming. Crosby started to rage inside. If this were one of his activist flunkies, he'd have already been all over the dude, screaming in his face. But there was something about Carly—his athletic build, his connection with Feliz, his appearance—out of nowhere, at Peet's. The way Carly was nonchalantly treating him now. There hadn't been a word uttered in about a minute. It seemed like an eternity. "I'm glad you're enjoying the Coors, Carly, but what about Feliz? What's going on?" Crosby tried not to have an edge in his voice, but it didn't work.

"What are you pissed, Tom? Holy dick, I'm the one who should be pissed. We grab your fucking cell phone and the listing for Frommer isn't valid? What kinda shit is this?"

Everyone's had the dream of being chased by Frankenstein— up the stairs, down the stairs... can't get *away*... But then there's the waking up, the smell of warm biscuits, the warmth of hearing

Mommy call out "Hurry, dear, you'll be late for school." Well, there were no warm biscuits, no Mommy, just the can of Coors and the suddenly malevolent Carly glowering directly at him. Carly's not gonna get him out of this. Carly *is* this. He tried to hide the panic no doubt evident in his face. Worse, he suddenly felt like his crap was going to come out liquid and right through his trousers. "I gotta hit the john."

"Go right ahead," Carly responded calmly, as if he were that police captain in *The Godfather*. "Hope you don't have a gun taped in there somewhere. But you people don't believe in guns or violence, ain't that right?"

Crosby had hurried into the bathroom and got to the can just in time. While he was going, despair overwhelmed him. What was he in for? Feliz and now Carly. How many more were involved, and how could he get out of it? He dreaded going back out there.

But Carly had mentioned a gun. How did he know Carly wouldn't be standing at the door and pump bullet after bullet at him? Or almost as bad, was Carly rummaging through his papers, his records? He couldn't think straight. He'd always been careful, remembering how he led his minions to bork anyone on the other side of the political fence. Then he remembered, it was just five minutes ago. *They want Frommer, not me.* He rushed back into the living room. Carly was sitting there, calmly enjoying another can.

"You don't mind, do you? I helped myself to another beer."

"No, err, no, I don't," Crosby responded.

"Okay, feeling better? Look, Tom, I could bring some boys up here within minutes to rummage through your shit to see if you've got a working number for that Frommer ahole, but—"

"No, Carly, I swear I—"

"Would you let me finish? Don't ever interrupt me again. Got it, you insignificant piece of shit?"

Seeing this side of Carly, even more menacing than Feliz, almost made Crosby wish for someone to put him out of his misery. He'd never been scared like this. It overwhelmed him. And it was getting worse by the moment. He started to breathe so heavily it became audible. He noticed Carly noticing. He thought he'd pass out, but no such luck.

"Look, Tom, we're not after you. As of now, you don't have to worry about any rough stuff. But if you're holding out on us… uhh, what's that trite expression, you'll wish you were never born? So I'll ask one more time, is there anything you know that can help us find—"

"A yoga teacher," Crosby blurted out, "a yoga teacher out past the tunnel. Walnut Creek, I think, some hotel or health club. Otherwise, he's dropped out of sight. Haven't heard from him in about six months. Now I guess I know why." His heart was pounding, his throat parched, and worse, there was Carly just sitting there, sneering.

Carly finally smiled. "Hey, you're not so dumb for a kooky Berkeley activist. You just bought yourself a two-week pass. We already checked that out. Did you say six months? That's what she said. He musta panicked all at once. Too bad about her. Some dish."

"You, you didn't—"

"Wash your dirty, faggoty mind with soap, you pathetic bean-bag. I meant that a luscious angel like that should even spend a minute with a dick like Frommer. You hinting we might have worked over that innocent beauty? Get one thing straight. We're the good guys."

They stared at each other. There seemed to be a meeting of the minds. "On the other hand, Tom, you're not an innocent beauty, are you? Nah, Tom, you're part of the whole Frommer crap that leads right up to Mellon, aren't you?"

"Mellon? I never—"

"Shut the fuck up. You had a real ball on the way up, didn't you? Now you'll find there ain't no free lunch, as they say in Joisey. We know a nothing like you would never get close to Mellon. But Frommer, we find him and—"

"But I swear—"

"Did I say 'don't ever interrupt'? A lot of ruined lives, a lot of people trying to effect justice. We got a lot of money, a lot of volunteers, our cause is just, or did I already mention that? No offense, Tom, but in the big picture, you're hapless. I got a little of that Stockholm syndrome. Know what I mean? Been around ya. We broke bread, so to speak. I don't want to see you get hurt. But we'll be back in a week or so. Better have something for us—or else… We're not the Senate hassled by Code Pink, or the DC government putting up with rowdies at your New Mobe. We got people who can hurt and enjoy hurting people bad. Oh, yeah, you already met Feliz."

Carly got up and headed toward the door. "See ya in about a week. Well, maybe not me, but someone'll pay you a visit. Oh, one more thing, you call the cops and you're dead, if you're lucky." He opened the door and looked back at Crosby. "Oh yeah, you don't buy another cell phone till we give the okay. We want to keep track of all your calls. It's easier on your landline. And no calls from any phone booth, even if they still exist. And don't try and get Phil to call the cops for you. First, you don't know if we've already gotten to him. There's no one you can trust. No Phil, no groupies, no one at Peet's."

"But what about my work? I can't just—"

"Oh yes, you can. You got the flu or some shit. Lie low, only a week or so. When you give us something, we'll give ya a pass. If you're empty-handed, your so-called work will be the last thing you'll be thinking about. Don't forget, have something for us in a week, or maybe we'll call on you in less than a week. See ya." With that, he was out the door.

Crosby looked at the door. He was calm. Still scared shitless, but calm. These sessions with Carly, preceded by that encounter with Feliz, had taken all the hysteria out of him. He had nothing left to give Mr. Fear, Mr. Panic, only the calm of an emotionally spent person. Now, all the grand plans, a national Progressive force, his own website, matching MoveOn and Daily Kos suddenly seemed far away, unimportant.

What was that about comfort food after 9/11? He went to the kitchen cabinet and looked for that box of dried mashed potatoes.

SLATS

Crosby tried a brandy that night. It had helped in the past when he thought he'd have trouble sleeping. Not this time. An hour went by, maybe two. The whole scenario kept swirling in his now-rabid mind. The worst part, although insignificant now, he'd been so turned on by that bimbo, a bargain at one hundred dollars, but nothing but tantalizing frustration came of it. Then back to the living hell—Feliz, the cell phone, Frommer, Carly, the deadline. His mind wandered to Carly's attempt at humor, before all hope and the roof fell in. He'd kidded about being reported to the *Berkeley Gazette*. *Gazette*, *Gazette*—why had he used that Dickens-era, old-fashioned expression? His mind was too active. He figured some more brandy. He opened the kitchen light and grabbed the bottle of Paul Masson he'd left near the sink. His eyes wandered to the headline in the *SF Chronicle* lying nearby. *Chronicle*, *Gazette*, two old-fashioned... Then it hit him: Frommer had boasted how he had it in for some reporter for some news rag called the *Gazette* something—*West Coast Gazette*? *California Gazette*? The guy had a catchy first name, something like Bats, but that wasn't it; he'd have remembered that. It wasn't much. But it was info. Might be enough to make Carly, Feliz, et al. happy and, more important, keep yours truly in one piece.

It was several days before Crosby had the nerve to go back to Peet's. He tried to remember Carly's "don't do" admonitions, but he didn't recall that included not showing at Peet's. He approached the entrance when Upshaw cried out, "Tom, where the hell you been?"

"Oh, hi, Phil."

"'Oh, hi'—is that all you got to say? I called you on your cell, it wasn't working, so I wondered—"

"My cell broke down, Phil. I'm trying to get it fixed. Why the hell didn't you call my land number?"

Upshaw blushed. "I don't have that number."

"Piss," Crosby sneered. "I thought I gave you—"

"Fuck you, Tom, you disappear while we got all this shit on the line and you cop an attitude 'cause I neglected to jot down your other number?"

"Jot down? All you had to do was enter it in your cell, you—"

"Can we cut this, Tom, and get on to business?"

"Fine." Crosby smiled. "Let's go in and find a seat." He was more relaxed now.

Being around Phil, with the usual banter—what a difference from the dread of the Feliz-Carly combo.

Turned out Phil was impatient about getting something together to meet and greet and, of course, harass, some nationwide tour that Shawn Hannity and Laura Ingraham, among others, were in the middle of. They were scheduled to appear in the Bay Area in about ten days, and Phil was concerned about mounting an appropriate protest to match the expected demonstrations by MoveOn, Kos, and other groups.

"Good cause, Phil, but it looks like you're going to handle this one on your own."

"What?"

"Hard of hearing, Phil? Let's just say I'm a little overwrought. Sort of need a rest. That's all."

Upshaw made one of those faces he was noted for. "A rest? What the fuck's going on here?"

"Shh, Phil, there's ladies present. Bad enough your language, but losing your cool to boot." Crosby grinned. "Got to learn to calm down, dude. It isn't the sixties anymore." He felt so good. Toying with the likes of Phil was such a blast compared to the recent travails.

He hadn't felt this good in years. Then his heart started pounding again. This Bats, or whatever, with the *Something Gazette*—what if it's not enough?

Crosby caught Upshaw glaring at him. "Hey, relax, Phil, the answer is final. I got to drop out for a while. I'll be back when—"

"Did someone get to you, you bastard?"

Now Crosby matched Upshaw glare for glare. But the hostility was mixed with a newfound fear. Did Phil know what had happened with Carly? "What the fuck are you suggesting, Phil?"

"What did you say about watching your language?" the suddenly grinning Upshaw asked. "I'm suggesting someone from the other side paid you off. How's it feel to be a damn Republican?"

Crosby laughed so hard. It was one of those tears-in-the-eyes laughing spasms that seemed to encapsulate all the dread of the past week with the sudden relief that Phil's not part of it. It took about a minute before Crosby could speak. "No, Phil, I'm not a Republican." He continued to wipe the tears from his eyes. "I'm... I'm not even a Demo—" Laughter overwhelmed him again. Crosby hugged his ribs as if it were a magic formula to stop the giggling. "No, Phil, I'm not a Democrat. After all, that evil Lieberman is or was a Democrat. I'm a Progressive, just like you, and—"

"Can I join in on the fun? Sounds like you guys are having a blast."

They looked up. It was a disheveled blonde. Nothing that would keep them up at night. But not bad, not bad. Crosby instantly had a hunch. Groupies usually latched on at demos or at planning for demonstrations. Carly had broken into their conversation. It was early in the week, but maybe, just maybe this was a similar deal. "You mean about that turncoat, Lieberman?"

"Well," she smiled, "I did hear the part about him. But I'm sure that, that wasn't that hilarious. He's just sad. What's with those people in Connecticut?"

She was also coming on like Carly, saying all the PC things. Crosby got up and grabbed a nearby chair. "Please, please sit down." He held out his hand. "I'm Tom, Tom Crosby. This here's Phil Upshaw."

She grinned and said "I'm Alma" while shaking their hands. She sipped what remained of her Frappuccino.

"Can… can we get you a refill on that Frap?"

"Oh, that's okay, guys," she answered. "I'll just toy with—"

"Don't be silly," Crosby countered. "What was that, a green tea Frap?" Crosby shot a devastating glare at Upshaw.

"Yes, it's a green tea Frap. I'll just—"

"Oh please, Alma." Upshaw had finally gotten the message. "What was that, a Grande?" Upshaw watched her nod. He got up and got on line.

There were five or six people in line ahead of Upshaw. Crosby figured he had at least five minutes. Alma had stolen a look at the line. She glanced at Crosby as if they were both on the same wavelength, happy that Upshaw's absence had given them…

"So, Alma, you new in Berkeley? I've never seen you around."

"We don't have much time, Tom." She almost giggled while briefly watching Upshaw waiting on line.

Crosby sighed. "Carly send you?"

"You're on the right track, Tom. Carlton, or Carly as you call him, just wants to make the point that we can pop up in any form at any time."

Tom drew a heavy breath. "I must say, this form is a lot more appealing than Carly or that Feliz."

"Well, Tom, I'll take that as a compliment. Got anything for us?"

"Racked my brain, Alma. Pass the word. All I could come up with was some guy named Bats or something like that. Works as a reporter for some paper called the *West Coast* or *California Gazette* or something like that."

Alma briefly looked at Upshaw; he was now second in line. Her expression turned serious. "If we don't finish, you know those benches near the French Hotel?"

"Yes, I do."

She issued a frozen smile. "I'll meet you there if Upshaw returns too soon. So what's this Bats connection to Frommer?"

Crosby felt his tension ease. Maybe if he gave her enough, this nightmare, this nightmare… "Well, apparently, Frommer knew this Bats well enough to hate him personally. But I sort of remember they were kind of working on the same issues, but obviously not on the same side of things."

She watched Upshaw waiting for the Frap. "I think we have enough. If not, maybe we can meet again for something else you might recall. How's about Thursday at ten at those benches? You free?"

He unwittingly went into the flirting mode. "Meet you at a bench anytime." She noticed Upshaw heading in their direction. "Well, based on Carlton, followed by Feliz, followed by me, none of us are sure just who will be there at ten in the morning, are we?"

Crosby blushed; all this James Bond / CIA shit was unending. He suddenly felt he had to take a crap again. "I'll expect anyone, obviously, based on the recent past."

"That's good." She smiled.

Upshaw plopped the gleaming green tea Frap in front of Alma. "Did I miss much?"

"Oh, thanks a lot, Phil. No, you didn't miss anything. We were just talking about the weather." There was a pause. "Well, I hate to eat and run, so to speak, but I'm running late. But since you guys are treating me," she glanced at her watch, "I can give you five minutes." She slowly and delicately licked the whipped cream off the end of the straw. She smiled inwardly at the effect this was having on her young male audience. "So, guys, how do we drum that dolt, Lieberman, out of the Democratic Party?"

The *Bats* and *Something Gazette* information had been forwarded to Captain Tumult. He called Chase. "Carlton, I mean Chase, even I'm getting confused. I think we got something on that *Bats Gazette* thing."

"So soon, Captain, after just two days?"

"We got some good googlers, Chase. And if we're right, it turned out to be pretty easy. I wanna give you your next assignment. Where are you staying? Did you clear out of Berkeley?"

"Instantly, Captain, I'm now in the refined atmosphere of Pacific Heights. A boutique hotel."

"Pacific Heights, boutique hotel. Wow, Chase, rough way to make a living, eh?"

"Yeah, Captain, rough terrain, but someone's got to do it."

Captain Tumult's tone turned serious. "So, Chase, can we meet this afternoon?"

"Sure, Captain. We don't even have to cloak-and-dagger an out-of-the-way restaurant. "There's a nice little park at Sacramento and Octavia. Nothing but teens and moms and their kids on a week-day afternoon. Not crowded. No one within earshot. Enter on Sacramento and grab the first bench you see. I'll bring my cell. We can call if perchance we don't see each other right off."

"Cool, Chase. I won't forget my phone. What time?"

Tumult spotted Chase right away. They found a convenient bench and watched the sporadic parade pass by. A stately blonde pushing a carriage was cooing her crying baby.

"Uhmm, Chase, do any good around here?"

"Comme ci, comme ca." Chase grinned.

They watched the passing scene until there was no passing scene. "Ever hear of the *Pacific Coast Gazette*, Chase?"

"No, Captain, although that *Gazette* thing rings a bell. Isn't that what Alma got out of that Crosby creep?"

"Right, Chase, and that so-called Bats turns out to be Slats Conners, who works for that paper."

"Shit, Captain, that means Crosby came through. Too bad, I was sort of hoping I'd have an excuse to go back and work over that blankety-blank."

Tumult frowned. "Just as well, Chase, like in *The Godfather*, save the physicality for those in the 'muscle end' of the equation. That certainly doesn't apply to a little America-hating creep like Crosby."

"But he did come through, Captain. I think Feliz scared the bejesus out of him."

Tumult chuckled. "That was quite a scam, Chase. Amazing how you pulled that off."

Chase knew it was time for "business." "So, Captain, is this Slats guy next on our radar?"

"Yeah, Chase. Trouble is, he's got to be handled differently than Crosby. It's not clear whether he's anti-Mellon, Frommer, Crosby like we are, but from what little we've read of his work, he's certainly no left-wing agitprop." He handed Chase a four-page dossier. "I'll summarize what's in there, Chase. He's spent most of the past year or so involved in coverage of Ann Sloan, the Chanteuse, and Josh Parker, who ended up killing her brother. Wow, talk about a Hollywood script."

"So I play it neutral with this Slats?"

Tumult's eyes narrowed. "Yeah, Chase, neutral, but even if you have to be more delicate than with the a-hole, Crosby, we still want something out of this Slats. Clear, Chase?"

Chase smiled. "A nuanced approach, Captain?"

"*Nuanced*—that's the word, Chase. I know you can do it."

***

Slats was in Leary's office. "Yeah, Slats, hot off the presses, as we used to say. Except it was picked up by our old standby, Lopat, on Google."

"About the missing scoundrel, Mellon?"

"None other, Slats. Seems he held a big press conference at some billionaire's private enclave in Aruba. The gist was 'Yo, guys, what's all this BS that I'm on the run? Sort of been lying low. Semiretired and all that. Taking time to smell the roses.' Lopat's probably got the full printout on your desk by now."

Slats grinned. "So he won't admit he's hiding/running for his life?"

"Yeah, Slats, but not fooling anyone. By the time the newsweeklies and the big papers jetted reporters down there, he was already gone."

"Sure, Tom, if he gave time to those big media types to get there, no doubt those gunning for him would join the crowd. Gee, Tom, I always wanted an all-expense-paid trip to Aruba."

"Get outta here, big spender, and come back with any ideas after you read Lopat's. stuff. And don't forget, Frommer and Mellon aren't just the hunted ones. They're also the hunters, they're gunning for that Beltran doc who's hiding somewhere."

"Yeah, right, we got a real donnybrook, Tom. Beltran after Mellon, Mellon after Beltran, Frommer pulling up the rear. Big money on both sides."

"Well, Slats," Tom grinned, "some twenty-first century, eh? We got Osama and his jihad, the Dems and 'impeach Bush and Cheney,' and the lawyers against the doctors et al. Go to it, Slats. Bye."

Yeah, right, easy for Leary to yap about the big scenario—jihad, impeachment, Mellon v. Beltran. Easy for you, Tom, sitting behind that big swivel chair overlooking the Pacific. Meantime, Slats was bored with the shrinking Mellon-Frommer trail. Plus, it was getting harder to find anything of interest regarding the Chanteuse's daily activities. In addition, without a big murder trial or other national attention, he felt he was not only a pathetic gossip hound but a two-bit one at that. And even worse, there hadn't been an excuse to compare notes with Spivey, thus giving him another shot at Ms. Rhea. He was hoping there wouldn't be another argument with Holly that night. Daydreaming in the heavy Robertson traffic, Slats suddenly decided to hang a right at the next light and stop at Wingdale's for a drink. It was a quarter to six, and the spot was pretty crowded with an enthusiastic after-work crowd. He tried not to notice any hotties giggling, flirting, and drinking up a storm. That crowd had already passed him by. *Settle for what ya got*—Slats, Holly, and maybe if the stars are aligned, the possibility of that delicious Rhea.

Slats found a quiet spot away from the bar and ordered a beer. The buzz assumed a background sound as Slats went deep in thought. The fact that Mellon had briefly surfaced made him wonder about Mellon's partner in crime, Frommer. It was no secret among the mavens in the media that Frommer was pulling a Mellon—running, hiding, and scared to death. It was impossible to get into his office. Security was as tight as Fort Knox or the HQ of Homeland Security. Scuttlebutt was that all the reporters, correspondents—print, radio, or TV—couldn't get within hailing distance. It was always "He's not available." Nothing more, nothing less. No one wanted to report that because the answer could always be "He's not hiding, just didn't have the time to talk to the likes of you or your paper." Combine that with the potential loss of business to a people-oriented business, and you had the possibility of an all-time lawsuit from the experts, the Mellon-Frommer team. So everyone stayed out of it, at least publicly. But the gossip and the rumors were rampant. Frommer was running for his life. For how long, no one knew. *One thing*, Slats thought as he poured what remained of his Budweiser into his glass, *even if Frommer was losing business due to all this, it didn't matter dollarwise.* He and his biggest client were in the same boat, and ol' Mellon, like King Midas, could never run out of money.

At work the next day, the morning seemed to fly by. That's the way it works when you can't seem to get going, no ideas are hitting, and that damn clock on the computer keeps announcing 10:00 AM, 10:45 AM, 11:15… *Shit*, concluded Slats, *pretty soon it'll be noon. What if Tom passes by and asks "What do ya got?"* He'd tried the usual googles, the usual websites, and some bloggers. No ideas, no idea what to do next.

Reminded him of that penultimate writer's block flick *Barton Fink. Well, at least I'm getting paid… Come to think of it, so was Barton Fink.* Slats was picturing that madman Hollywood mogul who employed Fink; he was so mesmerized he ignored the phone ringing on his desk.

"Ay, Slats, that's your extension."

"Oh, thanks, Dave, must have been in la-la land." He picked up the phone. "Hi, Slats here."

"Slats? Is this Slats Conners?"

"The one and only. Who's this?"

"Ahh, Munson, Carlton Munson."

"Yeah, Mr. Munson, what can I do for you?"

"Well, to get right to the point, Mr. Conners, I—"

"Please, Carlton, call me Slats."

"Okay, Slats, I'm representing someone interested in some aspects of the Josh Parker case. You know, all the interesting ramifications, Ann Sloan, and all that."

Slats was pissed. *I'm up against a wall, and I gotta help someone else?* "Like, what do you have in mind? I have some deadlines, and—"

"Oh, I wouldn't want to take any of your work time, Slats. How's about we meet at Spago's, like, right after work?"

"Spagos?" Slats almost shouted.

"Yeah, Slats, needless to say, it's on me. I got a big expense account, maybe tell whoever I saw a movie star when I get back home."

"Stag?" Slats blurted out.

"Well, Slats, I'm sure you've got a wife or significant other that you'd like to take to Spagos, but I think that would sorta get in the way of the 'business' aspect of our—"

"Oh, I understand that, Carlton. It's just that it'd be pretty hard to keep it from my old lady and there'd be hell to pay if—"

"Gotcha, Slats, how's about a compromise? Hardworking dudes like you—journalism and all that—must miss a lot of lunches, so ask your boss for some extra time since there'd probably be something in it for the *Gazette*. So we make it lunch at Spagos?"

Slats felt relieved, apprehensive, and greedy. A paid working lunch at Spagos—how could Tom object? Still, an anonymous caller, flush with money, interested in all that stuff… Slats felt he was starring in a movie and the audience was yelling, "Slats, dummy, can't you see what you're getting yourself into?" Nevertheless, he dived in. "Yeah, Carlton, that'll be fine. What day did you have in mind?"

Carlton had e-mailed his photograph to Slats, and when Slats arrived a little past one, he recognized Carlton at the bar to the left of the entrance to Spagos. They shook hands enthusiastically, Carlton grinning from ear to ear, Slats more hesitant.

"Read some of your stuff, Slats. Great meeting you. Been here before? First time for me. I feel like a kid at Disneyland. Maybe one of those babes I've seen in a darkened movie house will magically appear sitting next to me at lunch. You know, like those Woody Allen flicks where someone walks off the screen into real life." Carlton paused. "Oh, sorry, Slats, I'm not giving you a chance to get a word in edgewise. First time here?"

Slats had been eyeing the few ladies at the small bar; no one looked like they'd "walked off the screen" completing a horndog's sexual fantasy. *Probably a better shot at dinner*, he concluded. "No, err, Carlton, been here once before for my old lady's birthday."

"Well, Slats, the place sure lives up to its reputation. All that electricity and buzz. What's the name of that famous chef? Swedish or something?"

"Wolfgang Puck, German, I think."

"Yeah, Slats, that's it. A funny and famous name." Carlton looked at his watch. "Well, Slats, we're on for 1:30, the receptionist said they're running on time. What can I get you?"

"A Sam Adams, Carlton, thanks. Beer goes good with eye-talian food."

They were seated in fifteen minutes. Both men had glanced around the restaurant as they were led to their table. No celebs were in sight. They started out talking about Josh Parker, the Chanteuse, and the trials. Apparently, this Carlton guy had done his homework. Slats became uneasy. He sensed he was a batter being set up by a couple of soft outside pitches, to be followed by a high, hard one inside. Then it came. "Isn't the top end of all this some dude named Frommer answering to that billionaire on the run, uh, Mellon?"

Slats felt a jolt in his chest; he sensed he was blushing and had to answer correctly, fast. "Ahh, I'm sure you can see you rang a bell there, Carlton. Point is, coincidentally, our paper is trying to get up to speed on both those guys, sort of a follow-up to our earlier work."

"Please, Slats, call me Carly. Maybe it's no coincidence that—"

The waitress pulled up the cart. "And who had the ravioli?"

Carly buttered some bread as he watched her wheel the cart away. He dipped the bread in some olive oil and scooped up some of the marinara sauce on his plate and took a bite. "Like I started to say, Slats, it's no coincidence. We're sort of trying to find Frommer's trail."

"Who's 'we'?" Slats gasped. He looked at his plate of ravioli; his appetite was dissipating.

"Ah, you know, Slats, one of those internet entrepreneurs, like that Bloomberg guy—started his own blog, on the q.t., figures he'd make a big opening splash if he pulls off a Drudge with some info on that missing dude."

Slats suddenly felt woozy, glad he was sitting. "Gee, Carly, I'm not sure I follow. A guy opens a blog and wants it to be on the q.t.?"

"Well, Slats, he's always been a winner—wants to start off big, become famous, maybe have his own TV show, like Trump. If he starts a blog and everyone goes ho-hum? Well, it's like Steinbrenner if he ever ended up in third place."

"I guess I follow, Carly, but how do we, the *Gazette* and I, fit in? After all, it's obvious you've checked the archives, you know everything we know."

"Come now, Slats, I know a little about publishing. You come up with bits of information, then you wait for some more so that you can piece together a 'story.'"

"Well, that's probably true, Carly, but if your boss is the dynamo you described, he'd know that we wouldn't give out those tidbits before there is a story."

Carly toyed with some pasta hanging precariously on his fork. He took a bite and watched some of the pasta fall to his plate. "Maybe these type of restaurants ought to provide chopsticks, eh, Slats?"

Slats forced a smile.

"Well, Slats, let me get to the point. We're anxious to reach this guy, you know, scoop and all that. But no need to worry or to feel left out, Slats. Think of this as an employment opportunity. There's plenty of money there, obviously, you'd be amply rewarded."

Slats tried to hide his increasing anxiety. He'd barely bought the blogger cover. Now he suspected what it took him too long to suspect. Carly and whoever weren't after a scoop or a story about Frommer. They were after Frommer, the dude who was running/hiding for his life. "Thanks for the lunch, Carly, but I've got to get back to the office."

Carly's eyes narrowed. "Hate to sound like Mommy, Slats, but you've hardly touched your lunch. Besides, didn't you tell your boss this was a working lunch?"

Slats looked at his half-finished plate. His appetite had disappeared, and he was suddenly scared. This Carly looked so clean-cut, but if they were out to "whack" Frommer, was Carly the front man or the hit man? He was so anxious he didn't seem concerned about ploughing ahead. "Don't laugh, Carly, if that's your name. But we all know Frommer and Mellon are hiding for their lives. Amazing it took me this long to figure out you're not after a story, you're after the dude himself. I don't want to be a party to that."

Carly shoved his plate aside and gulped down some water. "I don't know what made you arrive at that conclusion, Slats. Look, I get paid handsomely, I don't deny that. But I'm a working stiff, not exactly white- or blue-collar. My experience, ah, expertise, wanders into other areas. But I'm still a working stiff. Got this boss paying me good money for me to complete an assignment. Now I know there's people out to get Mellon and Frommer, all this bad blood over this litigation shit. So what, my boss wants to reach him all the more, just for that reason. It's like when Paris Hilton's hot, before they go back to that Lindsay gal or whatever."

"Lohan?" Slats chimed in, happy to break the monologue.

"Right, Lohan." Carly grinned. "Almost forgot, you know all these scandals, working for a tattle sheet in Malibu, the Chanteuse, all that shit."

"The answer is still no." Slats was amazed at his coolness under potential fire. It was possible that any second, this so-called Carly would lose his cool, pull out a gat, and whack him right there in Spago's, just like Michael in that other eye-talian restaurant.

No more Holly, no more Rhea, no more anything… Slats repeated, "The answer is no. To be polite, I'll wait till you pay the bill."

Carly frowned, as if Slats was his son and had just announced he wouldn't do his homework. "Slats, Slats, what's the big deal? Look, we know your paper's about to be bought out. Who knows how and where you'll land? We got people here who won't forget a kind gesture. Lemme put it this way, I'm not asking you to give us anything that only you or your paper knows. What I'm asking is that you save us the time and legwork to find out something that's already out there but we don't know it yet. It's not in Google, but it's there. Can't you just do that?"

This fucker's good, Slats concluded. *Goes from being an all-American type to a menacing potential hit man, to a suave negotiator, a regular Joe College Henry Kissinger.* Slats decided, *What the hell.* There was something he knew that other reporters up in San Francisco knew...
"Well, there is something that's inside knowledge among scribes in the Bay Area. It's all I know."

Carly looked at Slats intently. "I'm all ears."

"It's up in Frisco, right near Baker Beach. You can google it or look it up in any city map."

"Baker Beach? What about it?"

"That's where he reportedly lives. Not on the beachfront, but there's a semiprivate enclave right near Baker called Sea Cliff, or something like that, quite exclusive. I think the likes of Robin Williams and other celebs live there."

"Good info, Slats. Sounds like the kind of area—"

"I think you got it, Carly. There's just one way to get in. I've been told Frommer, if it's him, has private dicks monitoring all traffic entering Sea Cliff heading in his direction. Of course, they know the plates and appearances of people who live in Frommer's vicinity, so in that small community, it's easy for them to kind of intercept outlanders and sort of—"

"Wouldn't someone complain—the capital of civil rights and all that?"

"Right on, Carly, but they're using some uniformed Pinkerton/Burns-type outfit. Supposedly keeping roving sightseers in line. Well, what person who lives in that kind of area would object to that?"

"I see." Carly frowned. "When it comes to making life easier for human rights celebs and elites, the concept of civil rights and right to know plays second fiddle to privacy and tranquility."

"I think you got it, Carly. And no one follows up 'cause it's not that important and not the Bash Bush and Halliburton news features that turn on the body politic up there."

"Meaning?"

Now Slats matched Carly in intensity. "Meaning that someone who's eager to find him doesn't work for and is restrained by a major paper and has the resources. Well, those uniformed guards aren't exactly Mafia or CIA types."

Carly waved for the waitress. "Check, please."

"Thanks for the lunch, Carly, I—"

"Come on, Slats. We should be thanking you. We got a lot more than expected. You'll definitely benefit from all this."

"Please, Carly, don't talk about money. I can't stand Frommer and what he's up to. So I helped you find him. But I'm still not sure I buy your story. We know he's the prey, and if you're the hunter and not representing a blogger, I won't be feeling good about it. Despicable as he is, I don't want to be a party to a killing or, should I say, a whacking."

Carly calmly looked at the check. "Umm, not too bad for a fancy dive." He got up. "I assume you drove here. Otherwise, I'll drive you back."

Slats felt an abyss at the pit of his stomach, as if he'd sold out to the Russkies during the Cold War. This fucking Carly, now that he had what he wanted, wasn't bothering to lie anymore. Slats felt his eyes moisten as they went out the door. He had a drink with that Frommer slime pit; they talked about broads… Now yours truly is gonna be instrumental in having the guy whacked? He cursed himself for his weakness.

THE REALTOR

Chase was exhilarated following the successful meeting with this Slats dude. He had planned to call Nancy, his latest pickup, that night, but the large portions at the lunch at Spagos, followed by the flight back from LAX, sort of obviated another large meal, and he did owe her a dinner. Bringing her up to the pad too often without some kind of outside entertainment might make her feel like a tramp. And he didn't want that. Probably check in with her tomorrow. Meantime, he did feel like letting off some steam, so he figured after a nap, walk down to Van Ness and catch the happy hour at Ruth Chris's.

He got there about six thirty and ordered an Anchor Steam; this West Coast brand was getting to him. He looked at the appetizer menu and considered the french onion soup, but he told the bartender he'd decide later. Meanwhile, in less than two minutes, he'd already ordered another beer. He looked around. Good buzz, a guy could get lucky here, but tonight didn't look too promising. He swiveled back around to face the bar and finished his first Anchor Steam. *Good thing I walked here*, he mused. *Didn't think I was that thirsty. Looks like a cab to go back up those hills in the condition I'll be in.* He felt so mellow he asked if that small corner table in the lounge was available. It was, and the waitress efficiently moved him there in a jiff. He was midway through his second Anchor Steam when he leaned back against the wall to reflect.

How many months had he been out here with Ol' Captain Tumult? The latest of many assignments with the good captain. A long ways from Bala Cynwyd in the Philly burbs where his first recorded ambition was to QB the Eagles to the Super Bowl. He barely made backup on his high school team, so his dreams turned elsewhere. After graduating from William and Mary, Chase thought consulting was the deal, but a one-year assignment with a regional firm soured him. Too many numbers and not enough excitement. To the disdain of his father, who had provided a pretty penny for the college tuition, he announced he was going to Cabo for about six months to hang with other expats while he "found" himself. Mom, who grew up in the seventies, had a more Progressive view and encouraged him to "explore," but she agreed he'd "only be supported for the six months." That made parting amicable, and in less than week, Chase was partying and enjoying the Cabo vibes as if he'd never even been to Philly.

Inevitably, by the fifth-month funds were getting low, and Chase started paying attention to the guys passing out the info on how to make money to extend their stays. A couple of rough characters at one of the gringo hangouts, Slims, occasionally bought rounds for fellow Americans. The two tough dudes were former SEALs who, for one reason or another, graduated or descended from their Navy careers to soldier-of-fortune wannabes. No one knew or dared ask what prompted their change of profession, and nobody seemed foolish enough to satisfy their curiosity. One night, downing some Coronas at Slims's, Chase met an American in his twenties who went by the first name of Adam.

They took turns buying rounds, and Chase found that they had a lot to talk about since they grew up ninety miles from each other. One day, they decided to have dinner before hitting the spots. Adam told him that he had hightailed it out of Brooklyn to escape some heat and had planned to return within three months. But cash was always an issue, and word passed quietly within the gringo community that these ex-SEALs were always looking for reliable and gutsy Americans for some "jobs" in South America. Adam apparently passed whatever "test" these former SEALs had in mind, and within a week, he was part of a team protecting some millionaire from a threatened kidnap in Medellín, Colombia. About ten Gs and expenses for two weeks' work. Adam was hooked. He took the name Captain Tumult, and after some fifteen months, he returned to the States with some fifty grand, a new attitude, and a new profession. The SEALs wished him luck as long as he confined his activities to North America. Chase had always dreamed of a nondesk-type profession and became one of Tumult's main associates. They returned to Philly on the same flight. After staying in Bala Cynwyd for about a week with Chase's happy and wary parents, Chase and Tumult went to Bensonhurst to see if there was any residue left over.

Inquiries were made. The gal in question was hitched, which didn't surprise Adam. She'd be in her twenties by now, and a mamma mia like that with the guys hanging 'round like bees around honey… well, Bensonhurst ain't exactly *Sex and the City* lifestyle for local beauties. Chase stayed around long enough to make sure the local toughs wouldn't gang up on the good captain—not that the good captain couldn't afford a penthouse on Fifth Avenue. Well, he'd still be visiting his mom and stuff. Well, he could move his mom anywhere. Maybe it was just a question of flexing some newfound muscle.

Chase and Adam walked into the storefront club of the local padrone, reviewed the happenings, and asked if anyone still had a wish to "discuss" any residual grievances. The local chief, seemingly impressed by the cool of the duo facing him, assured them it was all in the past. The host pulled out a bottle of Drambuie, which they all drank straight to seal the deal. Confident in Adam's safety, Chase went back to Philly, but not before being assured that he was now Captain Tumult's main man.

"Would you like another?" A waitress was smiling at him.

"Err, do you serve appetizers in the lounge?"

"We sure do."

"Good. I'll have the french union soup, some bread, and a carbonated Calistoga."

Chase watched her walk away. The lounge and bar were packed. *Did I nod off with all this going on? Well, maybe it was all those Anchor Steams. Good to reflect on the past*, he mused. Especially since he wasn't

231

sure how to follow up on what he'd learned from this Slats character earlier in the day.

All those beers and that soup had a calming effect on Chase, and he slept the sleep of a wide-eyed youngster, close to ten hours. His stomach was growling, and after a glass of OJ, he decided on breakfast. He drove down to Union Street and walked into one of those overpriced trendy breakfast nooks. It was midweek, so most of the talent would be at work. *Fine by me*, he concluded. After ham, eggs, and home fries, he'd pretend he was absorbed in the *Wall Street Journal* while sipping on coffee. But he wasn't gonna check the stocks or the featured articles. He was going to concentrate on figuring out how to find that Frommer SOB.

Chase looked at his Blackberry. He googled "Baker Beach," saw the nearby enclave called Sea Cliff, adjoining still another beach, China Beach. He roamed the Google Street Map. *Hmm, near the Presidio. How impressive can you get. What did Slats say, Robin Williams and the like? Wouldn't there be a realtor serving that kind of community?* He took Union to Van Ness and went north on Geary, hooking a right on Twenty-Fifth Avenue. After a block or two, he looked for parking. He spotted a sandwich place, ordered a shrimp salad on rye to go, and nursed a Coke while buttonholing other customers about "a good realtor servicing this area."

A gentlemanly senior with appropriate white hair offered, "Young man, everyone in these parts uses L. W. Perrin Associates. They've pretty much got this area locked up, for many years."

"Really? They're close to here?"

The senior responded, "Corner of Twenty-Seventh and Geary. Can't miss it."

"Thanks." Chase grinned. "Can… can I buy you a cup of coffee?"

"I'm fine," the man answered.

Chase got up. "Well, thanks again for the advice." With that, he was out the door.

When he got in his car, he took about ten minutes to figure out a cover story for every anticipated question. *Watch out, Frommer, I'm closing in.*

Chase took a right on Geary, passed Twenty-Sixth Avenue and quickly saw the Perrin Realtors sign at the next corner. He found a metered spot, good for only a half hour, and poured a bunch of quarters into the meter's slot. He passed the entrance several times to both catch the lay of the land and review his spiel. He walked in and took a seat, while the receptionist/greeter appeared occupied with another customer. Looking around, Chase spotted a tall brunette wearing black boots over Levi's and a white-and-black sweater/chemise, whatever. Chase was smitten.

The receptionist was ready for him. "Yes, do you wish to see an associate?"

Just saw one, and that's all she wrote, Chase mumbled to himself. "Ah, as a matter of fact, that young lady wearing that black-and-white outfit... I, err, met her recently, and she mentioned Perrin Realtors, and I am interested in this area, ahh, I'm relocating from back East."

The receptionist eyed him coldly, then a slight smirk creased her lips, which she seemed determined to quash. "Her name is Carrie, Carrie Woods. Just a moment, I'll call her."

Chase watched her pick up the phone. He was duly embarrassed and felt his face was flushed. This receptionist maintained a professional cool, but she had him covered, still another male animal turned to putty while entranced by a beautiful dame.

She arrived in no time and held out her hand. "Hi, I'm Carrie, Carrie Woods. You're new to the Bay Area?"

"Yes, I am. Bala Cynwyd outside of Philly. Name's Chase Wright."

She started leading him to the bull pen. Sometimes when beauty gets a close-up, it's not that beautiful anymore, but not in her case. All that BS about models and cheekbones—well, that was her, in spades. Plus, the best part, while still slim, she at least looked like she didn't skip meals like those rail-thin supermodels. They reached her cluttered desk. She pointed to a guest chair. "Please, Mr. Wright, have a seat." She started toying with her computer. What was she gonna do, google Chase Wright?

She suddenly looked right at him. Apparently, the computer thing was an "establish my credentials" feint. He felt the tension.

Listen, you horny bastard, I've got a profession here, trying to make a living. No fuckin' time for dickheads who follow me off the street just because I'm a 10 or most certainly a 9.

Her professional stance turned into a smile; she leaned back on her cushy swivel chair. "So, Mr. Wright, are you looking for a condo, a semidetached, or—"

He cut in, "I was sort of thinking Sea Cliff." He was sorry that he'd interrupted her but felt relieved that he seemed to have skated on the "I've met her" BS. No such luck.

"Rachel told me that we've met?"

"Rachel?"

"Yes, the receptionist."

Yes, in my dreams. He decided he was already in enough hot water without that kind of swarmy answer. He had nothing to lose with the truth. "In all honesty, Ms. Woods, Rachel was busy with someone, and I saw you pass by. Like any red-blooded American boy, I felt that the onerous, boring chore of looking for real estate could be, err, enhanced, ahh, with someone like you." She was about to reply. He held up his right hand, as if to shush her. "My mom always said honesty is the best policy. I hope you can never go wrong by being honest." Chase noticed a blush to her cheeks. She no doubt had spent a lifetime warding off unwanted advances, but apparently, his "honest" approach had thrown her for a loop.

"I must admit, you are a direct young man." Her demeanor turned serious. "We *are* here to do business, aren't we? You mentioned Sea Cliff?"

"Yes, I did. I like the privacy, and it's scenic. Those beaches and all that."

"You do realize, Mr. Wright, that you've selected one of the priciest enclaves in the nine-county Bay Area, which is also one of the priciest areas in the Nation."

"Huh?"

She giggled ever so slightly. "I'm sorry, it's been a while since I took English comp. What I meant was, the Bay Area is just about the least affordable real estate market in the Nation, and you've selected, aside from maybe Tiberon or Hillsborough, the toniest section in Northern California."

"But that's why I selected it." He feigned a sigh. "I can guess what's on your mind." He reached into his sports jacket. He pulled out a folded printout. "I think we're on the same wavelength." He handed her the sheet. "My social and other proprietary info has been blocked out, but this'll give you an idea of where I stand."

She started perusing the printout for Chase Wight, which was headed "Derrick Associates," regional discount brokers. Her eyes glazed over the money market holdings, the mutual funds, the stocks, Microsoft, Chevron, Starbucks.

"I don't want to bore you, Ms. Woods. Why don't you just skip to line 17?" Her eyes glanced down the page. "Hmm, over $1.2 million in the account. Impressive, but do you know what properties start with in Sea Cliff?"

"That sheet doesn't represent all my holdings. Also, I know that annual income is a major factor when we're at these levels." He shrugged. "When the time is right, I'll present my W-2s." Chase grinned. "After all, you've a right to know whether I can afford whatever listings are under consideration."

She leaned back on her chair and crossed her arms. "I think I've already established that Sea Cliff is la crème de la crème. May I pose a question?"

Chase grinned. "Shoot."

"Why not Pacific Heights or the Marina? Trendy areas near here providing more options at lower cost."

"Let me ask you a question. Does all this foreclosure stuff provide some bargains? I gotta believe that—"

"Interesting Bay Area stats, Mr. Wright," she cut in. "Prices have dropped precipitously in seven regional counties. Want to hear the exceptions?"

Chase blushed. "I got a feeling it's got something to do with Sea Cliff—n'est-ce pas?"

"C'est vraiment, Monsieur Wright. The two exceptions are Marin and San Francisco counties. Alors, Sea Cliff is, of course, in San Francisco County."

"Well, Ms. Woods, what we've just ascertained is that we both know a little French and the rich get richer."

"You've apparently done your homework, Mr. Wright. Marin and SF Counties have inherently been the highest priced in the area, and they invariably continue rising in value during housing downturns. Still interested in Sea Cliff?"

Is she seeing through me or what? Why would a young man on the loose bottle himself up in a staid enclave like Sea Cliff? Of course, if not for this hunt down Frommer gig, she'd be right as rain. Is this realtor con falling apart? Well, so what if it is? There are other realtors around and other 10s... "Obviously, I'm pondering this whole thing, Ms. Woods. Why don't you give me some printouts of what's available, two or three bedrooms in Sea Cliff, Pacific Heights, and the Marina. I'll think about it and get back to you."

"Sure." she smiled. "I'll get right on that. Would you care to wait, or shall I send it out to you?"

He sensed ad-Chase in the tiebreaker. She seemed to be taken aback. Our realtor beauty apparently sensed a little putdown, no doubt worrying how to terminate this little session. *Is he going to ask me out for a cup of coffee, whatever? Now it seemed unlikely. Now for the kill.*

He stifled a yawn. "Nah, that's okay, Ms. Woods." He took out a business card. "I've been staying at this hotel. You can send it out to me whenever." He got up and extended his hand. "Well, nice meeting you."

She looked at the card. "The Fillmore Hotel." It almost came out as a gasp. "You're... you're staying there indefinitely?"

Chase smiled and shrugged. "I've got a pretty generous employer." Now was the time to add, "And you must be familiar with that chic cocktail lounge adjoining the lobby. Care to join me for a cocktail?" She'd no doubt be expecting such a move from a horny, virile young man who's just met a 10—precisely the reason not to. "Well, nice meeting you. I look forward to receiving anything in the mail. I'll also do some checking of my own." He smiled and held out his hand. It rains, it pours, shake hands with a 10, and it's like there's a 10 marked on that lovely hand. He didn't want to think about the other possibilities. He waved as he walked away. "Be seeing you, and thanks."

There was a ticket on his windshield. *Right, I forgot, it was just a half hour.*

Should I ignore it? After all, a rented car. Nah, better pay. Remember that scene in Fargo, when they didn't have temporary tags on the new car? You never know what can screw you up.

Meanwhile, get Captain Tumult to get a couple of our guys, probably Durham and Bonds, in separate cars to see how much they can cruise around this Sea Cliff without getting hassled. At the same time, I'll be scouting the terrain under the cover of Miss Realtor Beauty. Plus, get Braverman, the accountant, to see if he and his dudes can crack SF or California realty sales records. Frommer probably didn't use his real name, but Braverman's sharp. He'll find the crack if it's there, assuming those records are available to the public.

29

MAJOR MELLON

William Mellon boarded a private jet for a flight to National. His son, Jack, had managed to get through all the security and succeeded in contacting him. Embarrassing as it was, Mellon just couldn't take the chance that his enemies had a bead on him and consequently would jump at the chance to take out Jack at the same time. So he planned to stay at the Key Bridge Marriott and meet Jack for dinner and, hopefully, more, like a visit from Jack's family. The thought of visiting Jack at his McClean home was too frightening. While there was no way they'd be able to follow his private jet, Mellon couldn't fathom even the 1 percent chance that they'd discover where Jack and his family lived.

It'd been close to two years since they saw each other, and apart from phone calls, e-mails, and live videos at Christmas or the grand-kid's birthdays, that had been the extent of contact with those he missed so much. He wondered what Jack wanted to see him about. He also wondered how long his game of cat and mouse would continue. Palmeiro and Frommer had done a brilliant job of moving him around, so far one step ahead of the so-called avengers, whoever they might be. Still, business and reputations were taking a pounding, snide remarks all around, and *ThisWeek* was reportedly in the process of doing another cover story on this whole shebang. Loss of sleep, no exercise, surreptitious vacations—everything was taking a toll. *Then there's this FISA thing that Burnitz and others are jumping into, feetfirst, while I'm indolent and hiding out of sight. The worst part, the only way·this could end satisfactorily is if our side gets this so-called Beltran, if that's the guy, before he gets me. I'd give anything or a good old summation to a trial jury.* He sighed. *How did it all come to this?*

He was driven to the Key Bridge Marriott by two Palmeiro-supplied bodyguards who had accompanied him on the flight. When they entered the hotel, Mellon quickly spotted the lounge and told the guards to go to a separate table. He said they'd meet at the car unless he left with his son. Mellon watched them select a table at the far end of the lounge. Apparently, there was no host station, so Mellon selected a small vacant table near the bar. He felt his heart pounding, worse than he could remember, about on par with the fear he felt some forty years earlier when he was about to address a jury for the first time. When the waitress approached, he ordered a double bourbon, rocks. While waiting, Mellon prepped himself on the first name of Jack's wife and the names of the children. He didn't want to add to the strained relationship with his son by fumbling for the names of those closest to him. It didn't take long for the bourbon to have its effect. The lounge appeared to turn into a beehive of buzz and activity, of which he felt more and more removed with each·swig of the liquor.

It seemed like five or ten minutes had gone by when he saw Jack striding directly toward him. He looked majestic—well over six feet tall, broad shoulders, and a plethora of campaign ribbons decorating his uniform. Mellon felt a gush all through his being.

As he strode to hug his son, he steeled himself to maintain composure. These infrequent meetings were tense enough without a show of unbridled emotion. "How are you, Jack? My, lemme look at you. Well, looks like there's no shortage of food at the Pentagon cafeteria."

"How are you, Dad?"

Mellon led Jack toward the table. "Jack, I... I, err, that didn't come out just right. What I meant was that you're looking great, great. Husky as usual, but certainly not fat or too heavy."

Jack sat down and smiled. "No problem, Dad. Sometimes small talk doesn't come out well. But I know what you meant."

The waitress came by, and they ordered their drinks. "Been a while, Jack. How are Linda, Doreen, and Jack Junior?"

"Everything's fine, Dad."

There was more small talk. Yes, Mom was still in Paris, and sister Arleen was still in LA at that fashion academy.

"Been to the new stadium to see the 'Skins?"

"Yeah, Dad, a couple of times."

The drinks had arrived. They paused to partake. Mellon toyed with the ice in his new bourbon as he watched his son take down about one-third of his vodka and tonic. "Anything special on your mind, Jack?"

Jack grinned. "The lawyer gets right to it, eh, Dad?"

Mellon shrugged. He sensed he'd be hearing something he didn't want to hear. "Well, not right to it, son, but obviously something's on your mind, or you wouldn't have—"

"You're right, Dad," Jack cut in. "It looks like your endeavors are the talk of Crystal City."

"Crystal City?"

"We're not all located within the confines of the Pentagon, Dad."

Mellon's heart started thumping as he caught Jack's glare. "Endeavors, you mean litigation?"

"*Litigation*'s a mild term for it."

Mellon felt his insides boiling. But this was Jack. He couldn't explode, as was his norm. "I'm sorry, I'm afraid I don't follow, son."

Jack made no effort to hide his glare. "It's that FISA stuff, Dad. It affects national security, or don't you notice or, for that matter, care?"

"Jack, so help me. I know I've pushed the envelope to unprecedented levels, accounting for my success, notoriety, whatever. But when it comes to the nation's security, I would never," Mellon's face turned red, "I'd never be a party to compromising our nation's security. Gosh, Jack, this has nothing to do with your being a major in the Army. Jack, I know where I came from. I know how much this country means to me. Son, your granddad was a black Irish immigrant. I grew up in the slums of Brooklyn. I owe everything to this wonderful country."

Jack's demeanor softened. "You guys are scaring the eyeballs out of the telephone companies. If any John Doe can sue for privacy, there goes our preemptive intel. You know that—"

"Jack, I swear on the Bible, I've had nothing to do with these suits."

"It's potentially affecting everything we're trying to do, Dad. No one's said anything, but I'd be in a pretty dumb intel outfit if virtually everyone didn't know I was your son and you're the main honcho in all these crazy lawsuits."

"I don't blame you or your associates for feeling the way you do. But, Jack, I wouldn't lie to you. This is one thing where I draw the line. Water's edge, so to speak. If I was still a young struggling lawyer, I'd never go against my country."

Jack frowned. "So how—"

"Oh, it's going on all right, Jack," Mellon cut in. "And I know who the culprits are. Would you believe me if I told you I was planning to confront the main asshole?"

Jack allowed a slight smile. "You're calling a fellow shark an asshole?"

"If the shoe fits, Jack, and it fits here. The name's Burnitz, out of Palo Alto. Been a burr on my side for a while. I'll appeal to his better half. Besides, Jack, how's the Army involved in this? What about the CIA, DIA, FBI?"

"There's a limit to what I'm prepared or, for that matter, allowed to talk about, Dad. But common sense would indicate that gathering information isn't just confined to the agencies you mentioned. After all, isn't sending out a patrol considered intelligence?"

"You know best, son. Sorry if I was out of line and made you uncomfortable."

"No sweat, Dad, Linda's already well trained. Since I got my new assignment, I no longer have to answer that inevitable 'What did you do in the office today, dear?' It all comes with the territory."

"Territory?"

"The territory of being a military wife, Dad. And Linda's been a real trouper. So what's your schedule like, Dad? Linda would love to have you over. It'd just be the three of us. The kids are on their own and out of town."

"That would be great, son. I'd love to catch up. But I'm sure you know what's been going on. I couldn't take the chance that anyone might follow us to McClean."

Jack smiled and looked toward the Palmeiro operatives. "Are those your bodyguards?"

"It's obvious you're a spook, Jack. Yes, they're with me."

"I'll meet you tomorrow, same time, same place. You can send your bodyguards to a strip club. Don't worry about anyone following us. There's a lot of spots to take evasive action between the Key Bridge Marriott and McClean."

Mellon spent most of the next day visiting Matt Thompson, who was recuperating in Bethesda. Thompson was coming along well enough so that they were able to set a tentative return date to the K Street office. Around three o'clock, Mellon's bodyguards drove him back to the hotel to await Jack, who planned to take several hours off and pick him up inside of four to beat the traffic to McClean and allow "quality" time with Linda before dinner. He told the Palmeiro operatives to have a ball if they so desired, but no brawls or police or their careers are over. He said they had to pick him up at seven sharp tomorrow since they planned a 9:00 AM flight back to New York.

Mellon had a continental breakfast at the hotel's breakfast nook the next morning. It was seven fifteen, and he planned to meet the Palmeiro boys at seven thirty for the short ride to Reagan National Airport. While chewing on an almond croissant, he was glowing over last night's McClean visit. Linda had been a real doll, and he felt that her typical Southern Virginia upbringing's "y'all make yourself at home, heah" had finally come fully to the fore. For years, Mellon had perceived an underlying tension under her Georgia Peach facade. As much as it hurt, it made sense. There'd been years of acrimony and tension over Jack's decision to pursue a military career instead of joining Mellon at the law firm. In hindsight, it might have been the typical rebellion of a youngster defying a career path outlined by his overachieving dad. Mellon had been a tyrant in those years and would brook no opposition, whether at home or at work. Now, it was wonderful that so much of all that was under the bridge and that Jack took him at his word over this FISA shit.

And the most important thing, his son was happy in his military career and his homelife. Mellon felt moist around the eyes.

"Mr. Mellon, we're ready." It was one of the bodyguards.

Mellon asked if they were checked out. They nodded. "Okay, let's blow this town."

Twenty minutes into the flight, Mellon put down the *Washington Post* and looked down at the lush terrain below. *No wonder they call it the Garden State*, he mused. He closed his eyes and began thinking of his next big "case"—his showdown with Burnitz over this FISA shit.

While Burnitz wasn't under the gun like he was, Mellon was aware that Burnitz also had to mind security. Any e-mail involving any Burnitz movements or meetings were to be sent to a "secure" site. Mellon found the site and wrote an e-mail requesting a meet.

Burnitz, rude as usual, responded, in effect, "I know you're on the run, not practicing, and under constant threats and duress. Why get me involved?"

"Because," responded Mellon, "we're still in the same fraternity, and you're giving our 'frat' a bad rep with your FISA crap."

"Oh, FISA—is that it? Well, I got news for you, Mr. Legal Eagle, I also want to discuss a four-letter word: *MTBE*."

"What the fuck's *MTBE*?"

"Mellon, you're embarrassing me and our profession. Send me your latest 'secure' cell number. Who's got the patience for all this e-mail crap?"

Burnitz called Mellon the next morning.

"Oh, hi, Derek, I've found out what *MTBE* is."

"Jolly good, old bean. Make that numero uno when we meet."

"Let's leave the agenda for the first plenary session, shall we? Your pad or my pad?"

"Very funny, Bill. But you should know I don't put out on a first date."

"But it's not a first date."

"Funny again, Mellon. Maybe you shoulda done stand-up instead of law."

"So that you can be number one instead of me?"

"Gee, Mellon, maybe you're not so funny after all. As for which pad, what with all those contracts on your head, I don't feel secure back East. C'mon out here. I'll send you an e-mail with the number of my security firm. It's still Palmeiro doing yours?"

Two days later, Mellon flew out to San Jose airport after deliberately "missing" his scheduled flight on United, just in case. Three first-class tickets, with the other two seats occupied by the same Palmeiro goons—again, just in case.

Among Burnitz's many hideaways was an out-of-the-way manse off a dead-end road in the secluded enclave of Pacific Grove.

"Not to worry," Burnitz had told Mellon, "any 'outsider' approaching my Grove digs would stand out like a sore thumb, and I've got security watching the approach when I'm there."

Burnitz's wife and daughter were due at eight for dinner after spending the afternoon in Carmel.

"You're welcome to stay for dinner, Bill. The chef was once with Alice Waters."

"Who's Alice Waters?"

Burnitz sighed. "Don't matter, Mellon. The point is, he's topflight."

"I don't know, I've got—"

"Your bodyguards are at the motel near the Aquarium in Monterey. They're not likely to starve."

"You win, Burnitz, I'll stay for dinner—on one condition."

Burnitz frowned. "What's that?"

"Can I call my food taster?"

Burnitz erupted in a loud guffaw. He rubbed his eyes and attempted to catch his breath. "'Call my food taster,' 'call my food taster...' Mellon, you're a card, a card. You shoulda been a stand-up!"

They retired to the study. An array of cold hors d'oeuvres, oysters, shrimp, fresh crab—all seafood oriented—were spread out on several tables. "What would you like to, uh, ease the tension, clear the cobwebs, whatever?"

Mellon eyed Burnitz coldly. "I'll have whatever you have."

"Comin' right up. You can't go wrong with vodka and tonic before dinner, right, Bill? You're not driving tonight, my guys'll drive you back. So how's a double suit you?"

Mellon delicately removed the lime twist from his drink while carefully biting into one of those shrimp kebabs. They watched each other, each wondering if one extra sip or gulp of the ol' vodka would make one of the barristers outmellow the other. Mellon broke the ice. "So before we get to FISA, what's all this about MTBE?"

Burnitz grinned warily. "Look, Bill, a lot of the junior league shysters are bustin' my balls over this MTBE shit."

"'How's that?'"

"They want to sue all the oil companies over the damage to the water supply, mostly in California, from the residue when they reformulate the gasoline using the additive."

"So? I thought lawsuits are your strong suit?"

Burnitz frowned. "Funny again, Bill, but I wouldn't feel right about these kinds of suits."

"Why not? Conscience never stopped you before."

"Nor you." Burnitz felt he had to dig back. "The point, Bill, is, in my view of things, my legacy, so to speak. There's one thing more important than conscience."

Mellon looked at him, as if to say, "Okay, I'll bite."

"What's the problem? You're going after deep pockets. What could be better?"

"Look, Bill, we're snakes, sharks, whatever. A drug company does twenty years' research, comes up with a drug that alleviates pain and suffering for millions of people. Then one or two get a headache or an itch, and we pounce. We advertise, promise penultimate riches to anyone coming forward with any BS, and—"

"I know the drill, Derek. Get to the point."

"The point is, I'd look like a fool. We can always get the right jury, the right verdict. But this thing has a catch."

"What's that?"

"The tree-hugging enviros forced the oil companies to add this MTBE. Now, those same idiots are leading the campaign to force the oil companies to pay up for the damage."

"C'mon, Derek, how's this different than any other—"

"The *difference* is that even if Sacramento, the enviros, the nets, the *Chronicle*, *LA* and *NY Times* all line up like the scared sheep that they are, *someone's* due to set the record straight. And I don't want to look like a dunce when a more reserved and unbiased history of these times is presented."

"Wow, Derek, I never realized you thought that far ahead."

"Well, now you know that I do. Can I count on you for a united front?"

"On that, Derek, but I want to make it clear—no support on the strike suits. I'm amazed that if you're worried about posterity, you'd lend your support to shysters suing 'cause the price of a stock dropped."

Burnitz grinned awkwardly. "Easy money, hard for those up-and-coming shysters to pass up. So I lend my support and get gravy off the top. What's the big deal?"

"But doesn't *that* embarrass you? Next thing you know, someone can sue if his horse doesn't win the Kentucky Derby."

"We've been through this before, Bill. A case can be made that the companies didn't have full fiduciary disclosure all that shit. At any rate, let's get back to today's agenda. Can I count on you on this MTBE shit?"

"Obviously, I've already said so, Derek, but you know for the immediate future, I've got to maintain a low, if not a no profile."

"Understood, but at least you won't be adding your prestige to those yahoos."

"You can count on that, Derek. Now are we ready for my four-letter word?"

Burnitz sighed. "Gee, Mom, do I *have* to brush my teeth?"

Smiling, Mellon shot back, "Yeah, and don't forget to clean behind the ears."

Burnitz shrugged. "You win, I'm ready for your four-letter word beginning with *F*."

"Okay, Derek, we've all made enough of the ol' *mahas* to last several lifetimes, so—"

"What the fuck is *mahas?*" Burnitz cut in.

Mellon grinned. "What we called money some fifty years ago, when I was growing up in the mean streets of Brooklyn."

Burnitz's eyes narrowed. "There's a reason you're using that term now?"

Mellon laughed. He got up and filled up another small plate with some crabmeat and red shrimp sauce. "You're on top of things, Derek. It definitely *has* meaning. When I was using words like *mahas* with my buddies in Red Hook, we all wanted new cars, beautiful dames—you know, the whole shmear."

"Another word you picked up in Brooklyn?"

"Oh yeah, lots of Jews in Brooklyn, you know."

"So you were up to the 'whole shmear.'" Burnitz showed a little annoyance.

Mellon glared. "Don't get ticked, Derek, you're the one that keeps interrupting."

Burnitz held his arms apart as if to say, "Okay, I'll listen."

"Well, even though we wanted the whole shmear, we had standards—maybe tough, rude ghetto standards, but standards."

"So you uncouth youths had standards. So?"

"So I'd like to get back to the days when we were animals but had ideals."

Burnitz rose to refresh his drink. "So I got a feeling I'm not gonna like what's coming next. You're perhaps suggesting that the likes of yours truly are exhibit A of this loss of ideals—"

"Give that man the Kewpie Doll prize," Mellon cut in while pointing to Burnitz as if he was a barker at a carnival. "But leave us not get into generalities where most of us big-time litigators are guilty as charged."

Burnitz downed a huge portion of his vodka tonic and bared his teeth with a leering, frozen smile. "Well, Mellon, it took a while, but we're finally getting to the heart of it."

Mellon nodded. "I don't care how much money you and your cronies are planning to rake in on this FISA shit. It's out, over with."

"Really?"

"Yeah, really."

"Gee, Mellon, not only don't I like your tone, would it be superfluous to remind you that as I recall, our two firms have never merged, leaving you with the upper hand, and therefore, *you are not in position to suggest, let alone demand, a course of action for some three hundred partners and countless associates and staff at Middleton & Burnitz.*"

"Got your goat, eh, Derek?" Mellon grinned. "You call it a demand? What if during the Cold War, I felt your firm was inadvertently, or advertently, giving confidential information to the enemy? If I told you to stop *that*, would it be a demand that's out of line?"

"Don't get philosophical with me, Mr. Brooklyn with the whole shmear, we're talking apples and oranges. We're representing the rights of litigants who feel their privacy has been violated and deserve their day in court."

"Cut it, Burnitz, save your legalese for hapless jurors or your left-wing sycophants in the media who—"

"*My sycophants?* What about you? Since when did you stop being a litigator and become Bush/Cheney?"

Mellon closed his lips and glared at Burnitz. "We're in an extra dimension here. It's like the Cold War, Vietnam, Korea—you're helping the damn enemy and putting Americans at risk."

"'Americans at risk'? Shove it, Mellon. When Homeland Security or the FBI tell me I'm aiding the enemy, then I'll cease. Meanwhile, full steam ahead."

"Damn you to hell, Burnitz, I—"

"I know what's fucking bothering you, Mellon. You're no different than me. *I know about your son—*"

"Don't bring him up." Mellon's lips quivered.

"Why not?" Burnitz smirked. "Does the great Mellon get his marching orders from a major now instead of the Chanteuse?"

Mellon rose and accidentally spilled his drink. "I told you to—"

"What's this? America's top two litigators are gonna come to blows? Bush, Cheney, Halliburton, and Limbaugh would really love that." Burnitz had also risen and was virtually nose to nose with Mellon.

Mellon looked up at the glowering Burnitz, who was about four inches taller than his six feet. His mind fleetingly returned to those brawling days in Red Hook when he took on all comers, but all those years, all that weight, all that flab—Burnitz looked like an oak and was about twenty years younger. Mellon caught himself. *You're a fuckin' billionaire lawyer, over sixty years old. What the hell are you thinking?* He backed up several steps, an unthinkable scenario back in Red Hook. He evinced an awkward grin. "On top of everything else, can you imagine, police, reporters, everyone would know where I am."

Burnitz watched Mellon intently. He sneered, "That was pretty close. I would have been subject to the realities of things, but who knows what would have happened if you had swung first? I was pretty worked up."

Mellon had sat down and was gulping down his drink. It'd been a long time since he needed liquor to steady his nerves and his voice. "So you won't budge?"

"Absolutely not." Burnitz scowled.

Mellon got up. "Looks like I won't be finding out just how good that chef is."

"Ow, gee, Bill, do you really have to go?"

"Should I call a cab, or can your chauffer drive me back to Monterey?"

Burnitz walked toward the oak-paneled door to the study. He opened it and yelled, "Karen, tell Timothy I'll be needing his services ASAP!"

A minute later, Karen, apparently a gofer with looks, walked in. "That'll be about ten minutes. Is that all right, Mr. Burnitz?"

Burnitz seemed to appreciate looking at the diminutive brunette assistant with high heels and a short skirt. "It's fine, Karen, we're not in *that* much of a rush."

Mellon watched Burnitz refresh his drink. "Since we've got a few minutes, Derek, what about your enviros' stunts outside of MTBE?"

"What the hell do you mean?"

"The price of gas is sky-high, affecting our economy and millions of hardworking people, plus giving aid and comfort to the backers of the terrorists who—"

"So?"

"So everything's supply or demand, both in terms of speculators and drilling and refining capacity."

"I'm lost, Mellon, what's all this got to do with—"

"They're suing every effort to drill, build refineries, go nuclear."

"I don't control those wackos, Mellon, and the whole shit doesn't affect my business so—"

"So you're worried about their stunts with MTBE but not about a serious energy shortage?"

"I told you, Mellon, the MTBE shit makes me look like a fool. Otherwise—"

"Otherwise, you don't give a shit?"

Burnitz bit his lips, his cheeks flushed. He glared at Mellon.

A tall young man walked in. "Hi, Mr. Burnitz, hope I didn't keep you waiting. Where to?"

Burnitz looked at the chauffeur immaculately spiffed in that gray uniform. He smiled. "It's not for me, Timothy. This here's William Mellon. He's staying near the Aquarium, and he's in a rush."

As Mellon got his jacket, Burnitz said, "I'll e-mail you what we agreed to today. Please confirm. You'll be using that encryption program?"

"Yeah, Derek, my software guru'll e-mail you to let you know which e-mail location has the latest encryption." Mellon wanted to deliver one last shot, but this Timothy looked like a nice kid. "I'm set, Timothy. Bye, Derek."

Burnitz added ice to his drink and grabbed some crabmeat and avocado on a rye cracker.

"Mr. Burnitz, your wife called to say she'll be about a half hour late."

"Fine, Karen, thanks. Anything else?"

"Well, as a matter of fact, Mr. Burnitz, I wasn't eavesdropping, but I think I overheard some acrimony amid some raised voices."

Burnitz smirked. "What gave you the main clue, what you just described or Mellon not staying for dinner?"

Karen blushed. "I guess both. If I may ask, was it something serious?"

"Nah, Karen, I think it' just the matter that Mellon's, uh, lost it, that's all."

Karen pointed her right index finger to her right temple. "Lost it?"

Burnitz shrugged. "No, Karen, not that way, although he may be getting close to that also. Rather, he's lost the fire in his belly. Perhaps it's passing the big 60, or maybe developing a new set if moral values or some combo thereof."

He looked at Karen for a response, but she seemed to be at a loss for words.

"Put it this way, Karen, he doesn't fit anymore. Can you imagine the CEO of Walmart not opening an outlet in, say, Sandusky, Ohio, 'cause some mom-and-pop stores might go under?"

"Well, when you put it that way—"

"There *is* no other way, Karen. I hired you before you passed your LSAT. Your grades, your demeanor—you appeared special. That's why I have you around me instead of climbing the normal ladder like the other new hires. I want you to see how we tick from the inside. I want you to *emulate* me."

He stared intently, focused on her eyes. "I wouldn't want to think my early appraisal of you was a mistake. You're being groomed to climb high, but if—"

"No problem, Mr. Burnitz, I'm not nearing the big 60, and I haven't 'lost' anything in the belly. I'm following you all the way." She smiled.

Burnitz smiled. "Good, Karen, and never hesitate to provide your input. Gonna join us for dinner or forsake us for that no-account boyfriend of yours?"

RAY WALKER

Steve Halpern was primed for another late-night prepping for that Fernandez presentation. It was barely five thirty, but Steve's stomach was already growling. He decided to go out to one of the ubiquitous Lee's Sandwich Shops around Market and Montgomery before the 6:00 PM closing. *A turkey sandwich with lettuce, tomato, avocado on a sourdough roll. Hmmm, that ought to last me through another couple of hours at the office,* he thought. *Deadline's approaching on that damn Fernandez account. Let's see, tonight's Monday. Probably another two or three sessions of unpaid OT for Frommer & Sons before resuming a normal existence by next week. No complaints,* Halpern figured, *I'm getting paid enough and probably just one step away from the real top accounts. Also, being between girlfriends right now, so there's no one to account to.*

Steve smirked at the dual use of the word *account* as he approached the Frommer Building. He looked at his watch. "Five past six," he muttered, "and security's still tight as a drum, plus all this fuckin' security money's coming out of the bottom line." *Did anyone say no pay raise or Christmas bonus this year? On the other hand, if they whack the boss, a lost bonus would be the least of it. It would probably mean the demise of Frommer & Sons.*

Steve got past the first Burns-type security guard after showing his Frommer picture ID. The second guard, the one just inside the door, wanted to see his driver's license in addition to his picture ID. No more going out for sandwiches after normal work hours, Steve vowed; security's too much of a bitch. Plus, since no deliverymen allowed in the building after five, he vowed to remember to pack his own snacks the next time he planned to put in several hours of OT.

He took the elevator to the third floor, entirely occupied by Frommer & Sons, where another gun-toting guard, hired directly by Frommer, smiled and waved him into the office. He reviewed what he had so far for Fernandez while beginning to attack that humongous sandwich. There wasn't much on the Fernandez firm in cyberspace, so Steve focused on Spivey and other competitors to anticipate their approach and how to at least match, if not beat, their expected proposal.

His train of thought was interrupted when he heard this black dude engaged in conversation with an elderly Hispanic-looking cleaning lady. The black guy was wearing a logo similar to that worn by the lady on her grayish-blue smock. Apparently, they'd agreed on a division of labor, and she left, presumably to clean another floor.

Steve was focused on the computer screen when he heard the sounds of cleaning get closer. He looked up. The black guy looked apologetic. "Sorry, sir, was I too noisy?"

Steve smiled. "Think nothing of it. You weren't that noisy, and even if you were, you got a job to do. I shouldn't even be here getting in your hair."

"I understand," the black guy grinned, "when you gotta have OT, no problem. Whoever said no to time and a half?"

Steve got up and extended his right hand. "Hi, I'm Steve. Sounds to me like you've had a nine-to-five existence, so all this isn't Greek to you."

The black guy nodded and shook Steve's hand. "I'm Ray, Ray Walker. Yeah, Steve, I used to work in an office. Came out West to try a little acting and screenwriting. So I'm doing this instead of waiting tables."

Steve laughed, grabbed an 8"×11" bond paper, and pointed it toward Ray. "An actor, eh? Too early to ask for your autograph? But why are you up here, Ray? Why not LA?"

Ray shrugged. "You're not the first to ask. Well, I got an uncle, in the Fillmore, used to play jazz. My mom finally stopped giving me a hard time when I agreed to let her brother keep an eye on me. Plus, I figured, since there's less Hollywood up here, there's less unemployed actors and writers competing with me."

"Sounds like good thinking, Ray. Any luck so far?"

"Well, I had a three-week run as an extra in the movie *Rent* and some work in *Milk*."

"Really? I never saw *Rent*, but I'll make an effort to see *Milk* just to look for you. But, uh, I can see why you have to supplement—err, that is, I hear the pay isn't much being an extra."

"You're right about that, Steve, but putting in twelve- to fourteen-hour shifts, with all those time-and-a-half and double-time rules, it can add up."

Steve smiled.

"Well, Steve, I don't want to take up too much of your OT time, but how does it feel to work for a firm that's so much in the news, and—"

"In the news?" Steve looked at Ray warily.

"Well, yes, I read the trades, and I've come across Frommer & Sons often in connection with PR for various showbiz types, and there's been some stories lately in the regular media about Mr. Frommer and—"

"Well, Ray," Steve cut in with an edge to his voice, "the paper's always looking for ways to fill all that space, you know, like all that Lohan and Spears coverage."

"Well, like I said, Steve, still sounds exciting to me." He started moving toward the other end of the office. "Good luck, and nice talking to you."

Steve tried a new website and printed out some promising information. As he got up to grab the printed data, he looked out toward where he'd last seen Ray cleaning. Ray was even farther away now. Steve sat down and reviewed the information. Reflexively, he turned toward Ray again, and he was gone, presumably to another floor. *Interesting guy,* Steve thought, *not the elocution and background you'd ordinarily get from the after-hours cleaners. Well, guess they're not all illegal immigrants.*

Ray had gone up to the fourth floor and found Amelia there. She told him to do the fifth and seventh floors while she finished the fourth and then the sixth and they'd finish the top floor together before calling it a night. Ray, while nodding profusely, smirked inside. He was actually beginning to see through the fog of her thick Spanish accent. They were finished at eight thirty, and Amelia said her husband was coming by and asked if he could use a ride.

"Nah," he answered, "I'll be talking Muni home, but thanks anyway." He left her waiting in front of the building and started walking slowly toward the multilevel garage at Fourth and Howard. He occasionally sneaked a glance behind him and stopped into several shops along the way. The chances of this Steve being sufficiently suspicious to follow him were remote, but in this business…

He walked up to the second level and easily found his late-model Lexus. As he waited for change from the twenty-dollar bill he gave the attendant, Ray sighed wearily. Just wouldn't do for this Steve character to catch an office cleaner tooling around in a thirty-grand vehicle. He zoomed out to catch the jazz at Sweetwaters in Mill Valley, making good time in the virtually nonexistent 9:30 PM traffic. He got there just outside of ten and reached into the trunk for a change into "cooler" threads.

The next morning, he dialed Captain Tumult. "Hi, Captain, this a good time?"

"Perfect, Ray. Any breakthroughs?"

"Maybe, Captain. I finally got to speak to someone who was still working at six thirty. The question, whatever kept him overtime, who knows how long that project will last."

"Yeah, Ray, it's a long shot, but remember, we don't want you to press. It's better you don't accomplish a thing than to make anyone there suspicious. Meanwhile, how are you doing with the other work—the cleaning?"

"Well, Captain, you asking work-wise or ego-wise?"

Captain Tumult chuckled. "Now that you mention it, Ray, both."

"Well, Captain, ego-wise, no problem. It's better undercover than dealing and a lot safer. As for the work, it's not exactly rocket science."

"Good, Ray. Don't pull any stunts like going to a lounge or something while you're on duty. They inevitably are gonna have supervisors making unanticipated visits. We worked too hard to get you the job. We'd lose too much time if we had to replace you."

"I got you covered, Captain, no high jinks. How long do you think the cleaning company will keep me in that building?"

"As long as it takes. Our contact's not edgy, we're paying him good. He'll continue to cooperate."

"You the boss, Captain. I'll call you the next time I have something."

Captain Tumult looked at the phone. He wondered when the breakthrough would occur. *You had Chase contacting that realtor to be able to wander around that Sea Cliff area.* Ray just made his first contact within Frommer's office. There wasn't yet an excuse to send a team of computer geeks to hack into Frommer's system. If Ray can find a time where there are no employees there and no chance of a coworker seeing him at a computer... Even then, there's the possibility that the ever-vigilant security could pop up at any time. Ray felt it would take about ten minutes to fuck up the system enough to require a repair team. Then one of our guys could hack into their system. Not that Frommer would volunteer his residence address in an e-mail. Plus, those MFs probably used encryption to keep outsiders, err, outside.

Tumult sighed. This gumshoe aspect looked too time-consuming. All the plants in realty boards and tax offices in SF and Sacto had so far come up empty. Several computer systems had been penetrated, but there was only that condo near the ballpark, which he vacated when the "troubles" started. All bills, taxes, and mail were subsequently forwarded to his "accountant" on Van Ness. Several walk-in attempts at a job there were laughed off. "We have a special referral service when we need someone," it was explained. Aside from that vacated condo, there was no hint of Frommer. Either the fucker's using an alias, or more likely, he's renting. Still, the State sends out checks once a year to renters, which means get to someone in that office? *Probably not*, he figured. *We can't get a plant in every office, and if he's using another name, what good would it do?* Tumult felt a chill. Was this "soft underbelly" thing a mistake? Focus again on Mellon or Frommer's brother in New York? Well, Frommer's brother wasn't important enough, and while in plain sight, his heavy security would result in a bloodbath even if an opportunity arose. As for Mellon, if Frommer can disappear like a groundhog with 1 percent of Mellon's resources, what chance was there of getting the big man?

Obviously, Frommer's and Mellon's businesses were hurting by all this, but so was our cause. How much longer would Beltran and his supporters continue to provide the big bucks?

Ray Walker was biting into his second slice of the veggie pizza he'd gotten at Zachary's, located near his pad in Rockridge. The Warriors were on the tube, and Ray shook his fist at the TV due to the team's lack of D. He chugalugged some Bud from the can, which sort of mellowed him, especially when the home team hit a trey. He grabbed another slice when he heard his cell. "Yeah, Ray here."

"Hi, Ray, it's Chase."

"Chase, my main man from Philly. What's up? Hey, this better not be business. I'm chillin' with some of the best pizza in the world, some Budweiser, and the aggravating Warriors on the tube."

"Whoa, Ray, sounds like some bad timing on my part. I finally got around to take up your offer to do the town around SOMA."

"Well, you got me covered, Chase. I'm gonna hang loose tonight. But one of these days, Chase, when our schedules allow, we'll blast a hole in the big SF." He heard Chase laugh. "Oh yeah, Chase, pardon my double entendre, the only time I'm half funny is when it's accidental."

"It's okay, Ray. Before I let you get back to the game, I hear you struck a little pay dirt."

"Me? Depends on your definition of *pay dirt*. I'm cleaning an office at night while you hit it with a top real estate babe. Yo, Chase, can we check with the captain to change assignments?"

Chase chuckled. "He's the boss, Ray, we gotta follow orders. It's like when the umpire makes a bad call on the home team. You can yell all you want, but it won't change a thing. But next time, it could be your team that gets the good call and—"

"Enough, Chase, rest on your laurels, the umpire called it your way, and you got the babe while I'm dusting off one office after another."

"Okay, Ray, talk to you next week."

"Yeah, Chase, either next Tuesday or Wednesday, bring all your credit cards and your best threads."

Chase closed his cell and put on the TV. It was past the *Nightly Network News*. Why do those idiots all broadcast at the same time, five thirty? He turned the remote to TCM. There's always a movie on. He fixed himself a Bloody Mary and started watching *12 Angry Men*.

Tomorrow I'll call Ms. Woods. We may not do the town, but we'll at least be doing Sea Cliff.

He called her at half past ten the next morning. She was with a client, he was told.

"Can Ms. Woods call you back?"

"Yes, she has my number," he responded and put the cell away. *Here we go*, he sighed. *Yeah, they all want commissions, but a babe like that will never hurt for money, and why should she put up with a panting a-hole who's making a fool out of himself?* This was no Woody Allen neurotic fit. Broads had never been a problem, but this was important not because she's such a stunner but 'cause she's the best conduit so far to reaching that Frommer SOB. He looked in the fridge to see if there was enough to eat dinner at home before going out. There was a little calamari salad left; otherwise, everything was frozen. Maybe the Marina Safeway—that joint's always jumpin', even if most of the gals were a little too young. Chase heard the ring on his cell phone. "Hi, Chase here."

"Mr. Wright? This is Carrie, Carrie Woods. I gather you've looked at my printouts?"

"Yes, Ms. Woods, I especially liked that duplex on Ridgeway Court, near Twenty-Seventh Avenue."

"Incredibly good choice at 1.5. The owner bought it as a can't-miss investment, Mr. Wright. Now he's in a panic with the subprime mess. He originally wanted 2.1, and that was only a month ago. I bet we can move him even lower."

Chase was ticked over this "Ms. Woods / Mr. Wright" dance, but it was too much of a risk to graduate to the Carrie-Chase verbiage. Might sound like a come-on and scare her off. "So how does your schedule look, Ms. Woods? I'd sure like to see the place."

"Well, I can see you almost anytime tomorrow," she almost chirped.

"That's good, Ms. Woods. How's about two-ish—I, uh, got a consulting gig in the Embarcadero."

"Yes, you have my cell, right? I may not be in the office when you call."

"No problem, Ms. Woods, your cell and pager are all on your card."

"Good, see you tomorrow. I'm sure you'll love it."

He called her around one the next day saying he was running a little late. "Would two thirty be okay?"

"Fine, Mr. Wright. Did you map out Twenty-Seventh and Ridgeway? Good, I'll meet you there."

Chase felt like crap 'cause he'd lied. But it had to look like he was busy consulting, and what's more normal than running late? When he turned onto Ridgeway Court, he quickly saw the Perrin Realtors sign and some banners to boot. *Well, I'm playacting*, he mused, *but that Woods hottie and that Perrin outfit* are *out to make a sale.* Again, he felt like shit. He wondered why all this conniving never bothered him before. Maybe it was that Carrie Woods. He felt his heart pounding and movement in his groin area. *Holy shit, am I falling for this dame?* His heart leapt when he spotted her. She was wearing one of those tacky green blazers, but that didn't change a thing; she still looked great. They shook hands.

"Hope you didn't have too long a wait."

She laughed. "Part of the job, Mr. Wright." She held out some forms and her cell phone. "Always something to do. She pointed to the duplex entrance. "Well, shall we?"

"Sure, Ms. Woods, can't wait to see it."

The place was in mint condition. Obviously, the sucker specu-lator had left it as good as new. Chase dutifully checked out the closet space, the fridge, washer-dryer, on and on. He had to look interested enough to keep this charade going. "Is the owner still asking 1.5?"

She grinned. "Just be the godfather."

"Godfather?"

Her dazzling smile was now triumphant. "Make him an offer he can't refuse."

Chase's face turned red. He was slow on the uptake on this "can't refuse" thing.

He sensed she noticed the blush on his face, and his wong was virtually bursting in response to that smile, that face, and the realiza-tion that he could follow up his desires since they were in an empty place. "Err, I guess you can e-mail me the latest comparables, but I'd guess I'll be offering around $950,000."

Her demeanor turned serious. "If you like, we have an agency that, uh, sort of checks on the overall financial status of sellers. We absorb most of the cost, but we add $500 to the client's commission cost."

Chase caught on right away but decided to affect a puzzled look.

"Well," she smiled, "if we ascertain the seller's really in trouble and desperate, we can lowball and—"

"Cost yourself some commission? Sorry for interrupting."

"Oh, that's all right, Chase. Can I call you Chase?"

"Sure, Carrie, but again, why would you want to cost yourself commission?"

"Obviously, Chase, a satisfied client is our first priority, and in the long run, we come out ahead. Satisfied customers inevitably come back, and then there are the referrals."

"Hey, this is fun, Carrie, I mean for the buyer. I thought real estate only goes up, especially in these affluent climes."

Her attractive face turned serious. "Most of the time, you'd be right, Chase, but I think this time, we may be facing an abyss, what with this subprime mess. I don't remember much from Eco 3.1, but I do recall learning that nothing goes up forever and—"

"And the longer it defies gravity?" Chase grinned.

"Let's not even think about that, Chase. The important thing is, you're looking at a beautiful duplex in a beautiful area in a beautiful city that—"

"You left out something else that's beautiful," he interrupted as he moved toward her. Her face turned ashen. She started to drop her papers; he put his arms around her waist. They kissed passionately; he held her slim form halfway to the floor, like one of those "French dips" from a foxtrot, circa the 1950s.

They separated as Chase looked over the empty premises. It's either the floor or one of those folding chairs snug up against one of those small portable tables. Reality superseded his fantasy right away.

"You bastard," she hissed.

"Huh?"

"It's the first time I've lost my professional cool."

"Well, I'm sorry if I—"

"Don't play innocent, Chase, you wanted to make me dance to your tune, and damn it, you succeeded."

"Carrie, I—"

"Please, Chase, let me finish. I know what I look like, and I know that your nonchalance was a gimmick to differentiate from horny, eager males. And it worked, boy, did it. You got me, big boy." She moved toward him and started with the ear bit, moving methodically to his neck, then showed her tongue, inviting the inevitable French kiss.

Whew, Chase thought afterward, *this is one beauty who's not passive.*

She left him and quietly picked up the fallen paperwork and put it on the little table. "Sorry for the outburst, Chase. It's just that I'm not used to being manipulated. Usually, it's the vixen who spins the web."

He watched her put her papers, cell phone, and other stuff on that suddenly crowded table that also featured a stack of flyers and her business cards.

"I'll be right back," she chirped. "Okay if I use one of your future bathrooms to get my game face back on?"

"Be my guest." He smiled. He sat down at the little chair opposite of the one she'd just vacated. He glanced at a flyer: "LUXURY LIVING IN THE PRIVACY OF SEA CLIFF. Isolation, yet just minutes all that San Francisco has to offer. Enjoy the—"

"Well, Chase, I'm back." She sat down on the other chair. "Enjoying the clichés of the real estate industry?"

"Well, Carrie, anything that's part of the private sector has got to eventually involve a sale of some product or, in this case, a house. And these brochures, mundane as they are, help close the sale."

"Wow, private sector, sales—I didn't realize I was involved in something that heavy. What did you major in, Chase, economics?"

Chase shrugged. "The dismal science? Not a chance. Let's just say I didn't fall asleep in *all* my business classes at William & Mary."

"William & Mary." She giggled. "It sounds so… so… colonial." They laughed.

The beauty's face turned serious. "Chase, when I mentioned putting my game face back on, I was referring to smeared lipstick. Now I—"

"I got ya," he cut in. "No monkey business until our professional relationship's played out, whether I purchase something or change my mind."

"I'm glad you're so understanding. It'll make things easier."

"Carrie, I might not be all that gallant." He pronounced it the French way, with the *ant* sounding like *aunt*. "My assignment, uh, that is, is sort of stressful, for lack of a better word. As you females love to say, now's not a time for me to be involved."

Even though she'd introduced the concept, his effortless acquiescence to the noninvolvement concept seemed to perturb her. "Fine," she said crisply, "I'll get back to you on the seller's latest price."

"Carrie," he answered softly, "we gotta go slow. It's best all around."

Her face showed a blush. "Don't be silly, Chase, I'm not put down. I bought it up, didn't I?"

They looked blankly at each other. Chase finally saw the light. "Can I walk you out, or are you—"

"I'm going to stay awhile—catch up on some text messages and phone calls. Are you heading back to your hotel? Oh, right, I almost forgot, you're now staying at that furnished flat on Octavia?"

"Right, Octavia, near California." Chase, concerned she might spot him, added, "Nah, Carrie, I won't be leaving the area for a while. I'd like to walk around. Sort of get the lay of the land. You never know what surprises you might discover that—"

"Chase, is there something going on I should know about?"

Chase shrugged and assumed a "What, who me?" expression. "Don't know what *you* mean, Carrie. Just want to walk around my potential new neighborhood is all."

"Well," she replied, "if you run into any other realtors, remember that Perrin's number one."

"I will." He grinned. "I'll wait for your call."

Chase walked down Ridgeway Court and decided to try Twenty-Seventh Avenue. He was sort of bothered that she didn't buy his rationale for "walking" around the neighborhood. *To hell with it, so what if she suspects? What's she gonna do, report me to Frommer?*

Wouldn't be half bad; at least he'd come out of his rathole. It'd been five minutes, and Chase hadn't seen a soul. Always that way in affluent neighborhoods; no one's ever outside.

He crossed the street for the second time and looked back so he wouldn't forget where he started on Ridgeway. Finally, the promised land. No pedestrians but one of those private security guards whose duty was to assure the privacy of this exclusive enclave. The guard was heading in his direction, and they met within two minutes. The guard exhibited a cheery smile. "Hi, anything I can help you with?"

Chase grinned. "I like it."

"Like what?" The guard's demeanor was no longer cheerful.

Chase pulled out the flyer for the Ridgeway duplex. "Well, I'm considering buying this property, and I was assured that there were personnel around to guarantee privacy and safety. Running into you reassures me."

"Well, you should rest assured, sir. The Neighborhood Association charges twenty dollars a month to each owner for the private security, and I haven't heard of a complaint yet." The guard studied the flyer. "Perrin's your realtor? Can't go wrong. They do a lot of business around here."

"Well, that's good to hear. They come highly recommended." Chase looked at the guard's name tag: Ted Dawson, Premier Security Services. "I was wondering, Ted, you see, I'm considering this type of area, 'cause while it's important I be in the city, my line of work generates all kinds of responses, some of them potentially unpleasant, if you know—"

The guard seemed reassuring. "It's fully understood, err..."

"Chase."

"Yes, Chase, you'll discover that Premier isn't the only security service in Sea Cliff, and of course, the SFPD patrols regularly, so you can rest assured that—"

"Oh, I read you on that, Ted. It's just that my concern lies elsewhere."

Ted frowned ever so slightly. "Well, anything beyond what we've just talked about is beyond my pay grade. So if you'd contact your realtor at Perrin, I'm sure that—"

"But, Ted, I'm definitely limiting myself to *your* pay grade."

Ted grimaced; his breathing became so heavy it was audible. "Okay, shoot. What are you driving at?"

"Here's my concern, Ted. You've assured me that I'm protected from strangers and/or enemies by patrols from the SFPD and private security provided by outfits like yours."

Ted stepped back and looked at his watch, as if saying, "I've wasted enough time with your loony tunes fantasies, I gotta move on." He cleared his throat. "Your point?"

"Well, don't be offended, Ted, but I've been around. What if someone looking for a man offered a security guard, say, $50,000 'cause the man ran away from his wife and kids? It's not a police matter, and yet $50,000 to a security guard is an awful lot of money and—"

"Mister," Ted almost shouted, "I don't know what's going on, but I'd never... Are you some kind of company spy?"

Chase blushed. "Definitely not a company spy. But I'll get right to the point—what if I were the one looking for the culprit and I offered the fifty—"

"Mister."

"Call me Chase."

"Mister, Chase, whatever, this damn conversation's gone on long enough. I've got a mind to—"

Chase grinned. "Fifty K's a lot of moola. It could even be more, depending—"

"Mr. Chase, nice—well sort of nice—talking to you. But 50 or even 100K won't do it if it results in a bust. I got a wife and two boys, and I'm going to SF State. You got the wrong cat. I'd report all this, but something tells me—"

"You're right, Ted, if you're not interested, let it go at that. Suffice it to say, I'm the good guy. You'd be doing the world a favor and your family a lot of good."

Ted was trembling. "You say it's not a police matter. And if it were Al-Qaeda or something like that, you wouldn't be screwing with the likes of me. Mr. Chase, goodbye."

Chase watched him turn to cross the street. "Hey, Ted, no hard feelings, huh? I'll call Premier in a week or two, maybe run into you before that. At any rate, I'll leave my cell number. Maybe you'll have reconsidered."

"No way."

Ted was now about fifty feet away, and no one else was in sight. "I'll just give you a name, Ted!" Chase shouted. "If you know where he is, the money's yours!"

Ted had just turned a corner and was out of sight. Chase grimaced. Maybe this hadn't been handled well.

LEGAL RECESSION

Derek Burnitz hadn't slept well for several days. Probably all that Mellon shit. He'd been in the office a half hour but still couldn't shake the cobwebs. While sipping black coffee and trying to figure what, if anything, besides Mellon, had kept him up at night, he heard the intercom. It was Karen Burnett. "Hi, Mr. Burnitz, just got an e-mail from Dennis Bradshaw's appointments secretary. It seems he wants to meet with you ASAP. I just forwarded it to you."

"Thanks, Karen, I'll read it right it right away." *Wonder what he wants?* Burnitz felt a little apprehension. First, troubles with the venerable old man, Mellon, the king of the hill. Now, here's Bradshaw, at the other end of the age equation. Bradshaw was a comer, young, about thirty-five, and ravenously hungry. He and his kind were the unseen eight-hundred-pound gorillas in his study during that tense meeting with Mellon several weeks earlier.

His e-mail read: "Hi, Derek, long time and all that. Look, how's about a meet real soon in SF? If your schedule allows early next week, please call. It's business and VI. Best Dennis."

VI Burnitz reflected, *That's fancy legal talk for Veddy Important.* He picked up the phone then decided, *Fuck it, there's that charity soiree tonight. I don't need that Bradshaw on my mind.* Tightening credit, the dot-com collapse, and now the financial crisis due to the housing mess. Major corporations were cutting back on outside legal costs as profits evaporate. Combine that with decline in mergers, IPOs, all that shit. The fucking rainmakers were running for cover, causing a lot of those firms to compete or lose out on new clients. Worse, the banks were calling in loans if too many partners quit. *It's only the tip of the iceberg*, Burnitz assumed. Year after year of more lavish office space, graduates showered with signing bonuses as if they were free-agent versions of Barry and A-Rod. Plus, the blue chips were demanding global representation—another factor in overspending and the consequent inability to withstand any slowdown in billings. That's why so many white shoes were lowering themselves to becoming fancy ambulance chasers, trying to get some of the class action revenue that yours truly and Mellon were so successful at.

Burnitz was staring blankly at Middleton & Burnitz's latest quarterly report. *Holy shit*, he ruminated. He didn't need Bradshaw on his mind and just spent the last five minutes thinking about the whole deal. Back to more "pleasant" thoughts, like fitting into that damn tuxedo while Sonja's gaga over that $14,000 creation designed by that French faggot who advertises his gowns through all those sexpots presenting and accepting those awards at the Oscars, Emmys, and those other waste of times.

Bradshaw, Bernstein, & Lowe were in the heart of the financial district, occupying the seventeenth to nineteenth floors at Embarcadero II. Word was that Bradshaw had contemplated financing the construction of his own Legal Towers at the corner of Market and Montgomery, but Burnitz had heard through the grapevine that the plans were on hold pending the end of the legal recession. The meet was scheduled for Tuesday at 10:00 AM, so on Monday afternoon, Burnitz got his chauffeur to drive him and Sonja the thirty-five miles from Palo Alto to the St. Francis Hotel in Union Square. Sonja had looked forward to seeing a show, but Geary Street was "dark" on Monday nights. So they dined at Michael Minna's fancy digs adjoining the hotel's lobby, and Sonja was happy. It wasn't a play, but she did see the "beautiful people" in their element in sophisticated SF, eager as she was to compare how she looked as opposed to the city's chick elite. If Burnitz remembered correctly, the dress she wore at Minna's was in the $3,200 range—not as spectacular as the $14,000 garb she'd worn last week but certainly good enough to match anything worn by the doyennes of SF at the theater or a fancy salle à manger.

After breakfast Tuesday morning, the Burnitzs wandered back to the hotel lobby, where Derek promptly relieved his wife of her credit cards. "You've got about four to six hours to wander around Neiman Marcus, Saks, and all the rest. For you, four hours, give or take, could result in ten to twenty thousands in credit card totals." He smiled. "A casual, unplanned shopping spree can result in quite a lot of damage when put in the candy store that is Union Square, am I right?"

"What are you up to now, Derek? What am I supposed to do while you're meeting with fancy lawyers? Ask for handouts like the homeless on Powell Street?"

Burnitz grinned and pulled out a one-hundred-dollar bill. "This is for you in case you decide you're hungry before, during, or after your shopping spree."

"And what am I to spree on without my credit cards?"

"Coming to that, hon, coming to that." He pulled out one of his personal checks made out for one thousand dollars. "The endorsee's blank." He grinned. "So who's the lucky winner, Macy's, Saks, Neiman Marcus?"

"Very funny, Derek. Just for that, I've a mind to give you your check back intact, but, uh, not yet. I'll kill the time just window-shopping, so to speak. And if I spot a buy, well, you know…"

"Yeah, Sonja, I know. Okay, my cell will be off, but I'll be checking for messages now and then. So if you have to reach me— well, not for another check. So I'll see you back at the hotel around five-ish, okay?" Burnitz concluded that her huffy expression meant his comment about another check bombed as he watched her head out to Post Street. *Well, Sonja,* he mused, *your limited mind isn't concerned about or following this, but if your hubby messes up at this and subsequent meetings, all that carefree shopping and $14,000 gowns will become a distant memory.* He glanced at his watch. It was 9:45 AM. He walked out and stepped into one of the cabs lined up in front of the hotel. "Embarcadero II, please."

It was the first time at Bradshaw's new digs, and Burnitz was duly impressed by the reception area. Naturally, the receptionist was a knockout, but even more impressive was the stylish seating, the self-serve choices of coffee and various juices, soft drinks, and bottled waters in a refrigerated case.

"Please help yourself, Mr. Burnitz. Mr. Bradshaw's finishing a call. He should be out any minute."

Ordinarily, Burnitz enjoyed playing "eye" footsie with a captive stunner like Bradshaw's receptionist, but not this time. He wanted all his focus on the meeting with Bradshaw. *Maybe next time, beauty.* He rose from the plush brown leather chair and pulled out a cold bottle of Fiji water.

Bradshaw appeared as Burnitz opened the cap. "Hi, Derek, sorry I kept you waiting." He looked at the beauty. "Thanks, Gloria."

As Burnitz followed Bradshaw to the conference room, he stifled a smirk as he wondered what Bradshaw "thanked" Gloria for—a good time last night?

Bradshaw picked a chair in the center of the imposing room-length conference table. Burnitz promptly pulled out a chair directly opposite, thankful that Bradshaw hadn't picked the seat at the head of the table, where, whether to the left or right of him, Burnitz would be seated in an inferior position. He appreciated the gesture, but his heart started pumping—why the meet, and what was this upstart pipsqueak up to?

Bradshaw leaned back. "Drive up this morning?"

"Nah, Dennis, our chauffeur drove me and the missus up last night. We're staying at the St. Francis."

"Dine at Minna's?"

"Yeah, Dennis, a first time and fantastic experience. Ever been there?"

"Several times, obviously a destination point whether you're local or from out of town."

Burnitz swallowed hard, hoping it didn't show. Small talk at the beginning of a big meet was often forbidding. One never knew when and in what form the sucker punch would jolt the participants back to reality. "So what's happening, Dennis?"

Bradshaw smiled. "It's probably no secret to all of us in the profession that things have slowed appreciably in the last year or so."

"Right, Dennis, and a lot of these trends have been discussed in prior meets among a bunch of us."

"Right, Derek, so I gather you'd agree that when there's a slow-down, we ought to do everything we can to maintain income."

Burnitz winced. "It's not hard to see where all this is going."

"Obviously, Derek, because, as you say, all this has been discussed before. There's a lot of Young Turks out there, and they've designated me to be the spokesman, err, spokesperson."

"So the point is…"

"So the point is, there's a mutiny out there on your sort of concord with Mellon."

"In what regard?"

"In the regard, well, it's that MTBE and FISA."

"Oh." Burnitz smiled. "So the word's out."

"Yes, it is, Derek, and those Turks are in no mood to lose out on all that, and neither am I."

Burnitz tried not to show irritation, but his grimace was visible. "Look, Dennis, Mellon, for some reason, thinks I can control all you guys. Based on common sense and today's meeting, it's obvious that I can't."

Bradshaw grinned. "We look up to you, Derek, obviously, but there's a limit to—"

"A LIMIT?" Burnitz boomed. "If not for our rainmaking, where the hell would all you MFs be?"

Bradshaw blanched; it was the first time he'd seen Burnitz lose it. "Cool it, Derek, please. I don't want this to turn out this way. I'm just a messenger. Bradshaw, Bernstein, & Lowe can easily survive without any MTBE or FISA action. It's just that the others are adamant… and then there's Zig Hermanski—"

"Hermanski, that weirdo Transylvania financier? I knew he was on our side and supplying lots of dough, but I never realized—"

"Well, realize it now, Derek. He's stirring the pot and providing his endless personal Fort Knox to keep all this shit, and the so-called pot, boiling."

"No shit, why?"

"Dunno, Derek, he started this Commie-type website, and I guess he's got all kinds of political aspirations. He's secretive but supplying all the moola in the world to our cause—mostly, to help Mellon while he's on the lam. At any rate, that's what I heard."

"Wow, let's get Oliver Stone. Sounds like it's a screenplay right up his alley. Anyhoo, getting back to your Young Turks. They're not going under, are they?"

"Not yet, right now the main problem is not being able to offer 200K to a topflight grad, European or Caribbean trips down to one or two a year, with the top hotels and first-class travel by the boards. So they're not at tin-cup levels yet, but there's additional worries out there."

"Like?"

"Like real estate. The shit hasn't hit the fan yet, but some of our consultants say this subprime mess may cause problems."

Burnitz blinked and exhibited a wry smile. "Really? Hadn't heard. In my neck, the peninsula, the bubble is still going gangbusters. Of course, even if there were a slowdown, it'd just affect the agents and the lawyers who make penny ante closing the deals."

"Maybe, Derek, this hasn't showed up in the mainstream or business media, but a lot of our colleagues are running into difficulties selling their homes."

"Like who?"

"Well, like Calvin Antonini. He's been trying to sell his three-bedroom in Manhattan for about a year. He paid twelve about three years ago, and he figured he'd ask fifteen. Now he's down to $12,500,000 just so he can have the mental comfort of a profit, but still no takers."

"Well, Calvin, he's got enough, he'll never have to worry."

"Not the point, Derek, we're talking a real slowdown. Cal's got ten years on us, easy, and he says he's never seen such a sluggish environment."

Burnitz frowned. "What part of Manhattan?"

"The East Side, natch, where else would someone of Cal's stature hang his hat?"

"That does sound like something to be aware of."

"And it's just not him, and it's just not Manhattan, Derek. I'm hearing this stuff from Chicago's Lakefront, Society Hill in Philly, and Georgetown."

"Well, let's not get carried away, Dennis. After years of nothing but up a pause is almost healthy, unless of course you're anxious to sell right then and there—so you come out even. At least you didn't lose. And besides, Dennis, happy days will soon be here again. What have we got, about a year and change before the election?"

"Yeah, can't wait. We'll be rid of that Bush crowd once and for all." Derek grinned. "Got an in, Dennis, or wishful thinking?"

"C'mon, Derek, the Reps are finished." Bradshaw laughed. "Two long-term wars. They don't stand a chance. Just look at history. Harry Truman, LBJ—both wartime presidents decided not to run 'cause they knew their goose was cooked."

"You got a point with the wars, Dennis, but that W got us out of a potential big dip with that tax cut when he came in, and I read that he's had the best unemployment numbers for a six-year period in US history, I think 4.1 percent."

"No shit. Still, even if true, there's no reason to worry, Derek, the wars will be the big issues, and any good jobless numbers will be buried by a hostile media."

Burnitz shook his head. "I'm not worried, Dennis, just trying to show off my nonlegal knowledge. Attended Stanford undergraduate, you know, and I didn't fall asleep in the eco classes. What about you, Dennis? You went to Berkeley before Harvard Law, right?"

"Right, and I fell asleep when those lefty professors talked down the good old USA and capitalism, not necessarily in that order. It was the only safe thing to do. If I had responded to all that stupidity, there would have gone my straight A's and admission to Harvard Law."

"So you think we'll be back in the saddle after the election. You think Clinton's gonna carry the banner?"

"Who else, Derek? She's got the name, experience, and all that fund-raising capacity, plus ol' Bubba backing her up."

"Who else?" Burnitz shrugged. "Biden, Dodd… What about that young black guy with the funny name?"

"Obama something," Bradshaw replied. "Yeah, he's got some charisma based on that keynote, but he's way too young. He's running, if he does, to get exposure for a real run in '16 after Hillary finishes her eight years."

"Sounds like you are on top of things, Dennis. What about the damned Reps?"

"Giuliani'll probably get it. He's got 9/11, all those Mafia guys he prosecuted, and he knows how to speak understandable English."

Burnitz giggled. "Unless he's wearing that dress, his divorces, and living with those homos, err, gays—"

Bradshaw held up his hand as if imitating a Stop sign. "If your argument is 'we never know,' well, you've got a point." He shrugged. "Then it'd probably be Romney or—"

"Romney, hey, he'd be tough."

"Maybe, Derek, but he'd never get the nomination."

"Why the hell not?"

"The third rail of Republican politics, Derek, abortion. Romney's for choice, or at least he was, in Massachusetts."

"Massachusetts, well, that doesn't mean squat—you know, Dennis, when in Rome… What about the other guy, you know, who ran against Bush?" Bradshaw's face was impassive. "Err, you know, the old guy, the war hero?"

"Oh, McCain, yeah, he might give Hillary some problems, but he's no threat."

"No threat? War hero, personable…"

"Because he's got no money, Derek, and he's too clean, against earmarks and all that. Plus, the base hates him. Who the hell's gonna give him the loot while there's other Reps in the running?"

Burnitz leaned back and grinned. "So we got Hillary. Will she play ball?"

"Certainly, she's a lawyer. Her husband's a lawyer, hip-pocket, or whatever that phrase is."

"Any producers in her circle?"

"Not to worry, Derek, there are no producers among the Dems. The only power players there, if they aren't attorneys, are financiers—you know, Lehman Brothers, Goldman Sachs. Have not fear, Democrats do not produce."

"Jeez, Dennis, you sure know your shit. But what about Bill Gates, those Google guys?"

"Yeah, they produced. Notice the tense, Derek? I said they *were* producers. Now that they're beyond big, they can go along with anything bad for business. No matter what happens, Gates and those kids at Google will weather the storm, and in the meantime, they get invited to all the right social events, get treated right by the mainstream press, and so on."

Burnitz smirked. "You got it down pat, Dennis. If I ever go into politics—"

"No thanks, Derek," Bradshaw cut in, giggling. "No politics for me. Couldn't ever match my present income as a consultant, and who wants to get by on four hours' sleep in a freezing Iowa January?"

Burnitz leaned back and looked at his watch.

Bradshaw's laugh had turned into a frown. "I'm glad we were able to shoot the breeze, so to speak, Derek. But before we conclude, I have to have your word or something to take back to the guys. They're hurting, and they mean business."

"They can have MTBE, as long as it's clear I'm not involved. As for FISA, Mellon's like the Rock of Gibraltar, something about his son who's in the military. I'm pretty sure he won't budge."

Bradshaw sighed. "There's too much telephone money out there waiting to be had. They're not gonna listen, Derek."

"Well, pass the word, Dennis, Mellon's a tough guy—at least he was in his younger days. It could get rough."

"Don't look at *me* in that tone, Derek. I'm talking about the hungry Turks, not me. Besides, it would be a one-way rough stuff. No one knows where he's hiding," Bradshaw grinned, "unless we get word the next time you guys meet."

"What is the 'we,' Dennis? Freudian slip? I thought it was just the Young Turks, not you. Besides, if you're hinting—that is, if there's an attempt while we're meeting, I could get caught in the cross fire.

Or if it's before or after and if he survives, guess who he's going to come after. Forget it, Dennis, get him on your own, if you guys can. What was that movie? *Catch Me If You Can?*"

"Jeez, Derek, your imagination's really running wild. No one ever said anything about—"

"Let's not lose sight of why Mellon's on the run, Dennis. It's that damn Gyno, Beltran, and all that antilawsuit money that's behind him. They've apparently hired pros, and while Mellon's number 1, I don't think they'd lose any sleep over getting any other lawyers involved in class actions."

"Okay, okay, you saw the security here, we're alert."

"C'mon, Dennis, penny ante, you don't think a determined… Well, you think they'd be dissuaded by what's out there?" Burnitz pointed to the door leading to the hallway. "Besides, why make a frontal assault when they can get at you and your family at home?"

Bradshaw blanched. "You… you trying to scare me? You didn't have to bring my family into this."

"Forget it, Dennis, it's Mellon and this guy Frommer they're after. I… I was just giving an example of possible—"

"Who the fuck's Frommer? I never heard of—"

"Well, he's not a hotshot attorney, Dennis. That's why you never heard of him. He's—"

"Well, how does he fit in?" Bradshaw's voice was cracking.

"Well, to go to the well one more time, Dennis, Frommer's like a button, a soldier to Mellon, the godfather."

"A button?"

"Yeah, you know, Dennis. The button does the dirty work while the capo, or godfather, theoretically keeps his hands clean."

Bradshaw still looked puzzled.

"Look. Frommer's a PR guy, but that includes a lot of endeavors, not just being a wordsmith."

Bradshaw looked pensive and leaned back on his chair. "Oh yeah, Frommer & Sons. I guess I have heard of him. So they're after him also?"

"That's what I've heard. He's sort of dropped out of sight." Bradshaw looked at his watch. "Past noon. Wanna grab some lunch?"

"Sure, Dennis, why not? But not for too long. I gotta make sure the wife hasn't emptied every store on Union Square."

They both cackled.

THE LEGAL SCENE

William Mellon, the top litigator in the nation, is MIA. He's been missing for nearly six months. The founder and chief honcho of Mellon, Caldwell, & Cunningham was last seen while "vacationing" in the Caribbean, where he granted a brief interview to breathless reporters denying he was on the run. He hasn't been seen since *ThisWeek* did a cover story on Mr. Mellon nearly a year ago (May 19, 2007) following the abortive assassination of Matt Thompson, the firm's representative in their Washington, DC, office. (Mr. Thompson, severely wounded in the attempt, has since returned to work under heavy guard.)

All this had led to speculation that the controversial attorney fears for his own life and has accordingly disappeared from public view. This line of speculation had been denied by Drew Jurgensen, a spokesperson at Mellon, Caldwell, & Cunningham's Fifth Avenue headquarters in Manhattan. Mr. Jurgensen had continually asserted that Mr. Mellon's unavailability is a result of his desire not to exacerbate whatever ill feeling led to the unfortunate attempt on Thompson's life. The inference that he's "on the run" was portrayed as "sheer nonsense."

Meanwhile, *ThisWeek*'s Los Angeles bureau sent an investigative reporter to San Francisco to get some background on Stuart Frommer, another player in these legal shenanigans. Frommer, along with his brother, Phil, run the bicoastal Frommer & Sons, one of the leading public relations firms in the nation. Reportedly, Stuart Frommer had disappeared from plain sight, while his brother, Phil, had declined requests for interviews at the firm's Madison Avenue offices. A week's investigation by the intrepid reporter didn't elicit a clue as to Stu Frommer's whereabouts. The firm issued several press releases asserting that Mr. Frommer was on "special assignment" and visits to the firm's Market Street offices yielded no clues. Years of investigations and reporting had provided a strong business and financial link between the two firms leading to speculation that if Mr. Mellon is concerned for his safety, so is Mr. Frommer.

Reportedly, another missing player in this narrative was Dr. Craig Beltran, an ob-gyn who left the state of Pennsylvania amid much adversity and furor after allegedly vowing vengeance against Mellon and "his kind." All this followed what Beltran's supporters labeled a spate of frivolous lawsuits that ruined his practice and led to the suicide of his wife. Repeated queries to Federal, state, and local law enforcement officials as to the whereabouts of any of these individuals had come up empty. Off the record queries by *This Week* and other national publications had similarly run into a stone wall. This brouhaha had obviously been going on since before May of last year (see above reference to the May 7 cover story) and drew the attention of a wide assortment of bloggers immediately after that unfortunate shooting, but as is/was the nature of internet attention spans, the bloggers readily descended to the more popular showbiz topics like Brangelina, who's been dumped by whom, and who's had "work" done.

On a more macro level, this legal melée, if indeed that was the principal issue, underlined a chasm in the nation's legal/cultural collective that will inevitably come to a head. Perhaps not in the upcoming presidential race, where Iraq and the economy promised to be the principal issues. Still, the economic and political perspectives at both extremes threatened both the economic and social fabric of the nation. At one end, you purportedly had the "sue at any cost and any pretext" trial lawyers and their fellow travelers in the Democratic Party. Fighting them tooth and nail were corporate lawyers, medical associations, a collection of business groups, and of course, the Republicans.

Reportedly, with so much at stake and the abundant funding behind both sides, it was no wonder that Messrs. Mellon, Frommer, and Beltran have so far been able to evade their pursuers.

***

Slats was perusing *Drudge* online when he heard the phone. "Yeah, boss, I'll be right in." He headed toward Leary's office wondering what was up, since nothing was due today. For a change, Leary wasn't relaxed, feet on the desk, checking out the tranquil Pacific waves on the Malibu shoreline. Eerily, he was staring right through the glass partition, focused on Slats's approach. "Aw, shit," Slats mumbled, "there goes my soft, easy day." Leary pointed Slats to a chair. "Yeah, boss, got something new?"

Leary smirked, "What'sa matter, Slats? Is our great scribe, our local Hemingway, bored covering the Manhattan Beach flower show or the Pacific Palisades auto antique show?"

"Err, make that the South Bay Automobile Antique Show, boss."

"Auto, automobile, same piece of crap. I'd be bored out of my gorge if I had to—"

"So why are you assigning me to—"

"Listen, you miserable ingrate, check your bank account lately? Are the checks coming in?"

"Yeah, boss, Holly checks the bank account online. What's your point?"

"Don't get uppity with me, Conners."

"Me, uppity? Who the hell just called me a miserable ingrate?"

Leary's made-up frown dissipated into gales of laughter. He had to get up to wipe away the tears. "Slats, Slats, what would I do without you? When they give me the gold watch, I'll come in for free just to be entertained." Leary was hit with another spasm of laughter. "Slats, you MF, you MF slay me."

Slats shrugged. "Well, boss, you'd pick up a sense of humor if you were covering antique cars or daffodils in Manhattan Beach."

Leary wiped tears from his eyes one last time. "I asked you about the checks for a reason, Slats."

"Yeah, what's that?"

"To prove that you're better off than so many of your colleagues at the *Times*, as in *LA*, *NY*, and *Seattle Times*, who may have been working at more prestigious newspapers but are either already or about to walk the pavement—y'know, as in being jobless, y'know, like when their significant others check out the bank account online, there is no *fucking account*, because there are no more paychecks."

Slats checked out Leary's countenance and his sudden loss of temper. "Wow, Mr. Boss Man, just a minute ago, you were Jay Leno. Now you're like a—"

"Correct that, Slats," Leary interrupted. "*You* were like Jay Leno. That's why I was the one that was laughing. I'm a little worried, Mr. Conners. Are you still my iconic reporter, or are you slipping into ennui or senility?"

Slats grinned, his cheeks flushed red. "Hey, boss man, I'm still that mild-mannered reporter who's up to most tasks and capable of entering the nearest phone booth if things get hairy."

Leary frowned. That laughing spasm suddenly seemed ages ago. "Okay, Superdude, before you go home to Lois Lane, lemme repeat a point I was trying to make perfectly clear." He pointed his finger at Slats, Nixon style. "You may never be a guest on Larry King or a panelist on *Meet the Press*, but like I said, those dudes are either out of a job or about to be. Be thankful for what you got, Conners. What's a little flower or auto show compared to hitting the bricks?"

Slats inadvertently scratched the back of his hair. "Mr. Leary." He sighed. "It's a good thing I'm the one sitting in your office right now."

"Yeah, why's that?"

"'Cause I'm the only MF on this earth who could follow what you just said." Leary grinned. "Touché, Slats, but look at it this way—you're the only Monday–Friday on this earth that I'd speak to this way."

"Don't know if that's a compliment, or… are we through here, boss man?"

"Not by a long shot. Did you read *This Week*'s latest edition?"

"Err, no, I subscribe to it, so it don't, ah, doesn't arrive till Tuesday."

"You know what one of their features is in this week's *This Week*?"

Slats was about to pun this week's *This Week* but sensed that the boss man was no longer in the mood for all that. "No, err, something about the Chanteuse?"

Leary leaned back and swiveled his high-back chair for a view of the Malibu coastline. "Remember when you were skeered out of your gorge, Mr. Conners?"

"Gee, boss man, it's been so often, like, gimme a clue."

Leary leaned forward and smirked, "Remember a dude named Frommer, a hotshot culprit named Mellon, and some working lunch you had at Spago's several months ago?"

"Holy shit, Mr. Leary, is it that guy, that hit man that scared the shit out of me?"

Leary displayed a wide grin. "Damn, Slats, you must really be frightened. You haven't called me Mr. Leary since, well, since quite a few years."

"Matter of fact, boss man, I'm pretty easygoing and not prone to worrying, but when you're sitting with a Daniel Craig look-alike in an eye-talian restaurant and you realize he's out to whack my old nemesis Frommer, it's easy to imagine some Corleone type coming out of the restroom and…" Slats touched his chest to stop the pounding.

Leary looked at Slats sympathetically. "It's been a while, Slats. If you had been on their hit parade, someone would have no doubt called on you by now. Furthermore, according to *This Week*, your pal Frommer's successfully evaded his pursuers so far."

Slats gulped and couldn't hide his frown. "What are we getting at, boss man?"

Leary leaned back on his swivel chair. "Your old friend the Chanteuse has disappeared from view, and no one gives a shit. That's why my ace reporter is down to covering automobile and flower shows. So what'll it be, ol' Slats, being bored to death or covering a live-wire story?"

Slats almost giggled. "Well, you see, boss man, if the choice is being bored or being six feet under, I'll take boring every time."

"Makes sense, Slats," Leary elicited an icy grin. "Only trouble is, you think all that goes on around here is that you got to answer to me?"

Slats made like he was puzzled. "Err, I don't follow what you're—"

"What I'm saying, Slats, is that I got to answer also, you know, to the fourth floor. I don't pay yours, mine, or any other salary around here. It's the folks upstairs and the media holding company in Cincy or wherever the fuck they're hanging their hats nowadays."

"Which means?"

"Which means when they ask me why our senior reporter is covering auto shows instead of using his connections to get our tails into a story hot enough to be featured in *This Week*, I wanna be proactive."

"Proactive?"

"Yeah, proactive, they know you met with that thug, James Bond, or whatever he was/is."

Slats showed exasperation. "Why the hell do they know?"

"C'mon, Slats, you don't think they've been preparing for cuts? They gotta know who's productive, who's increasing the bottom line. Their knowing that you ran into a hit man, well," Leary leaned back and grinned, "it's like hitting the lottery."

"Oh, jolly good, boss man, I get whacked, and it increases the bottom line for the old corporation."

Leary sighed. "I love all this jousting, Slats. Sorta makes my day. But," now the sigh was audible, "considering your background, you're making, what, about $1,200 a week. That doesn't go far, specially in this area, but you get travel, per diem, and other bennies."

Now Slats showed annoyance. "Your point?"

"Well, you're in the ballpark with firemen, policemen. They make about the same as you and are always in a lot more physical danger. And that's not counting combat correspondents, say, in areas like Iraq and Afghanistan. So what's the infinitesimal chance of getting whacked to cause you to act like a worrywart, after the easy life you lead compared to those other professions most of the time."

"Man, you sure got a way of making a point, boss man, if one forgets the dangling participles of your last comment."

Now Leary was back to leaning back on his swivel chair; he stole a look at the Malibu shoreline, looked back at Slats, and smiled. "C'mon, Slats, all this Sopranos' usage of the term *whacked* is an exaggeration. At most, if things go awry, they'll lump you up a little. They got no reason to kill, err, whack you."

"Well, thanks for getting rid of my fears, boss man, but what does 'lump you up' mean?"

Leary shrugged. "It was in one of those film noire novels, circa the 1950s, as I recall. It's New Yorkese for a severe beating."

Slats just shook his head. "I'm sure Holly would appreciate the difference."

Leary looked at his watch. "Okay, Slats, do you know what you gotta do?"

"Sure, boss man." Slats grinned. "Get Travel to set me up in that dump in Frisco again, and do my best to find Frommer or find someone who can, uh—"

"You got it, Clark Kent. If you can't find Frommer, find someone who knows something... either about Frommer or someone who knows of Frommer or... Well, you know the drill."

Slats started to walk out and turned. "I... I might need a car trying to track him down."

Leary shrugged. "I hear you. Drive up, it's about six hours. Do it next Sunday so you'll be ready Monday morning. Get a weekly rate on parking. Meantime, clear it with Holly and whatever else you got to take care of before you go."

"For how long?"

"That residential dump has weekly rates, right?"

"Right."

"Plan for two weeks, then we'll see if you've made any progress. Now git, but make sure you're in this Friday in case there's anything I forgot."

Slats was at the door and turned again. "I thought you never forget any—"

"Correct that," Leary interrupted, grinning. "Anything I so-called forget is anything the fourth floor wants me to tell you before you go. Later."

CASSADY'S

Ann Witt looked at her watch. It was slightly past five. Another half a block to the precinct, but it had already been a hot, stressful nine-hour day, and mindful of her parched, thirsty throat, she smirked as she stole another look at her watch. That inviting Cassady's Bar & Grill sign loomed just above her. It was the precinct's local watering hole, but showing up before 4:00 PM was dicey. Even if you'd started at six and 4:00 PM represented ten hours, there'd be too much explaining to do, especially if brass from nearby precincts didn't know what you've been up to all day. But five, that was safe.

Even those working the night shift, a beer was like a coffee break, and it *was* a coffee break as long as there was another of New York's Finest there to shoot the shit with.

Ann found a spot in the center of the virtually empty bar. "Hi, Ann, the usual?"

"Nah, Dusty, still got to go back to the precinct and hit that computer. My Blackberry's on the blink. I'll just take a small Michelob draft to clear a dry throat. Damn, was it hot today."

She watched Dusty pour the draft. "Lucky you, Dusty. You work in an airconditioned place all day, carefree atmosphere. What more could anyone ask for?"

Dusty answered her grin with a slight smile as he deposited the beer on the coaster. He watched her delicate frame down about a third of the beer in one swig, as if she were a longshoreman who'd just finished unloading a ship. "Tell ya what someone could ask for, Ann, how's about a Dick's pay with bennies and pensions I could only dream about?"

He grinned and shrugged. "Now that you mention it, *that's* something yours truly could ask for."

Ann blushed. "I guess the grass is always greener, or however that saying goes."

"Be back in a sec, Ann."

She watched him turn his attention to a solitary drinker who'd yelled out "Bartender!" She pulled out a pen and pad and started to jot down some notes. *Insurance scam.* She sighed. So routine she gets sent out without a partner. Might as well leave the .38 snubby at home. Those insurance execs were about as dangerous as Andy Hardy. Her mind pictured Mickey Rooney as the young Frank Merriwell type as she looked at several business cards: "Hal Rhodes, Vice President, Casualty Division, Gotham ReAssurance Company." It was basically a Fed matter, but Captain Sullivan got a call from on high asking her to meet an assistant DA, Bernie Rappaport, and some FBI agents and work Gotham ReAssurance's 120 William Street headquarters to look for a local angle. It figures, she concluded. What DA wouldn't want to make headlines in the tabloids going after insurance scammers? Good for benign headlines and a no-contest situation. As opposed to minorities, lawyers, organized labor, it was a no-lose deal against defendants with virtually no constituency. The Feds didn't see a local angle, but what would you expect, they want all the glory. Trouble was, neither did Rappaport. He said he'd google some stuff, but he didn't appear too confident. What was the name of Rhodes's lawyer again? She thought she'd put his card somewhere…

"Hi, ever been here before?"

Ann turned and looked at the intruder. She was somewhat pissed and flattered at the same time. Nonencroachment would entail sitting in the middle of all the empty barstools. This dude sat himself down just one stool away, not totally gauche but not strictly kosher either. Pickup attempt, here we come. On the other hand, he appeared to be young and was well-dressed and, most important, cute.

"Yes, I sort of work around here." Her slight courtesy smile quickly turned into a self-deprecatory frown. *Way to go, Ann, why not tell him whether you sleep in the nude, what your sex fantasies are, and whether or not you exaggerated your deductions on Form 1040 last April 15.*

"Yeah, me too." He grinned. "I'm on an advertising gig that brings me to the West Side pretty often. I like this place. Unwind before I get on the packed Long Island. Usually, if I wait till about six thirty to seven, I get a seat."

"Oh, you live on the island?" She hadn't been able to notice a wedding ring or not, but this looked promising. Maybe he was just a "friendly" guy.

"Yes, I do. Roslyn. The little lady went back to her mom in Ohio for the near term. Meanwhile, I'm the sole inheritor of that beautiful split-level three-bedroom in the island's bucolic South Shore."

Ann knew exactly where all this was going, but she couldn't help herself. "Oh, your wife's on vacation?"

"No." He shrugged, evincing a slight smirk. "Trial separation." He got up, moved toward her, and held out his hand. "Name's Terrence, Terrence O'Boyle, but my friends call me—"

"I know," she cut in as she shook his hand, "Terry. My name's Ann, Ann Witt."

"Okay if I sit next to you? I'm a real gentleman. Just don't feel like shouting, and the buzz is acting up now that it's almost five thirty."

"Sure, but I'm gone as soon as I finish this beer and—" Ann had turned and saw "Stretch" Rizzo, Jillio, Nowitzky, and that new guy at a center table staring right at her.

They couldn't contain their grins.

"Something wrong, Ann? You look like you've seen a ghost."

"Ah, just noticed some coworkers and—"

"Oh, that bunch at the center table looking straight at us?"

"That's the bunch, all right. So tell me, Terrence, what part of Italy did your family immigrate from?"

Terry grinned from ear to ear and put on his most exaggerated brogue. "Well, if there's a Counnnty Caaaark located between

Naples and Rome, that's where they came from." He watched her steal another tentative glance at her grinning "coworkers." "You a cop, Ann?"

Startled, Ann blushed but quickly regained her composure. "Yes, I am, and you're under arrest." She meant it as a joke, but there'd been an edge to her tone. She tried to recover. "What made you ask me that?"

Now Terry blushed and shrugged. "As I've said, Ann, I've come here more than once, and I recognize your 'coworkers.' They're all cops, probably from the Sixteenth Precinct, down the street."

She smiled inwardly. Now she had something to needle them with. Boy, you guys can really work cover; some nerdy ad dick made you guys right off. "How'd you figure all that out, Terry?"

"Easy, my uncle was a cop, Astoria. There was this place, right on Northern Boulevard, sort of like Cassady's. Soon as I turned eighteen, I made my uncle's day, or should I say early evening, when I'd drop in for a beer, sometimes with my dad, sometimes by myself. Heard the war stories, the banter. Your associates over there fit the mold, like from central casting."

"Well, let's hope you stay on the 'right' side of the law, Terry. We plainclothes types don't appreciate being made right off the—"

"You kidding?" He giggled as he cut in. "I got something that's gonna revolutionize the ad business."

"Oh?" she whispered, glad that the conversation had shifted from New York's Finest.

"Yeah, Ann, ever hear of the four-minute mile?"

Dusty reappeared. "Another, Ann?"

Terry pushed a twenty dollars forward. "Yeah, another all around."

Ann pushed the bill back toward Terry. "No offense, Terry, but I pay my own way." She looked at Dusty. "Make it a large draft, Dusty, and have the waitress deposit it on that table with all the grinning baboons."

Terry's cheeks flushed red again. "That doesn't give me much time, does it?"

"I guess not," Ann answered evenly, trying not to appear bored. "Now what is this about a four-minute mile?"

"Well, Ann," Terry beamed, "about fifty years ago, some English guy ran the mile in four minutes. It was a big deal at the time, a nice round figure, like Babe Ruth hitting sixty home runs."

"No offense, Terry, but you look a little too stocky to be a long-distance runner." Terry held up one finger as if he were a professor about to make a point. "Well, you see, Ann, coincidentally, if you watch any TV, you'd notice that, depending on the program and the time of day, commercials usually run between three and four minutes. Well, the barrier right now is four minutes, but it was three several years ago. I say with the trend being what it is, why not skip five and jump to six minutes—you see, the six-minute ad, the four-minute mile."

Ann noticed his enthusiasm, a good kid, so to speak. She tried to be pleasant. "It does sound like an interesting—"

"This guy bothering you, Ann?" Ann looked up. It was Jillio. Before she could answer, Jillio had moved to the right of Terry. She gasped as she saw Jillio flash his badge. "Watch yourself, dude, this is a nice, respectable—"

"Jill," she snapped, "will you get the hell out of here and join those grinning baboons? I'll be there in a sec."

Ann watched the smug look on Terry's face. He was staring at Jillio and, while not threatening, was clearly not intimidated.

Jillio shrugged and waved off the "gang" howling at a table about forty feet away. He held out his hand toward Terry. "Name's Charley, Charley Jillio. Sorry if I was out of line. It's obvious you're a good sport."

"And obviously not intimidated by the likes of you," Ann offered delightedly.

Terry, his cherubic face beet-like now that he was the center of all this attention, looked right at Jillio. "Think nothing of it, Charley. If ya can't kid around, what a boring place this world would be."

Jillio nodded and sort of saluted Terry by moving his beer stein up and down and turned to face his tormentors. He pointed to them as he headed back toward the beerfilled table. "Will you guys get off my Monday–Friday back, or I'll call the cops."

"Call the cops!" Stretch howled. "Oh, that's a funny one."

That Stretch is always the worst when they're loaded. Ann sighed. She looked at Terry and held out her hand. "Well, nice meeting you, Terry. Believe it or not, I got to join those imbeciles." She pointed at the table that had suddenly turned quiet after Jillio sat down.

"Well, Ann, can I get your number? Maybe we can—"

"Just give me your card, Terry. I'm sort of involved, but maybe we can have some coffee—"

"But, Ann—"

"No argument, Terry." She stood up and turned toward the "baboon" table. "And I'm not listed. Either give me your card or…"

Terry's wide grin had returned. "Sold America." He reached for his wallet and pulled out a business card. She grabbed it as if she were a wide receiver as she headed toward her coworkers without a glance back.

Someone had pulled up a chair from another table and deposited it next to the full beer stein that still had a head on it. Ann sat down and watched the suddenly quiet and sullen bunch look at her awkwardly. Her anger at Jillio and the "baboons" resulted in a thirst that the just-finished draft hadn't quenched. She smiled inwardly as she chugalugged the fresh draft while trying to maintain the look of a schoolmarm in charge of a bunch of junior high "incorrigibles" held over for detention. Ann had a lot to say, but she'd be damned if she'd be the one to break the silence.

Nowitzky broke the silence. "Just letting off a little steam, Ann, is all." Ann's only response was a sudden angry glare.

"Ay, c'mon, Ann," Nowitzky sort of pleaded, "don't take it that way."

"How should I—"

Stretch suddenly leaped up and pointed at Jillio. "It's your fault, Jill. You gotta take the rap. We ain't gonna be written up just 'cause you had one beer too many and…"

Ann waved her hand and obtained the required silence. "Jill," she hissed, "going all the way back to the class clown pulling my pig-tails I've never seen—"

"C'mon, Ann," Jillio cut in as if he were responding to Mom for being five minutes late for dinner.

"Pulling out your badge for no reason while under the influ-ence," Ann hissed, "a three-month suspension without pay, if you're lucky."

Jillio, suddenly appearing sober, said, "Ann, you don't think that guy—"

"You're a lucky MF, Jill. Not only is that dude a nice guy, but his uncle was, maybe still is, a cop. Next time you complain about a perp skating 'cause of a lawyer or a jury, remember this one, Jill. Remember the time *you* skated."

Stretch smirked, "Even if the dude is quiet, your worries aren't over, Jill. Ann's also a wounded party, and she's on the inside. Make it up to her, Jill. Next time you get a plum detail, she's first in line, right, Ann?"

Nowitzky held out his arms, as if he were an umpire deciding a close call. "A bribe would be nice, if offered, to make Ann forget this whole shebang. But we don't have to worry about Ann, right, Jill? Tell us why."

Jillio gulped, as if he were starting a big lecture. "Yeah, Skee, you nailed it. What happened today, well, you're one of us, Ann. You know what kind of life we lead. Yeah, we let off steam like we're still in junior high, but half the time we're out of the station, our 'signif-icant others' don't know whether we'll make it back for dinner or breakfast, depending on the assignment."

"I'm sorry, and I know I went too far with that badge shit, but you're not who I'm worried about, Ann." He pointed toward Stretch, Nowitzky, the new guy. "Speaking of wives, girlfriends, whatever, we're all closer than any of those relationships. Our wives, much as we might love them, don't carry our backs. Our wives might make love to us, take care of the kids, but when it's life-and-death," he pointed at everyone again, "that's the biggest bond there is. I... I... I love these guys. You too, Ann, you too."

Ann gasped. She fought back tears. "Excuse me, I have to…" She almost jumped from her chair and raced toward the ladies' room. No one was in there, and she paused at the wash area and stared at the mirror. She noticed her flushed cheeks, her heavy breathing, and worst of all, that slight indication of teardrops. Too ladylike in front of those male, chauvinist, pig, grizzled veterans? Well, whatever, Jill said she belonged. Jill said she belonged. Her insides tingled like the first time she knew there was a Christmas and she'd rushed to the tree that morning to find out what Santa had brought her.

Ann powdered her nose, and voilà, not a trace of a delicate damsel in distress.

She put on her game face and headed back. Skee kicked Ann's chair out toward her as she rejoined the crowded table. "Ann, you're back just in time. We could use your input."

"What is it now, Skee? The last time I—"

"C'mon, Ann, we're not foolin' around." Skee pointed toward the new guy, Molina. "Believe it or not, Ann, Mo wants to quit the force, just two years after getting his detective's stripes."

"Oh?" Ann wanted to ask "Too stressful? Not enough pay? Too many baboons around?" but decided to leave it at "Oh?"

"Yeah, Ann, the greedy SOB is considering accepting an offer from Palmeiro Protective Services."

Ann looked puzzled. She stared at Molina, who rolled his eyes while looking at Skee, as if to say "You got the floor."

Skee grinned. "Yeah, Ann, we're trying to talk this mother out of it." He edged closer to Molina until he was virtually in his face. "Pedro, Pedro, we're all taking it personal. Ditching us for a lousy five grand a week."

Jillio leaped up. "Five mother grand a week? Sign *me* up. Ay, Pedro, show me the…"

"Shut the fuck up, Jill, you're not as funny as you think you are."

Skee waited till Jillio was properly chastised. "Y'see, Ann, Palmeiro's one of them amorphous outfits that, uh, takes care of things that law enforcement or lawyers can't quite handle."

"Oh, like that Blackwater in Iraq?"

"A little more shady, Ann. Blackwater does what the Pentagon or Bush wants done that requires a little civilian finesse and resources that… Well, the point is, theoretically, Blackwater, depending on your politics, helps the USA implement foreign policy and—"

"Implement?" Stretch cut in. "When the fuck did you conduct foreign policy seminars?"

"Enough, Stretch." Skee scratched his head. "None of you fuckers is funny. What is this? A tryout for a guest spot on Leno? No more interruptions. I'm trying to explain all this to Ann. Ah, pardon my French, Ann."

Ann let out a slight smirk. "No offense, Skee, you're doing a good job. Go ahead."

"Well, Ann, while natch everything Palmeiro does is under wraps, there's a big thing going on that Palmeiro's hugely involved in."

"I'll take it from here, Skee." Stretch looked at Ann. "You heard about that big fuss that's been going on for at least a couple of years? Involves that big-shot lawyer Mellon."

"Right, just read about it in *This Week*."

"Well, Mellon uses Palmeiro's outfit for bodyguard and more proactive services. Who the hell knows what kinda jobs they're gonna give to Mo over here?" Skee leaned over and tapped Molina affectionately on the shoulder. "Jeez, Mo, don't put us in a spot where we'd have to arrest you. At least stay outta Manhattan."

"Not to worry, Skee." Stretch smiled. "Palmeiro's not paying out that kinda dough for just any cop. Mo speaks Spanish fluently, looks like a spic leading man, and is already trained in firearms and all the other qualifications we got." He looked at Molina, who was blushing and grinning. "So where they gonna send you, Mo? To some hellhole like Calli or Medellin to joust with those coke cartels?"

Molina took in all the eyes focused on him; he was enjoying the silence and the attention. "Caballeros *et* senorita," he affected his best Spanish accent, "d'ju left out a closer location. *Et*, senors, what about all the action a little closer, Mehico?"

"Damn right," Jillio chimed in, "they're stealing all the action from Columbia and—"

Molina cut Jillio off and held up his arm. "Okay, guys, enough kiddin' around. They haven't told me a thing yet. But I was assured I'd never be in any of that. On the other hand, we might be protecting or, well, people involved in that shit, ah, pardon my French, Ann. Or be protecting the embattled law enforcement. Well, that's all I'm prepared—"

"There ya go, Mo. You're already on the other side of the fence, you're taking the Fifth." Jillio cackled. "Well, guys, we shouldn't be too hard on old Mo. At least he's not going to Internal Affairs." Everyone laughed.

When the laughter subsided, Jillio looked at Ann. "It was before your time, Ann, but Mo's connection with Palmeiro reminds us of the Sixteenth's unfinished business. You all remember that a-hole Josh Parker who walked after killing Officer Manny Santana from the Twenty-Fourth Precinct."

"I remember that," Ann offered. "Didn't all of Hollywood come to his aid 'cause he sprouted poetry out of his cell?"

"Right, Ann, led by that bee—ahh, rhymes with *witch*—Ann Sloan, a.k.a. the Chanteuse."

"I remember," Ann said excitedly. "Then after he was free, this Josh character killed the Chanteuse's brother in some Ripley's one-chance-in-a-million accidental coincidence."

"Your memory's good, Ann. Well, the brother's killing was in our precinct, and Sully pulled out all the stops. He went to city hall to get the best DA in Manhattan. It was LWOP—we couldn't get death 'cause it wasn't planned."

Stretch picked up the story. "So the Chanteuse natch turned against Josh, so she was ostracized by the Hollywood weirdos who went bonkers for their latest cause until they lost interest, but there's still enough dough for continued appeals, but that fucker'll never walk quietly in, say, ten or fifteen years."

"Why not?" Ann smirked, guessing the reason before Stretch answered.

"Because every judge who'd love to be a hero at Columbia or Elaine's with the glitterati would think twice... that Josh, in effect, skated after killing one of our own. The PBA and every precinct in the city would come down so hard on that freakin' judge, nah. The LWOP is gonna hold on this one, irrespective of the ACLU, ACORN, PBS, NPR, or any of those Hollywood ghouls."

"Wow." Skee stood up and grinned. "Make an Italian a cop, he makes a speech."

"Yo, Skee, ready for some Pollack jokes?" Jill and Stretch responded virtually in unison.

"Ay, c'mon, guys, no offense. I seen it in a movie… ah, let's see, yeah, *Cry of the City*, with Victor Mature, and—"

"Victor Mature?" Ann interjected, looking puzzled.

"You all seen that old movie *Samson and Delilah*?" Skee grinned, catching the nods from his rapt audience. "Well, Victor Mature was Samson, and Hedy Lamar—"

"What's all this got to do with dago wops?" Stretch cut in impatiently.

"Yo, gimme a chance, guys. So Victor Mature and this guy Richard Conte grow up poor in Little Italy, and as is normal with Hollywood, one becomes a crook and the other a cop."

"Who's Richard Conte?" Ann grinned, sheepish that'd she'd interrupted again.

"Lemme finish the story, Ann," Skee responded pleasantly. "So Conte busts out of a hospital jail and makes it back to his ma in Little Italy. Mature tracks him down there and won't get into a gunfight in Mama's tiny apartment, vowing not to violate the sanctity of Mama's home. But before he leaves, he goes into the usual BS about growing up poor, and while some dedicate themselves to lead an honest, productive life, some take to the streets for the easy money. After all this tongue-lashing, the camera shifts to an embarrassed Conte, who's just been humiliated in front of his ever-forgiving mom. So not knowing how to answer, he simply grins and says, 'Make an Italian a cop, he makes a speech.'"

"Wow," Ann gushed, "you ought to review movies for the *Times*, Skee. So who's this Richard Conte?"

"Easy. Ann. All you dudes seen *The Godfather*?"

"Ah, he was the dude who smacked around Sonny's sister?" Molina giggled.

"Good guess, Mo, but this Conte guy musta been sixty by the time *The Godfather* was made."

"I got it." Stretch grinned. "The Vegas guy."

"Good guess, Stretch, but that's not it. You guys remember that big meeting in that huge office building when Brando and the other family chief hug and everyone claps?"

There were murmurs of "yeah'" all around.

"Well, it was the guy who ran the meeting… err, he made some joke about 'After all, we are not Communists.' *That* was Conte." Skee caught all the blank expressions. "Okay, guys, rent the freakin' movie… and look for that scene. That was Conte."

"How'd we get derailed into this Conte guy?" Ann looked at her watch. "It's past seven. I'm not hitting the computer tonight. Time to go home."

Skee responded, "Yo, Ann, guys, just tryin' to pay homage to Stretch over here. I liked his tirade against the Hollywood elites working for scum like Parker."

"Thanks, Skee." Stretch walked over and hugged Nowitzky, who rose to meet him.

"Jeez, I'm glad I'm gonna be outta here," Molina cracked. "Hard-boiled dicks huggin' like a pair of gringo fairies—too much for my macho mentality."

They all laughed as they pulled out their cells to announce just how late they'd be for dinner tonight. Ann pulled out her cellphone absentmindedly. She had no one to call to say she'd be late, because she lived alone. She again fought back tears, but since everyone was busy calling home, she knew she'd win the battle. She stared at her phone, still emotional over her "acceptance" and watching the "hard-boiled dicks" hugging. Two hours ago, these guys were "baboons." Now she'd go through a wall for any of them.

34

THE GRAMMAR LESSON

Stu Frommer took a cab to Enterprise Rent-A-Car in downtown Walnut Creek and approached the counter.

"Are you a previous customer?" The young man was looking down at the computer, ready to find him in the database.

"I really don't recall," Frommer replied with an edge. "Is all this necessary?"

"Well, if we find you, it'll be a time-saver," the rep answered cheerily, as if to say. "Stop being a jerk. If you'd given me your name right away, I'd already be asking you what kind of car and for how long, and I'd be that much closer to the next customer."

Frommer cracked a slight smile. *Damn Stu, stop falling apart. You think this young kid is gonna recognize your name and, under instructions from Beltran, take out a Glock from beneath the counter and plug you right then and there? Bad enough I'm so paranoid I gotta rent a car and drive to Sacramento for a flight back East 'cause they're "perpetually" casing SFO, Oakland, and San Jose airports.*

"Err, Frommer." He smiled. "Stuart Frommer"

"Ah, yes, are you still on Third Street in San Francisco?"

"Nah, I moved. I was staying at the Marriott on Main. I just checked out. I need the car for one way to Sacto Airport. Can I drop it off there one-way?"

"Sure." He smiled. "And there's no surcharge."

Frommer was in a new Lexus within ten minutes. *Good kid*, he reflected as he headed back to his pad to pack. *Let's see, if I'm on the road by eleven, I should be at the Sacto hotel by early afternoon.* The flight was for JFK at seven thirty the next morning with a connection in KC. He had a full load of work for the afternoon and checked his Blackberry to make sure he'd inserted the name of that trendy restaurant near the airport. He finished his packing and the other BS by ten thirty and was out the door when… *Damn, gotta record the next two weeks of Mad Men. Big meet with Mellon, whatever. Ain't forgettin' ol' Don Draper and all those shenanigans on Madison Avenue.* Double-checking his DVR, Stu was satisfied, and he headed toward the Lexus rental with his two flight bags.

He crossed Treat and was on 680 North in two minutes. He reflected on his caution in telling that Enterprise kid he was staying at the Marriott, which was BS, but he hadn't wanted to give Enterprise his Walnut Creek address. The kid could have asked for a more permanent address, but he didn't. *Guess they're trained that a valid credit card is sufficient.* Within five minutes, Stu saw the 80 East sign for Sacramento. He put the car on cruise control, inserted a Beatles tape, and was comfy for the next fifty minutes until his reverie was broken by seeing the first signs for Sacramento.

He called brother Phil that night and during the next day's layover in KC.

"Yeah, Stu, you said you didn't wanna stay with us and the Plaza's known as one of your haunts, so Mellon found a dump on the Upper West Side that's guaranteed to make you 'safe at home.' It's such a dump that if they had two agents covering every hotel in Manhattan, they'd need five thousand or more operatives before they'd get to the level of that hovel."

"Gee, thanks, Phil. Why don't you tell Mellon I'll remember the both of you in my will?"

"That's the point, Stu. That's the point. We don't want your will to be an issue until you're gray-haired and walking with a cane."

Stu smiled, recalling Phil's smart-aleck answer as he found the entrance to the West Side Highway in Lower Manhattan. He got off the highway on Ninety-Sixth Street and took West End Avenue down to Ninety-First Street. There it was: the Seneca Hotel. All the usual BS associated with a dump. Weekly rates, monthly furnished rentals available... *Yikes, Beltran, if I had no reason to hate you before, making me stay in a place like this... What a freaking way to make a living.*

There was a typical New York type luncheonette on the premises, and Stu salivated at the prospect of enjoying *one* of the treats not available on the Left Coast, but Stu's elation at the prospect gave way to wariness. All kinds of signs in Spanish, Chinese, or whatever Asian country, even the distinctive Arabic signs—this wasn't your uncle's Brooklyn, where everyone was either Irish, Jewish, or Italian and Irish bars, kosher delis, and pizzerias doted the landscape.

"Got an egg cream?" he asked hopefully.

"What size?" the counterman responded.

Right then, Stu coulda kissed the SOB. He asked "What size?" instead of "What the hell's an egg cream?" Well, granted, it won't taste like the ones at Sy's on Ocean Parkway; still, Stu started salivating. "Err, large."

"Vanilla or chocolate?"

Chocolate, what else? he thought, but limited his answer to "chocolate."

"That'll be just a minute," the counterman replied as he turned to grab a new glass.

Stu started scanning the *New York Times*'s front page. As promised, the egg cream came within a minute, give or take. Frommer started sipping. Ahh, nothing like Sy's, but even an average egg cream's better than no egg cream. Hey, that'd make some ad if egg creams could be merchandised nationally like pizza and burgers. Feeling mellow, Stu figured he'd review some of Syms's notes on the Adams account while slowly downing the fulfilling egg cream. Stu felt good about the progress on the Adams approach; Carpenter was continuing his fine handling of the...

"Hey, mister, you can't do your work at the counter. This ain't no Starbucks or—"

"What about that guy?" Stu almost shouted while pointing to a man farther down the counter reading the tabloid *Post*.

The counterman shrugged. "A paper's okay, just—I got instructions people can't just sprawl out there and make like this is their extended office." He looked at Stu. "No offense, mister, I do as I'm told."

Stu felt lousy over snapping at the counterman. *How'd you like to be middleaged and being a counterman at an ordinary luncheonette attached to a dingy hotel in a slumlike neighborhood?* He smiled, hoping that would overcome his harsh response. "Yeah, my mistake. A place like this obviously has a different business plan than a Starbucks. Ah, speaking of which, is there one around here?"

"What, a Starbucks?"

What else we been talking about, ya dummy? "Yeah, a Starbucks."

The counterman pointed to his left. "Right down the avenue, about two blocks. You can't miss it."

"Thanks, thanks a lot." Stu started perusing the *Times* as the counterman moved on. *Damn, Stu, you actually processed the "what else we been talking about?" stance with that hapless working stiff you were feeling sorry for just two minutes ago? Don't know what Mellon wants, but I know this—I gotta speak to somebody about everything that's going on. Can't fuckin' sleep, heart beating like a drum, paranoid about meeting anyone, going anywhere... On the other hand, those things are temporary, as long as you're your old cool self most of the time. Yeah, most of the time. Something to latch on to before I see a shrink or end up in a loony bin. Loony bin—that ain't good. Beltran's boys would know where I am. See that? There you go again. Maybe a night's sleep, maybe it's the jet lag...*

As to why Mellon wanted to wait till the morning, who knows? The three-hour time difference would have led to a late arrival, even with a nonstop. What with the layover in KC, it was already past ten, and all he had so far for "dinner" was that appetite-busting egg cream. Well, it was only 8:00 PM West Coast time, but Stu started to feel hunger pangs. He opened one of his travel bags to find a fresh T-shirt to sleep in and took out his toiletries. That was all he needed for the AM since Phil had said Palmeiro would pick him up by 9:00 AM. The rest would stay packed for a quick getaway. *Just got here and can't wait to get out of this dump.*

Stu felt better as he checked out the neighborhood in the early evening breeze. He passed that Starbucks and decided he'd have something there if he couldn't find anything else. *We're not talking the Duck Club*, he mused. *Anything, anything that looks half decent… Ah, Godfather's Pizza, the Best in the City.* His heart soared like that proverbial eagle—next to an egg cream or a knish, nothing like a local Big Apple family pizzeria.

It didn't even have to be the "best in the city." He walked in and saw it was strictly takeout. The only seats were for those waiting for their orders. He ordered a small vegeterian sans the olives. He knew he was in for a treat; the aroma of quality pizza permeated the place.

He had real trouble falling asleep. It was twelve thirty when he'd finished eating and the just-digested pizza and his 10:30 PM body clock kept him up. He tried to finish that movie he'd been watching with the pizza, and it ended within ten minutes. *Damn*, he muttered, *I gotta take a walk, sort of "work off" all those delicious calories.*

He hit the street around 1:00 AM, and joints were starting to close. He saw a bar, but the clientele and the atmosphere didn't remind him of Perry's in Frisco or P. J. Clarke's on Third Avenue. *In other words, you've had your walk and fresh air, Stuey, don't go risk your chin or other bodily parts by partaking in an after-dinner drink in a dive populated by yahoos.*

The wake-up call caught him groggy at 7:00 AM—jet lag. That's why he'd asked for another call at seven thirty just in case he fell asleep again. But he was up at seven fifteen and had an extra meticulous shave; this was no big date, but he was seeing the Big Man, which, from a financial standpoint, was certainly more important than a night with a babe. He hurried down to the luncheonette and ordered coffee and a muffin. His cell rang as he was pouring cream into his coffee. It was Phil. He said the Palmeiro ETA was going to be around eleven, two hours later than planned. "Don't hassle me!" Phil had screeched. "They said something came up. I gave them your cell. They'll call when they're about fifteen minutes from your hotel."

Shit, Stu mused as he bit into his muffin. *I'm not gonna wait around this dump another three hours.* He figured that Starbucks, even in this neighborhood, would have a nice vibe. Plus, he could do some work, since that's what everyone does there. He pictured walking the two blocks with his two carry-on bags. *Not good*, he concluded. He'd stand out too much. *Could take a cab, for two blocks? To a Starbucks? "Hey, Johnny, listen to the jerk I just had for a fare. Goes from that Seneca hotel to that Starbucks two blocks away carrying two flight bags. Well-dressed dude. Think something's up? Should I call da cops? Could be a reward…"*

Well, the most obvious choice was to check the bags at the hotel and come back for them. Trouble with that was, you start yapping with Palmeiro's boys as soon as they pick you up and you're halfway down the FDR before you realize you left without your bags. Finally, Stu concluded Palmeiro has high-quality operatives; if he enters their limo without luggage, they'd question it. He went back up to the room, took out Syms's notes and his Blackberry, and took the elevator down to the lobby, where he checked his bags.

It was a crisp morning, but the sun was coming out. He looked at his watch as he approached the Starbucks; it was a quarter to nine. *Shit, two hours to kill, and that assumes they'll be on time. Well, maybe I'll have some questions for Syms and have to call him. That'd kill some time*, he concluded. Now *to decide what to get. Those egg sandwiches look interesting. Get to Mellon's around noon. When do we eat and where? The richest dude in New York, give or take Donald Trump and a few others, and he's got nowhere to eat. Brother Phil had surmised that Mellon had takeout food delivered to various Palmeiro boys, who then surreptitiously delivered it to Mellon's digs, or maybe some of their wives cook dinner and the Palmeiro operatives aluminum-foil it and deliver it or… Mellon also couldn't be using his own live-in chef, the guy would have to get a day off and…* Stu was getting a headache. *What a fuckin' life for Mellon and, of course, for me.*

"Lemme have that egg sandwich with the spinach and the latte that goes with it."

"You want the combo?"

"Ah, right, the combo."

"That'll be $4.40. Your name?"

"Stuey."

"Fine, Stuey. I'll find you when the sandwich's ready and look for the cup with your name on it at that counter." She pointed to the right.

Stuey smiled. "Thanks." He put the change in the cup. He found an empty table and took out his work papers. He shook his head at the "efficiency" of the "host person," or whatever they're called. *Well, I guess that's how that Schultz dude built that winning organization.* The paper-wrapped egg concoction was there in no time, and Stu got up and found his latte.

Fifteen minutes had gone by, and Stu had already entered several questions for Syms in his Blackberry when he heard something come through the ordinary Starbucks' background din. It was that heavy "Nuu Yawk" accent like out of Red Hook or Greenpoint—guess it reaches all the way to the Upper West Side.

"So she goes 'That dress you're wearing is so out of fashion it's unbelievable."

"So I go 'You should tawk. I seen your whole family's outfits. Tawk about being out of fashion.'"

"Then she starts tawking about Franky, and I says, 'Angie, you keep my boyfriend out of this, like you should tawk.'"

Frommer was staring in disbelief. The banter had been coming through the hubbub for about five minutes and looking at the relaxed yenta on this end; it looked like no end in sight. He decided to bite the bullet and see if he could concentrate despite the "tawk"… Syms had highlighted some portions of the Adams account. Stu tried to focus, but that yenta was still yapping up a storm. He looked around. There were some empty tables outside. It wasn't that cold when he'd walked over from the hotel, and that was about a half hour ago. For sanity's sake, he scooped up the notes, the half-eaten sandwich, and the latte and settled on a spot in the fresh air and away from the din.

Frommer used the latte cup as a paperweight against the breeze blowing away any of the papers. Back to Syms. He seemed confident that the Adams account would add about 10 percent to the bottom line and there was more where that came from; apparently, the board had approved another $10–15 million for another campaign in the next fiscal. Frommer suddenly looked up. He'd been aware of some background coughing since moving outside, but now it seemed louder, deeper, like what you'd hear at a TB Sanitarium. He caught the dude with the hacking cough. He was glaring all around as if to say "I'll cough all I want. Whatcha gonna do about it?"

Be my guest, Frommer concluded, *cough in good health*. He went out of his way to avert the man's glare. He did look to his right and spotted the last Starbucks table next to the entrance to a small toy store. He moved his latte and papers to that table and looked at his watch. *Almost ten. Got about an hour before Palmeiro's boys arrive and—*

"What are you, wise guy?"

Frommer did an automatic "huh," like when you're half asleep on a swing on a lazy sunny day and you automatically swat a fly without even thinking and...

"What are you, wise guy?"

Back to reality. In the next second or two, a thousand thoughts seemed to have been processed through Frommer's cerebellum. Panic, flight, fear, yes, but also "stategic depth" to avoid a possible opening sucker punch. Frommer hadn't looked up yet, but he could gauge from the coughers' shoes that the threat was far enough away to give him a chance to—he quickly jumped from his chair and backed up two steps. It had all occurred in five seconds. They faced each other. *How far was PS 116 from this forsaken hole? Time to remember everything you learned in the schoolyard, dude. Pull out a cell phone to call da cops, and he'd have swatted the phone out of your hands before the first touch of the keyboard.*

"What's the problem?"

"Problem? No problem, I'm just gonna kick your ass. You know why?"

"I can guess. How's this, some two-bit whore turned you down for a date, and you're looking to take it out on someone half your size. Can I get another guess? You're insulted 'cause I didn't continue to sit next to you and absorb all your fuckin' germs. Am, am I getting close?" The thud in Frommer's feverishly pumping heart was losing some of its thud.

The cougher, who, just moments ago, was an affronted wise guy, appeared to be losing his mojo. Unbelievably, he repeated himself. "You wise guy?"

Now Frommer tried mightily to suppress a grin. Wouldn't do in the middle of a standoff. *This guy's pathetic, but he's big and obviously been through the wars before or he wouldn't be acting so belligerent. Just continue to rattle his cage, Stuey, Brooklyn style.*

"Where's the article, you twit?"

"Huh?"

"Article, article. You harda hearing in addition to your lack of grammar—you know, article, adjective, preposition."

"Proposition? You fuckin' faggot *and* wise guy?"

"I'm a fuckin' faggot and a wise guy. *A* is an article, and *preposition* is a grammatical word. *Preposition*, not *proposition*, you twit. What were you doing in school while my taxes were paying for your education? Can't you even speak English? There's more to life than hanging on the corner and saying 'What's happening, guys? Let's bust some chops.'"

The cougher was edging toward Frommer but wasn't sure what to do next. Some green-clad Starbucks's employees, apparently summoned by wary customers, peeked out to see what the ruckus was about and quickly disappeared inside. It was obvious da cops would soon be arriving.

"Ay, doofus, ya ain't gonna land a sucker punch, and time's a-fleeting. You don't think Starbucks has called the cops by now? Dollars to doughnuts, you got a record… and… this ain't exactly a good time for me. So back the fuck up a couple of feet so I can pick up my shit and cut the scene."

Sirens were coincidentally heard above the traffic's din. "I'd get the fuck outta here if I was you, and don't forget to check yourself out for TB, and for heaven's sake, go back to school and learn some grammar. I'm positive you quit school when you got to be sixteen." Frommer had been edging backward while continuing his harangue. Now there was about twenty feet separating the two, and he figured he could finally turn his back to the big man and head back to the hotel.

"Hey, mister." It was the big man's voice.

Frommer turned quickly to face him. He glared defiantly. "Yeah?"

"No hard feelings, huh? Ya got balls and a big moud. I like that."

Frommer just stared in disbelief. "*Moud?* The education and elocution—challenged bruiser probably meant *mouth*."

"Just one question before you go, what the fuck's a *twit?*"

Frommer just grinned. This confrontation was obviously over. "That's a British word for *mook*, big fella. See ya around."

The squad car had just arrived. The big cougher quickly turned and started walking in the other direction. "Holy shit," Frommer concluded, "never a dull moment." He crossed the street; the Seneca was a block away. His cell rang. "Yeh, it's Frommer. You're a half hour early? Okay, I'll meet you in the hotel lobby. What? Don't apologize for being late. I had a nice, quiet cup of coffee in Starbucks."

Two minutes after Frommer had gotten his bags, the Palmeiro limo pulled up. "Hi, guys, been to the stadium this season? Hear Derek Jeter's lost a step."

THE MEETING

One of the two Palmeiro operatives sat in the back of the limo next to Frommer, while the other drove. "Still gin and tonic, Mr. Frommer?"

Well, I like vodka and tonic, Frommer reflected, *but why correct the guy? His memory, while not perfect, was virtually spot on. Besides, most people do prefer gin and tonic.* The ice maker in back of the front seat was dispensing the ice cubes like those ubiquitous soda stations at McDonald's, Burger King, et al. *An ice maker in the back of a limo—now I've seen it all,* Frommer mused, *even the twist of lime.* Before Frommer finished his second sip, the driver pulled over. The shades were drawn in the back of the limo.

"Nothing personal, Mr. Frommer. I do hope you understand, but we do this with all passengers visiting Mr. Mellon."

"I understand fully." Frommer grinned. "Mellon's version of Homeland Security."

The Palmeiro dude, blindfold in hand, winced but allowed a small grin. *Well, that's why comedians like Leno try out their material at local nightspots before using it on TV—you never know when a joke's gonna bomb.*

He put the blindfold over Frommer's eyes. "Is it comfortable, Mr. Frommer?"

"Quite, Sandy. How long do I drink my gin and tonic in the dark?"

SLATS AND THE CHANTEUSE

"Well, Mr. Frommer, we might be ten minutes away or twenty-five minutes away. It all depends on what kind of evasive action Artie takes." With that response, both Sandy and Artie laughed as if in unison.

Talk about trying out your material. These guys must think they're at the improv. Frommer leaned back and kept downing the drink in the darkness and silence. Frommer estimated they were on the FDR for less than ten minutes. Of course, "evasive" could mean anything. For instance, they could have passed the proper exit on the FDR so that a pro who later went back and simulated the trip couldn't guess what exit was taken after entering the highway on Ninety-Second Street. *For a better man than me,* Frommer reflected. *I didn't even look at my watch just prior to the blindfold, and besides, even if the time on surface streets was five minutes from the exit, how the hell do you know which way they went after exiting the FDR? Besides, I'm not after Mellon. Let the potential hit man have all the headaches.* But just for the sport of it, Frommer counted five stops at red lights (or Stop signs?) after the FDR. In fantasyland and slowly sipping his drink, Frommer suddenly experienced the whoosh of a down ramp. It must be the garage. About a minute later, the limo came to a stop.

"Okay, Mr. Frommer, I'll be taking the blindfold off now."

"Thanks, Sandy." Frommer had to blink for several seconds to return to visual reality.

"Yeah, wow, all those movies where they ask the dude if he wants a blindfold before the firing squad begins firing."

"Which option would you choose, Mr. Frommer?" Artie asked.

"No blindfold for me, Artie. I'd want to glare at those SOBs so they'd have something to remember me by."

The elevator went up to the seventeenth floor. The Palmeiro boys didn't seem to care that Frommer saw the blinking elevator lights stop at 17. *But of course,* Frommer realized, *anyone would figure the floor, since when they rang the bell, it was for unit 1710. Duh, but how many 1710s are there in Manhattan? Ten thousand, fifty thousand? Cut it out, Stuey, you'll give yourself a headache even before meeting the big man.*

A butler type opened the door and greeted the trio. He led them into the "study" and excused himself. Frommer started heading toward a chair. "Just a minute, Mr. Frommer." It was Sandy. "We're gonna have to frisk ya before you sit down. Hope you understand."

"Sure." Frommer grinned. "I understand."

"Could you take your suit jacket off, please."

"Sure, Sandy." The moment Frommer took off the jacket, Artie grabbed it and quickly patted it down. Meanwhile, Sandy was dutifully patting Frommer from head to toe, like any good cop in the movies. Frommer was about to ask whether he should take his shoes off but decided there might be a limit to Palmeiro types' sense of humor when they're in the midst of their security duties.

"Sorry for the hassle, Mr. Frommer. You're okay. Sit anywhere you like."

"It's okay, Sandy. You guys obviously know your jobs."

"Thanks, Mr. Frommer. The butler will be right in." With that, Artie and Sandy disappeared from view.

Within a minute, the butler appeared.

"Vodka and tonic," Frommer replied when the butler asked what he'd like to drink.

"My name is Harold, Mr. Frommer. Mr. Mellon will be right in. Will there be anything else?"

"Nah, thanks, Harold, I'm fine." Alone in the room, Frommer looked around. There weren't shades on the windows. There were dark bamboo-type window frames.

They seemed to be sealed shut with what looked like a key latch where the frames met.

So that's it. I'll bet all the windows are similarly sealed when company arrives. If you see so-and-so restaurant or dry cleaners across the street or a hotel sign nearby, it wouldn't be that impossible to figure out which building belongs to 1710. Wow, all this is too much for me. Stuey, baby, forget the CIA as a second career. Be happy with...

There was a knock. Frommer looked up. Mellon walked in.

Frommer leaped up from his easy chair. "Nice seeing you again, after all this time, Mr. Mellon." They shook hands.

"Please, Stuart," Mellon blushed, "call me Bill."

Frommer wanted to answer "What is this Stuart business? My pals call me Stu or Stuey." But he reasoned, "If a billionaire with Palmeiro types at his disposal wants to call me Stuart, who am I to—"

"Please, Stuart," Mellon pointed to the plush leather chair Frommer had just vacated, "make yourself at home. Did Harold take care of you?"

"Sure did, Bill." Frommer held up the virtually full glass of vodka and tonic.

"Well, Stuart, if you'll take your left hand and feel toward the middle of the side of your chair, you'll find a little button. Just push it if you need more ice or something."

Meanwhile, Frommer watched Mellon do that very thing, pushing the white button. Although silent at this end, the buzz was evidently heard outside the study since Harold came in within a minute.

"Yes, Mr. Mellon?"

"Johnnie Walker Red on the rocks, Harold."

"Yes, Mr. Mellon."

Harold looked at Frommer. "I'm fine, Harold, thanks."

Mellon grinned. "The last time I ordered Johnnie Walker Red in public, someone pointed out that Joe Namath once said he likes his Johnnie Walker Red and his lady friends blond."

Frommer laughed. "Whether apocryphal or not, sure sounds like Broadway Joe. Been to any Jets or Giants games recently, Mr. Mell—err, Bill?"

"Not since they moved to Joisey, Stuart, although our firm does have a luxury box at Giants' Stadium. I guess I'll have to go once just to see what the suite is like. But for me, it's not worth the trip. I'll let the junior associates use the boxes for rainmaking purposes." Mellon paused. "Of course, with present conditions, I don't think I should be sitting in the Mellon, Caldwell, & Cunningham suites. Might just be too easy and tempting a target."

Frommer didn't know how to answer that, so he just mumbled, "Good point."

"Well, Stuart, that leads me to why I wanted to see you." Mellon paused to see if Frommer would respond. "What's it been, over a year since we both got involved in this imbroglio?"

"Sounds about right, Bill."

"Well, to get to the point. What the hell have we been doing? If this was a fuckin' movie, everyone in the audience, except for some lawyers, would be rooting for Beltran. I feel like I've been in a fog. No, not a fog, more like on autopilot. This guy's lost everything and then some and wants revenge, so we use all our resources to get him before…"

Frommer wasn't inclined to interrupt, but Mellon had evidently paused. "Before he gets us?"

Mellon's jowls quivered; he allowed himself a slight smirk. "Precise and to the point. Did you say you were in PR?"

They both laughed. "If I may ask, Mr. Mell—err, Bill, when did you arrive—"

"I got you covered, Stuart, as we used to say in Red Hook. About three months ago. My son, who's a major in the Army, had me come down to DC to meet with him. Seems he and his colleagues were up in arms over FISA and all the ambulance chasers going after the tel companies for allowing our spooks to eavesdrop without a warrant on suspected… ah… You're familiar with the FISA shit?"

"I am, Bill, and I was also uncomfortable—"

"Well, that's it, Stuart, talk about autopilot. I'm suddenly on the wrong side of our security, my son… Not that I was, mind you, on the wrong side of this FISA shit, but the *fuckin' legal establishment was* led by your neighbor, that Burnitz out of Palo Alto. Well, I straightened him out, but where the hell did I stand *before* it was cleared up?"

Frommer watched as Mellon virtually chugalugged the rest of his scotch. He toyed with the ice while reaching for the button. Frommer decided right there to finish his drink. He'd look too square if, after taking Mellon's request, Harold looked at him and he answered "I'm just fine, Harold."

In Shakespearean enunciation, Mellon tipsily rose and hoisted his glass, as if to commence a toast at a festive wedding or similar affair. "Here's to our noble youth and our noble hopes and aspirations. When all young lawyers strove to follow in the footsteps of Clarence Darrow and help all the downtrodden and discards of a cruel society. Set things right helping the poor and gut-checking the rich. When, dear Stuart, when did it turn from helping the helpless to billable hours, rainmaking, and yes, class action and frivolous lawsuits?"

Frommer felt a chill through his veins. The Great Man, the one and only Mellon, was losing it, falling apart, but he dared not interrupt as he watched Mellon smack his lips after a large gulp of the Johnnie Walker.

"How does it happen, Stuart? We were all good guys when we grew up, right?"

Frommer nodded.

"Think back, Stuart. When did you make that first choice? You know, like a liar starting with a little white lie. Well, this guy's probably not guilty, but I need convictions to move up the ladder in the DA's office. Well, maybe my client's guilty of murder, but if I get him off, can you imagine the fee I command for my next case?" He looked at Frommer. Frommer was transfixed but tried not to show it. It didn't work. His breathing, despite his efforts, reminded him of the sounds he uttered when he was dry-humping Hotsy, the cheerleader, in the back seat of that '87 Buick that was shared by the guys because of the ample space in the rear.

Mellon caught the drift. "You okay, Stuart? Want me to open a window?"

Frommer's uncontrollable breathing had subsided, but that was only because it had been replaced by a look of dread. "Err, the window, well…"

"But you figured it out, right, Stuart? The fuckin' windows *don't* open. And you know why?"

"'Cause you got company. You don't want any visitors to figure out where this building is." Frommer had replied coolly—his self-confidence had returned.

"Absolutely right, Frommer—I mean, Stuart. Is this any fuckin' way to live?"

"I think it's time for me to say what's on my mind, Bill."

"Yeah, Stuart, go right ahead. I've been monopolizing the floor."

Frommer watched Mellon sit himself down and press that stupid button again.

*What kinda host. Haven't eaten since nine this morning. Three, or is it four, drinks since then. My stomach's yelling "*Gimme some food!*"*

"Err, Bill, I just saw you buzzing Harold. Any chance for some food?"

"*Aw shit, Stuart,* I wanted to start off with a drink, loosen things up. I just… Well, you saw me—I just got carried away."

Mellon noticed Harold, who'd been standing there for several minutes. "Yeah, Harold, sorry I didn't see you come in. Is the food ready?"

Harold allowed a meek, butlerian smile. "For a while, Mr. Mellon."

Mellon blushed. "Gee, Harold, my apologies to the cooks, staff, everyone."

"Quite all right, Mr. Mellon. Shall we?"

"Sure, bring it in now." Mellon rose and gestured to Frommer to also stand up. He put his arm around Frommer. "C'mon, Stuart, lemme show you the nearest restroom. I'm sure you want to clean up before we eat. Then I'll show you around these digs, and then, as they never say in our hometown of Brooklyn, we can dine, ah, that is, grab a bite."

Mellon was heading toward another "restroom" and pointed toward a settee in front of a plasma TV, where they'd meet afterward. Frommer was out' first and sat uncomfortably in front of the large screen wondering whether and/or how he should turn it on. Mellon quickly appeared and roared, "Hope ya like shish kebob, Stuart. One of the Palmeiro guys knows this caterer. It's the best in the city. Of course, we also have cold cuts and burgers, if that's more to your liking."

"The shish kebob sounds just fine, Bill. Looking forward to it." *The best in the city,* Frommer mused. *Where have I heard that one before?* Frommer watched Harold direct some food helpers into the study, rolling those covered hot food casseroles with them as they entered. Frommer was in a daze as Mellon showed him around. His stomach was churning as never before, and he wondered when he'd get a chance to say what was on *his* mind. But most of the apprehension had dissipated. He'd wanted to tell Mellon he was through, he'd had enough. There was always the chance the big man would strongly object. *It's like the Mafia, Frommer, there's no getting out. You're in for life.*

They were back in the study and hovering over the shish kebob steamers. "I guess you've had enough liquor, Stuart." He pointed to the left of the food tables, where Harold was standing next to an array of tall bottles of Coke, Diet Coke, ginger ale, club soda, and bottled water. "Just tell Harold your preference, and he'll get you started on your first drink."

"Diet Coke, Harold, thanks." Frommer watched the butler add ice and a lemon peel to a large glass of the Coca-Cola. After serving the Coke to Frommer, Harold, without prompting, provided what looked like ginger ale to Mellon and then excused himself. Frommer had started on his first stick of shish kebob as he watched Harold exit. There was silence as they both chewed on the lamb.

"Before we get back to business, Stuart, my little speech, about how all this started before we became corrupted, jaded, whatever, reminds me of those good old days. You know, when we played kick the can, Johnny on the pony, ring-a-levio—"

"Ring-a-levio." Frommer was embarrassed that he'd cut in but continued, "It had such a ring, eh, pardon the pun, but we never did play and to this day—"

Mellon laughed out loud. "Same here. We'd heard about it, but never... Well, as we got older, we'd go to the parade grounds for touch or real football."

"Yeah, Bill, couldn't play football on the streets of Brooklyn, so we played off the wall, stickball, and punchball so that—"

"Punchball?" Mellon roared. "What the hell was that?"

Frommer smiled. "Well, Bill, you're familiar with stickball?"

Mellon grimaced. "Well, we never played it. But I think I've seen it. Willie Mays and all that."

"Right, Bill, Willie Mays. Well, in stickball, the sewer man-hole cover is home plate. There's a catcher back of the plate, and the pitcher shoots it in from about sixty feet away."

"A baseball?"

"No, Bill, a Spaldeen. So if you picture the "batter" standing at the plate with a broomstick as his bat. He faces a first baseman about seventy-five feet away on the right side of the street, and similarly, a third baseman on the left side. Then you have a 'shortstop' in the center of the street a little further back and an 'outfielder' about twenty feet in back of the shortstop."

"Then it's just like softball in a schoolyard or playground?"

"Right, Bill, but in the latter, you don't have to worry about being run over by a car."

"So, Stuart, that was Willie Mays stickball. So what was punchball?"

Frommer paused and sipped some Coke to wash the food down. "Gee, Bill, since we're talking ring-a-levio, stickball, punchball, could you call me Stu or Stuey?"

"Sure, Stu." Mellon's face evinced a blush.

"Well, Bill, if you picture the stickball setup, punchball's the same, except there's no pitcher or stick."

"Huh, so how do you—"

"That's why they call it punchball, Bill." Frommer stood up and grinned. He threw an imaginary ball in the air and then swatted at it the same way a tennis player does when serving.

"Gee, Stu, wasn't that difficult?"

"I guess so, in retrospect. But if you start young enough, it's second nature. The real test was the two sewers."

"Two sewers?" Mellon seemed fascinated or, at least, wasn't bored by all this reminiscing.

"Yeah, Bill, you see, any guy acquired a rep if he could punch the ball two sewers."

Mellon closed his eyes momentarily, as if picturing the feat. "Wow, Stu, that wasn't too easy, was it?"

"Nah, Bill, that's why the two-sewer guys had such a rep. The best I ever did was one and three quarters sewers, and I'm proud of it to this day."

"I'm sure it was a feat, Stu, and you should be proud. Well, in Red Hook, most of our, err, activities were indoor—"

Frommer produced the expected X-rated laugh.

"No, Stu, not that. That came later. Once we outgrew Johnny on the pony, we, uh, went indoors to every pool hall in Red Hook or South Brooklyn. So you see, while you middle-class Flatbush guys were emulating Willie Mays, we were all sinfully trying to become the next Willie Mosconi."

Frommer now felt he had to show he'd also been around. "Straight or progression, Bill?"

"Straight, Stu, progression's for faggots. And I don't mean what they call gays in today's vernacular. I mean sissies, guys without balls." Mellon, suddenly all wrought up, paused and regained his composure. He grinned. "At least that's what *we* thought about guys playing progression."

Frommer tried to change the subject, even if only slightly. "That movie have any effect on you guys?"

Mellon gulped down some ginger ale. "Oh, you mean *The Hustler*?"

"Yes, the one with Paul Newman."

"Oh yeah, we all flocked to see it. We sounded our parents, older siblings, 'See, we weren't wasting our time.' But I was nineteen by then and going to Hofstra with two part-time jobs. No more time for dingy pool halls. What about you, Stu? Ever see that movie?"

"Sure did, Bill, but only on cable. After all, it came out a decade before my parents even met."

They both laughed.

Mellon grabbed some potato salad and looked at his watch. "Sorry, Stu, you've been here quite a while, and I'm afraid I've monopolized the—"

"Once a trial lawyer, always a trial lawyer," Frommer interjected.

Mellon looked at his watch again, this time for emphasis. "Try some potato salad, Stu. It's real good. You've been here quite a while, and over a half hour ago, you were gonna say what's on *your* mind. Now I'm gonna finally keep my big-shot litigator's trap shut. Shoot."

Frommer toyed with his potato salad. He looked directly at Mellon. "Bill, hearing what you had to say really made my day. I felt a little trepidation preparing for this meeting. You see, I was afraid I'd disappoint you by telling you that after a year or so, I've also had it." He waited for a response, but Mellon just gently sipped his ginger ale. "Well, in your case, Bill, it seems conscience, your son, and all sorts of guilt feelings led to your change of heart. In my case, well, I didn't mind the hiding, the conflict. I was all 'get those MFs before they get you.' But I'll give you an example. So recent it happened *this* fuckin' morning, ahh, pardon my French, Bill."

Mellon just juggled the ice in his drink and smiled.

"I'm sure you're aware that your Palmeiro guys were going to arrive two hours later than originally planned." Frommer paused and looked at Mellon, who nodded while toying with the ice in his drink. "So I went to the nearest Starbucks to do some business and kill time. And you know what kind of neighborhood I was in."

"We can't always stay at the Plaza or Pierre." Mellon guffawed. "Right now your safety comes first."

"I appreciate that, Bill. I was just trying to set you up for what comes next, considering the neighborhood. I moved to an outdoor table because of the noise inside. So I'm sitting next to a lowlife who's coughing like he's got TB or something."

"Not too pleasant, I'd imagine."

"Right, Bill, so I unobtrusively, I thought, moved to a further table when the dude, a burly cat, starts sounding me and promising he'll kick my behind and all that."

"Sounds bad." Mellon laughed. "But you're here and apparently in one piece, so I'd imagine disaster was averted."

"Yeah, Bill, disaster was averted, but it was a hairy scene. Not from him. After his initial BS, I did most of the yapping. I used every trick we all learned in Brooklyn, Bill. Yap so hard and so confidently that the dude starts thinking he made a mistake."

"Yikes, Stu," Mellon bellowed, "you sure you didn't grow up on my block in Red Hook? I guess it's the same wherever."

"Well, Bill, the a-hole started thinking the better of it. But, Bill, I was so outta sorts I didn't tone it down when the guy lost his nerve. I had to get extra licks in there. Had to sound him, rank him, let 'em know who's boss."

Mellon chuckled. "Sounds like par for the course."

Frommer took a deep breath and swished on some of the ice in his Diet Coke. "I'd leave right now and go to a shrink, Bill, only—"

"I know a good one, Stu—Park Avenue, y'know, the $500-an-hour type."

"Thanks, Bill. I'll wait till I get back to Frisco. My point being, well, when you summarized your first case before a jury, was your heart pounding?"

"Worse than a drum, Stu." Mellon seemed to wince at the long-ago memory. "Well, Bill, a shrink or a speech teacher would probably tell you 'No need to get upset over the speech, and no need to get further upset over being upset. After all, the only bad thing that's gonna happen is your view of yourself if the audience thinks you're a nut or a nerd. But that's your view. Doesn't make it so—"

"And the less you care," Mellon interjected, "the less you get those butterflies."

"Right, Bill, but the difference now is not that I'm imagining the horrors that will ensue if I give a lousy speech or presentation, but the dangers, horrors I'm thinking of now aren't made up, they're out there. One slip and..." Frommer demonstrated an imaginary knife slitting his throat.

"I read you, Stu. What we're facing isn't just in our minds, it's fuckin' out there. Well, Stu, a meeting of the minds. Since you're in the same frame of mind, we're calling the whole thing off, at least from our end. When, by whatever nefarious means, word gets out to the other side that we're calling it off, well, you and I won't have to be in hiding. You're obviously tired and freaked out, and so am I."

"If the other side buys it." Frommer sighed.

"Well, Panmunjom, Paris Peace Talks, Israelis and Egyptians, talks that ended wars. Why not us and Beltran?"

"What about the class actions making it up to Beltran?"

Mellon shrugged. "We can't make it up to him. You don't lose your practice, your wife, your way of life and then call it even when the other side blinks."

"So what can we—"

"We can do what's right. Maybe to ease our consciences, maybe to save money, maybe not to have to seal windows." Mellon pointed to the shuttered windows. "Maybe to return to our lives before this so-called war started."

Frommer stared at Mellon. "You'd still have enemies, there'd still be danger. You're considered the king of torts, with apologies to Grisham."

"Maybe, maybe, but at least I'd sleep good at night knowing those MFs are after my livelihood. I'm successful and wealthy from an honest, if controversial, profession. Maybe, probably, we went overboard with Beltran, but finding redress for wronged consumers and others is an *honorable* profession, and I don't apologize to no one." He glared at Frommer.

Frommer felt a knot in the pit, or however that phrase goes. Suffice it to say, he was shaken. Mellon's public persona, the cool, efficient, successful litigator was a veneer; his Red Hook traits were still there, beneath the surface, but still there.

"Sorry, Stu, for hitting you with the old Red Hook 'death glare.' It may be fifty years since I first did it, but every once in a while, the feeling, the glare—they come back." The tension on Mellon's face seemed to subside as he toyed with his drink. "It looks like I'm pun-king out, Stu, but I ain't. I got my family, my rep, my grandchildren, Mellon, Caldwell & Cunningham—all of it. I'm not throwing in the towel, just calling off this senseless war."

"I see what you—"

"I hope you do, Stu, I hope you do. I don't want you walking out of here and spreading the word the old guy's lost it."

"I'd never," Frommer barely gasped, "even if I believed it, which I don't. I see another ten, twenty years—"

"Don't patronize me!" Frommer bellowed. "Lucky if it's five years. Shit, I'm pushin' sixty-seven, but the old dude ain't slowing down or giving in."

Frommer felt still another chill at Mellon's belligerent attitude, especially being addressed as Frommer again. *Well, this guy's my main meal ticket. It's all good. The old fart hasn't lost it.* "I got you covered," Frommer replied softly.

"Good." Mellon smiled. "As for your retainer, it'll stay at current 'wartime' levels for another twelve months. Then, depending on whatever you're doing for me, we'll probably continue at the levels before all this shit broke out. Sound fair?"

"More than fair, Bill." An elated Frommer stifled a grin.

"Okay, in about a month, after a review by our financial people, we'll send you an e-mail or letter with specific details." Mellon looked at his watch. "Going to see your brother?"

"Where are Palmeiro's guys gonna drop me off?"

"Who knows. I guess you want the heart of Manhattan? At any rate, they know better than any of the major hotels."

"Good. Wherever. Phil's standing by, waiting for my call."

Mellon suddenly smirked. "It'll probably take an hour for Phil to pick you up. Maybe they'll drop you off at a Starbucks."

Frommer clapped his hands together and giggled. "I'm not worried. Lightning ain't gonna strike twice." He noticed Mellon glance at his watch again. "Mrs. Mellon in town?"

"Err, no, Bill, she's still hanging her hat in Paris. Won't be back till the opera and symphony seasons begin." Mellon paused and exhibited an X-rated smile. "But if you're wondering, I am expecting some company."

Frommer joined in the amusement. "Does she have a girlfriend?"

"Sure, Stu, that can be arranged. Did you bring fifteen dollars in cash with you?"

"Wow, Bill, fifteen large ones. Gotta be a 10 on a scale of 10. For just a night?"

Mellon leaned back on his chair and briefly closed his eyes. "Nah, Stu, it's full service. She stays around for a tumble in the AM, if I so desire."

Frommer sighed. "Well, Bill, I'm gonna drop the subject. But sometime in the future, maybe you can e-mail me a photo of tonight's call girl, or her equivalent. I'd love to see what kind of beauty $15,000 buys."

"It's a deal, Stu. Going to spend a few days with Phil and his family?"

"Yeah, Bill, Phil's coming with the wife and kids, and we're gonna spend the night in Scarsdale with a relative. Then it's off to Nantucket after a brief layover in Hayanispaart."

"Hayanispaaart." Mellon chuckled as he repeated the Kennedy / New England affectation of that lovely resort destination.

Frommer rose. "Well, I guess that's it. So I'll be getting a summary and details in the mail?"

"Most definitely." Mellon held up his wristwatch for effect. "I still got time, and there's something else."

Aw shit. Frommer suddenly felt like his gut had been hit with a sledgehammer, with the inevitable guillotine about to descend in an upcoming coup de grâce. I was literally out of here in one piece. Now what the hell…

"Believe it or not, Stu, I got to clear all this with Zyg Hermanski."

"Hermanski? The devious currency speculator? How does he fit in?"

Mellon sighed. "The partners at Mellon, Caldwell, Cunningham have approved only so much for all our nefarious undertakings in the past year. A lot has come from my personal assets. But the costs are staggering. So Hermanski stepped into the breach. With his resources, money hasn't been a concern. It's as if we're the US Treasury or the State of California. No matter how much we spend, there's more where that came from."

"Yeah, I can see that, Bill, but isn't he hated by both the Left and Right? And an American making untold millions betting against the US dollar."

"Yes, Stu, that's the cat. Only I'm not sure he ever became as US citizen. Point is, he's a one-worlder. Y'know, we're all in this together. Carbon footprints, global warming, world government—no room in all this for the Eagle and the Land of the Free. I know his rep, but he denies he hates the US. Just our capitalistic form of government."

"Well, don't that beat all, as the granny in Iowa is prone to say. The dude hates capitalism, and he has more money than you."

Mellon chuckled. "Never knew I was the yardstick, Stu. But yeah, if having more loot than someone like me is the comparison, the dude's filthy rich."

"Where does he live, Bill?"

"Well, Stu, he sort of hangs his hat anywhere—the Riviera, Davos. But when in the US, he's got this estate on twenty-or-so acres at the furthest point in Montauk, overlooking the Atlantic. That's where I'll be meeting with him next week."

"Whew, twenty acres. Well, one thing's clear from where he hangs his hat."

"What's that, Stu?"

"If the dude's gotta live in this capitalistic hellhole, he wants to be as close as geographically possible to his Socialist buddies in Europe."

"Hmm, you might have something there, Stu, but I think the answer lies elsewhere. Reportedly, the best saltwater fishing on the continent is right there off the coast of Montauk, and apparently, he partakes of that sport quite often from his yacht. Plus, there's plenty of empty real estate two hours past the Hamptoms, and that allowed him not only to build a mansion and guesthouse but include subsidiary structures such as a heliport."

"A heliport? Wow."

"Yeah, Stu, matter of fact, I'm probably gonna be driven to Islip Airport, where his helicopter will pick me up. That's what happened the last time we met."

Frommer just sighed.

"What'sa matter, Stu? Never heard of the Gilded Age?"

"Sure I did, Bill. But there were no private jets, limos, or private helicopters back then."

Mellon took a deep breath and looked at his nearly empty drink. "There'll always be filthy rich people and, unfortunately, desperately poor ones. We can't change that, Stu. All we can do is live our lives as best we can."

36

ZIG HERMANSKI

Mellon looked at his watch. Didn't matter. *Habits are habits*, he concluded. No need to worry about the time. It's not like catching a scheduled flight. That copter will be waiting at Islip no matter what time he arrived. He rang for Harold and asked for some more coffee. Palmeiro had called and asked if it'd be all right for a new man to take Sandy's place. "Name's Pedro Molina. He's sort of new with us, but he had several years with the NYPD, and he's had outstanding fitness reports. This drive to Islip is sort of a walk in the sun, and Artie will show him some of our evasive techniques and, of course, fill him with all sorts of information on Palmeiro operations on the drive back. Okay with you?"

"Sure," Mellon had replied, "no problem at all." *Point is, the Palmeiro guys are only driving me to Islip. Once they see me board the copter, they drive back. Since I'm staying at Hermanski's estate, a whole crew of Palmeiro operatives wouldn't help. If Hermanski were to turn on me, it'd be the old "behind enemy lines" analogy. Our side would be helpless with all the assets Hermanski could call on. But he's not going to do anything. By definition, too many people know about this meeting. So the Palmeiro dudes will go back to the city and meet me in Islip in a day or so. Last time, I was there three days. Got seasick in the heavy waves off Montauk Point accompanying Hermanski on a fishing jaunt on his yacht. This visit's sure to be shorter, but with the anticipated afternoon arrival, surely there's going to be at least one night's stay at Hermanski's digs.*

They left the next morning at nine thirty and were on the LIE by 10:00 AM. "Moving pretty good, eh, Mr. Mellon? We should be in Islip in no time." There was no audible response from Mellon. Artie tried again. "One thing about the Long Island's been disproved this AM, Mr. Mellon."

"Really? What's that, Artie?"

"It's not the world's largest parking lot all the time."

Molina giggled at the joke, but only after hearing a grunt of a chuckle from Mellon sipping coffee in the back of the limo.

They approached the outskirts of Islip Airport by 12:30 PM, and Artie got on his cell to call one of Hermanski's employees. "Yeah, is this Dalton? Good. This is Artie with Palmeiro. We should have an ETA of about 12:45. Same lot as last time? Good, see you at the terminal then."

They were met by Dalton, a businessman type, appropriately wearing a suit, tie, and trench coat. He stood next to a hulking apparachnik appropriately called Serge and the copter pilot who looked like he'd seen action in the past decade. *Yeah, but on which side?* Mellon wondered.

Dalton moved toward Artie. He looked at his cell phone. "This number you just called me from. I'll be able to reach you on it in a day or so?"

"Right, Mr. Dalton. Gimme at least two hours so I can be at Islip before Mr. Mellon arrives."

"Will do." Dalton, with a slight smirk, put his left arm around Mellon's waist and pointed toward the helicopter. "This way, Mr. Mellon. Next stop, Montauk."

Mellon was led to his "quarters" in the spacious estate, which featured a Jacuzzi, a sauna, and of course, a shower. Mellon settled for the sauna and shower. At his age, he feared "accidents" at unfamiliar Jacuzzis. Refreshed, Mellon tried some mints left on a coffee table as he glanced at a magazine.

The phone rang.

"Mr. Mellon? This is Theodore. If you're rested and comfortable, Mr. Hermanski is waiting to greet you in the drawing room."

"That's fine, Theodore."

"Good, Mr. Mellon. I'll be there promptly."

Theodore led Mellon into the "drawing room," where he observed Hermanski in one of those fancy maroon "housecoats" as if he'd just walked out of a Sherlock Holmes tale.

Hermanski rose and approached as if enthusiastic. He grabbed Mellon's right hand with both his arms. "Bill, how have you been? How's the wife, the family?"

Mellon, feeling relieved that Hermanski had let go of his hand, blushed slightly. "Everyone's fine, Zig. Thanks for asking. Justine is still hanging her handbag in Paris. That time of the year, you know."

"Correct, Bill, I now remember. She only returns during the fall season." Hermanski started toward one of the spacious seating lounges, turned, and looked at Mellon. He waved his right arm. "Sit down, Bill, sit down. Please, feel at home."

Mellon mumbled a barely audible "thank you" and selected a plush nearby chair. "I'll get right to business, Bill, if you don't mind."

"Go right ahead, Zig. That's what we're here for."

"Sorry to state, Bill, but I've been hearing things, disturbing things." Hermanski appeared to be waiting for a response, but Mellon remained silent. "I've heard from Mr. Burnitz and other contacts that, err, you are no longer fully cooperative in our endeavors."

Mellon shrugged. "Some parts of it, yes. You heard right."

Hermanski's eyes narrowed. "Inform me, please."

Mellon didn't appreciate the edge to Hermanski's tone, but it wasn't unexpected.

He had a hunch when this meet was agreed to that Hermanski had something on his mind. He appreciated the fact that Hermanski had come right to the point. Now he wondered when it'd be best to spring the really big news at him, something that Burnitz and his shyster friends most likely weren't aware of. *Our side, that's me, with the concurrence of Frommer, have declared a unilateral cease-fire. It's over with, Zig, over. Just look at all the money you're gonna save.*

"Well, Zig, if you've spoken to Burnitz, you know about our disagreement over FISA and—"

"Not just FISA," Hermanski cut in. "It's also your attitude—it has... it has changed. Your son, apparently—"

"Keep my son out of this." Mellon was surprised at the tenor of his response.

Hermanski's dark countenance showed some color. "No need, no need, Bill." He picked up an intercom attached to his chaise. "Theodore, yes, Theodore. The martinis, are they ready? Good, please, Theodore, bring them in." Hermanski looked at Mellon and stroked his fingers through what was left of his jet-black hair. "I hope you like Theodore's martinis. Three parts Beefeater for every half ounce of Vermouth. You're not driving, right, Bill? So enjoy."

Mellon *was* thirsty. It'd been several hours since he'd sipped some coffee in Palmeiro's limo. The martini tasted tart, strong. What was all this about three parts for every half ounce? The standard was two and a half gin to half ounce of Vermouth.

Everyone knows that. Besides, vodka martinis are the rage now. Lighter, easier down the gullet. "Tell Theodore he's got the touch," Mellon lied. *Well, maybe it'll break the tension.*

"I'm happy you approve, Bill. Theodore's been with me many years." Mellon clocked Hermanski staring at him, apparently expecting a response.

Mellon just took another sip of the martini. *I'll stare this mother down*, Mellon vowed. *Nobody beats this barrister at liar's poker or, more colloquially, at putting on a game face.*

"I-I'm sorry about bringing up your son, Bill. You are correct. It was not appropriate of me to—"

"Think nothing of it." Mellon gurgled as he almost spilled some of the martini while waving to Hermanski. *Holy shit, my head's spinning. Is it that extra half ounce of gin, or did this Theodore spike the damn concoction?* "Well, Zig, can I get to the point?"

"Well, of course, Bill, please do. We are all busy people. Please, I'm anxious to hear what is on your mind, if there's more than FISA and those kind of things."

"Well," Mellon smirked, "it is more than Burnitz, those shysters, and FISA. The war is over."

"What war, Iraq?"

"Our war, Zig, our war. You know, Beltran, the doctors, the chamber of commerce, the NAM. No more hunting, no more being hunted. It's over."

"But how?" Hermanski's response was almost a screech. "They're after you. Beltran... Beltran and his people. They must be stopped, destroyed."

Mellon gulped down some more of the martini, put the glass down, and effected a puzzled look. "Why is it so important to you, Zig? They don't even know you're alive. Well, I mean they've no doubt heard of you but have no idea you're part of this mess."

Hermanski' s lips tightened. It looked to Mellon that Hermanski was trying to stifle a sneer. His dark visage effected some color. *Here it comes*, Mellon reflected.

"I do not count. If I may be so bold, neither do you, Burnitz, or the rest. What is important is what we're trying to do."

"You mean beat Beltran and his sort?"

"No!" Hermanski virtually shouted. "Not Beltran, not the lawsuits, not useful idiots like the Chanteuse. What we're trying to do is *change* this country for the better."

"This country? You mean our country," Mellon countered. "Oh, right, I almost forgot. You never did become a US citizen."

Hermanski seemed to regain his composure. He allowed a slight smirk. "Yes, I've never taken the time. At every stage since I arrived, knowing who was the second president of the US seemed trivial compared to the work I was doing."

"Like bringing down the dollar?"

Hermanki's response was a glare. "If you'd done your homework, like you do in your legal cases, you'd know I was a currency trader whilst I lived in London."

Mellon, whose combative juices were aroused by Hermanski's glare and general attitude, replied, "Currency trader, I thought *currency speculator* was the more traditional term."

Hermanski swished the latest swig of his martini around his closed mouth as if he were obeying a dentist's order to rinse after a procedure. Only he didn't spit out as in a dentist's office; he eventually swallowed the drink.

Playing for time, Mellon surmised. Typical lawyer's trick when trying to figure out what to say next—the main difference, lawyers generally make out like they're studying their notes when stalling. Hermanski, it seemed, was trying to regain his composure. Billionaire Gecko-like financiers are no doubt not too used to impertinence in their face.

"*Speculator* isn't a kind word the way it's used in the English language. But speculation, Bill, is a guess as to where conditions will be in the future. All capitalistic markets couldn't survive otherwise. Like you know, Bill, the price of oil and, yes, the dollar."

"So if a 'speculator' thinks the stock market is going to go down, he sort of… sort of helps it along."

"You should understand—"

"Well, Zig, what I'm thinking of is driving the price of a particular stock down—the people, the job losses."

"Only because it was going to happen anyway, Bill. If a so-called speculator thinks GM's going down because of Toyota or the economy. Well, it's like betting on Real Madrid, err, I mean the Yankees. The bettor reaps the benefit of his insight but has no influence on whether the Yankees win the cup, uh, I mean—"

"The pennant and the World Series," Mellon smirked.

"Ah, yes, correct, the World Series. It reminds me that—"

"Mmm, before we get all involved about baseball, soccer, or other pastimes, I'd like to get back to short selling. It's true you have no control over whether the Yankees have a successful year by betting against them, but when you bet against GM or Ford, if enough traders join in, it could have a cumulative effect on the stock price and the well being of the company."

Now Hermanski made no effort to hide his annoyance. "I thought I had made myself clear. Law is your game, finance is mine. Trust me, I know more than—"

"Maybe you do, Zig, about trading and/or speculating, but not about the morality of it."

"I have been called names worse than *immoral* by the reactionary forces in this count, err, in America, so your attack on my profession will just slide off my back, Bill. My principal effort, I thought *our* effort is to improve the flaws in this country. To make it a Progressive beacon for all humanity, instead of the reactionary, militaristic, oppressive regime answerable only to the corporate establishment that—"

"What corporate establishment, Zig? The same one that existed for eight years under Bill and Hillary?"

"There is only so much an administration can do, Bill. It's the system of financing campaigns. The powers that be will never give up their influence."

"Oh?" Mellon chuckled. "Like the trial lawyers and the SEIU instrumental in electing 90 percent of 'Progressive' Democrats in the past decade. Not that I'm complaining, it's been the trial lawyers, my funds, and of course, your assistance that's financed this whole Beltran thing for the past year or so."

"So what's your objection, Bill?"

"Not objecting to the immediate issue, Zig. I'm a greedy MF. I want to sue at will. I'll use any financial or political aid to accomplish that task. But that's my profession, not my outlook. I love the good old USA and everything it stands for. It's not a flawed, oppressive, or whatever you Lefties are always ranting… Uh, I've read some of your dot-org organizations—it seems we're always wrong, and of course, the Israelis… and… and the others always have, what do you call it, 'legitimate' grievances."

"I and my organizations stand for justice."

"Sure, Zig, but leave us not get bogged down in political discourse. I have just one question for you. If we so bad, how come the whole MF world wants to come here if we so bad?"

"If we so bad? I'm afraid I don't understand."

"Just some jargon from the old neighborhood, Zig, just some slang." *Of course now, what with ghetto slang, "we so bad" means "we are the best." But how to explain that to a ghoul from Transylvania?*

"What I'm saying is that no one ever wants to come to the 'oppressed' countries. It's always the other way around. They willingly come to the so-called oppressor."

"I'm afraid I don't—"

"My point, Zig, twenty or thirty years ago, when I was still taking cabs, it seemed every cabdriver was from Nigeria or elsewhere in Africa. Now apparently, they're from the Middle East."

"I still don't—"

"Don't you see, Zig? Nigerians and other Africans come to the most antiblack racist country in history, while Middle Easterners come en masse to a country full of infidels allegedly at war with Islam."

"I don't approve of your sarcasm. These are decent people. All they're trying to do is improve their—"

"You so right, Zig. All they're trying to do is improve their lot in life, take care of their families. But they come *here* to do that when they've got the whole world to choose from, let alone their native habitat."

"I see your training has gone beyond the law and courtrooms." Hermanski seemed grudging in his observation.

Mellon swirled his nearly empty martini glass and took a deep gulp to finish the drink. He put the glass down on a nearby end table. "Please, Zig, a big-time trial lawyer has to be aware of world and national developments. After all, jurors aren't empty suits. Mention 9/11 in the middle of a sentence and they know what's happening."

"Empty suits?"

"That's a phrase, Zig, a colloquialism. An empty suit is someone with a blank head. No lawyer wants an empty suit sitting on a jury."

Zig appeared to be at a loss for words. Close to a minute went by. "Your drink is empty, Bill. Would you like another—"

"I'm good, Zig, I'm good," Mellon smirked. "What time is dinner? Will Mrs. Hermanski, uh, Ingrid, be joining—"

"Ingrid's in Manhattan catching a show with our daughter, 'A Chorus Line,' I think…" Hermanski allowed a slight grin. "Of course, there will be time allocated for Saks, Bloomingdale's, and other such stores."

"I read ya, Zig." Mellon almost giggled. "I draw the line at Tiffany's. Saks and Bloomies are penny ante compared to the possible damage at Tiffany's or Cartiers."

They both chuckled.

Hermanski looked at his watch. "In about two hours, Bill. We'll be dining alone tonight. Sir Herbert Montague of the London All Futures Exchange will be joining us tomorrow. Will you still be here?"

"That depends on how much we accomplish tonight, Zig. What's for dinner?"

"Lobster flown in from Maine, but if you prefer, steak tartar is—"

"Lobster's just fine." Mellon smiled.

Dinner began around seven thirty with a wine steward suggesting choices for the foie gras appetizer and the lobster avec les petit pois et pommes frites. The lobster was delectable, but Mellon, after the appetizer, refused a second helping of the "delicious" lobster. He used the compliments to the chef cliché while patting his ample girth. "I'm afraid I can't pack it away the like I used to when younger, Zig." They both vetoed Theodore's inquiry as to dessert and retired to the library, a more intimate setting than the drawing room.

"Brandy, Bill?"

"Sure, Zig, that'll wash everything down."

Hermanski approached the liquor cabinet. "Napoleon or Courvoisier?"

"Either's fine, Zig."

"With or without."

"No ice, Zig, thanks."

Mellon watched Hermanski pour the drinks. He braced himself for some more heavy discourse. The banter had been light during dinner what with Theodore and the waiters and bus boys hovering around like fleas. Now they were alone.

"Thanks, Zig."

Mellon tasted the brandy. "Ah, just what the doctor ordered. I can feel that lobster melting away, Zig."

"No doubt, Bill, no doubt. Through the centuries, the best after dinner and the best nightcap."

They both swirled their glasses and contentedly sipped their brandies as if they were starring in a commercial for a particular brandy. The silence was deafening. *Here it comes*, Mellon concluded.

"Are you planning to go to Copenhagen for the Climate Summit, Bill?"

Mellon tried to hide his astonishment. He was glad no jury was present. Even the best litigator can't hide his unease when suddenly facing a surprising witness or new evidence. *That's sure out of left field. What's Hermanski up to?* "Hadn't thought of it, Zig. When is it?"

"About two years from now. Late '09 as I recollect. I was in Kyoto, you know, and—"

"No, Zig, I did not know that."

"Well, I was there, and it was a good beginning, although certain forces in the Congress have not followed up with the proper support in the past decade and—"

"Excuse me, Zig, don't mean to interrupt, but the mention of these different geographical areas reminds me that I still don't know where you're from. Romania, Poland, Hungary? Your last name does sound Polish."

Hermanski appeared set aback. *Perfect, Zig's always been reticent about his origins. So I'm surprising you, Zig. You deal with that while I recover from the Copenhagen ploy. Whatever the fuck that is, what's he up to? I'm a damn lawyer. What the hell do I know about climates?*

"Apparently, you are well versed in my background, Bill. I am from Hungary, but my family was originally from Poland."

"Yes, Zig, wasn't there a story about your father and anti-Semitism?"

"I don't know what lies you've been subject to on the internet, Bill. It's the Fascists, anti-Progressives who are calling me and my father Fascists and anti-Semites. It's... it's like the kettle is black or whatever."

"I think it's the pot calling the kettle black, but I follow you, Zig."

Hermanski smiled sheepishly. "Yes, the pot calling the kettle and so on. I don't know where these accusations come from. They have followed me ever since I arrived in London. And now here. Such calumny, such lies."

Mellon succeeded in hiding his inner smirk. "Why? Why spread such slander if there's nothing to it?"

"It's the Jews."

"If I was your lawyer, I'd keep that kind of response out of the courtroom. You're denying anti-Semitism by saying it's the Jews who are spreading the lies."

"Well, my father was forced to be a member of the Iron Cross, and naturally, the Jews came after him after the war."

"How was he forced to join?"

"He'd been a policeman in Budapest, and of course, with his training, he'd have labeled a Bolshevik and/or a Jew lover if he hadn't joined the fight against the enemies of Hungary."

"But wasn't the biggest enemy of Hungary the invading Nazis? Sounds to me like the Iron Cross was the equivalent of Vichy France and the Copperheads during the Civil War. Furthermore, I can't understand why—"

"I don't know what these Copperheads were, but I strongly resent your comparison of Vichy France to members of the Iron Cross."

"But why do you resent it? You implied your father was forced to join. So why are you defending a right-wing, racist, anti-Semitic organization?"

"Don't play your courtroom tricks on me in my own home. I'm one of the richest men in the world. Who do you think you're dealing with?"

Mellon tried to hide his rising anger, something Hermanski wasn't successful at, since his face had turned ashen while one of the veins on his neck showed more blue than the Pacific Ocean. "Okay, Zig, I'll ask again. How can you defend—"

Hermanski suddenly leapt from his chair. "I really don't want to talk about Hungary, the Iron Cross, or the Jews. The subject is changed."

Mellon tried to hide a sudden smirk. A minute ago, his own anger had been rising, and then Hermanski leaped from his chair as if he's about to physically throttle yours truly. Mellon was ready to jump from his own seat if Hermanski took one step toward him.

Mother of Mercy, two billionaires, one over sixty-five, getting into a brawl in a library of a mansion. How would that look in the tabloid NY Post? He watched Hermanski sit back down. "I'm all for changing the subject, Zig. No more Iron Cross, Hungary, and all that. But the subject of anti-Semitism sort of carries me back to the old days."

"The old days?"

"Yeah, Zig, when we were kids in the neighborhood. We hated Jews, only we didn't even grant them that title. They were kikes, Hebes, and other terms I don't recall. And that wasn't all. There were the spics, dago wops, jigs, Polacks. We hated them all." Mellon watched Hermanski wince. "Err, no offense on that last one, Zig."

"None taken," Hermanski sneered.

"Well, we even hated the Micks if one was dumb enough to show up in Brooklyn when he was from the Bronx."

"Your point?"

"My point is, once we no longer protected our turf, our neighborhood, once we grew up, things changed."

"In what way?"

"When I started my own practice, one of the up-and-comers was a kid named Irv Ross. I remember the name because it had been shortened by his father before Irv was born. It was originally Rossfeld or something like that. We were both young and on the loose, and we hit the joints in Manhattan and Yankee and Mets games. We also went to the Garden to see some boxing matches. Irv told me he tried some boxing in memory of his father, who'd shortened the name to Ross in honor of Barney Ross, a great Jewish boxing champ in the thirties."

Mellon watched for a reaction from Hermanski, but the latter remained silent.

"So Irv just loved John F Kennedy, said he once shook his hand on Kings Highway when Kennedy was campaigning in Brooklyn in 1960. When Johnson escalated in Vietnam after Kennedy was shot, Irv was enthused about the war because he said if JFK sent nineteen thousand Green Berets there, the cause had to be just. He volunteered, and by '67, he was in charge of a pacification program around Da Nang. The camp was overrun by the VC, and Irv was butchered. They kept the details from his family and—"

"VC?"

"Yeah, Zig, stands for Vietcong, you know, who we were fighting in Nam."

"I'm sure it's a sad story, but what has it to do with our conversation?"

Mellon took a deep, audible breath, as if to advertise his exasperation. "The pemt, err, point, dear Zig, is that Irv's my lifelong message in bigotry. When starting law, I'd lost contact with a lot of my childhood buddies, Irv, a Jew, was my best friend when he died. A loss I'll bear forever."

Hermanski looked at his watch. "I think it's time we enjoy the crisp air and walk off our dinners. Before we do, I was wondering about Copenhagen."

"In what sense, Zig?"

"Well, whether you're planning to attend and lend support."

"Support? Lend support to what? What do I know about weather? I know to wear galoshes when it snows, but my dear departed ma taught me that."

"We're not talking about weather, Bill, we're talking about climate, as in climate change and/or global warming."

"Fine." Mellon shrugged. "Go for it. But I'm an attorney, remember? Not one of those geeky weather—err, pardon—climate scientists."

"I'm not a scientist either, Bill, but I care about the future of the human race."

"I don't follow. How will my attending affect the future of the—"

"Let me explain," Hermanski cut in but smiled benignly. He leaned back and assumed the air of a lecturer. "It's twofold, Bill. First, the US and other Western powers must help the underdeveloped nations pay for their attempts to go green."

"Huh?"

"Well, it's the capitalistic nations with their carbon imprints/footprints that put the poor nations in an economic/weather predicament that's going to cost *beaucoup d'argent*. You could call it climatic racism."

"You don't say." Mellon had to bite his lip to stifle a smirk. "Racism gets attached to quite a few issues, but I never realized... Err, is the climate different in Harlem than midtown Manhattan?"

"Very funny, Bill, but we're not referring to that kind of racism. It's that the poor nations are paying climactically for the sins and output of the West, basically their carbon imprints."

Mellon sighed heavily, audibly. *No jury here, but at least let this idiotic ghoul know that I'm exasperated.* "Racism, poor nations? You're referring to Africa?"

"Yes, Bill, Africa and South America, principally."

"South America? What the hell's that got to do with race? They're all from Spain, Italy, or Germany, if my knowledge of Evita Perón and her Nazi sympathies..."

"Yes, the Euros dominate, but not much longer. The indigenous peoples are rising to the fore."

"Granted all that Zig. I'm getting a headache. How does Africa, South America, and the so-called West fit into all this?" Mellon looked at his watch for emphasis.

"Yes." For the first time, Hermanski laughed out loud. "You see, Bill, the US and the Western nations emit more than their share of polluting carbon emissions. These emissions eventually foul the atmosphere and then the climate of nations in Africa and South America."

"So?"

"So the wealthier nations should, must provide financial compensation to the poorer nations in the form of carbon credits."

"What?"

"You see, Bill, if a nation emits above a specified level, it must provide compensation to the innocents affected."

"Jeez, I thought trial lawyers were slimy. You guys make us look like pikers. Ever hear of the term *extortion*?"

"To ask US Steel to clean up Pittsburgh, was that extortion?"

"Zig, come on. We're an industrialized country. It's industry that provides our wealth. You think I'd have this kind of dough if I was a trial lawyer in Bangladesh?"

"What is dough?"

"Money, Zig, money."

They glared at each other. "We can't balance our budgets at the Federal or state or local levels, and you want us to put money down a bottomless—"

"Like Iraq, Afghanistan, Vietnam?" Hermanski's response came out like a hiss.

Mellon started to boil but wouldn't let his inner turmoil affect his game face in front of the jury, in this case the one-person jury of Zig Hermanski. "Is there something behind all this, these carbon credits and the rest of the BS?"

Hermanski grinned and leaned back on his chair. "Perceptive, Bill, perceptive. In Kyoto, a caring cabinet minister for one of the Scandinavian nations stated the policy clearly. What we, the caring citizens of Western nations, must do, are *obliged* to do, is to level the playing field. Money must go from the rich, developed nations to the poor, underdeveloped—"

"What about Asia? Why haven't you mentioned Asia?"

"Well, Bill, Asia is in between. You've got China, India, Japan—"

"But the US has always given generously to poorer nations—floods, earthquakes."

"Yes, Bill, but now the US would be obliged to give, systematically."

"So the global weather thing is bullshit, a con."

"I never said that. But who said 'never let a crisis go by without taking advantage'? We always wanted income redistribution. Within nations is a good start, but among nations is the final goal. Will you come to Copenhagen to help us achieve worldwide justice?"

Mellon tried equanimity. Years of practice had taught him the importance of and how to maintain an expression of serenity. If the other side had just come up with a whopper or, conversely, a telling point, don't let on in any way. If a jury sees anger, despair, contempt, whatever, there goes the case. He'd just decided he was through with

Hermanski and surely wasn't going to attend this Copenhagen thing, and that was *before* this "level the playing field" BS.

"I don't think so, Zig. I think I'll leave it in your capable hands. You seem more expert and enthused over this weather, err, I mean climate stuff."

"I'm not talking about the climate part, Bill. I'm talking about economic and political justice. Building a better, fairer world."

"Sorry you keep harping on that part of it, Zig. This climate stuff I mostly don't understand and could conceivably go your way on it, but this 'level the playing field' crap is way beyond—"

"You're calling economic justice crap?"

"Let's not get into semantics, Zig. I don't go against the good old USA. If some future prez and Congress want to buy your shit, fine, I'm a good citizen. I'll go along. But to think that I'd go to some conference—"

"So we agree to disagree."

"It goes beyond that, Zig. Since I know you, since we've worked together, it'd be my duty, my obligation to work against you." Mellon calmly absorbed Hermanski's worst glare yet. "But umm, that shouldn't affect our personal relationship."

Hermanski was about to respond but then held back. *Oh, oh, here comes some bullshit*, Mellon concluded. *Obviously, Hermanski's going to plan B. He doesn't want to say what's on his mind.*

"Fine, Bill, all this shouldn't affect our friendship. Come on now. Something tells me you'll be leaving in the morning. Let's get some air. There's a wondrous spot where we can watch the waves of the angry Atlantic Ocean punish the puny shores of Long Island."

IRS

Artie and Pedro met the helicopter just before noon the next day. They spotted Dalton escorting Mellon to the terminal and approached them. After a brief discussion, Dalton walked Mellon and the Palmeiro operatives to the limo in the parking lot, where he watched the trio get into the car and drive off. Dalton watched smugly as the limo pulled away. His job was done. He could now report that to the best of his knowledge Mellon had been "successfully" delivered from the boss's mansion. He turned back and spotted Serge downing a can of Coke. "Yo, Serge, job done. Let's blow."

There was silence in the limo for about ten minutes while Mellon perused the *Wall Street Journal*. "Thanks for the paper, boys. Looks like yesterday was pretty quiet in the world and in the markets."

Artie replied, "Must have been pretty productive, eh, Mr. Mellon? You finished in one day."

Mellon sighed. "That's one way to look at it. The other way is that we ran out of things to say or to argue about."

"That bad, Mr. Mellon?"

"Yeah, Artie, that bad. Maybe even worse. I'm gonna catch a little shut-eye now. Wake me when we hit the Apple."

Mellon pretended he was taking a nap, but sleep wasn't an option right now. His mind was agitated evoking the discussion with Hermanski after dinner. Discussion?

Clash was more like it. Hermanski had been evidently peeved when he learned that Frommer and I were dropping out of the fracas with Beltran. But the mood got uglier every time ol' Zig cornered me as to what degree I'd oppose him from here on in.

"Depends," I had answered. "I'll cross that bridge when *you* get to it." He didn't like the flippancy of that answer, and when he berated me some more, I finally had dropped an f-bomb. In summary, I had shouted, "Since I'm 'connected' to you, whenever I'll see you working against my USA to fulfill some left-wing crackpot fantasy, count on me to oppose you tooth and nail." On it went; he kept interrogating me, and when I reacted vaguely, he screamed he was "dissatisfied" with my answers. Finally, after I'd responded I wasn't one of his office boys in London, there was more name-calling until Hermanski shouted for Theodore, "Please take Mr. Mellon to his quarters!"

The stress had taken its toll on the sixty-seven-year-old lawyer. The feigned shut-eye led to a real sleep that lasted until the limo arrived at the garage in Mellon's building.

That afternoon, Hermanski summoned Dalton. "Matthew, still up on your accounting skills?"

"That depends, Mr. Hermanski. I'm not up-to-date on the latest arcane portion of the revenue code, but I'm still capable of fulfilling my duties as a CPA for routine matters."

Hermanski leaned back on his chair. He put his right fist to his chin. "Hmm, I have a plan. If you don't feel you have enough background, let me know."

"Well, Mr. Hermanski, that depends on—"

"I know, I know," Hermanski smirked. "I'll fill you in as we proceed. Meanwhile, round up about a dozen of your operatives fully versed in white-collar jargon. At the appropriate juncture, I shall introduce you to Timothy Cain, who used to head an accounting firm specializing in high-end IRS disputes. From here on in, no e-mails on this project. All discussions will be in person or on cell phones." Hermanski watched Dalton nod and begin to walk out. "Just a moment, Matthew, I almost forgot. Bundy & Associates will handle the funding for this project. Your budget is unlimited. You don't even have to worry about keeping track. Bundy will keep count of the money. Your only concern is spend as much as you need to make this operation believable and successful. Your other concern, you do not discuss any portion of this operation with Bundy. Clear, Matthew?"

"Clear, Mr. Hermanski. Now of course, I'm really curious as to—"

"In due time, Matthew," Hermanski grinned, "in due time."

***

Pedro Molina had just returned from an assignment in Sonora, Mexico. He went straight to his desk and started to wade through the mountain of piled-up paperwork.

"How's the old veteran doing?" It was Artie. "How was Mexico?"

Molina looked up and exhibited half a smile. "Weather-wise, nearly perfect, Artie, but otherwise, it's on a need-to-know, and that don't include anyone not in the operation."

Artie blushed then grinned. "That's my boy. Pedro, you is now a full-fledged Palmeiro operative. And now I got good news. We got another stint with Mellon. There's gonna be four of us: me, the usual other suspects, and good old Pedro Molina."

"Wow, with Mellon again."

"Yeah, your name was mentioned and heartily approved by Mellon."

"He remembered my name from two months ago when we went to Islip?"

"Not only that, Pedro, but apparently, Palmeiro himself was so impressed by your results from Sonora that he specifically told Mellon you last saw Molina when he was still a novice, now he's graduated to being among our best, or something like that."

"What do you mean, 'something like that'? Did you overhear it or not?"

"Cool it, Pedro. Just be happy with the compliment. Let's just say how I got any details of their conversation is on a need-to-know basis."

Pedro looked up and grinned. "Touché. Ya got me. Was that the appropriate word? My English, signor, still bad. I'm only in this country a short deestance."

"Okay, wise guy, talk like that in front of Mellon, and there goes our biggest account."

A chastened Molina adopted an appropriately serious look. "What's it about, Artie?"

"IRS."

"IRS?"

"Yeah, Pedro, beats me. We'll be getting details."

The next morning, Pedro, Artie, and six other staffers met at Palmeiro's meeting room on the third floor of the Jefferson Building on Madison near Forty-Seventh Street. Dick Willows was conducting the briefing. "Four to six of you guys are gonna be selected for this assignment. The ones not selected will be first alternates. You know, like on a jury. So we want all of you well versed in case someone drops out for whatever reason or… if they decide four to six isn't enough."

Snuggy raised his hand.

"Yeah, Snuggy?"

"Who's the 'they,' Dick?"

Willows pointed a stack of collated papers on the front desk. "All the details we can give out at this juncture are on this desk. Grab a set and memorize what's in those handouts. It's all we know so far." Willows looked at Snuggy. "But to answer your question, Snuggy, the 'they' are Mellon and his crew. Apparently, the criminal Investigation Division of the IRS has a bug up their ass about tax evasion at the high finance level."

"But, Dick, Mellon's a lawyer, not—"

"Yeah, Artie, you're thinking… But that came up when we first heard about it. Mellon's a bigger name than anyone at Morgan Stanley or Goldman Sachs. An election's coming up in '08—wouldn't hurt to nail a dude like Mellon. Think that would make the first page of the *Times*?"

Artie grinned. "In other words, Artie, shut your piehole and don't ask stupid questions until you read the fuckin' handout."

Willows tried to maintain a stern expression. "You said it, Artie, I didn't." Everyone cracked up.

"Okay, fellas, simmer down. I'll give you guys some dope since the handout. We went over to 77 Nassau where this IRS task force has set up temporarily. Nassau Street's a stone's throw from Wall Street, so it makes sense figuring they'll be calling in mostly financial types."

"Am I right that this is the first time Mellon will be seen in public since we went to Code Vanish?"

"Absolutely keerect, Pedro, all the more cogent since we went to Code Vanish easily a year before you came on board."

"Take a bow, Mo." Artie cackled.

"Okay, guys. So as you say, Pedro, this will be Mellon's first appearance since he ran to ground a year ago. So we got our work cut out. This ain't a case of 'we foul up and Mellon disses us and gets a new team.' If we fuck this up, *there is no Mellon*. So for the sake of your retirements and the kids' college education, be and stay on your toes. Clear?"

A staccato of "Clear, boss" rang out in reply.

"Yeah, Artie, what is it?"

"Dick, you say you've been over to 77 Nassau. How's the setup there?"

"Good question, Artie. I was just getting to that. They got the typical airport/courthouse/government building system you're all familiar with. You know, put the coins and metal objects on the moving container, then you go through the sensors, just like at JFK."

"Did they let you through?"

"Nah, we didn't try. Behind the TSA types manning the sensors were a couple of burly, well-dressed dudes who insisted no one comes through without an appointment cleared in advance. They were standing under a portrait of Bush, you know, like in all Federal buildings."

"So we can only get Mellon up to the checkpoint?"

"Right, Snuggy. I assume Mellon's preapproved CPA types and others of that ilk will accompany Mellon to the appropriate auditor."

"Why can't Mellon's CPAs take care of it while Mellon stays to ground?"

"Well, that's the point of this whole operation, ain't it, Artie? Apparently, this task force and type of audit insist that the subject of the inquiry be there, probably to sign some perjury and related shit. When the Feds mean business, they mean business. Any questions before we go? Yeah, Artie."

"It's probably in the handout, Dick, but what evasive procedures—"

"Good question, Artie." Willows grinned. "Although it's in the handout, there's no harm in reviewing it here and now. Depending on availability, there'll be three or four black limos with the shades and all that shit stopping in front of 77 Nassau fifteen minutes apart. There'll be two or three of us getting out of each limo. Mellon'll be in one of those limos. We'll work out the clothes, shades, all that shit, so if there's a sniper, he's got about ten seconds before we're inside, and most of the time, we'll be trying to figure which one is Mellon. And yes, that's why we have some of you portly dudes in on this assignment."

"I, err, resent, eh, resemble that statement!" Snuggy bellowed.

"We all bring our various assets to various assignments, Snuggy. Be happy that you're well-endowed. Okay, guys, we meet here in two days at nine sharp. There'll be a quiz on the handouts."

There were some chuckles.

"None of you MFs will be laughing if you don't pass the quiz. Now git."

***

Ann Witt had just come out of the shower. She went right to bed to grab some ZZZs before dinner. It'd been a rough day. She freshened her pillows and blissfully laid her head down and pulled the covers over her when the phone rang. *Oh shit*, she mumbled, *let it go, let them leave a message. Nah, it might be something from today. I'd better…* She opened her cell and didn't recognize the caller.

"Hi, Ann?"

"Yeah, who's this?"

"It's Mo."

"Mo?"

"Pedro Molina, you remember, from the station. Stretch gave me your number."

"Oh, yes, Mo. How have you been? How are things with Palmeiro?"

"Good, Ann, good. Interesting work. Which is the reason I'm calling, Ann. I remember that someone you were seeing was some biggie with the IRS. I remember all the jokes."

"Yes, Mo. Lenny Carpenter. I remember the jokes also. Hey, Annie, get that IRS guy over to my house to show me the ropes. I pay too much in taxes and all that BS. They weren't exactly jokes, just another chance for those baboons to rattle my cage."

"Yeah, Ann, that's what I remember, and you've always been a good sport."

"So what's it about, Mo?" Ann tried her best to hide any exasperation in her voice.

"Well, Ann, you know that guy Mellon, the big-shot lawyer?"

"Sure, Mo, who hasn't?"

"Well, Ann, it turns out that I'm part of security for him. And it turns out that IRS has some special program going on where they're auditing big shots and the big shots have to appear at some temp offices near Wall Street."

"Hasn't he been out of sight for a while?"

"Well, that's just it, Ann. Me and some others at Palmeiro are a little worried about Mellon having to show up."

"He's going to be in plain sight?"

"Well, not exactly, Ann. We'll be pulling our usual stunts to keep him under wraps until we deliver him to this Nassau Street IRS location, and then of course, we'll deliver him back to where he's safely out of sight."

"So where does Lenny come in, Mo?"

"Right, Ann, I'll get to the point. The Mellon people have been told this is a special treasury task force designed to catch big shots either weirding up expenses or not declaring all income properly."

"Why a special task force, Mo? I thought that's what IRS does all the time."

"Well, that's just it, Ann. I jotted this down. It's called the Comprehensive Audit Team, Treasury Department, subunit IRS special investigatory task force."

"Wow." Ann virtually giggled. "Those bureaucrats sure can come up with some impressive designations. But not much different than the impressive titles within the NYPD when the mayor's office wants to do something similar. You remember all that, right, Mo?"

"Sure, do, Ann. Looks like pompous bureaucrats come in all size, shapes, and entities. Was *entities* the right word, Ann?"

"Sure be, Mo. Your English is *mucho bueno*." Ann heard Mo's chuckle. "So you want me to see what Lenny knows?"

"Ann, you read me like a book."

"Trouble is twofold, Mo. We broke up a couple of months ago. We weren't that hot and heavy to begin with. He found someone new but insists we remain friends."

"And what's the second fold, Ann?"

"Well, Mo, hope you're not in a rush. Lenny's in Boulder at some training session with—"

"Boulder? What the F is 'Boulder'? A big rock?"

Ann giggled. "Boulder, in Colorado, silly. The U of Colorado is holding a special audit seminar for accountants with clients subject to potential heavy audits. Ain't that a coincidental hoot, Mo?"

"The University of Colorado teaches that kind of stuff?"

"Well, it's a Colorado U extension, Mo. Extensions get into all sorts of—"

"Why Colorado? Why not around here?"

"Well, Mo, welcome to the real world. Speaking of audits, the high-power accounting firms deduct the cost of the travel and training and, most important, during the three-day weekend, take in the skiing and the sights at nearby glamour locations like Vail, Aspen…"

"Wow, what a life."

"Don't be jealous, Mo. There's more chance you'll get a deal like that at Palmeiro than I'll ever be offered at NYPD."

"So there's no chance you can—"

"Don't jump to conclusions, Mo, it's not that bleak. Len and I still text, but under the circumstances, I don't think he'll be answering that quickly."

"I catch ya, Ann. Thanks in advance for anything you can do. Bye, and… nice talking to you again."

"Same here, Mo. Take care. Oh wait, this is all too complicated for three-way. Lemme have your cell so Lenny can call you directly."

"Right, Ann. Got a pen handy?"

Molina and Artie were still in the limo after delivering Mellon for the second day. "Any of Mellon's accountants tell you what's happening, Artie?"

"They say the usual hassle, Mo. But a special emphasis on travel. They want breakdowns beyond what hotels and restaurants ordinarily provide."

"What? Sounds like they're out to break balls."

Artie shrugged a weary shrug. "How do you spell *ball-breaker*, Mo? An I, an R, and an S?"

Molina chuckled a perfunctory chuckle.

"I don't blame you, Mo. Not even Leno can be funny about those three letters."

The next day, Snuggy and Willows were the "lucky" guys. They delivered Mellon at ten fifteen in the morning giving the Mellon accountants and the IRS auditors two hours' heads-up. The timing was good. That nearby Coffee Shoppe near the parking lot was relatively empty at a quarter to eleven. They were having coffee when Willows's cell rang. It was Aaron Horowitz, Mellon's CPA.

"Yeah, Willows here."

"Hi, Dick, it's Aaron."

"Yeah, Aaron, how's it going?"

"Well, Dick, I got some good news and some bad news."

Willows looked at Snuggy and sighed. "Okay, Aaron, lemme have it."

"Okay, I'll start with the bad news. We may be here till eight or nine tonight. So get ready for a long day. Just keep your cells on and enjoy all the fine restaurants around Wall Street."

"And the good news?"

"Well, since we're gonna go late tonight, it means the IRS bean counters think they can wrap this up tonight. I gave Landry your and Snuggy's cell numbers, in case I'm tied up. We cool?"

"Thanks for the vibe, Aaron. Have a good day."

"Hope so, Dick. Talk to you later."

"What'd he say, Dick?"

"Late night tonight, Snuggy."

"Aw shit."

"Nah, Snuggy, the opposite of shit. Late tonight, but it'll probably be wrapped up. So back to the office tomorrow 'stead of hanging around Manhattan like we're a couple of hoboes. And… for the first time on this assignment, a chance to dine at one of Lower Manhattan's prime expense-account locations, Les Deux Enfants."

"Shit, Dick, French, gonna burn a hole in my wallet."

"Cheer up, Snuggy. When the waiter comes with the bill, just pull out your gat. The waiter'll shit in his pants and comp us."

"Right, very funny."

Willows looked at his watch. "Almost four, Snuggy. Whatdaya say we walk down toward Wall Street and be in there when they open probably at five? I wouldn't want Horowitz to call saying they finished early while we're still on appetizers."

Snuggy shrugged. "You the boss. I'm just along for the ride."

They got out of the limo and stretched out. "What we been in there a couple of hours since lunch?"

"Sounds right, feels good to be standing."

"C'mon, Snuggy, Wall Street's that way."

They got to the entrance to the parking lot. Willows went over to the attendant. "See that limo we just came out of?"

"Yes, sir, the black one in the third row, right?"

"Right." Willows flashed twenty dollars in front of the attendant. "You keep an eye out?"

"Yes, sir." The attendant happily grabbed the twenty. "There's always someone here till midnight during the week. Those Wall Streeters keep late hours."

"Good. What's your name? Oh yeah, there it is on your uniform. I'm Dick. Nice meeting you, Leon."

Dick pointed at Snuggy. "C'mon, Snuggy, let's hang a left on Nassau Street. It's a little longer, but I know the area. We got time to kill, and the honeys that walk out of those office buildings are, well, honeys."

"Ain't we early for that, Dick? Don't they usually pour out at five?"

"Yeah, most do, Snuggy, but the ones that work for brokers, well, ya got all those foreign markets. So they start early."

"Dick, you're incorrigible. Not that I'd rat, but ain't you worried your wife'll find out you're a horndog?"

"Jenny knows, Snuggy, she knows. As long as it's just oohing and aahing, but no further, she's okay with it."

Snuggy grinned. "A lotta married guys must envy you, Dick, an open-minded wife."

"Well, Snuggy, it ain't just one-way. When she sees a cool dude, she goes into the old 'I wouldn't mind if he put his shoes under my bed' and all that malarkey. But I know she don't cheat, so…"

"That's yours, Dick. It's not my tone."

"Right." Willows put his cell phone to his ear. "Yeah? Willows here."

"Hi, Dick, it's Mo."

"Hi, Mo, *que passa*? You're not on till Thursday, right?"

"Right, Dick, but I'm not calling about—"

"Well, Mo, lemme cut you off. There's a good chance this shit'll be over tonight, so you won't have to worry about Thursday or any—"

"Oh, thanks for the info, Dick. That's sort of a relief. You see, I'm calling 'cause I'm worried."

"Worried? Happy-go-lucky Mo worried? That's something new. What's bothering you, amigo?"

"Well, this whole thing smells to me, Dick. I know all the accountants jump right to it for a guy like Mellon, boning up on the law, deductions, all that accounting mumbo jumbo."

Willows and Snuggy got to a red light, where they ogled the beauties crossing, when Willows held his cell up in the air and shot a look of exasperation toward Snuggy while shaking his head.

"Yeah, Mo, so what's your point?"

"Well, Dick, I figured I'd earn my Palmeiro pay by maybe contacting the IRS office that's conducting this whole deal."

"What for, Mo? You're not a big-time auditor or accountant."

"Yeah, Dick, that's true, but we're paid to protect Mellon, and you know, I kinda worry that this whole deal is a plot to to force Mellon to the surface."

"Just a minute, Mo. Okay, Snuggy, there's the place across the street. Let's cross here. Sorry, Mo, we're at the restaurant. You gonna be much longer?"

"No, no, Dick, enjoy your meal. Since this is the last night, I guess I was concerned for no good reason. Believe it or not, I was worried this was a setup to bring Mellon to the surface."

"*What?* What you been smoking, amigo? This IRS shit happens all the time. Why are you alarmed?"

"Alarmed? That's a strong word, Dick. I just wanted to be, what's the word, preemptive?"

"Preemptive?"

"Right, preemptive. I couldn't find this so-called task force on any IRS or treasury website."

"Well, Mo, you know how those bureaucrats, and this is, as you say, a Task Force, so—"

"Well, Dick, I called a detective at my old precinct. She gave me the number of an IRS guy she used to date and—"

"And he didn't know heads or tails?"

"Yeah, right whatever that means."

"That, Mo, means he didn't know diddly-squat, which is no big deal. I'd imagine there must be thousands of workers at IRS and—"

"Well, you're at the restaurant, and it's the last night. So I won't keep you any longer."

Willows rolled his eyes while looking at Snuggy. "Hey, it's cool, Mo. I always got time for you, and I like your zeal. You're going above and beyond. I'm doing your PE this go-round, and you're definitely at the highly effective level with a shot at 'outstanding.'"

"Well, that's nice of you to say, Dick. It makes me feel good. And I'll feel even better if this wraps up tonight with Mellon okay, and all I am is a nervous grandma. See ya, Dick, and thanks for hearing me out."

"Cool, Mo. I appreciate your input." Willows put his cell on mute, pointed toward the restaurant's entrance, and grinned. "C'mon, Snuggy, let's chow."

Aaron Horowitz approached Mellon sitting in a small anteroom outside one of the IRS offices on the fourth floor. "Good news, Mr. Mellon. Tidrow says we will finish tonight. You'll be out of here by seven at the latest. So you can have dinner at—"

"What happens between now and seven, Aaron?"

"Ralph, err, that's Tidrow's first name, says they got all they need. Basically, all that remains is that you sign some more forms and we're all going home."

"I have to sign some more…"

"Not to worry, Mr. Mellon, my associates are carefully reviewing everything you'll be signing. There'll be no perjury trap, not that I know what this so-called task force is about. After all this BS and reviewing three years' worth of records, they've barely come up with about 20K in 'adjustments.' There's no fraud alleged, so I guess they can't go back to DC with nothing, so they want the 20K, probably as a 'face-saver.' We could fight it and—"

"Are you kidding, Aaron, twenty thousand's chump change to our firm. Can… can we write out a check and get the heck out of here right now?"

Horowitz chuckled. "Wish it was that simple. They still got to review it in DC and then send out a formal declaration asking for the exact payment, plus penalties." He looked at his watch. "It's about five to six. If the guesstimate was right, we'll be out of here in just about an hour. I'll be right back after I find out what room they want you to go to sign all those forms. There's a lounge on the third floor with a catered coffee setup. Would you like to wait there?"

"Nah, Aaron, I've had my fill of coffee. I'll wait for you here."

Mellon was perusing an old Grisham paperback when Aaron reappeared.

"Mr. Mellon, this is Ralph Tidrow, who's sort of running this whole show for the IRS."

Mellon rose and shook Tidrow's hand. "Glad to meet you, Mr. Tidrow. Is the rumor that all this is close to ending true?"

"Absolutely." Tidrow grinned. "We're rounding third and heading home. If you'll follow me to room 409, it'll take about twenty minutes for you to John Hancock where indicated, and we'll still be able to catch a late dinner at home."

"Okay, guys," Horowitz said. "I'll be back in twenty minutes to see how things are going."

They watched Horowitz head toward the elevator. Tidrow pointed down the hallway. "C'mon, Mr. Mellon, 409's that way."

"Please call me Bill, Ralph."

Tidrow blushed. "Pardon the rudeness, Mr. Mellon, but when we're on an audit, we don't get to be on a familiar first-name basis. I hope you understand."

"Oh, sure, Mr. Tidrow. I should have been aware of that."

Tidrow reached for a key and opened room 409. He pointed to the leather chair behind the large table dominating the small room. "Please make yourself at home, Mr. Mellon. Don't be intimidated by all those papers. I've been told your people have reviewed all the forms and they concluded they're ready for your signature."

"That's right, they've reviewed—"

"You'll notice those little yellow stickers—they're there to make it easy to spot exactly where to sign, Mr. Mellon. Of course, you're welcome to read the forms if—"

"Nah, it's all right, Mr. Tidrow. As you say, my people have checked it all out. Looks like about twenty of those little stickers. It shouldn't take long."

"Good. I'm going to step out into the hallway to make a call. I'll be right outside if you have any questions."

Mellon watched Tidrow walk out into the hallway. *Let's see. Five already signed, about fifteen to go.* Mellon had actually enjoyed this "audit." It gave him a place to go every day. Hopefully, some of the initial responses from the Beltran camp would lead to a peace, or at least a cease-fire, so he could continue his career in the open. Retirement isn't...

Mellon heard the door open and watched Tidrow enter the room.

"Well, Mr. Tidrow, did you take care of your calls?"

Tidrow showed a wide grin. "Sure did, Mellon. Everything's in place."

Mellon dropped the pen and looked up. There was a tone to Tidrow's voice that Mellon hadn't previously heard. Plus, he called him Mellon. "Is there something…"

Mellon gasped as he saw Tidrow pull a revolver out of his suit pocket. Tidrow's grin was still wide. "You a praying man, Mellon?"

Mellon instinctively tried to get up. The last thing he heard was "Say your prayers." A fuselage of bullets entered his body. The first one stung like hell, but the others seemed like little pinpricks. He was obviously dying. *Is this the end of Rico?* he fantasized, repeating that famous line from *Little Caesar*. He was inelegantly perched on the floor, one leg still on the chair he'd fallen off. Tidrow had walked around the large desk and stood over him, still grinning. Clearly, he was about to administer the coup de grâce, Mafia style.

Mellon was in fantasyland, beyond recovery, but hoping for a few more moments… *Brooklyn, Red Hook, the parade grounds, Billy O'Shea, my son, my daughter, the grandchildren, Justine—will I never see them again? Sweet, holy Mary, Father Gilbride, I'm here for confession… if there's time…* Tidrow bent down, put the pistol to Mellon's temple, and squeezed the trigger.

THE BLOGGER

Slats had gotten the e-mail late Friday afternoon. It was from Leary and concluded with the request: "See you in my office first thing Monday morning." *Jeez, haven't heard from the boss man in a while. He's jealous I'm now spending all my time with Osborne now that I got my own blog? Fuck it, I won't even mention it to Holly. Now that we're hitched, she tends to worry too much. She's been looking forward to seeing a revival of Fiddler at the Long Beach Rep this Sat night—no way I'm putting a damper on that. But those "first thing Monday morning" thing was always subject to angst and/or worry… He's pissed at one of my blogs?*

Slats was promptly in the office at eight thirty, and Leary waved him on in. No sooner had Slats sat down than Leary got a call from upstairs. Watching Leary on the phone and viewing the calm Pacific waves washing onto the Malibu coastline, Slats began to speculate. He had a hunch—it'd been over a week since Mellon met his maker. *Dollars to doughnuts, Leary wants my take on the whole shebang. After all, Leary knows I still get occasional nightmares after that Spagos lunch with the dude looking to bump off that asshole, Stu Frommer, who just happens to have been Mellon's right-hand man, or henchman, as they'd describe it in the Batman comics.*

It had been about two weeks since he'd been face-to-face with Leary. The "yeah, boss" syndrome had changed. Leary was still nominally in charge of him, but Slats also now reported to Osborne on the sixth floor. In the three months since Slats had started *Slats Blog*, he sometimes reported to Osborne, sometimes used his old desk opposite Leary's office, and more often than not, stayed home, becoming, in effect, a home-office computer geek. In the time since Mellon's slaying, Slats had checked out *Drudge*, *Huffington*, and some of the other national sites. He figured he still had time to address the Mellon affair in his blog after the dust had settled. After all, people went to Slats's blog for assorted drivel, but with a local angle, which wasn't the case with this Mellon/Beltran thing. *Best of all was the timing*, Slats concluded. *Two days earlier, ThisWeek had arrived in the mail with a comprehensive, nonfrenetic report on l'affaire Beltran/Mellon. If Leary wants a briefing, I'm ready.*

Leary had hung up his phone. As usual, he leaned back on his swivel chair and observed the waves hitting the shoreline. "Well, big-shot blogger, you finally deemed yourself ready to slum and hang out with the proletariat facing deadlines every day?"

Slats answered Leary's grin with a smirk. "Natch, boss man, first of all, 'cause you requested my presence."

"And second?" Leary was losing his grin.

"Err, I said that wrong, boss man. There is no second. But there is a second point. Ya don't think I got deadlines on my blog?"

"Okay, okay," Leary snapped. "So you got deadlines. But if you're behind or didn't do your shit, you can always just write what's on your mind. That's why it's called a freaking blog. So don't bullshit me, Mr. Slats's Blog."

"Gee, boss man, what an outburst. I didn't realize you still cared."

Leary smiled. "Slats, Slats, what am I gonna do with you? Six months ago when I called you in, you were like a whimpering puppy. Now, since you married Holly and got your blog, you've... you've become... a regular big shot. A Monday–Friday highfalutin married big shot of a blogger who's no longer afraid of his boss."

"Gee, boss, I didn't realize the extent—"

"And furthermore, if Holly was too good for you as a girlfriend, she's certainly too good for you as a wife. Enough screwing around, Slats. How's Holly, and how's married life?"

"Couldn't be better," Slats smirked. "All that tension's disappeared."

"What tension?"

"Well, you recall l'affaire Rhea Simpson and assorted other fantasy indiscretions? Well, now that Holly's got me legally hog-tied, it's sort of understood that any more screwing around and…" Slats blushed and used an imaginary knife toward his groin area and winced. "You know Holly's temper."

"Easy, Slats." Leary grimaced and sort of pointed toward his groin. "I'm not sure I like that analogy. After all, Lenore's been known to lose her temper."

They looked at each other for almost a minute. "Bet I can guess why you called me in this fine, sunny Monday morning."

Leary leaned back on his chair and took a swig of his water bottle. "How many months has it been since you had the fright of your life with that dude who was after Frommer?"

"Two or three." Slats blushed. "Who remembers, I try and repress frightful memories."

"But your memory can't be that obliterated that you don't know why I called you in today."

"You right, boss man, my memory ain't *that* obliterated. The Chanteuse was ours virtually from the beginning. Then we were all over her brother's killing, then there was Crosby, then Frommer—the more the tale got national, the more we hung to the local angle. It was great while it lasted… Err, did I say that right, or is it still lasting?"

"Give that man a Kewpie Doll!" Leary exclaimed. "This is so *Page One*. How the hell do we get in on the deal? And not for your freakin' blog. For your old paper, for your old colleagues, and for… ah, your young boss."

"Clear it with Osborne?"

Leary grinned. "What do you think? Okay, it's been over a week. What do ya got?"

"Stop me if you've heard—"

"Don't gimme that crap." Leary looked at his watch. "It's barely nine. I got all day. Filibuster all you want."

"Okay, then I'll start from the beginning. Apparently, Mellon had already sent out peace feelers to Beltran and his hit men, probably including my nightmare guy from Spagos. Then, by coincidence, or whatever, the IRS supposedly calls for a special audit. You know why I say 'supposedly'?"

"Yes, I do, Slats. Just continue."

"So Mellon had been in hiding for all the past year plus, but evidently his presence was required for this 'special' audit. Well, the Palmeiro Protective Services, the outfit protecting Mellon all this time, reportedly used all their nefarious talents to get Mellon to the IRS audit site and then whisk him out of there."

"Where, where, Slats, was the site?"

"Uh, Nassau Street, near Wall Street. I, uh, remember that 'cause Nassau is the biggest county in Long Island."

Leary could no longer maintain his poker face. "Slats," he grinned, "you're too fuckin' much."

"You right, boss, I am too much. Can I continue?"

Now Leary virtually giggled. "You most assuredly may continue. So Mellon and the Palmeiros couldn't detect a setup?"

"Well, actually, *This Week* revealed that there was one guy at Palmeiro, an exNYC police detective who was leery from the get-go. I... I don't recall his name. It's Hispanic."

"No sweat, Slats, you're doin' fine. Go right ahead."

"Okay, so except for that ex-cop, all the Mellon accountants and Palmeiro guys who either weren't there and/or survived that day were comfortable with the whole deal. Apparently, the higher you are in the wealthy class, the greater you're used to these dramatic IRS sweeps and task forces. Evidently, that Nassau Street building had all the accoutrements of any Federal building—portraits of President Bush, airport-type screening... the whole megillah."

"Wow." Leary smiled. "Accoutrements, megillah—I'm being briefed by a virtual thesaurus."

Slats blushed. "Well, you know I grew up in Fairfax. That's where I picked up the 'megillah' word. As for 'accoutrements'... Yikes, boss man, don't sell me short. Ain't I your top wordsmith?"

"I guess," Leary sighed. "Go on."

Slats stole a glance at his watch. His stomach growled, reminding him it was almost time for his 10:00 AM latte. "Well, to skip to the most interesting part of the *This Week* piece, this IRS gambit happened once before."

Leary's eyes narrowed. "Happened before?"

Slats displayed a big grin. "Ever hear of Lucky Luciano?"

Now Leary's cheeks flushed red, a sure sign of his Irish temper. "What the F does Lucky Luciano got to do with all this? It's an organized crime?"

"Hold on, boss man." Slats held up his right hand. "I'll explain. It seems when Luciano was moving up the ladder, there were two old-time mafioso running things. One was Joe the Boss something, the other... err, forgot his name. I have it in my computer if—"

"Go ahead, Slats, I don't care about the name."

"Well, one of the bosses was mowed down by Luciano mobsters in a restaurant. The other," Slats paused and showed a wide grin, "the other boss had had a history of problems with the IRS. So a couple of Luciano associates made out like they were IRS agents, walked breezily past the bodyguards, and whacked him in his office."

"Come on, Slats, you putting me on?"

"Nah, there it is, well researched in *This Week*. Plus, I think I saw it depicted in a movie, with Christian Slater playing Luciano and Anthony Quinn the boss whacked in the restaurant."

Leary leaned back on his chair and giggled. "Christian Slater as Luciano? That's a stretch, but Quinn... what a dude, started in pictures in the early forties. What's that, about sixty-five years? Incredible."

"And speaking of movies, you wanna hear something else?"

"Shoot, Slats."

"Lore has it that one of the IRS hit men was Bugsy Siegel—you know, the guy Warren Beatty portrayed in *Bugsy*."

"No shit, what a small world. Plus, there's all that affirmative action. Siegel doesn't sound like a Sicilian name."

Slats's face was beaming, like he was about to impress the teacher and the other classmates with a well-researched book report. "Well, that was the point, you see. Luciano was the only big-time mafioso to

LEE BORNSTEIN

hobnob with Jewish gangsters. So any of the eye-talian hoods would have been recognizable while posing as IRS agents."

"Gee, Slats, I'm starting off this week with a doozy of a head-ache. Christian Slater, Anthony Quinn, Lucky Luciano, Bugsy Siegel... Can we get back to the late, lamented Mellon?"

"Sure, boss man. As you recall, Mellon had put out peace feelers to Beltran and his associates. Reportedly, Beltran had tentatively responded. Apparently, both sides were weary of the stalemate. All the hiding, all the fear—that's why the timing is sort of suspicious."

"How's that, Slats?"

"Well, just when there's evidence that both sides are about to call off the feud."

"That's just it, Slats. They figured Mellon's guard was down, and—"

"Well, that's not it, boss. This IRS con would have worked no matter when it was pulled. The Mellon people were completely hoodwinked, figuring if the IRS wants you in person, you don't fuck around."

Leary made a strange sound. It sounded like a "harrumph," not typical for the likes of Leary. His eyes seemed to wander. He turned his chair toward the ocean. *Leary's losing patience*, Slats concluded. *Fuck him. He called the meeting, I ain't wasting his time.*

"So what's the latest on law enforcement? Has—"

"Well, Beltran's turned himself in, maintaining his innocence. He said not only didn't he order the IRS fake-out, but even if any of his crew wanted to pull it off on their own, they wouldn't have the money, the capacity, and so on... and certainly not without his knowledge."

"Are they holding him?"

"Who?"

"The Feds, the cops—I don't know."

Slats grinned impishly. "Well, the Feds have had a low profile. I'm guessing there's enough to go RICO on Beltran, but his wife's suicide, his ruined practice, and the Republican's antipathy toward lawsuits... well... It looks like the Big Apple has stepped in to fill the breach."

"How's that, Slats?"

"Well, he's not in that notorious Rikers' holding pen. The Manhattan DA has arranged for him to stay in a middling hotel in Manhattan while outfitting him with all the latest monitoring devices, bracelets, all that shit. Plus, reportedly, there's a surreptitious twenty-four-hour watch by the NYPD. The DA kept hemming and hawing between 'suspect' and 'person of interest.' But it's obvious they don't have enough to officially charge him."

"You get all this from *This Week*?"

"You kidding, boss man? When you called this 'first thing Monday morning' crap, I had a hunch this'd be the topic, so I went online to all the NY papers to be fully prepared. I also checked out some blogs."

"I take my imaginary hat off, Slats, you Monday–Friday sure came in here prepared." Leary was grinning.

Slats, watching Leary's beam, felt a glow inside, like the first time he got a gold star in kindergarten, or was it the first grade?

Leary looked at his watch. Surely a sign this meet would soon end and Slats could calm his growling tummy with a Cinnamon Dolce Latte.

"Okay, Slats, we don't have enough to go on at the moment, especially since *Pacific Coast* is two-thirds of the moniker of our fish wrap, which reminds me, what's up with the Chanteuse, and is there any way we can make her part of the story?"

"You hadn't heard?"

"Heard what, Slats?"

"About her move to Florida?"

"I guess I heard something. Is that of any use?"

"Well, boss man, it's a sad tale. The ol' Chanteuse has had a fall worthy of some Shakespearean tragedy. Supposedly, she was changing her domicile to be near her youngest son who had just moved to Miami. Turns out that with her lifestyle and her income down to about $2 mill a year, some of her accountants and/or advisers pointed out that she could save $200,000 a year, give or take, by moving to a state with no income taxes like Florida."

"Makes sense if you're willing to give up the Golden State for a lousy 10 percent in tax savings. So what's the big deal, and where's the story?"

"Well one of her accountants ratted her out."

"Ratted her out? An accountant?"

"Yeah, the cover story, as I said, was that she was moving to Florida to be near her son. But this Hollywood blogger, YouSeekAndIShallTell.Com broke the story."

"What story, Slats?"

"Well, the story that she was BS-ing as to why she moved to Florida. She went to Florida to be near her son, all right, but only after she used some connections to get him a job down there so she'd have the excuse to move down there."

"How'd I miss all this, Slats?"

Slats shrugged. "You got a big-time newspaper to run. Me? I'm either blogging or reading blogs all day long. Anyhow, she's yesterday's news. That's why it hasn't been page 1 all over."

"Granted, Slats. But what's the big deal? Rush Limbaugh moved to Florida and never stopped boasting about the savings by not paying those humongous New York taxes."

"Sure, boss man. But Conservatives are anti-tax and proud of it. Conversely, Libs just love high taxes. It's a sign of their compassion. So when their erstwhile darling turned on Josh, that was bad enough. But to *openly* take 10 percent off the table, that's a blow in the eye socket of every Progressive's raison d'être."

Leary smiled. "Easy on the analogy, Slats. Methinks you're getting carried away. But did I catch a little emphasis on the word *openly*?"

"Sure did, boss man, sure did." Slats beamed. "You don't think those Hollywood types are begging their tax preparers for every loophole, every angle? But in public, they have to rant about Bush's tax cut for the rich."

"I thought it was Reagan's tax cuts for the rich?"

"Both." Slats giggled.

"But… but didn't everyone get a cut? Not just the rich?"

"Touché, boss man, touché."

Leary looked at his watch. "It's almost ten thirty, and I still haven't accomplished a thing. Think of an angle, Slats, think of an angle. We wanna get Mellon, Beltran, and the Chanteuse into the same story."

"Gee, boss man, a two-hour traffic delay on PCH and Bellflower isn't enough to boost circulation?"

"Get outta here and lemme get some work done. Yeah, and all my love to Holly."

"I'll let her know, thanks. Now I'm on my way up to the sixth floor. Osborne owns my ass for the rest of this blue Monday."

39

ON THE MAKE

Chase Wright tried to make heads or tails of it. Captain Tumult was back in New York. Beltran was a suspect confined to New York, and most of the "volunteers" had returned to their former lives. Meanwhile, virtually all the contributors had pulled in their heels, and Chase's pay and expenses had ended as of last Friday. Still, Chase decided to stay in the Bay Area, at his own expense. Money was no problem, and even if it was, he'd stay in San Francisco to clear up what was going on in his fogged-up mind. It was the matter of the unfinished business.

Yes, no more chasing Frommer, no more dealing with that pathetic Crosby, and no more being wary day and night in case someone's after *me*. Captain Tumult had said everything was okay back East so far. There was still enough money and New York–based volunteers to help Beltran in any upcoming legal and/or criminal hassles. The captain had retained counsel but seemed assured that Bloomberg and/or whoever would never get to his level—especially since they still seemed uncertain as to whether or how to proceed against Beltran.

Although the name had come up before, Captain Tumult repeated the name of that infamous billionaire left-wing blogger, Zig Hermanski. To wit, some ex-cop named Molina, now with Palmeiro, was screaming to the heavens that Hermanski was behind Mellon's death. There had been rumors that with all of Mellon's wealth, and the moola from the zealous lawyers supporting him, a great deal of money in Mellon's treasure chest had come from Hermanski. According to Molina, Mellon had paid a visit to Hermanski's estate about a month before the slaying, that it didn't go well, and this IRS feint so soon afterward was Hermanski's response. The *Times* and *ThisWeek* never covered that part of the story. Several New York tabloids briefly picked up on it but quickly reverted to the standard sexploitation of various showbiz and sports personalities. The last Tumult heard, Palmeiro Protective Services had no comment, and Molina was reportedly no longer employed by Palmeiro.

As to whether he had cause to worry, the captain assured Chase that any investigation wouldn't get down to his level, at least not until someone higher up had been convicted. And there was slim chance of that since the captain was the operational head of the anti-Mellon clique, and he *knew* no one in the group could have pulled off the hit 'cause no one knew where the fuck Mellon was. "So don't worry, Chase. It'll never get to you unless they want to pull off a massive frame, not likely."

Chase grinned, so no near-term chance of hearing a knock on the door, followed by "Chase Wright? I have a warrant for your arrest." *With that worry theoretically in abeyance, why am I breathing so hard? It's the MF unfinished business. How the hell do I win her back?*

Chase didn't want to think about it, but he had to. To know how to proceed, you gotta review what went wrong. What went wrong? Everything. When he first told Carrie that the Sea Cliff real estate ploy was, well, a ploy, to say she hit the roof would be an understatement. The only reason she didn't scream was because they were in Perry's on Union Street. But the way she hissed "I don't ever want to see you again" before storming out was bad enough.

He'd sent flowers to Carrie at Perrin Realtors, but they were returned with a curt message that he couldn't remember. No doubt a classic case of repressing an awful memory. Natch, she wouldn't accept any of his phone calls and didn't answer any of his e-mails—they hadn't advanced to the texting phase when things were good, so no chance of that.

Don't chicken out now, Chase, he admonished himself. *As discomforting as a public humiliation might be, this is definitely worth it. Scene or no scene, rant or no rant, it's just not a question that she's worth it. You've never felt this way before. Your body has never tingled this way before. Walk the plank, dingbat. Just do it, no debate.*

Well, there is a debate. I don't beg. Tail's never been a problem. Why should I lower myself like I'm a helpless, lovelorn puppy—there's more where that came from. Chase smiled. *Those silent sentences weren't helping and weren't truthful. You're hooked, you pathetic creature. It's like my broker once said, "You can't fight the tape."*

After dinner, Chase hit some spots on Chestnut. He had two or three Bailey's Irish Cream. Not at the top of the after-dinner drinks, status-wise, but Chase felt he didn't have to impress, especially when by himself. He just liked the damn taste of Bailey's Irish Cream. *Easy, fella, what are you getting bent out of shape about? You know what it's about. Gotta figure out a way to get back to Carrie.*

Several comely wenches gave Chase the eye, but he wasn't in the mood. This was going to be a lonely, brooding, feel-sorry-for-yourself type of bender. Chase's mind was reeling; his head was spinning… Or was it the other way around? He felt like another Bailey's. *Better not,* he admonished himself. *Even if you're not driving, you don't wanna stagger out of here like a hobo from the Tenderloin.* He asked for some ice water, and the cool drink got rid of some of the cobwebs.

Forget about a Carrie plan for the moment. Just review how you got here. Let's see, there was that America-hating Dick, Tom Crosby. Then there was his flunky, Phil Upshaw. Upshaw, Upshaw—how did he remember that name? Easy. Dale Carnegie says you think of something that sounds like the name. Then you recall the name. So with Upshaw, you think of a rickshaw. With Crosby? Too easy. Just think of Der Bingle. Let's see, who was that lanky babe I met when I first got to Peet's? Yeah, Longley, wasn't he a QB for Dallas or something? But no small talk. She might have turned out to be a football fan, and there'd be no end to the conversation.

That would not have fit with the covert infiltration plan. Chase toyed with his water. Suddenly, the Bailey's didn't look that inviting. He felt a chill. Was he getting somewhere? Let's see, didn't she have a funny first name? Not funny, but it didn't fit with her last name. It sounded Jewish, doesn't go with Longley. A lotta Jewish broads in Cherry Hill. He'd heard that name more than once when he socialized around there. *Rachel—that's it. Rachel, like out of the Old Testament. Rachel Longley, Rachel Longley—Monday-Friday. I MF got it. There's* another *Rachel—the* blasted *receptionist at the realty firm.* Chase got so excited he literally foamed at the mouth. He didn't care if someone caught the embarrassment. He was okay with the childish manifestation; he was bubbling over. This lead, this link, would, *had to*, lead to something good.

A week went by. Chase had contacted Ray Walker and had gotten the name of the best jeweler in town. They talked about what they'd be doing from here on in. They surmised they'd be in limbo till all this Mellon shit played out. Meanwhile, they agreed it was nice of Tumult to continue them at reduced pay pending another assignment. "That is, if Tumult ain't in Leavenworth or some other facility at taxpayers' expense." Walker cackled.

"Well, let's hope it don't come to that, Ray," Chase had responded. "On the other hand, Ray, while wishing the good captain the best, it may be academic to me if I change my profession." Chase then explained his quest for the realtor Carrie Woods and that if she took him back, leaving this dastardly profession might be part of the price.

"But I got it so bad, Ray, I'm gonna ask you a favor."

"Oh, was that the babe you tangled with while I was undercover as an office cleaner? Think nothing of it, Chase. Something to tell my grandchildren. Make them think their grandpappy was a good Joe. What do you want me to do?"

Ray had recommended Kravitz Jewelers, right off Union Square. "It's not Tiffany's, but their attention to detail… Well, anyone who grew up in the Bay Area knows Kravitz."

It took several weeks before Chase had the rock in the setting. It was a Tuesday morning when Ray called. "All set, bro. I asked for an appointment for this afternoon, and the receptionist said she'd be out with a client. Would tomorrow be okay?"

"Fine," I answered. "What's your name, by the way?"

"Rachel," she answered.

"Did I come through, bro?"

"What can I say, Ray? You more than came through. I owe ya a lot. One way or another, I'll find a way to repay you. Keep on truckin', Ray. Hope ol' Tumult reunites us soon. See you later."

Chase couldn't have felt better. It was a two-prong plan. Carrie had to be out, and Rachel had to be in the office. *Finally. The parlay, the combo hit. Chase looked at his watch. It was a quarter to eleven. Try to get there inside of two. If Carrie gets back while I'm still with Rachel, it'll be a melee for all time. Of course, Rachel could be taking a late lunch. What else could go wrong? Cut the shit, Chase. Don't sweat what you can't control. Besides, if the plan blows up, no one will be blowing you up—a possibility quite extant just a few weeks ago.*

Chase was sorry he hadn't shaved after his morning shower. Lately he'd been shaving every other day. He was about to approach the sink when he decided a little fuzz might bring out the compassion in a young lady like Rachel. *The young man is so distraught. Look at him. He's not even shaving. What can I do to help?*

Chase smirked while shaking his head. *Gee, Chase, all this conniving… You're like a male version of Bette Davis or any of those scheming wenches in Desperate Housewives. Yeah, well, true love—it's worth all the worry and the scheming. Enough of all this BS. Don't forget to bring the rock.*

He knew of a parking garage about a mile from Perrin. He drove there and then called a cab. Didn't want a repeat of the half-hour parking meter hassles. Chase got there at a quarter to one and approached the entrance. He pulled out his cell phone and made out as if he were listening to someone while he checked out the scenery. When a customer opened the door and walked in, Chase was right behind.

Rachel was there, and the best part, the customer, after a brief greeting, walked into the bull pen area to see one of the realtors. Rachel looked up and saw him. There was shock, embarrassment, some blushing, and naturally, a reluctant smile. Chase took a deep breath and approached her.

"Well, if it isn't Mr. Outcast, Mr. Get Lost, Mister—"

"I get the picture, Rachel." Chase put on his best "aw shucks" smile.

Now she really blushed. "Wow, you remembered my name. So obviously, you're not a total jerk. Carrie's not here. Not that it would do you any good if she were."

Chase sighed. It was a deliberate and audible sigh meant to convey a message—the message being "Forget the handsome young daredevil swashbuckler in front of you. Appearances can deceive. What you see in front of you is a helpless whimpering puppy, a puppy who needs all the help a compassionate young lady like you is capable of providing." It worked; her antagonism had changed to puzzlement, mixed in with a sprinkling of sympathy. "Look, uh, Rachel," he stumbled and mumbled, "maybe, err, it's for the best that she's not here. I-I'm not sure I'm up to doing with Carrie what I'm about to do with you."

"What, what on earth are you talking about?" The compassion was descending into annoyance.

"This," he replied as he pulled out the fancy case holding the ring. He opened the case.

"Wow," she almost screamed, "what a rock!"

Chase slowly closed the case and put it back in his pocket. "I'm the 'Get Lost' Guy, and I'm so in love that I spent you can guess what on this ring without any assurance she'd even respond, let alone respond with a no." She was hooked.

"Is… is there something you want me to do, to say?"

"Yes, there is."

Her eyes narrowed. The wariness had evidently returned. "I'm all ears."

Chase focused on her eyes. He was locked in. He had to appear sincere. It helped that he *was* sincere, but she had to be convinced. "You saw the ring, Rachel. I bought it with no assurance Carrie would ever give me the time of day."

"It's quite a gesture, like something out of a movie. What do you want me—"

"Just tell her I showed you the engagement ring. I'll be at the Top of the Mark this Saturday night from seven on. I'll be there till closing, waiting for Carrie."

"How... how do you know she doesn't have a dinner date Saturday night? It's already Tuesday, and Carrie's a popular, eh, person."

Chase allowed a slight smile. "If keeping a dinner date is more important than meeting someone who loves her and wants to marry her, then I'd have my answer."

Rachel quivered, then blushed. "You're... you're magnificent. I've seen every episode of *Friends* and reruns of *Seinfeld* but never experienced anything like this. I... I wish Carrie was here. You'd win her over. But... you apparently wounded her grievously. She, Carrie, didn't give me the details, but you have a lot to overcome."

"Absolutely, Rachel, I was duplicitous, but I... Well, I don't want to burden you with any of it. If Carrie does show, it doesn't mean she's accepting the ring or accepting my apology, but at least she's willing to hear me out. It's all I ask."

Rachel gasped. "I'll... I'll do my best." She looked at her watch. "It's almost three. Carrie said she'd be back inside of three thirty. Maybe you'd better. If she shows up and sees you talking to me, I don't think you'd be able to overcome the eruption."

Chase rose and grinned. "You're a wise gal, Rachel. I'm out of here. And... and thanks for listening, and thanks for whatever you can do."

Chase arrived at the Top of the Mark at a quarter to seven. He'd reserved a table for two and explained that his date had "business" and might be late. He was worried about having had two hours of drinks by the time she'd show, say, at nine—the last thing he needed for her to see him tipsy. Then he thought about having to hit the head after two hours. *What if she shows and I'm not there? Cut the shit, Chase. You'll worry yourself to death. Just imagine you're facing a drug runner on assignment for the captain. That never bothered you. Yeah, sure, subconscious, but in the latter, the worst that can happen is I'll be killed. This is worse than losing your life—this'd be losing the love of your life.* The conversation with his "subconscious" caused him to smirk.

Talk about getting carried away. Still, he decided, if he had to go, he'd just find the waiter or whoever and say that if an unaccompanied young lady shows up looking for Chase Wright, there's his table. He was in the mood for a beer, but that wouldn't look right in a ritzy place like the Mark. He considered a martini, but if he had to get another, on an empty stomach, before she showed, he concluded he'd be too out of it. When the waitperson appeared, he ordered J&B, rocks, water chaser.

The service was prompt. Chase quickly downed some of the scotch, and he felt relieved. The scotch cascading through his body seemed to mellow him out. *Guess that's why drunkards drink*, he smirked. *It just feels good, makes problems recede.* He looked at his watch. It was seven fifteen. He had another swallow. *Well, Chase, you decided to be extemporaneous—no notes, no cheat sheets.* Not that it wasn't considered. *But stumble trying to remember something, and it'll look like you're untruthful again. Nah, the truth is on your side. You can't go wrong if...* He saw her. She was heading straight for his table. He'd faced pistols and similar dangers in the past, but his heart never pounded as hard as this moment. He rose to meet her. Her detached expression gave way to a smile. In an instant, they were in a fond embrace. The cool/warm effect of her closeness changed everything. His pounding heart was a distant memory. Now his heart floated; it soared. She pulled back. He looked at her and was about to say how much he cared... He saw it out of the corner of his left eye. Her right hand landed on his left cheek. He was caught flat-footed—talk about a sucker punch / slap. He succeeded in suppressing a smile as he staggered backward. Wow, just like the movies. Does that make her Scarlett and me Clark Gable or whatever his name was.

"You louse," she hissed, "you think a lousy ring can make me forget what you put me through?"

Wow, the highs and lows in this thing called love. Just a minute ago, the hug that made everything okay, followed by the slap of the century, as the song asks, "What Is This Thing Called Love?" Not knowing what to do, Chase exhibited a wan smile. It was rewarded.

"Are you all right, Chase? I'm sorry if—"

The server broke in. "Is... is everything okay?"

Now Chase was in his element—dealing not with the love of his life but with a young dude that he'd just as soon deck as blink. "Everything's cool, thanks for asking."

Chase's tone conveyed the message. "Get the F outta here before I…" The waitperson split.

He looked at Carrie and tried his best "aw shucks."

"I'm fine, Carrie." He put his hand to his cheek and allowed a slight smirk. "You pack quite a wallop."

They sat down. She blushed and held out her hand. Chase quickly squeezed it. "I'm hooked, beauty," she said softly. "But I had to take the risk that my rage of the century wouldn't keep you away forever. If… if I hadn't blown sky-high, I'd have lost my self-respect, and probably, deep down, so would your estimation of me. Maybe not now when we're at the height of physical attraction, but later—"

"Carrie, you're… you're obviously quite a person, aside from your looks. I'm doubly hooked."

They stared at each other. "Omigosh, Carrie, I think I scared that waitperson away. What'll you have? Champagne?"

"Haven't you forgotten something?" She smiled and held out her hand. Chase eagerly held on to her hand. A minute went by. Her smile was now radiant, enchanting. Chase sensed there was something that he'd…

"The ring, Chase, the ring. After all, I've heard so much about it."

"Omigosh, I can't believe my stupidity." He hurriedly pulled the case out of his pants pocket. He gulped as he opened the case. He pulled out the ring and put it on what he thought was the appropriate finger. Now her smile really dazzled. It was like something beatific. He felt his heart pounding; his legs had given out. Good thing they were sitting. "Will… will you marry me?"

MERGER

Stu Frommer finally showed up at the office. It had been nearly a year since the heat got so bad that Stu had decided that discretion was the better part of… well, whatever.

He tried a quiet entrance around nine, but virtually the entire staff was all over him, visiting him in twos and threes, all with the same message: "Welcome back," "You're looking great," and "Hoping all this stuff's behind us." Stu tried his best "Some people will do anything to goof off away from their desks. The productivity in this office is going to hell" and other attempts at abrasiveness. It didn't work, especially since virtually every female member of the office insisted on hugging him, some even adding a smooch or two.

By ten thirty, the senior staff had closeted themselves in Frommer's office in an intensive review of current accounts and the financial condition of Frommer & Sons.

"See, Mr. Frommer, your management is so right on that we continue to roll with our top guy… err… offshore, so to speak."

Frommer blushed and felt a lump in his throat. "What can I say? You've all been magnificent. End of the year, assuming we're still in the black, I'll hold back half a mill for my 'salary' and operating expenses—all the rest is going out in bonuses…"

"We another Goldman Sachs?" Syms grinned.

"Not quite at that level, Charley." Frommer blushed. "But we'll do the best we can."

The meeting ended at noon, and Syms remained in the office. "You feeling safe now, Mr. Frommer?"

"Well, Charley, what can I say? As the song says, there's a time for loving, a time for living." Charley looked blank. "Okay, Charley, it's like this. There's a time for hiding and then a time for living. Ever since Mellon bought it and the subsequent heat from the authorities, plus the peace feelers, well, it's like you're buttoned up for a hurricane, and there's a tentative all clear. Some people are gonna stay holed up until the tentative all clear is a total all clear. Not me. I did what had to be done. Now, well, it's a new setting—when Mellon hid, I hid. When in Rome... Well, rest in peace, Bill Mellon. No more Mellon, no more Rome."

Syms blushed and chuckled. "You sure have a way with words, Mr. Frommer."

"Yo, Charley," Frommer was thinking of his last meeting with Mellon, "after all this, please call me Stuey."

"Okay, Stuey. You going to continue the extra security?"

"Sure will, Charley. I still worry about you or any other innocents getting caught in a cross fire if they try anything here in the office. But, but, I wouldn't have shown my ugly face here if I didn't think the coast was clear. Is... is anyone in the office nervous?"

"We all are, Stuey, but if incoming flak is part of the job, no one's punking out. We... we took a job, and we're ready to handle any incoming that goes with it. That goes for everyone, including twenty-one-year-old Joan Manion."

"Who's Joan Manion?"

"Our newest associate. I told her there might be fireworks, although I was vague. She grinned and answered, 'Thanks for the heads-up. When do I start?'"

Frommer tried to hide his emotion. He didn't think he was successful. "Charley, I can't find the words right now. Well, I... I appreciate everything..."

"Want to be alone for a moment, Stuey?"

"Nah, it's okay, Charley." Frommer looked at his watch. "Wanna hit Rickenbacker's for lunch around noon?"

"Sure, Stuey, bet you miss the old routine."

"How's about we hit Fredo's for a drink after five?"

"Love to, Stuey, but tonight's the start of the big West Coast Public Relations Jamboree at the Moscone. Manion and some other junior staffers will be setting up our display, and I kinda feel I should lend a hand."

"Oh, yeah, sure, Charley. I've always noticed a blip in billings after the jamboree. I guess we do a good job in spreading the word."

"Yeah, Mr. From—err, Stuey, the new billings, more often than not, cover the $1,500 cost of the display space. Especially this year, since, unlike last year, no hotel costs when it's at Moscone."

"Right, where was it last year again?"

"Modesto."

"I remember, what with travel, hotels, it set us back about four grand. Did we get any new customers?"

Syms blushed and grinned. "Nothing yet, but we're still dickering with Oddessa Convertibles… About $5,000 a month for two years. It's a family business, and some uncle or something is still holding out."

"Oddessa Convertibles? What kinda name…?"

"They're Russian émigrés." Syms shrugged. "They're located in Turlock. They sure know the furniture business. But they need us, as I tried to convince them. A good rep means more customers. The holdout uncle's probably an unreconstructed Commie. Can't grasp our wonderful capitalistic ways. At any rate, we'll do a lot better this year—better setting, classier companies, and good flow."

"Did you say flow, Charley?" Frommer grinned.

"Well, Stu, our business does attract a lot of beauties, but I was referring to the general public. Spivey's the big attraction this year, and with his rep, it should draw a lot more of the general public than usual."

"Humm, Spivey & Associates, the white shoe outfit from LA. You're right, Charley. It should draw—"

"And one of their young hotshots, someone named Rhea Simpson, is going to be the keynoter."

"Rhea Simpson?" Frommer flashed a devilish grin. "I think I've heard that name before. I-I'm sort of tied up till Tuesday. So I'll miss the keynote, but tell the people at our display I'll be there first thing Tuesday. We don't want anyone goofing off when the boss shows up, do we?"

Frommer spent the weekend and Monday contacting the cable company, restocking the fridge, and about one hundred or so other mundane chores involved in reestablishing a normal routine. His "breaks" consisted of checking out the old/new neighborhood, mostly to check out any new trendy eating and/or hanging-out spots. On Monday night, he dined with his insurance broker at the Paragon near PacBell Park to review his newly revised homeowner's coverage needs.

On Tuesday morning, Frommer walked over to Moscone and, after showing the appropriate badge, was directed to Moscone South, room 300. He casually wandered through the area testing himself as to whether he was familiar with the assorted company names displayed at the various booths.

Then he saw the Frommer booth and watched the young staffers enthusiastically buttonhole passersby, giving them the canned spiel and handing out brochures—"Frommer & Sons, Opening Up New Vistas Using the Written Word."

"Wow," Frommer sighed. "That's a little far out. Let's hope Charley tested that campaign slogan with some consultants."

Frommer stayed with the troops until Syms showed up around noon. Frommer asked him if he'd like to go out to lunch soon. Syms took Frommer aside and whispered he wanted to see how this group handled the banter until the more senior associates showed up around three. "But there's a big wine-and-cheese shindig at Moscone North between noon and two. Your badge'll get you in. We paid a little extra to get a Blue Badge. Just show it and you're in."

"What about you, Charley?"

"My cousin Howie and his wife are staying at the St. Francis. Janie and I are meeting them at five. When Howie comes to town, he likes to tie one on. He lives in Phoenix, and there's been too many DUIs since there's no public transport. So gimme a rain check, Stuey, I don't wanna be plastered afore the evening even starts."

Frommer smiled. "Wow, what a complicated life we're all—"

"It's a complicated web we all weave." Syms giggled.

"Just the words I was looking for. Okay. Charley, best to Janie. See ya tomorrow."

"Not coming back?"

"Probably not, Charley. Still got some chores to be taken care of on the home front. Starting Wednesday, back to the ten-hour days. Can't wait."

Frommer crossed the street to Moscone North. He was about to ask the guard where the wine and cheese was when he saw the sign:

WINES FROM NAPA AND OTHER ENVIRONS—JOIN
THE FUN FROM TWELVE TO TWO. ALL WELCOME.
EXHIBIT HALL 100A, LOWER LEVEL.

Frommer saw the escalator leading down and wondered about how un-PR a sign can get. *Assuming Syms is right, you need a Blue Badge. So not everyone is welcome.* Turned out no badge was necessary. There was no one manning the door. It was nearly twelve thirty, and everyone seemed to be into it. The buzz, noise was deafening, reminding Frommer of those good college mixers when everyone's tipsy and feeling great.

Sure enough, the hall was divided into two sections. The arrow pointing left indicated Wines from the Napa Valley. The one pointing right read Wines from Other Environs. His curiosity led him toward the "other environs." His eye caught one table setup featuring Chateau Ste. Michelle, a Chardonay, and a Riesling from the Columbia Valley. *Columbia Valley—that rings a bell,* Frommer reflected. Now where—oh yeah, up north somewhere, maybe Oregon, probably Washington. A Pinot Noir setup also caught his eye—Wild Horse, Central Coast. He decided on a taste of the Riesling. As expected, the servers were as delectable as the wine they were offering. *Well, what would you expect?* Frommer concluded, suddenly wishing he were a least ten years younger. He passed up the crackers and cheese offerings for now.

He sipped the Riesling as he headed toward the Napa area. *Oh yeah, Cabernet Sauvignon, just my type of wine. Let's see, Robert*

Mondavi or St. Supery. He hurried his Riesling and was starting to feel appropriately tipsy as he approached the Mondavi table. There she was. Munching on a tiny slice of French bread topped with what looked like soft Brie cheese. His knees went wobbly. It was Rhea Simpson. He'd seen photos of her in the trades, but being next to her… She wasn't a kid like Sharon, the yoga teacher, but she still looked cute as a button even wearing one of those stodgy blue business suits and short heels. The apparel didn't matter; Frommer knew that if she was buck naked, she'd compare to…

"Aren't you Stuart Frommer?" She allowed a slight smile while tasting her newly acquired glass of Mondavi.

"Yes, yes, I am." Frommer tried a sheepish grin while berating himself for daydreaming and letting her initiate the conversation. "And you're Rhea Simpson. How was your keynote? I missed it."

"It was the best keynote in the history of the Moscone Center." She giggled.

"Well, Ms. Simpson, then I'm doubly sorry I missed it." He pointed toward some empty tables. "Care to join me while enjoying some Napa Cabernet Sauvignon? Perhaps I can catch some of your expertise, especially after having missed the keynote. After all, I've heard so much about you."

She blushed, and her expression showed a little edge. "Not as much as I've heard about you, Mr. Frommer."

Frommer sighed and munched some cheese. "Please, Ms. Simpson, under these conditions, I'd like to call you Rhea. At the same time, while we're enjoying this relaxed atmosphere, could you possibly call me Stu?"

The deliberate wimpish response from the individual with the Frommer-type rep seemed to startle and disarm her. "I'm not so sure." She blushed. "After all, I *have* heard so much about you."

"Oh yeah, what have you heard?"

"Well, if you must know, I—"

"Please, Rhea," Frommer cut in; he pointed to the right. "Why don't we amble over to that nice, empty table? After all." He grinned. "Your answer might be so devastating I could need a chair to, so to speak, cushion my fall."

"All right, Stu." She shrugged. "Lead the way."

After she put her wineglass on the table, Frommer pulled out the nearest chair and hovered over her until she sat down. "Okay." He grinned. "Now that we're all sitting and comfy... err, shoot."

"Well," she hesitated and took a sip of the wine, "there's just so much I don't know where to begin."

Frommer turned his hands over, as if in a plaintive manner. "We're not in a sissy business, Rhea. As you know, a client wouldn't come to us unless, well, aside from some furniture chain out of Turlock, unless they were in difficulty or potential trouble. Publicists get their names out into the media and public awareness. We, on the other hand, smooth things over when the going gets rough and sometimes... uh, more."

She seemed impressed by his little presentation. He paused for her to respond. "It's the more that I have qualms about, Stu. For instance, everything that just happened."

"So I had Mellon, and you had the Chanteuse. Ann Sloan had lots of headaches, and you all did a good job until—"

"Until someone snookered her in that traffic incident."

Frommer tried to maintain his cool. Obviously, he hadn't wanted the conversation to take this turn. "Well, in addition to us, Mellon had private detectives, Palmeiro Protective Services, and who knows what else. Who knows who plotted all that, assuming it was contrived?"

"Oh, it was contrived all right. Someone you met, once or twice, Slats Conners, got to the bottom of it."

"How is Slats? I sorta heard you two were, umm..."

"We were never, umm, and he's now happily married to his long-time fiancée. And stop trying to change the subject." She grinned.

"Okay, okay." He shrugged. "Let's get back to generics. We're in a tough business. Our clients, well, when they go to their accountants, they don't expect an audit on their taxes. When they go to their lawyers, they're happy if that DUI is fixed. With us, it's more ambiguous, and with *our* clients' nebulous needs and desires, they expect, almost demand, a more spirited, aggressive attitude." He paused, thinking he had said too much. He did.

"But we're here to make our clients look good. Aggressiveness, belligerency, whatever—how does that make our clients more acceptable to the GP?"

"Because the general public, or GP, as you call it, only sees the results. Not the unpleasantness that got the so-called good results."

She started to respond. He held up his right arm as if he were a traffic cop. "Let me give you an example, Rhea. Political operatives use every trick in the book. They're nasty, scurrilous and make the *Enquirer* look like a Boy Scout publication. But when that beneficiary of all that becomes a senator or a president, does anyone really care what happened during the campaigns, except historians or book writers?"

She sighed and seemed to stifle a grin. "Your point?"

"Lemme change the subject a little, Rhea."

She looked at her wineglass and took a sip while demonstrating a little tedium.

Frommer gulped. *Make it good, you MF. It's the bottom of the ninth, and you're facing Rivera with the bases loaded and two outs.* "If you had Mellon as a client and let's say you duplicated some of the rough and tumble things I may have done, there'd still be one difference, wouldn't there?"

"The difference?"

"You'd still be the personable, sweet, easy-to-like young lady I see before me when the job is done or it's after hours. Me, well, I'm guessing you're from California, growing up in a post-industrial, bucolic environment..."

Her bored expression quickly turned to a smile. "And you?"

"Well," he shrugged, "I concede I cut a much more malevolent figure than most, but ya gotta look at the background, the deprivations. After all, here we sit in San Francisco, the capital of excuse making and the blaming of society for whatever faults a person can have, unless, of course, if he's in the Bush administration or working for Halliburton."

"What... what are you talking about?" She was grinning as she took another sip of wine. "Did... did you grow up in a ghetto, a slum?"

"No, Rhea, Flatbush is middle class, as middle class as it comes. But when you're dating girls from the Eyyyyland, that's Long Island to all of you West of Hoboken, you sort of get reminded of where you stand, status-wise. So if I seem driven professionally in a take-no-prisoners manner, don't chalk it up to the typical Hollywood melodrama of the son 'proving' things to his father. Rather, you get enough experiences like some Bs, rhymes with Rich, asking 'Do you lyyyyke it' when I tell them what I do for a living while going to school at night... Well, it builds up."

"So that's why you—"

"Nah, I know what you're asking, Rhea, but it wasn't those skanks or their obnoxious moms that drove me..." Frommer grinned and gulped down some wine. "It was just an excuse to drive myself. Basically, Rhea, we are all lazy. We need deprivation, maintaining lifestyle, and/or impressing others to get off our keisters. Well, I used those petty put-downs, insults, whatever, to get off my behind and become driven."

"I-I've never met anyone quite like you." She gasped.

He tried a friendly smile. "Got time? There's a lot more where that came from."

She looked at her watch. "Well, there's a workshop at two thirty. Just a minute, let me refresh my wine. It's only a quarter to two. Enough time to finish your soliloquy?"

"Plenty of time, Rhea. I don't beat around the bush." He watched her walk back toward the wine setup after he responded "I'm good" when she asked if he wanted another glass of wine. He chided himself for not offering to get the wine himself but concluded in this day and age of women's rights even that might have backfired. *Might as well stick to being the hard guy, Stuey. It's sink or swim.*

She headed back to the table delicately holding that nearly full new glass of wine. Frommer noticed she had a smile on her face. *Well, that's two pluses*, he reflected. *Not only did she come back, but she's smiling.*

"So... so you were saying something about keisters?" She grinned.

379

"Yeah, well, you see, Rhea, most of my neighborhood, most of Brooklyn for that matter, was divided between the four-eyed nerds who spent all their evenings in the library, studying who knows what—prelaw, premed—and the others who called themselves tummlers."

"Tummlers?" It hit her as if he had literally spoken Greek.

"*Tummlers* is a Yiddish word for hanging around with the guys, bustin' chops, whistling at every pretty girl that passes by. Tummlin' was our way of being who we were, as opposed to those fags—err, nerds—spending all their time studying and worried about their careers."

Rhea smiled and shook her finger as if she were admonishing a child in kindergarten. "Did I hear you say *fag*? That's very un-PC in this day and age, especially in the Bay Area."

Frommer shrugged and blushed slightly. "Ahh, we had a different meaning for fags back there. It referred to guys who didn't play ball, weren't tough. There was no sexual connotation."

"I haven't learned so much sociology since I was a frosh at Cal State Long Beach." She gulped down some wine. "Go on."

"Okay, Rhea, now I'm gonna get to the point of this sociology dissertation. When you hang with guys, when you're tummlin', you pick up certain attitudes, certain behaviors, some because of habit and some for self-preservation. You see, everyone's trying to outbit the others. Not like poker in Vegas, where you bid, b-i-d. I'm referring to *bit*, b-i-t. As in 'listen to this bit,' 'watch this bit.' A story where you picked up a girl, said something funny, put an a-hole down—these are all bits."

"I can't believe all this, Stu. Is it the wine going to my head, or did we grow up in two different universes?"

"Probably the latter, Rhea. At any rate, there's always new guys around, new situations, new bits. Except for your closest of friends, you learn to look and act swarmy. Have an attitude, no matter how much balls you got—err, pardon my French. You'd always prefer to avoid a fight than not. So you find you act in a certain way—establish turf, so to speak. It keeps the peace." He grinned. "Still with me, Rhea?"

"Barely, Stu. I-I've never met anyone like you, or have I already said that half a dozen times?"

"Well, that's probably not a compliment. But lemme get to the point, an important point in our relationship."

"Relationship?" Her eyes narrowed. "Who said anything about a relationship?"

"Well, Rhea, when you said 'I've heard about you,' I have no doubt you were referring to more than my dealings with Mellon. It's how I come across… but," Frommer grinned, "but there's the question of the girls, the chicks, the dolls. Whether you like it or not, whether you admit it or not, Rhea, girls, ladies, women like guys with an edge, with balls. You learn that the nerds might get someone when they set up their practice, but in the meantime, the gals invariably go for the flashy guys, the guys who put them on edge. They… they wanna please. Some of it is human nature, some of it is primeval. It… it's probably got to do with the survival of our species. The maidens gravitate toward mates who'll protect them from wild beasts, other marauding tribes." Frommer grinned. "Am I putting you on? No, I'm not. Just trying to understand why invariably the wise guys get all the girls."

"And our so-called relationship?"

"Well, I would like to get to know you better, Rhea. But the whole point of my little diatribe is to explain what's on the surface, and potentially, a put-off to a nice person like you might not reflect what's truly inside of me." He pointed toward his heart.

She seemed flustered. "You… you are good with words."

He deliberately made his voice crack. "This, Rhea, this is one time my words mean more than satisfying a PR client."

She looked at her watch. "Well, Stu, it's a quarter after. The workshop starts at two thirty."

"What's it about?

"Oh, nothing you'd be interested in… how to get new clients."

He pointed at her and grinned. "Touché. Yeah, right, who'd be interested in getting new clients? Is it one of those preregistered things?"

"C'mon, Stu, it's obvious you haven't gone to many of these conferences. You just walk into any workshop anytime."

"Well, what are we waiting for?" He got up and inadvertently grabbed her hand to help her up. They started walking, and to his surprise and elation, she didn't pull her hand away.

She pointed to the escalator. "That way, Stu. It's in the South Building across the street."

"This workshop got me thinking, Rhea."

"Why? Frommer & Sons needs new clients?"

"We always do, Rhea, especially now that we've lost the Mellon account, rest in peace. But I was sort of thinking of expansion. You know, studying the SoCal market."

"Oh really?" She feigned anger. "Moving into our territory?"

They got to the escalator. He reluctantly let go of her hand. They both turned back to catch the swarm of people at the basement level of Moscone North. "Well, Rhea, I wasn't thinking along the lines of muscling into someone else's territory. I was sort of thinking of a possible merger."

They were about to cross the street to the South Building; they waited for the light to change. "A merger?"

"Yeah, Rhea, how does the firm of Frommer & Simpson, Public Relations, sound? That is, when you're ready to go out on your own."

They started crossing the street. "Hmmm, not as good as Simpson & Frommer."

Frommer grinned. "You got me on that one. Well, Rhea, you always got to be thinking of the future, professional mergers, uh, personal mergers. Who knows what's down the pike?"

She stared at his eyes and exhibited a bashful smile. She grabbed his hand. "Come on, Stu, it's almost two thirty."

About the Author

 Lee Bornstein is a labor economist who has always been fascinated by the political scene in the United States. He was born in Belgium and grew up in Brooklyn, New York. Prior writing credits include the US Bureau of Labor Statistics' *Monthly Labor Review* and the World Book Encyclopedia. He currently resides in Walnut Creek, California.

CPSIA information can be obtained
at www.ICGtesting.com
Printed in the USA
BVHW081209130519
548119BV00002B/109/P